chibi Vampire

VOLUME 13

CREATED BY
YUNA KAGESAKI

HAMBURG // LONDON // LOS ANGELES // TOKYO

OUR STORY SO FAR...

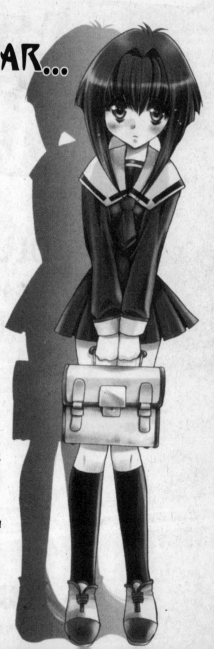

KARIN MAAKA ISN'T LIKE OTHER GIRLS. ONCE A MONTH, SHE EXPERIENCES PAIN, FATIGUE, HUNGER, IRRITABILITY—AND THEN SHE BLEEDS. FROM HER NOSE. KARIN IS A VAMPIRE, FROM A FAMILY OF VAMPIRES, BUT INSTEAD OF NEEDING TO DRINK BLOOD, SHE HAS AN EXCESS OF BLOOD THAT SHE MUST GIVE TO HER VICTIMS. IF DONE RIGHT, GIVING THIS BLOOD TO HER VICTIM CAN BE AN EXTREMELY POSITIVE THING. THE PROBLEM WITH THIS IS THAT KARIN NEVER SEEMS TO DO THINGS RIGHT...

KARIN IS HAVING A BIT OF BOY TROUBLE. KENTA USUI—THE HANDSOME NEW STUDENT AT HER SCHOOL AND WORK—IS A NICE ENOUGH GUY, BUT HE EXACERBATES KARIN'S PROBLEM. KARIN'S BLOOD PROBLEM, YOU SEE, BECOMES WORSE WHEN SHE'S AROUND PEOPLE WHO HAVE SUFFERED MISFORTUNE, AND KENTA HAS SUFFERED PLENTY OF IT. MAKING THINGS EVEN MORE COMPLICATED, IT'S BECOME CLEAR TO KARIN THAT SHE'S IN LOVE WITH KENTA...AND THIS BECOMES PAINFUL TO KARIN AS SHE SOON DISCOVERS THAT LOVE BETWEEN HUMANS AND VAMPIRES IS FROWNED UPON BECAUSE CHILDREN BETWEEN THE TWO SPECIES LACK REPRODUCTIVE ABILITIES. BUT KENTA'S LOVE FOR KARIN SURPASSES ALL BOUNDARIES AND THE TWO EMBRACE FOR THEIR FIRST KISS...

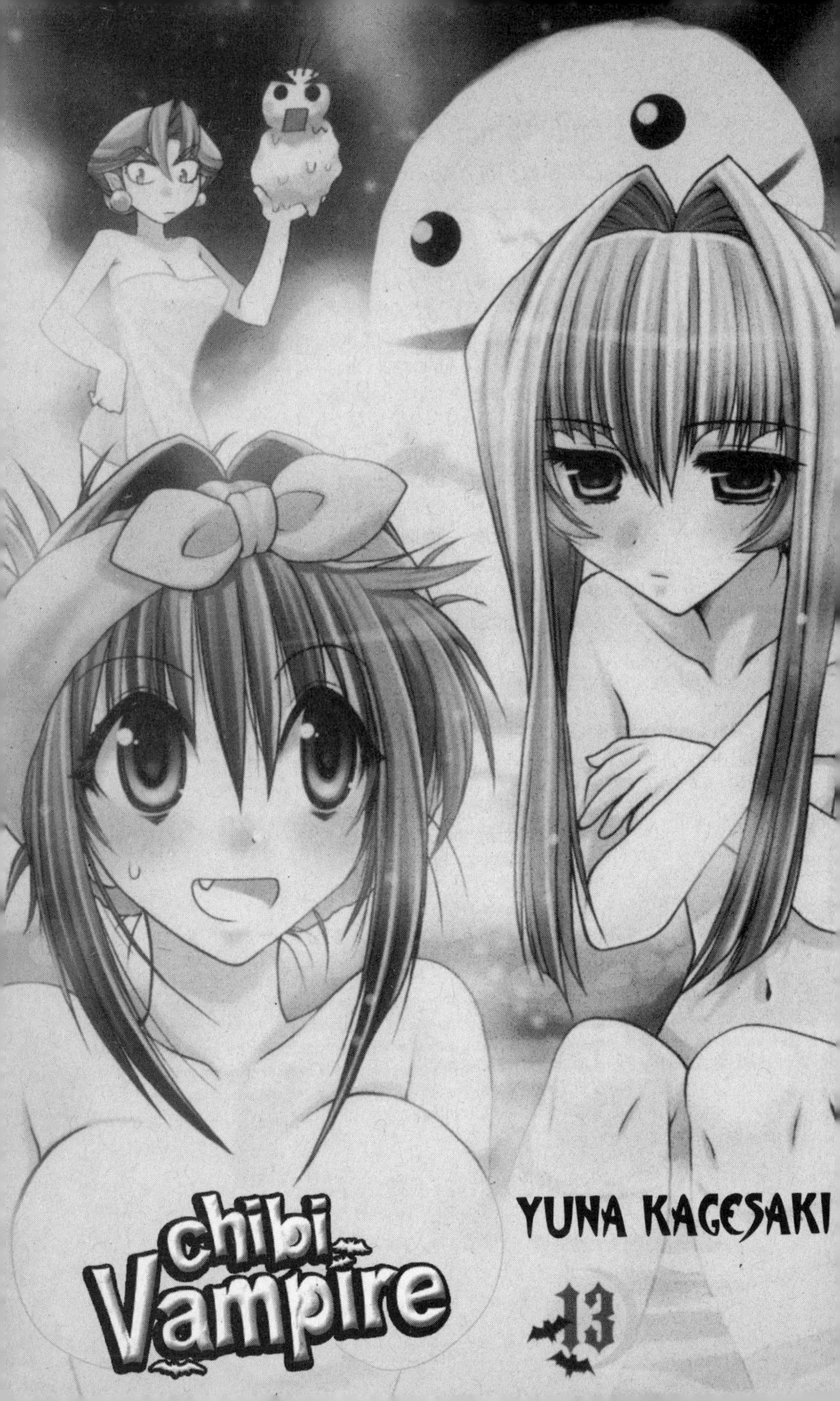
chibi Vampire
YUNA KAGESAKI
13

Chibi Vampire Volume 13
Created by Yuna Kagesaki

Translation - Alexis Kirsch
English Adaptation - Christine Boylan
Retouch and Lettering - Star Print Brokers
Production Artist - Michael Paolilli
Graphic Designer - Louis Csontos

Editor - Alexis Kirsch
Print Production Manager - Lucas Rivera
Managing Editor - Vy Nguyen
Senior Designer - Louis Csontos
Associate Publisher - Marco F. Pavia
President and C.O.O. - John Parker
C.E.O. and Chief Creative Officer - Stu Levy

A  Manga

TOKYOPOP and  are trademarks or registered trademarks of TOKYOPOP Inc.

TOKYOPOP Inc.
5900 Wilshire Blvd. Suite 2000
Los Angeles, CA 90036

E-mail: info@TOKYOPOP.com
Come visit us online at www.TOKYOPOP.com

KARIN Volume 13 © 2007 YUNA KAGESAKI
published in Japan in 2007 by FUJIMISHOBO CO., LTD.,
vo. English translation rights arranged with KADOKAWA
EN PUBLISHING CO., LTD., Tokyo through TUTTLE-MORI
AGENCY, INC., Tokyo.
English text copyright © 2009 TOKYOPOP Inc.

ISBN: 978-1-4278-1279-7

First TOKYOPOP printing: April 2009
10 9 8 7 6 5 4 3 2
Printed in the USA

THE MAAKA FAMILY

CALERA MARKER

Karin's overbearing mother. While Calera resents that Karin wasn't born a normal vampire, she does love her daughter in her own obnoxious way. Calera has chosen to keep her European last name.

HENRY MARKER

Karin's father. In general, Henry treats Karin a lot better than her mother does, but Calera wears the pants in this particular family. Henry has also chosen to keep his European last name.

REN MAAKA

Karin's older brother. Ren milks the "sexy creature of the night" thing for all it's worth and spends his nights in the arms (and beds) of attractive young women.

KARIN MAAKA

Our little heroine. Karin is
vampire living in Japan, bu
instead of sucking blood fror
her victims, she actually GIVE
them some of her blooc
She's a vampire in reverse

ANJU MAAKA

Karin's little sister. Anju has awoken as a full vampire, and is usually the one who cleans up after Karin's messes. Rarely seen without her "talking" doll, Boogie.

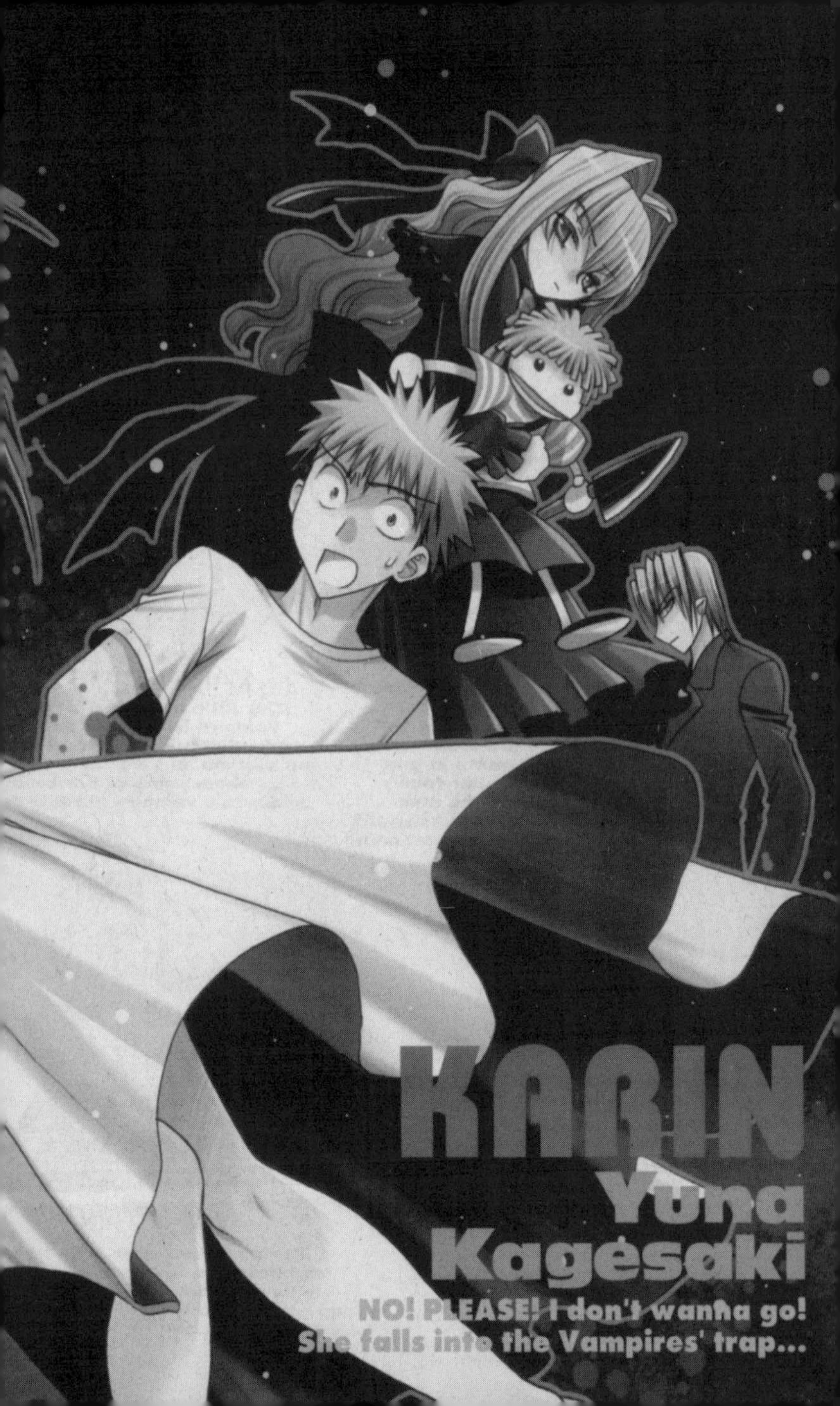

KARIN
Yuna Kagesaki
NO! PLEASE! I don't wanna go!
She falls into the Vampires' trap...

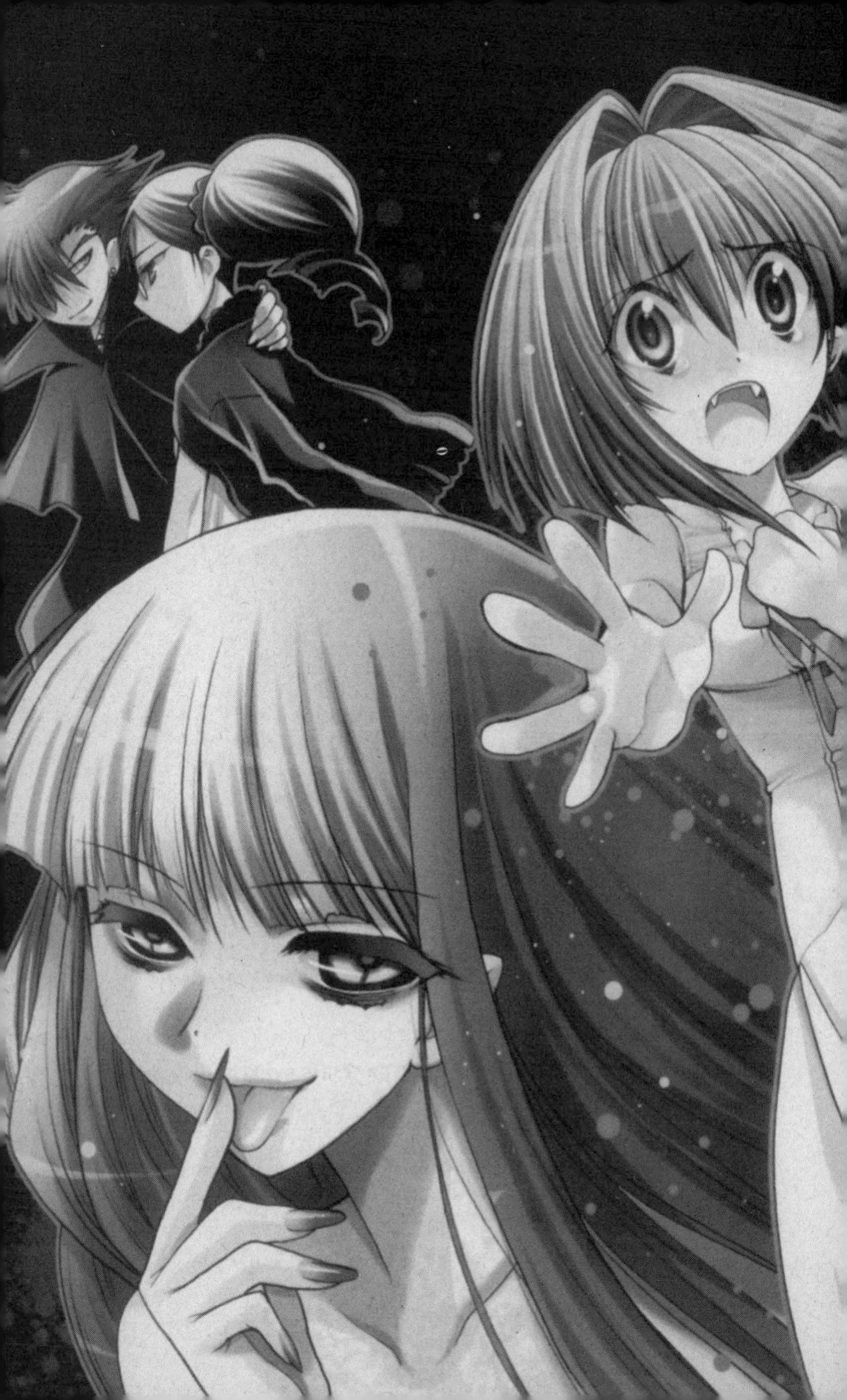

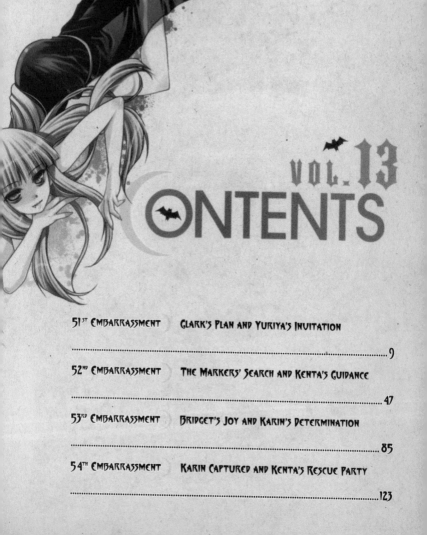

VOL. 13

CONTENTS

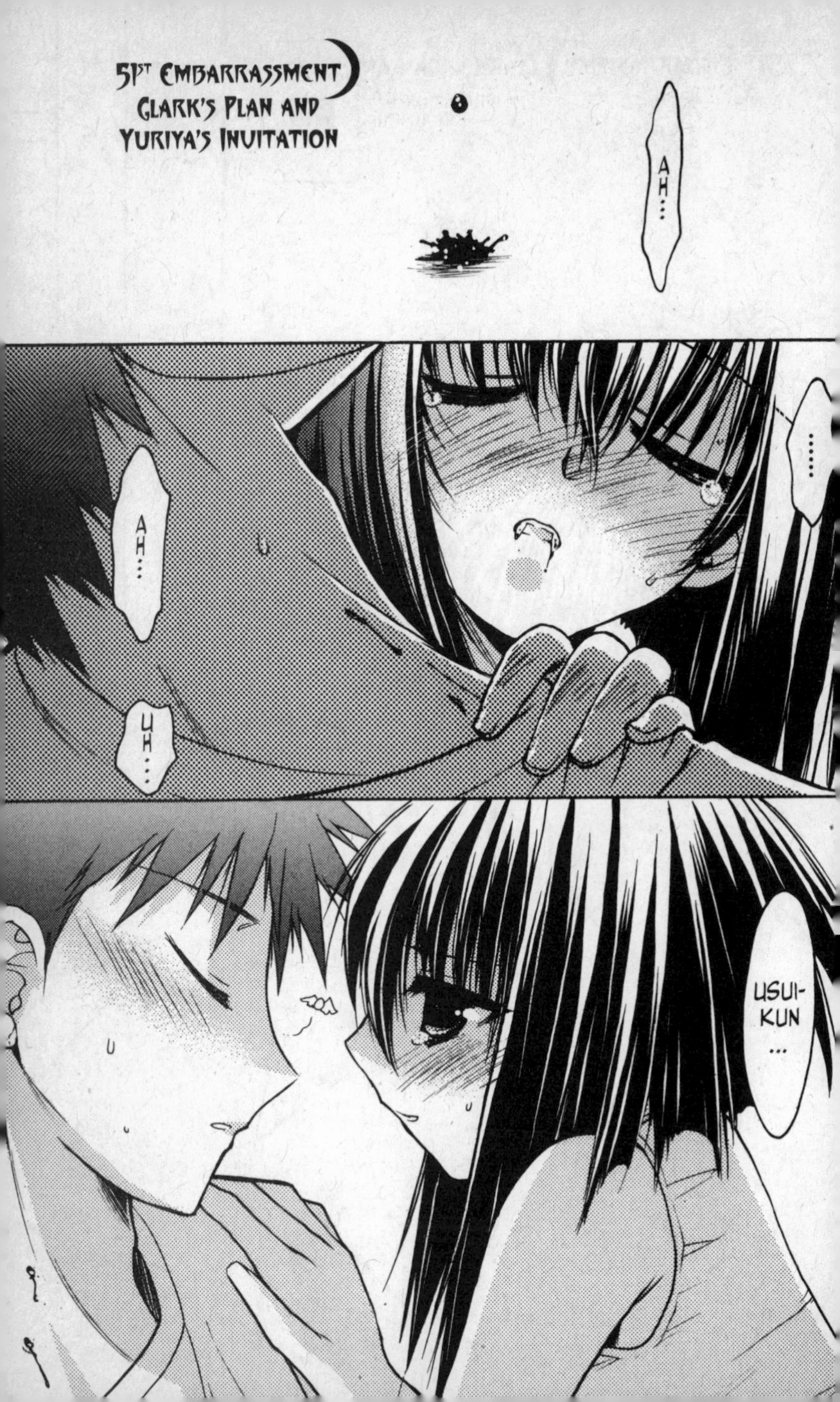
51ST EMBARRASSMENT
CLARK'S PLAN AND YURIYA'S INVITATION
AH...
......
AH...
UH...
USUI-KUN ...

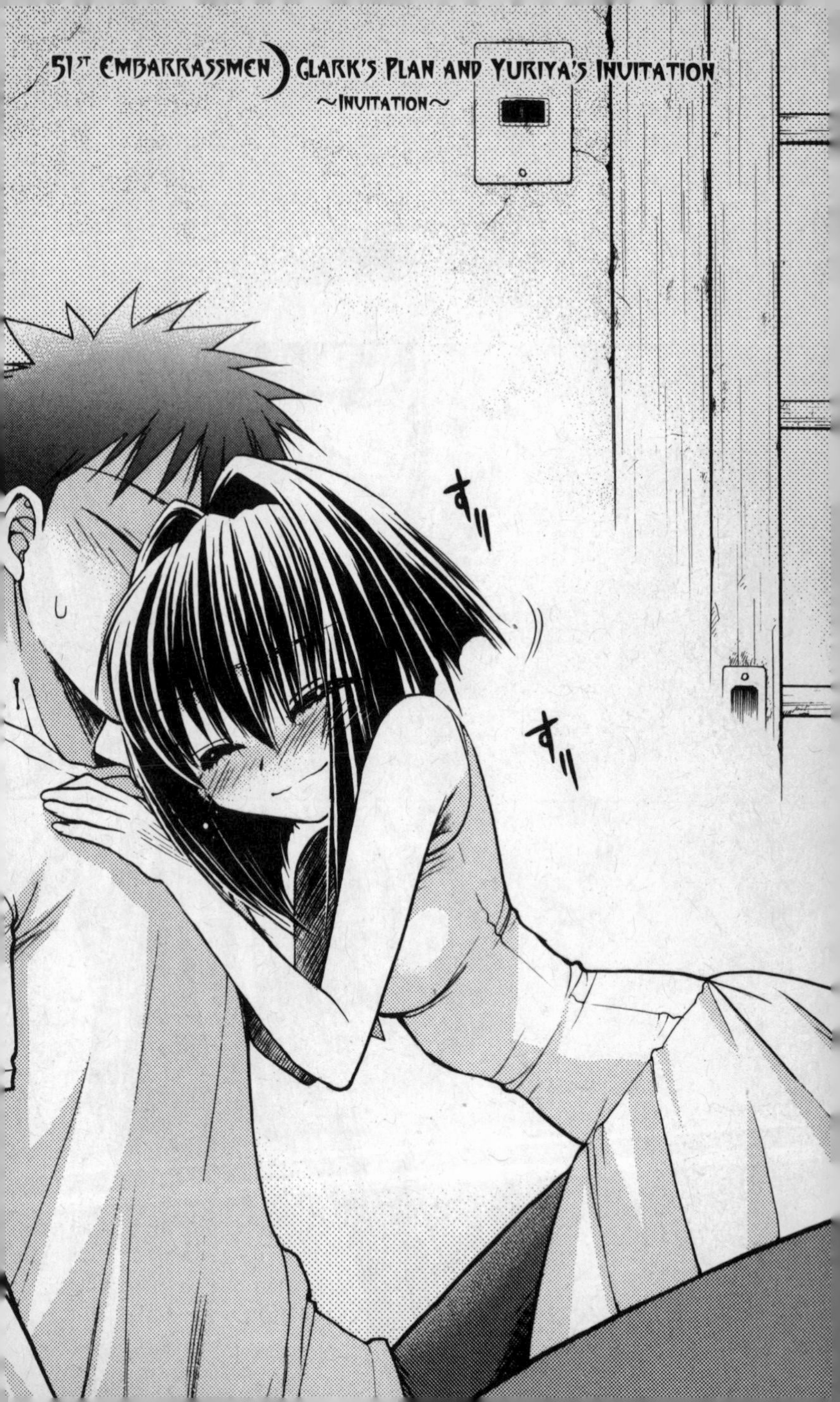
51ST EMBARRASSMEN) CLARK'S PLAN AND YURIYA'S INVITATION
~INVITATION~
すり
すり

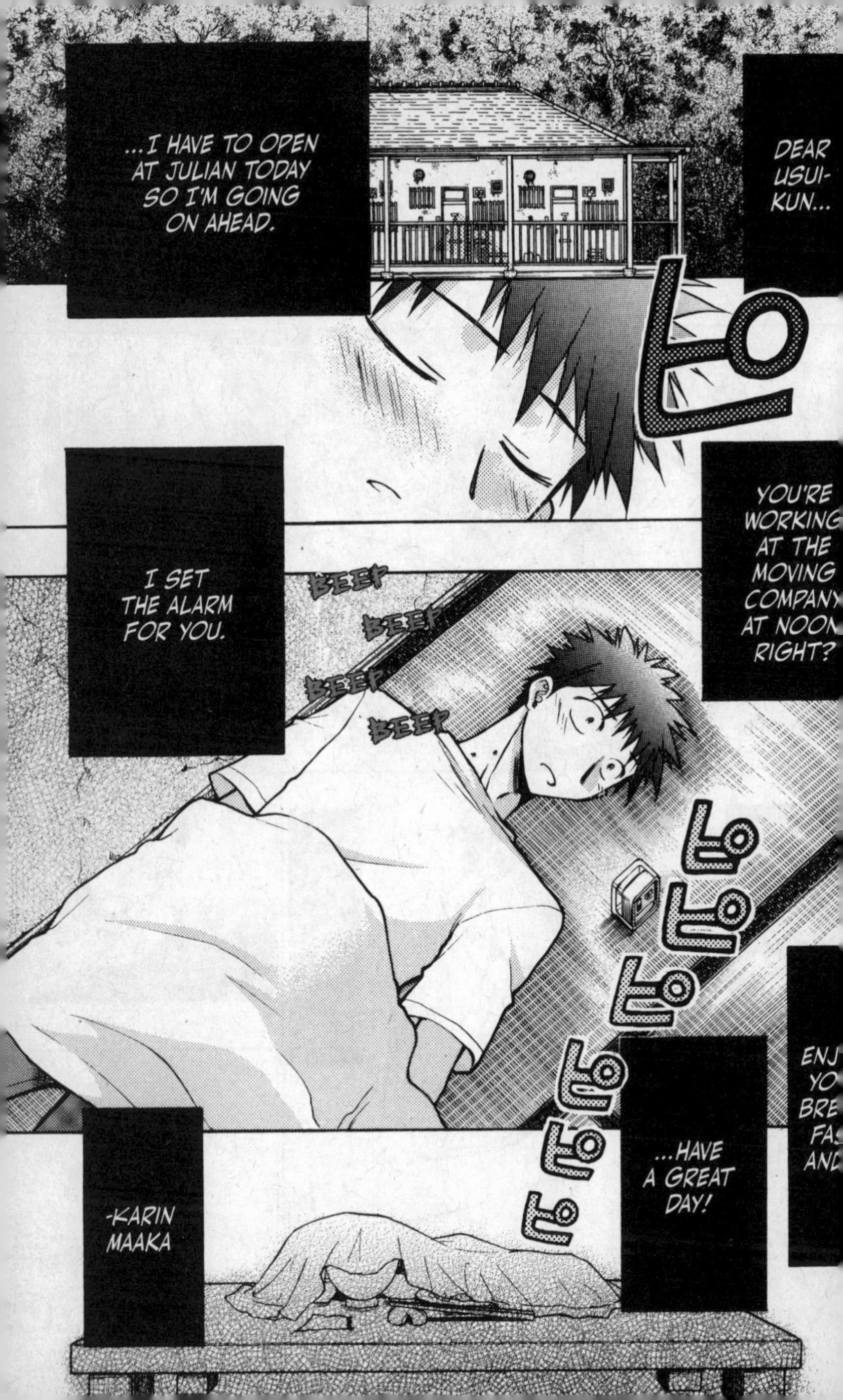
DEAR USUI-KUN...
...I HAVE TO OPEN AT JULIAN TODAY SO I'M GOING ON AHEAD.
ピッ
YOU'RE WORKING AT THE MOVING COMPANY AT NOON RIGHT?
I SET THE ALARM FOR YOU.
BEEP
BEEP
BEEP
BEEP
...HAVE A GREAT DAY!
-KARIN MAAKA

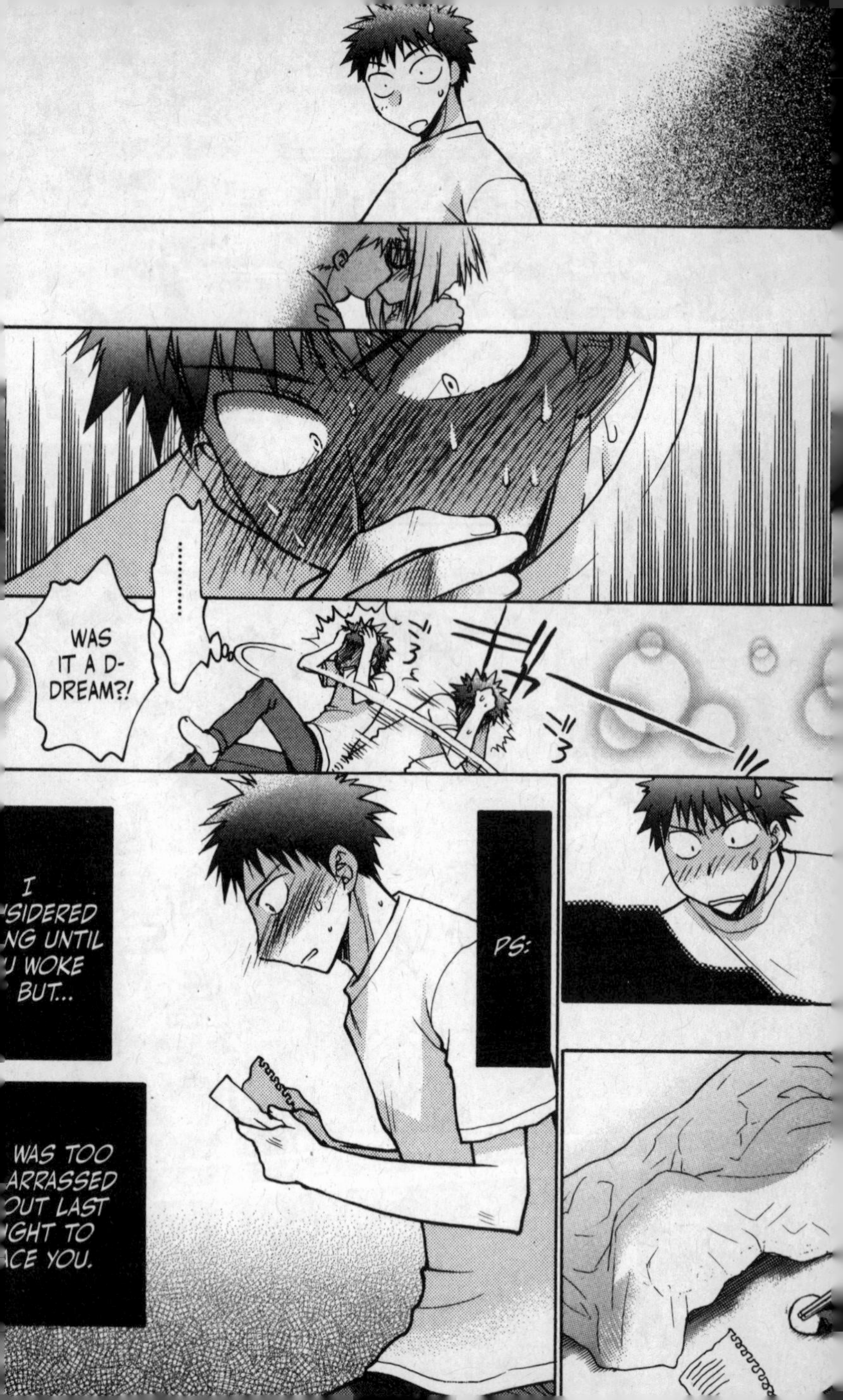
……
WAS IT A D-DREAM?!
PS:
I
SIDERED
NG UNTIL
U WOKE
BUT...
WAS TOO
ARRASSED
OUT LAST
GHT TO
CE YOU.

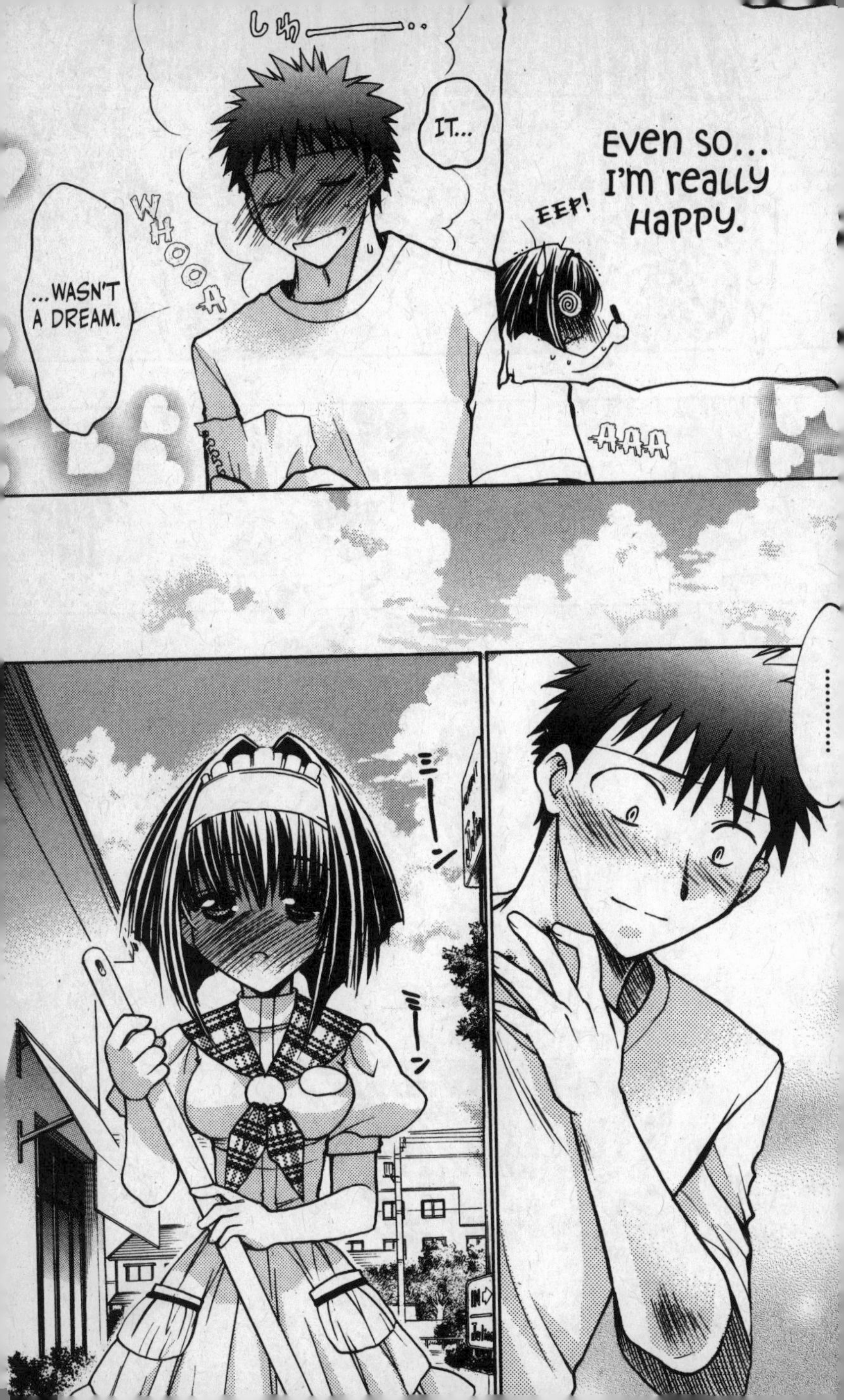
Even so... I'm really happy.
EEP!
AAA
しゅ——。。
IT...
WHOOA
...WASN'T A DREAM.
....
ミーン
ミーン

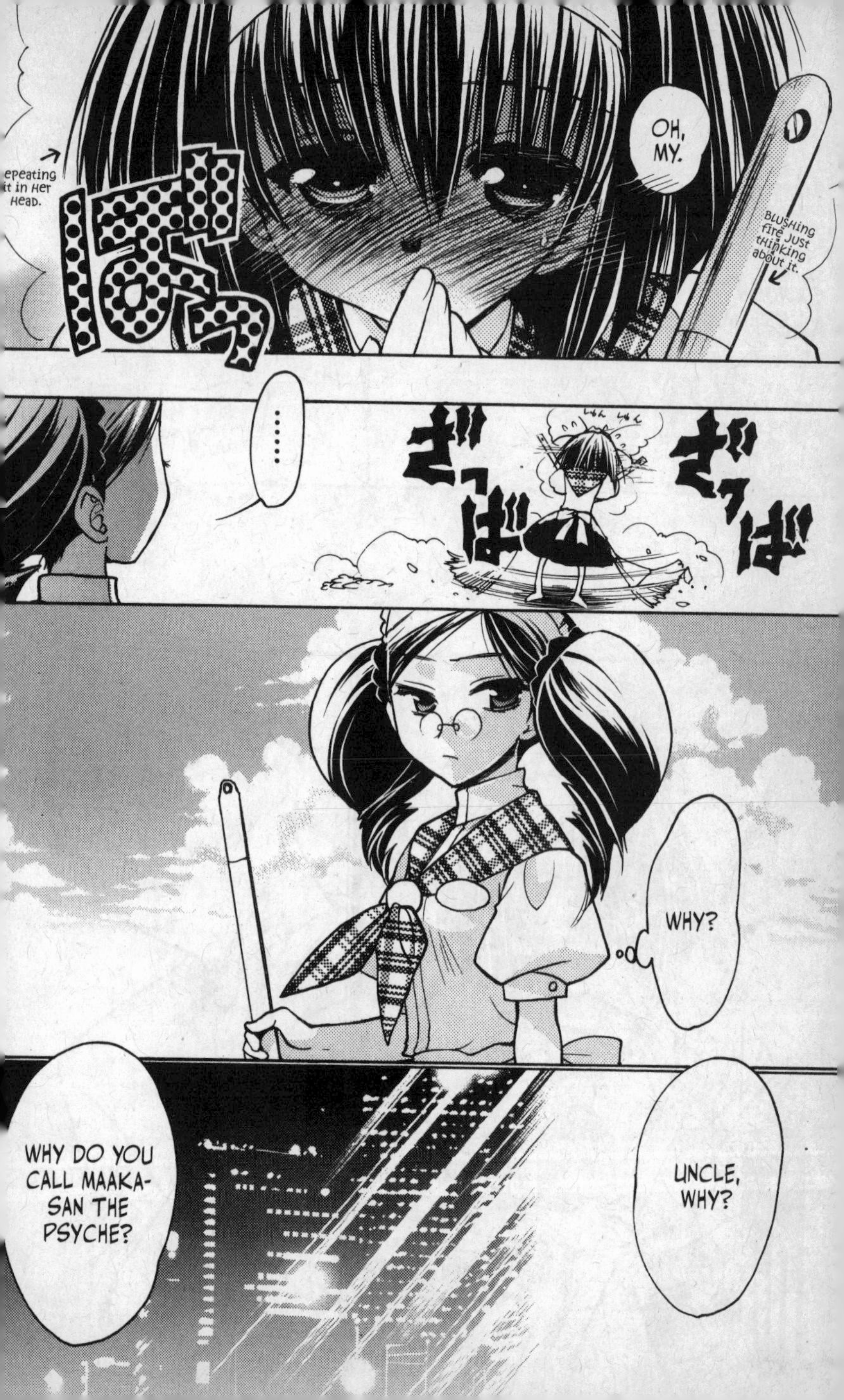
OH, MY.
BLUSHING fire JUST thinking about it.
ばっ
epeating it in Her Head.
ざっ ばっ
ざっ ばっ
......
WHY?
UNCLE, WHY?
WHY DO YOU CALL MAAKA-SAN THE PSYCHE?

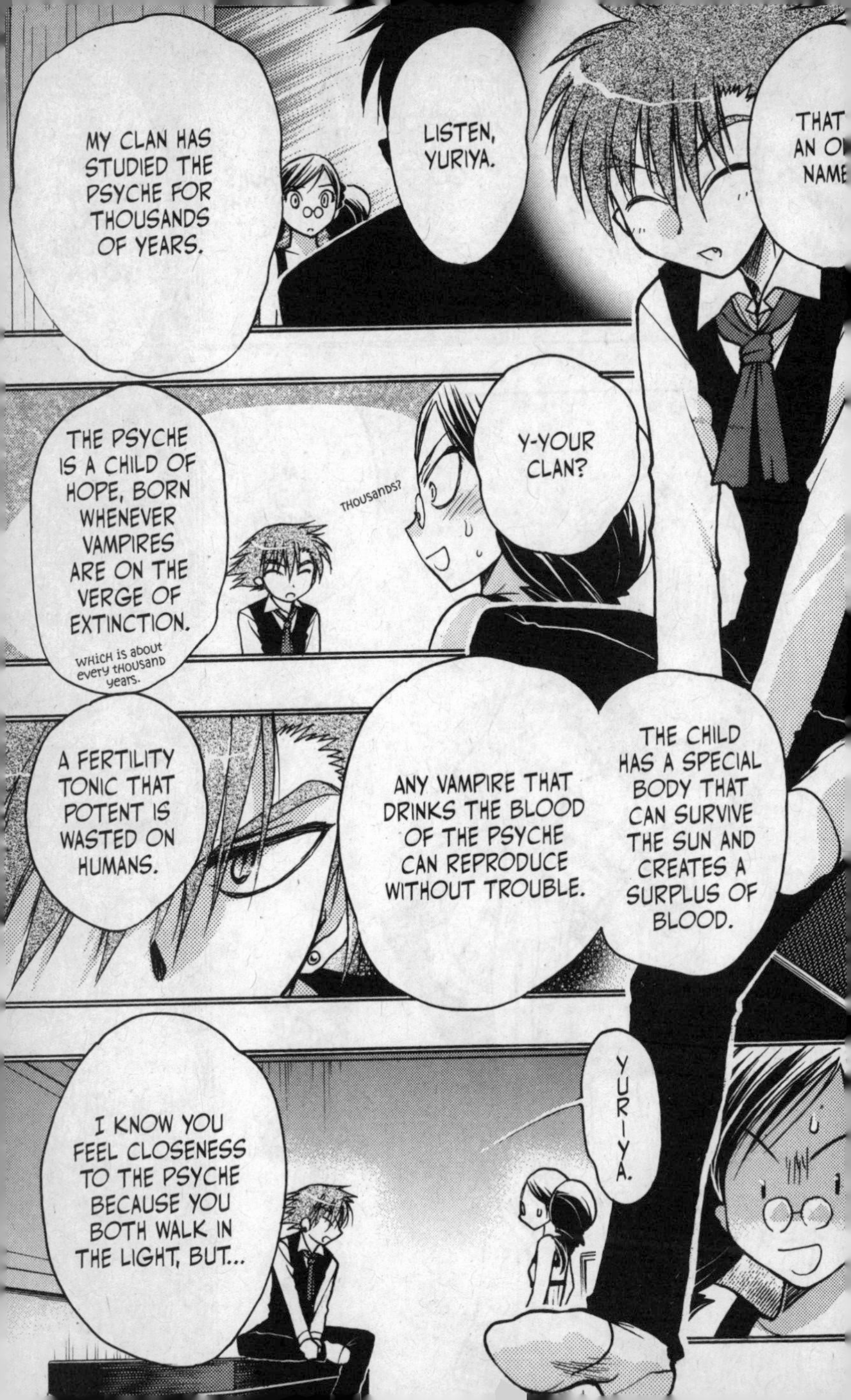
THAT AN O NAME
LISTEN, YURIYA.
MY CLAN HAS STUDIED THE PSYCHE FOR THOUSANDS OF YEARS.
Y-YOUR CLAN?
THOUSANDS?
THE PSYCHE IS A CHILD OF HOPE, BORN WHENEVER VAMPIRES ARE ON THE VERGE OF EXTINCTION.
WHICH is about every THOUSAND years.
THE CHILD HAS A SPECIAL BODY THAT CAN SURVIVE THE SUN AND CREATES A SURPLUS OF BLOOD.
ANY VAMPIRE THAT DRINKS THE BLOOD OF THE PSYCHE CAN REPRODUCE WITHOUT TROUBLE.
A FERTILITY TONIC THAT POTENT IS WASTED ON HUMANS.
YURIYA.
I KNOW YOU FEEL CLOSENESS TO THE PSYCHE BECAUSE YOU BOTH WALK IN THE LIGHT, BUT...

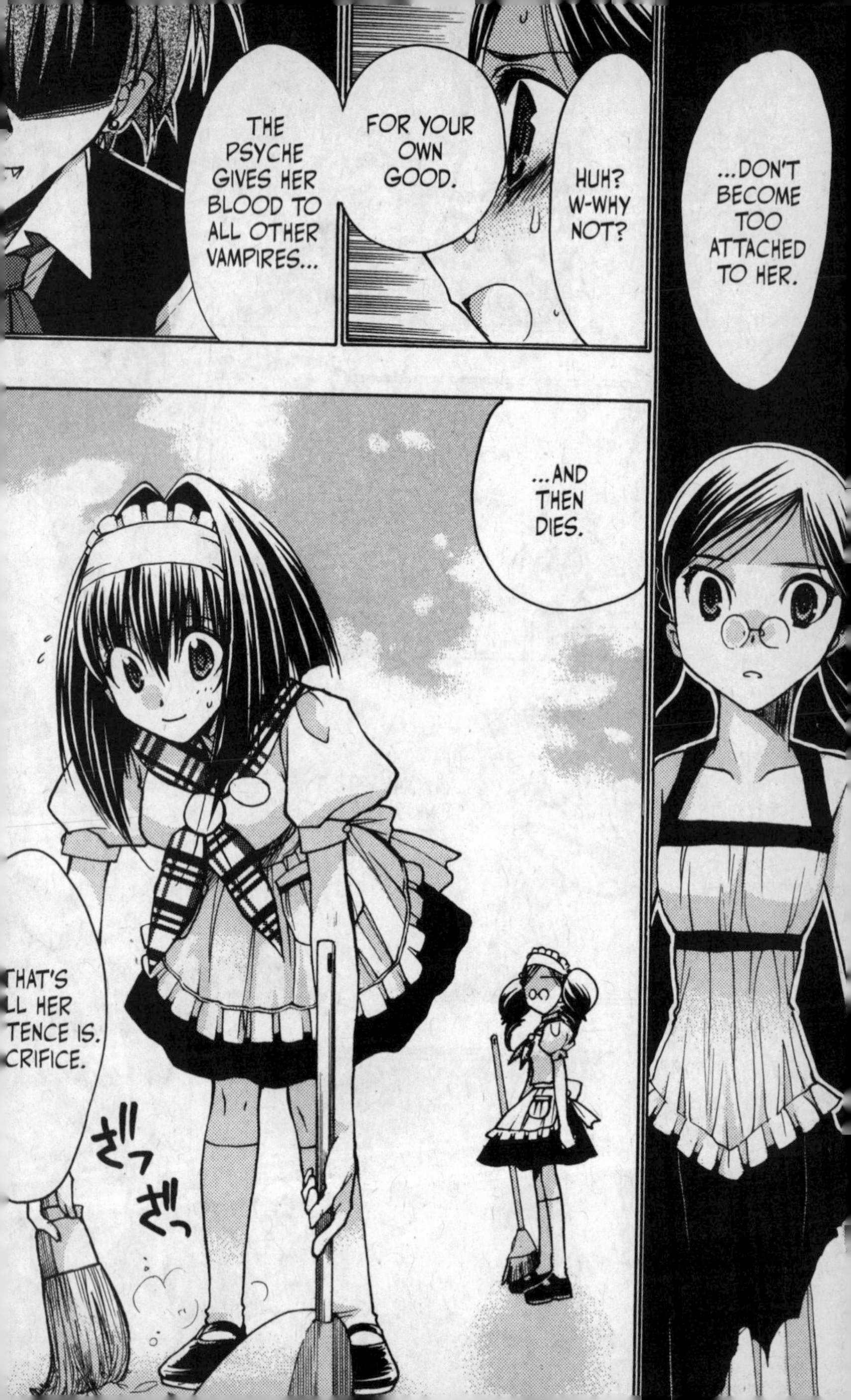
...DON'T BECOME TOO ATTACHED TO HER.
HUH? W-WHY NOT?
FOR YOUR OWN GOOD.
THE PSYCHE GIVES HER BLOOD TO ALL OTHER VAMPIRES...
...AND THEN DIES.
THAT'S LL HER TENCE IS. CRIFICE.
ざっ ざっ

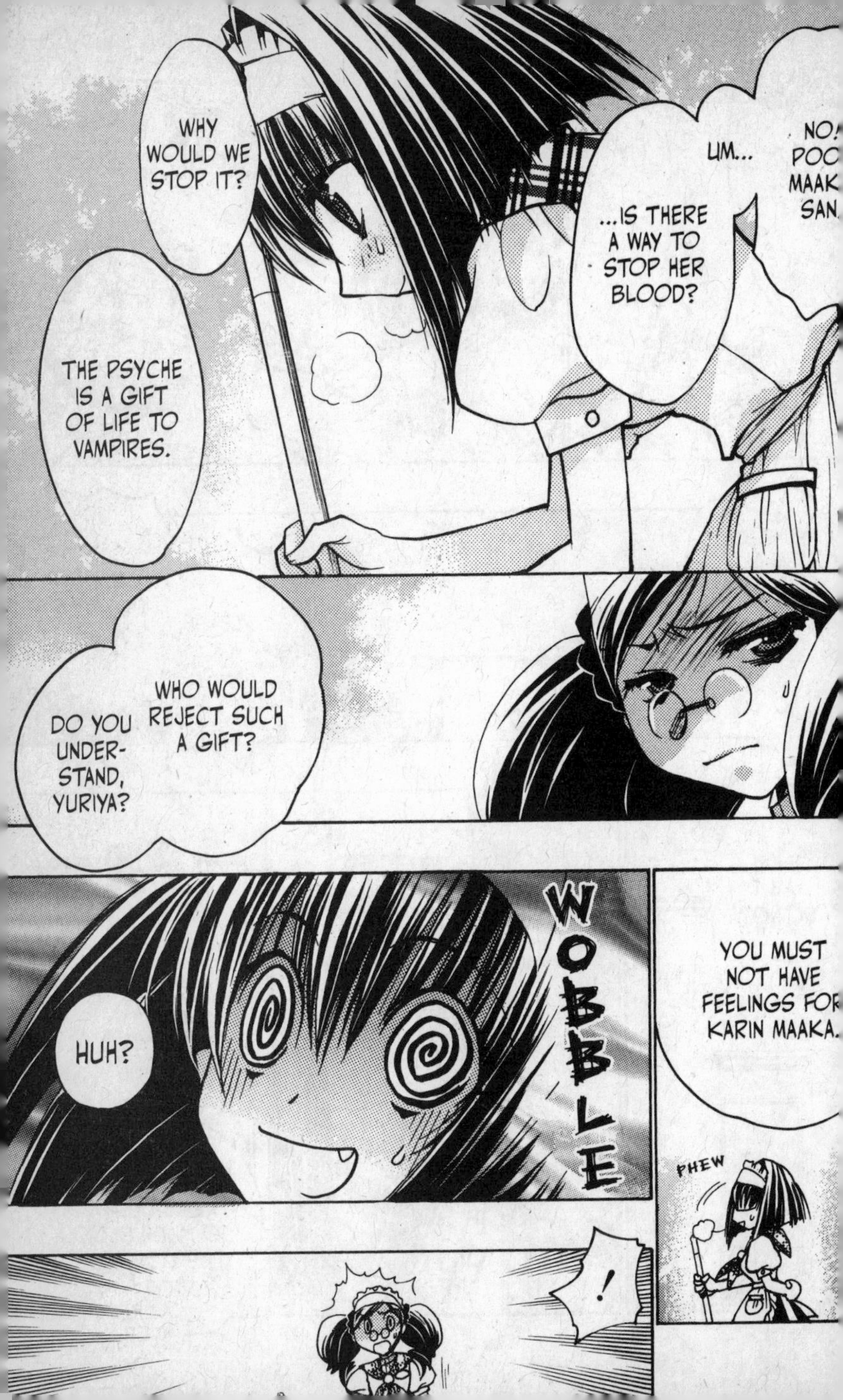

NO! POO MAAK SAN.
UM...
...IS THERE A WAY TO STOP HER BLOOD?
WHY WOULD WE STOP IT?
THE PSYCHE IS A GIFT OF LIFE TO VAMPIRES.
WHO WOULD REJECT SUCH A GIFT?
DO YOU UNDERSTAND, YURIYA?
YOU MUST NOT HAVE FEELINGS FOR KARIN MAAKA.
PHEW
WOBBLE
HUH?
!

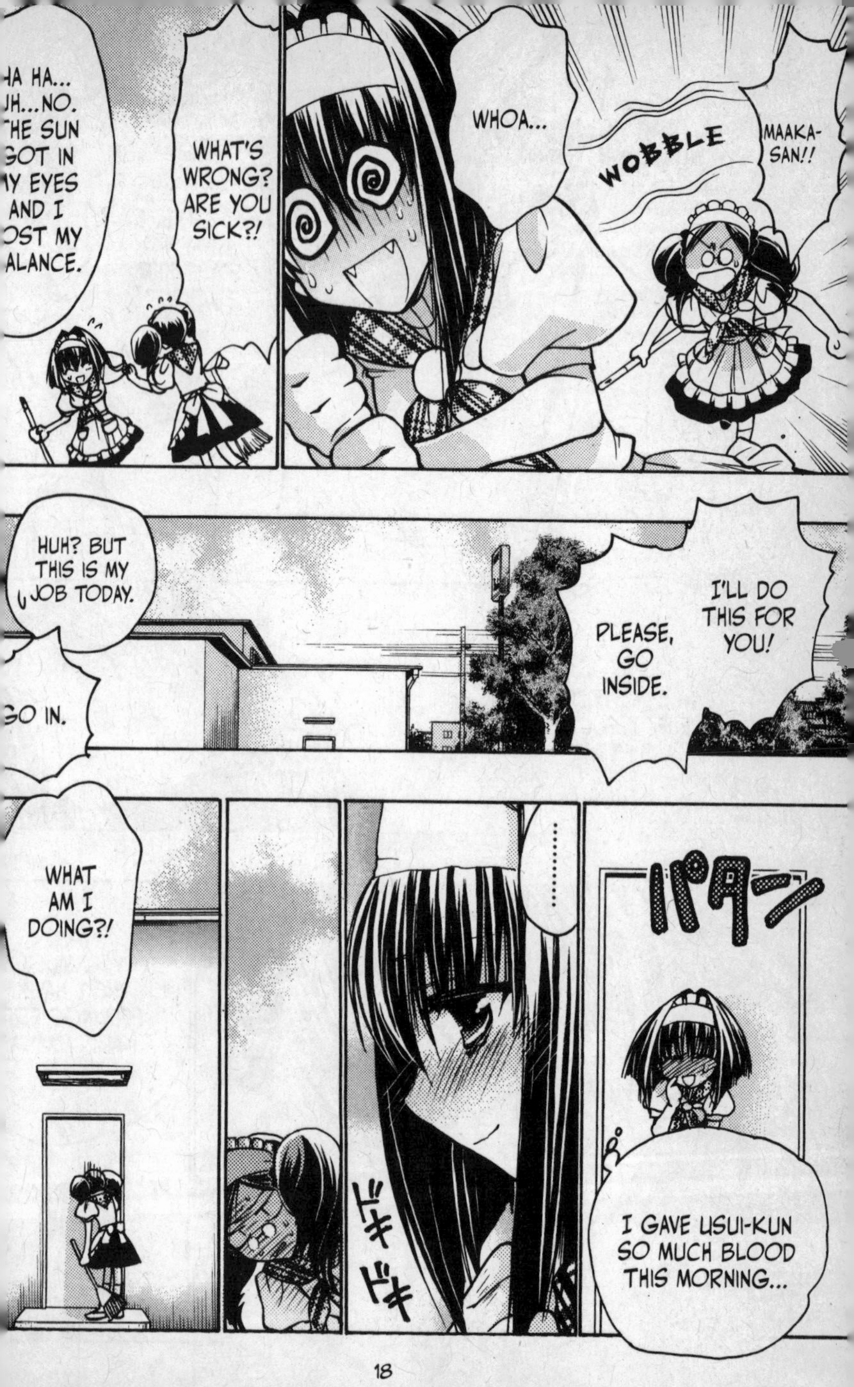
MAAKA-SAN!!
WHOA...
WOBBLE
WHAT'S WRONG? ARE YOU SICK?!
HA HA... UH...NO. THE SUN GOT IN MY EYES AND I OST MY ALANCE.
I'LL DO THIS FOR YOU!
PLEASE, GO INSIDE.
HUH? BUT THIS IS MY JOB TODAY.
GO IN.
パタン
I GAVE USUI-KUN SO MUCH BLOOD THIS MORNING...
......
ドキドキ
WHAT AM I DOING?!

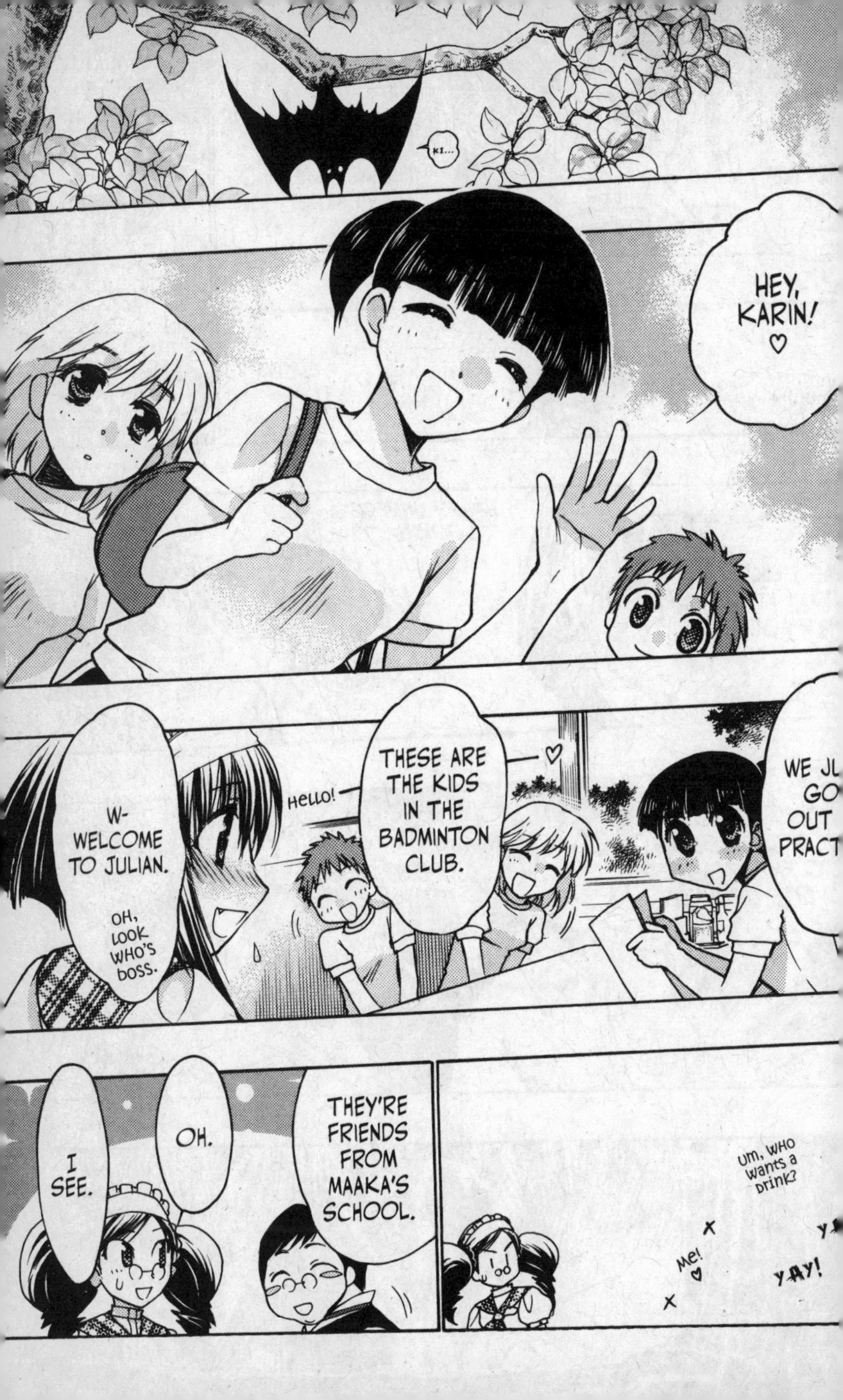
KI...
HEY, KARIN! ♡
WE JU GO OUT PRACT
THESE ARE THE KIDS IN THE BADMINTON CLUB.
♡
HELLO!
W- WELCOME TO JULIAN.
OH, LOOK WHO'S BOSS.
Um, WHO wants a drink?
Me! ♡
YAY!
THEY'RE FRIENDS FROM MAAKA'S SCHOOL.
OH.
I SEE.

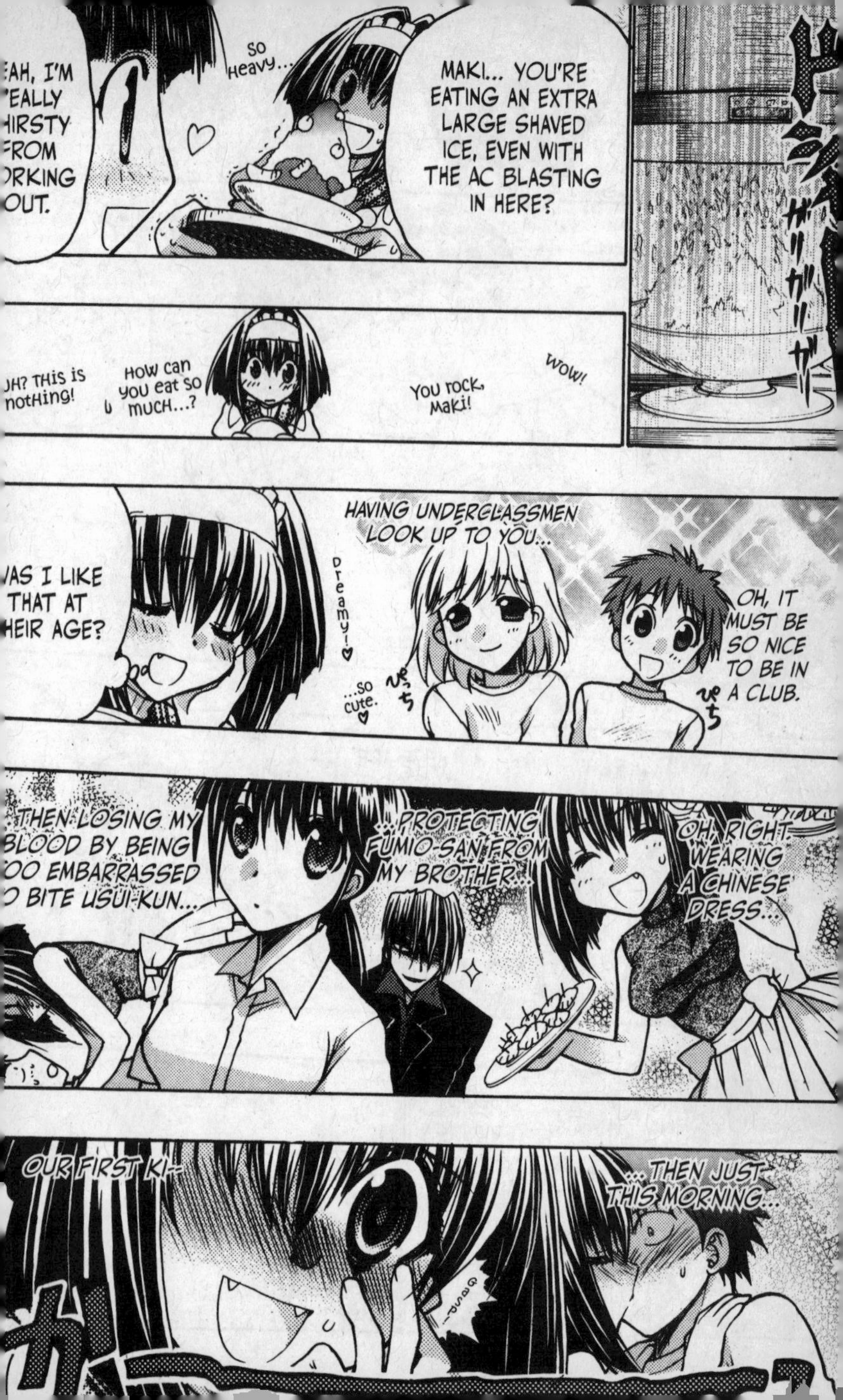
MAKI... YOU'RE EATING AN EXTRA LARGE SHAVED ICE, EVEN WITH THE AC BLASTING IN HERE?
SO Heavy...
EAH, I'M EALLY HIRSTY FROM ORKING OUT.
WOW!
You rock, Maki!
How can you eat so much...?
JH? THIS IS nothing!
OH, IT MUST BE SO NICE TO BE IN A CLUB.
HAVING UNDERCLASSMEN LOOK UP TO YOU...
Dreamy!
...so cute.
VAS I LIKE THAT AT HEIR AGE?
OH, RIGHT WEARING A CHINESE DRESS...
...PROTECTING FUMIO-SAN FROM MY BROTHER...
THEN LOSING MY BLOOD BY BEING OO EMBARRASSED O BITE USUI-KUN...
...THEN JUST THIS MORNING...
Gasp...
OUR FIRST KI-

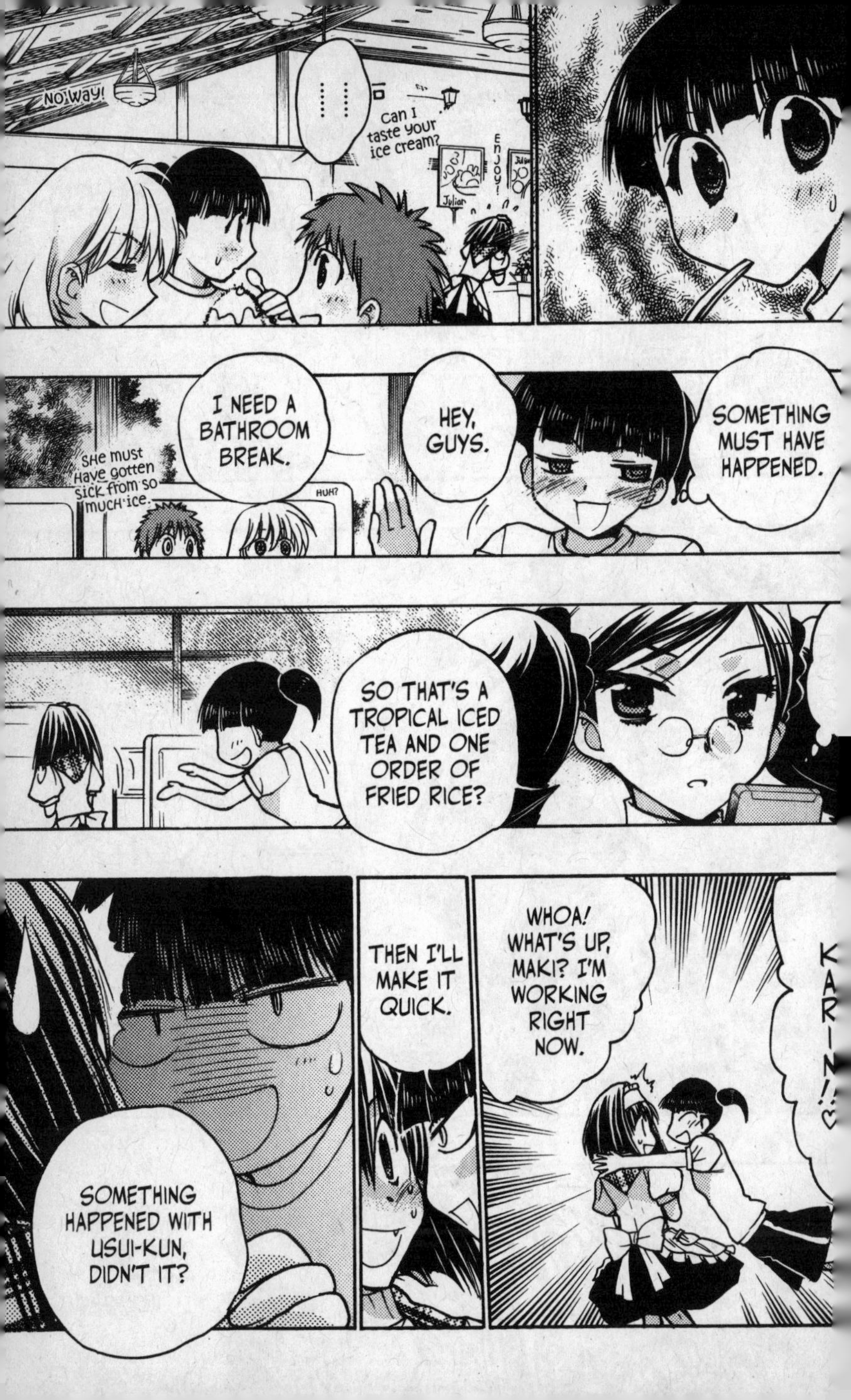
Enjoy!
Can I taste your ice cream?
......
No Way!
SOMETHING MUST HAVE HAPPENED.
HEY, GUYS.
I NEED A BATHROOM BREAK.
HUH?
She must Have gotten sick from so much ice.
SO THAT'S A TROPICAL ICED TEA AND ONE ORDER OF FRIED RICE?
KARIN!♡
WHOA! WHAT'S UP, MAKI? I'M WORKING RIGHT NOW.
THEN I'LL MAKE IT QUICK.
SOMETHING HAPPENED WITH USUI-KUN, DIDN'T IT?

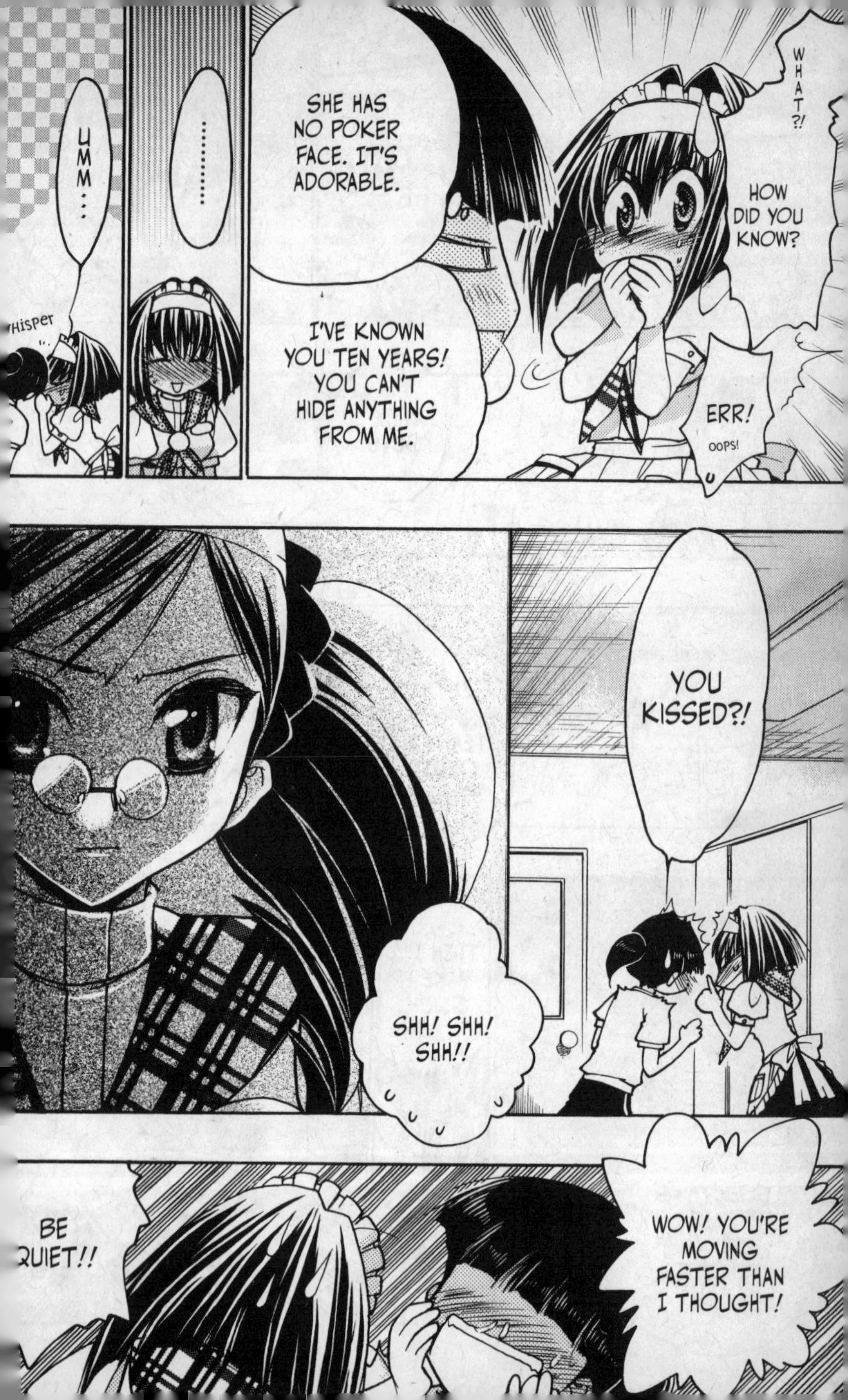
WHAT?!
HOW DID YOU KNOW?
ERR!
OOPS!
SHE HAS NO POKER FACE. IT'S ADORABLE.
I'VE KNOWN YOU TEN YEARS! YOU CAN'T HIDE ANYTHING FROM ME.
......
UMM...
WHISPER
YOU KISSED?!
SHH! SHH! SHH!!
WOW! YOU'RE MOVING FASTER THAN I THOUGHT!
BE QUIET!!

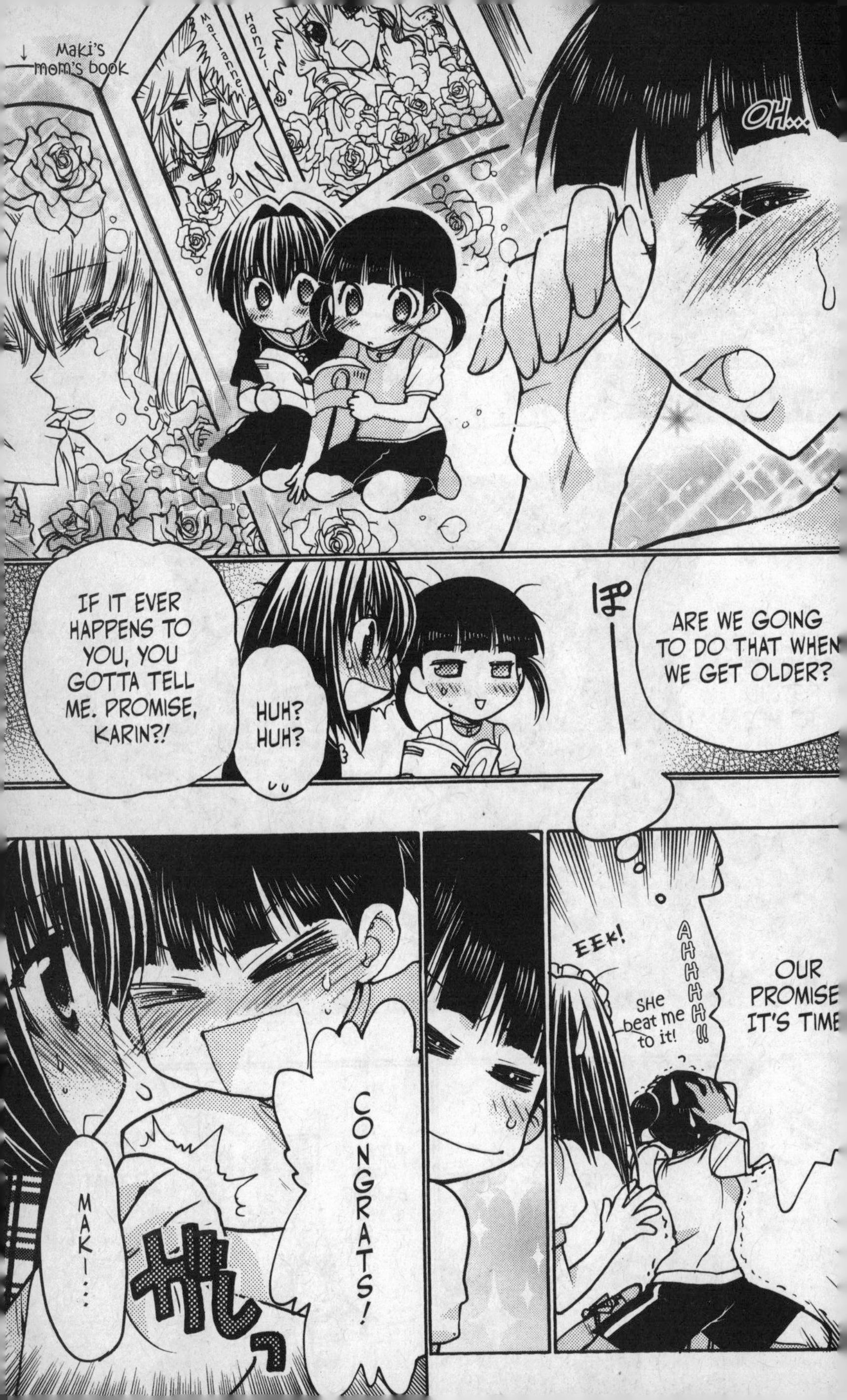
OH...
Hanzi!
Marianne!
Maki's mom's book
ARE WE GOING TO DO THAT WHEN WE GET OLDER?
ぽー
HUH? HUH?
IF IT EVER HAPPENS TO YOU, YOU GOTTA TELL ME. PROMISE, KARIN?!
OUR PROMISE IT'S TIME
AHHHHH!!
EEK!
SHE beat me to it!
CONGRATS!
MAKI...
ガしっ

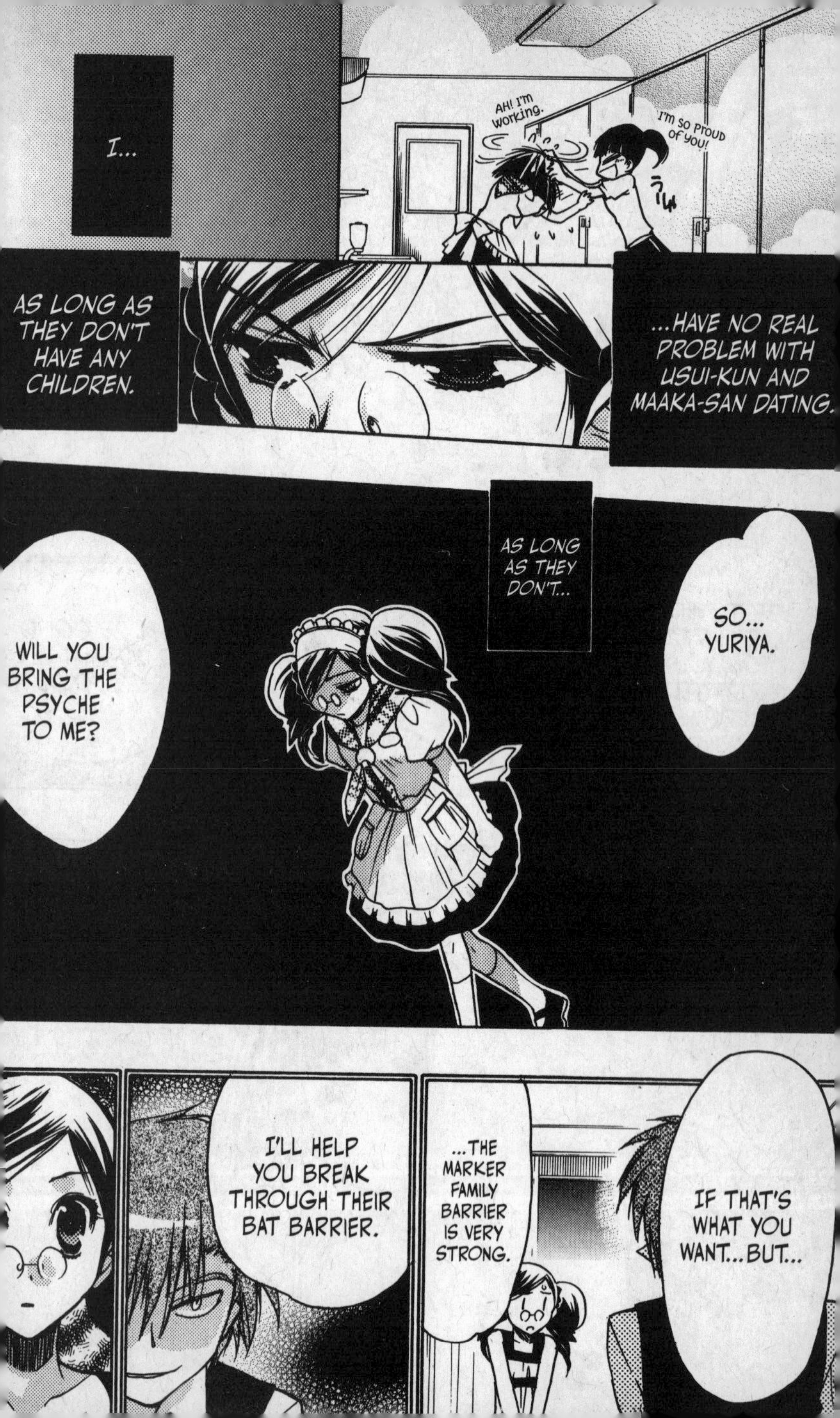
I'M SO PROUD OF YOU!
AH! I'M WORKING.
I...
...HAVE NO REAL PROBLEM WITH USUI-KUN AND MAAKA-SAN DATING.
AS LONG AS THEY DON'T HAVE ANY CHILDREN.
AS LONG AS THEY DON'T...
SO... YURIYA.
WILL YOU BRING THE PSYCHE TO ME?
IF THAT'S WHAT YOU WANT...BUT...
...THE MARKER FAMILY BARRIER IS VERY STRONG.
I'LL HELP YOU BREAK THROUGH THEIR BAT BARRIER.

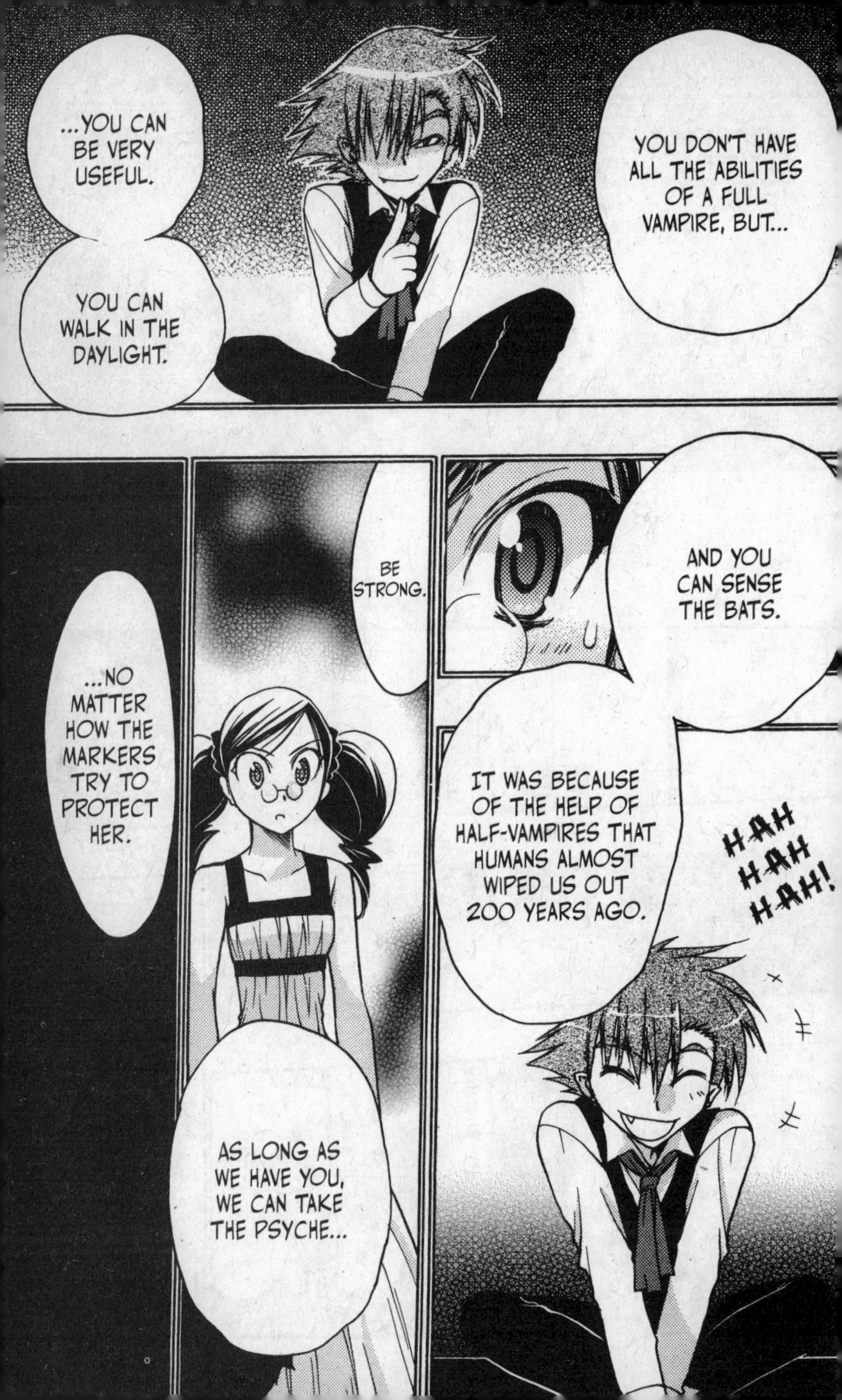
YOU DON'T HAVE ALL THE ABILITIES OF A FULL VAMPIRE, BUT...
...YOU CAN BE VERY USEFUL.
YOU CAN WALK IN THE DAYLIGHT.
AND YOU CAN SENSE THE BATS.
IT WAS BECAUSE OF THE HELP OF HALF-VAMPIRES THAT HUMANS ALMOST WIPED US OUT 200 YEARS AGO.
HAH HAH HAH!
BE STRONG.
AS LONG AS WE HAVE YOU, WE CAN TAKE THE PSYCHE...
...NO MATTER HOW THE MARKERS TRY TO PROTECT HER.

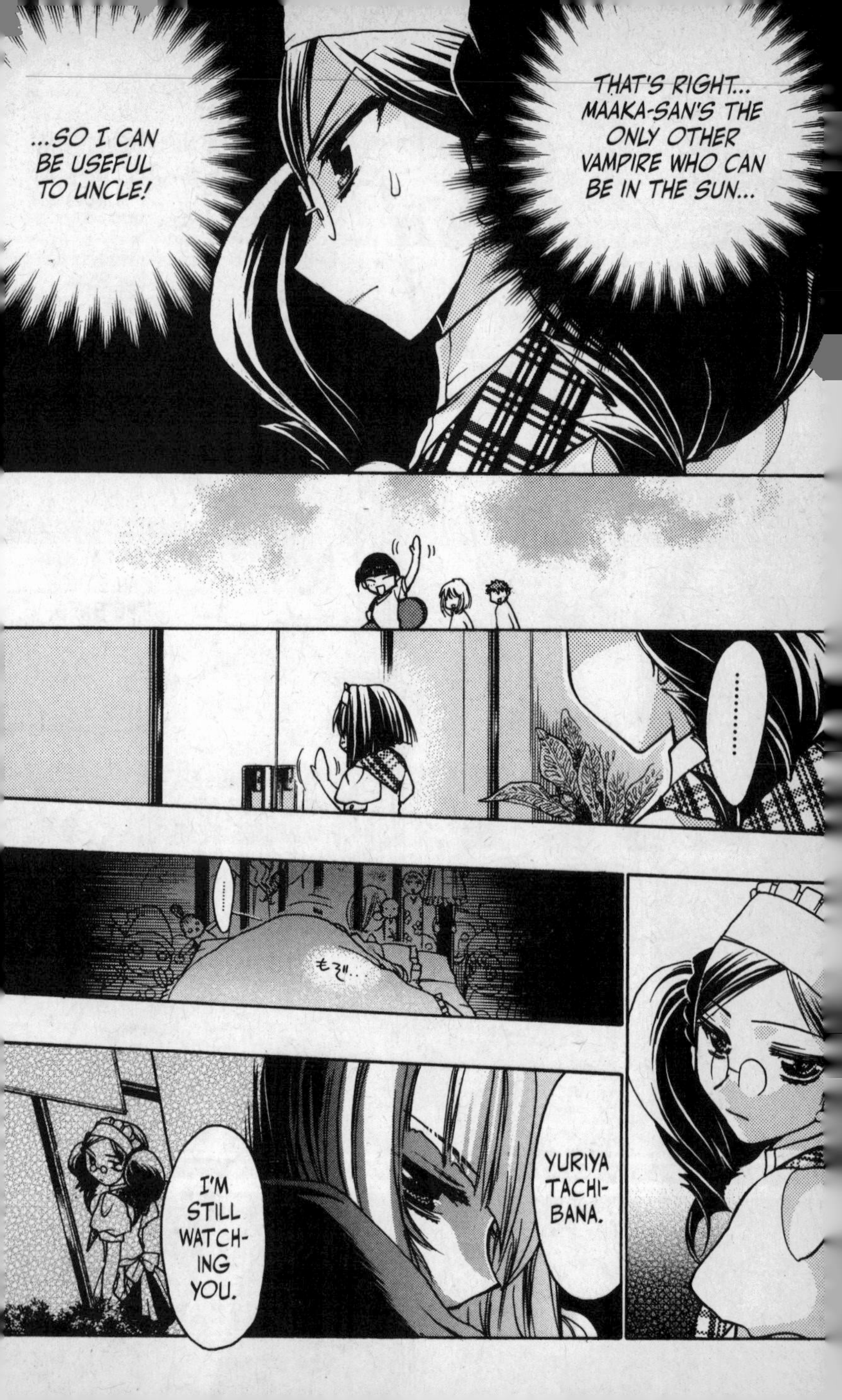
THAT'S RIGHT... MAAKA-SAN'S THE ONLY OTHER VAMPIRE WHO CAN BE IN THE SUN...
...SO I CAN BE USEFUL TO UNCLE!
......
......
もぞ...
YURIYA TACHI-BANA.
I'M STILL WATCHING YOU.

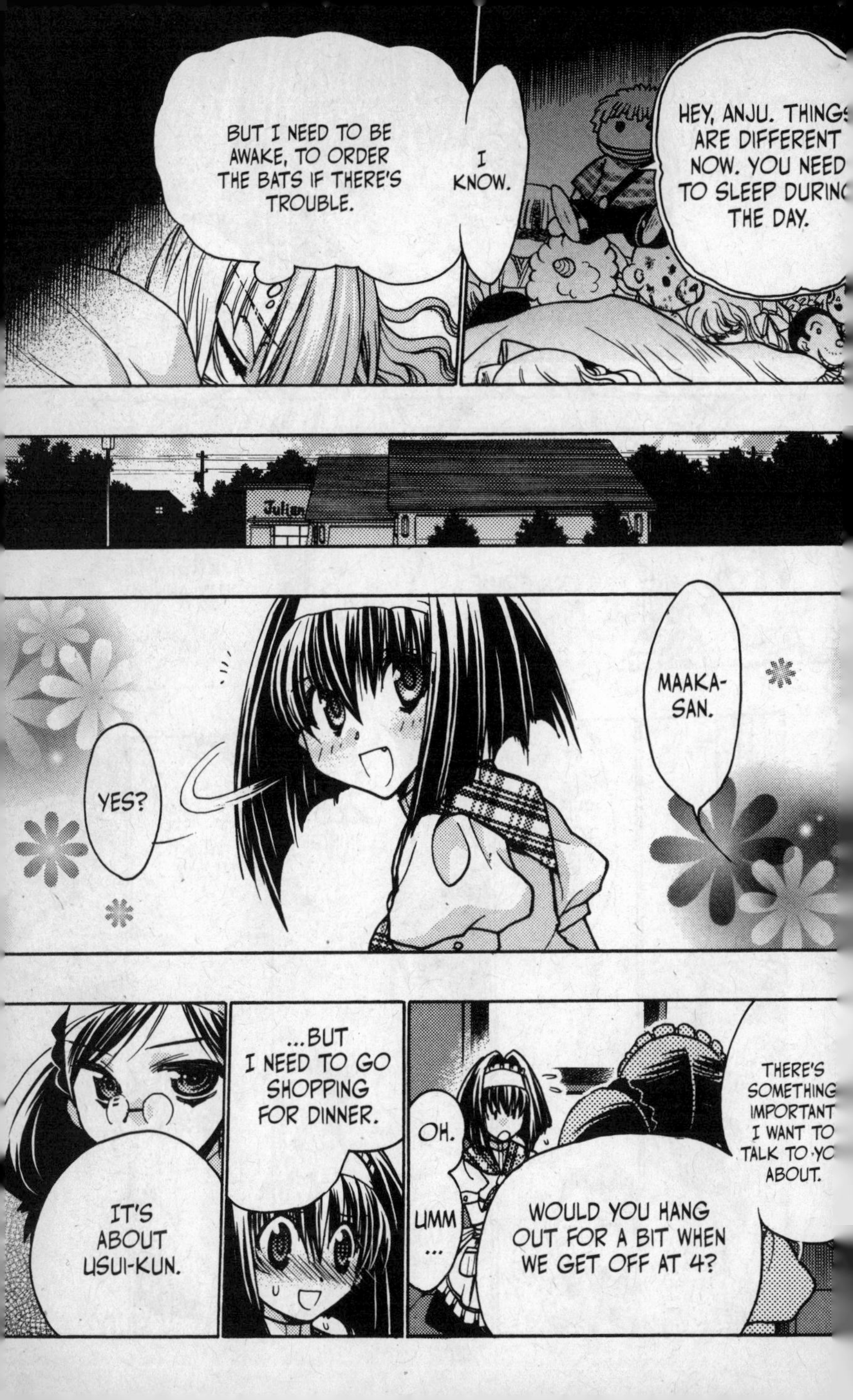
HEY, ANJU. THINGS ARE DIFFERENT NOW. YOU NEED TO SLEEP DURING THE DAY.
I KNOW.
BUT I NEED TO BE AWAKE, TO ORDER THE BATS IF THERE'S TROUBLE.
MAAKA-SAN.
YES?
THERE'S SOMETHING IMPORTANT I WANT TO TALK TO YOU ABOUT.
OH.
WOULD YOU HANG OUT FOR A BIT WHEN WE GET OFF AT 4?
UMM ...
...BUT I NEED TO GO SHOPPING FOR DINNER.
IT'S ABOUT USUI-KUN.

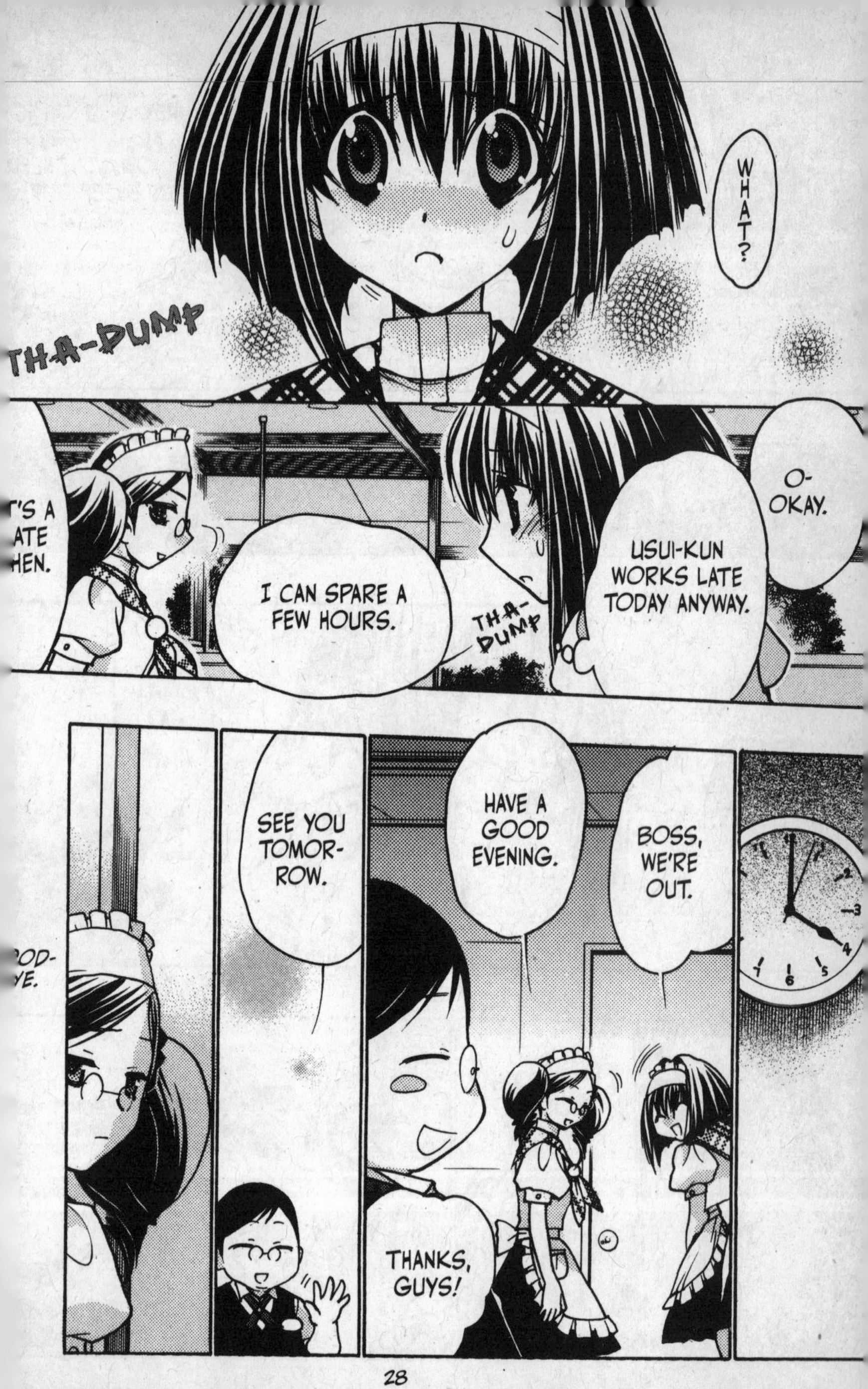
WHAT?
THA-DUMP
O-OKAY.
USUI-KUN WORKS LATE TODAY ANYWAY.
THA-DUMP
I CAN SPARE A FEW HOURS.
BOSS, WE'RE OUT.
HAVE A GOOD EVENING.
THANKS, GUYS!
SEE YOU TOMORROW.

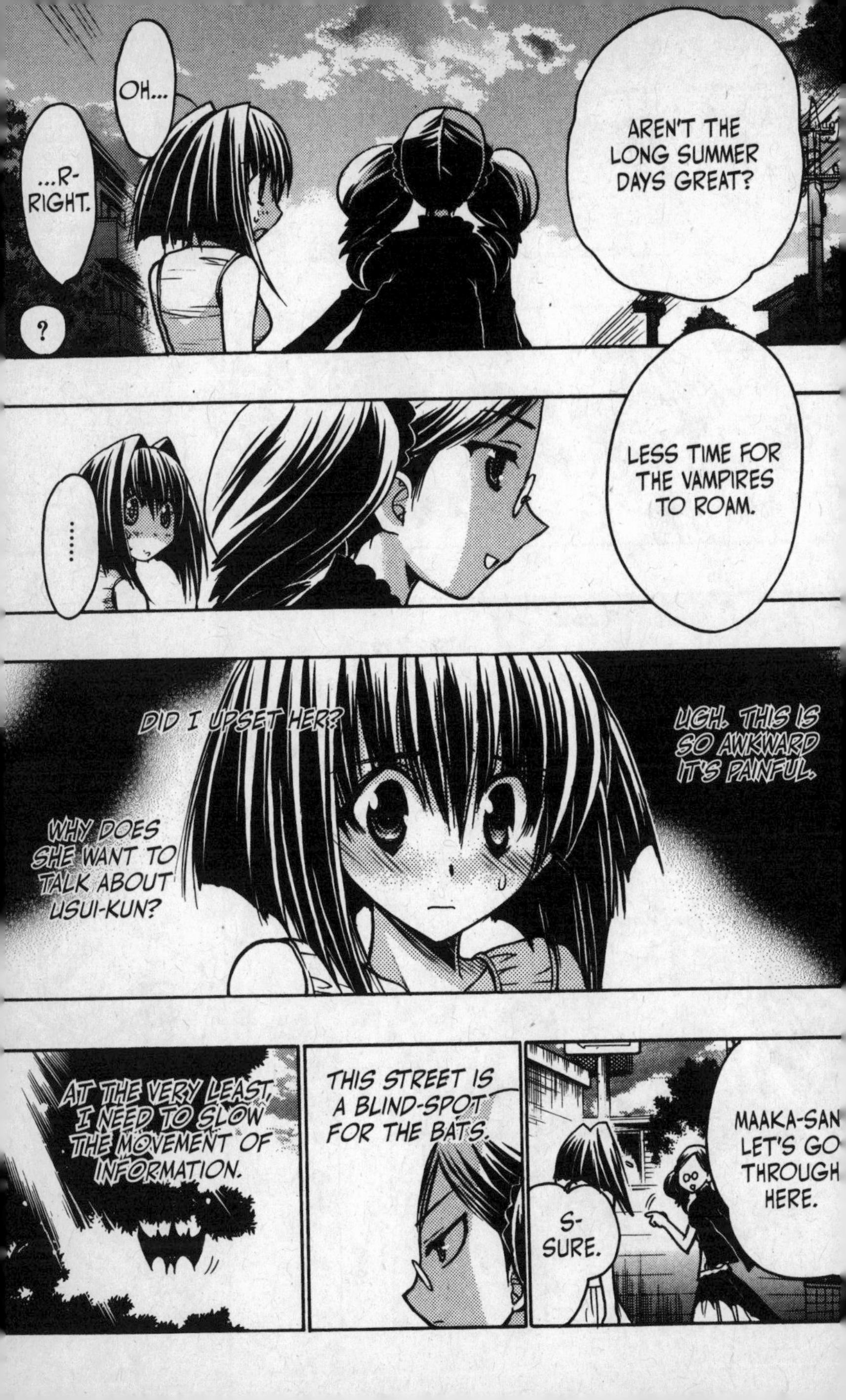
AREN'T THE LONG SUMMER DAYS GREAT?
OH...
...R- RIGHT.
?
LESS TIME FOR THE VAMPIRES TO ROAM.
......
UGH. THIS IS SO AWKWARD IT'S PAINFUL.
DID I UPSET HER?
WHY DOES SHE WANT TO TALK ABOUT USUI-KUN?
MAAKA-SAN LET'S GO THROUGH HERE.
S- SURE.
THIS STREET IS A BLIND-SPOT FOR THE BATS.
AT THE VERY LEAST, I NEED TO SLOW THE MOVEMENT OF INFORMATION.

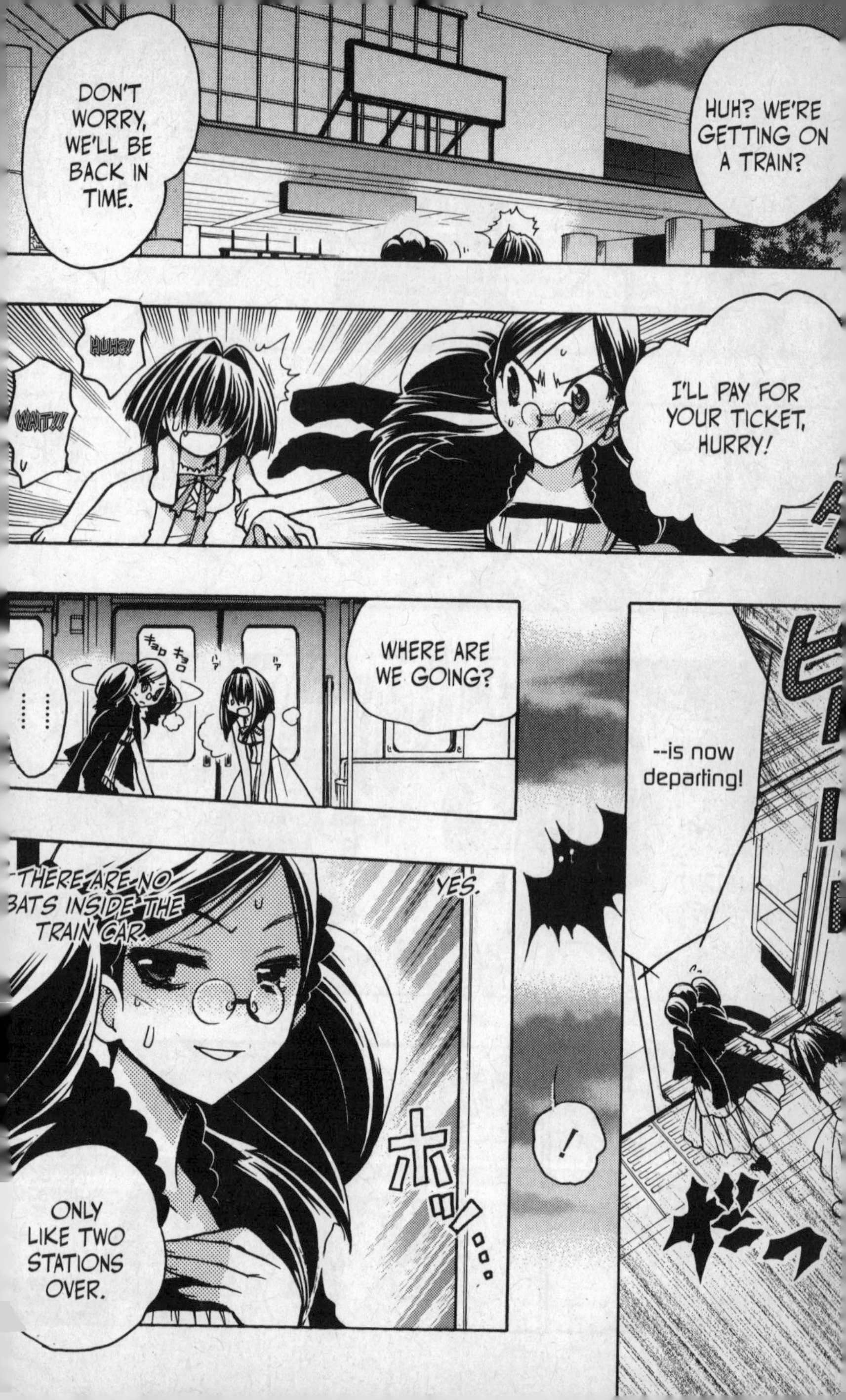

HUH? WE'RE GETTING ON A TRAIN?
DON'T WORRY, WE'LL BE BACK IN TIME.
I'LL PAY FOR YOUR TICKET, HURRY!
HUH?!
WAIT!!!
--is now departing!
!
WHERE ARE WE GOING?
......
YES.
THERE ARE NO BATS INSIDE THE TRAIN CAR.
ONLY LIKE TWO STATIONS OVER.

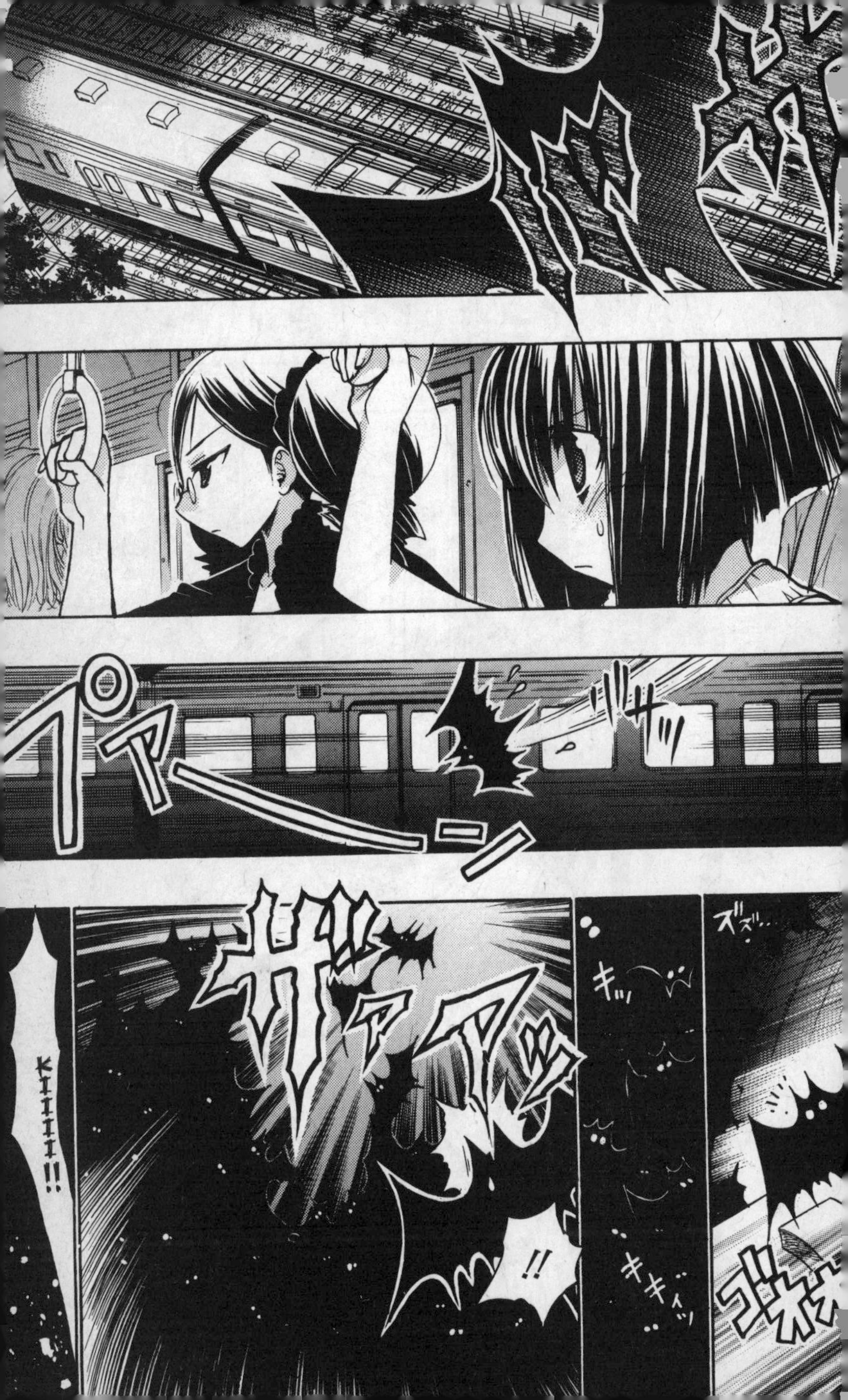

ザッ
パァーーーン
ズズ…
ゴォ
キッ
キキィッ
ザァアッ
!!
KIIIIII!!

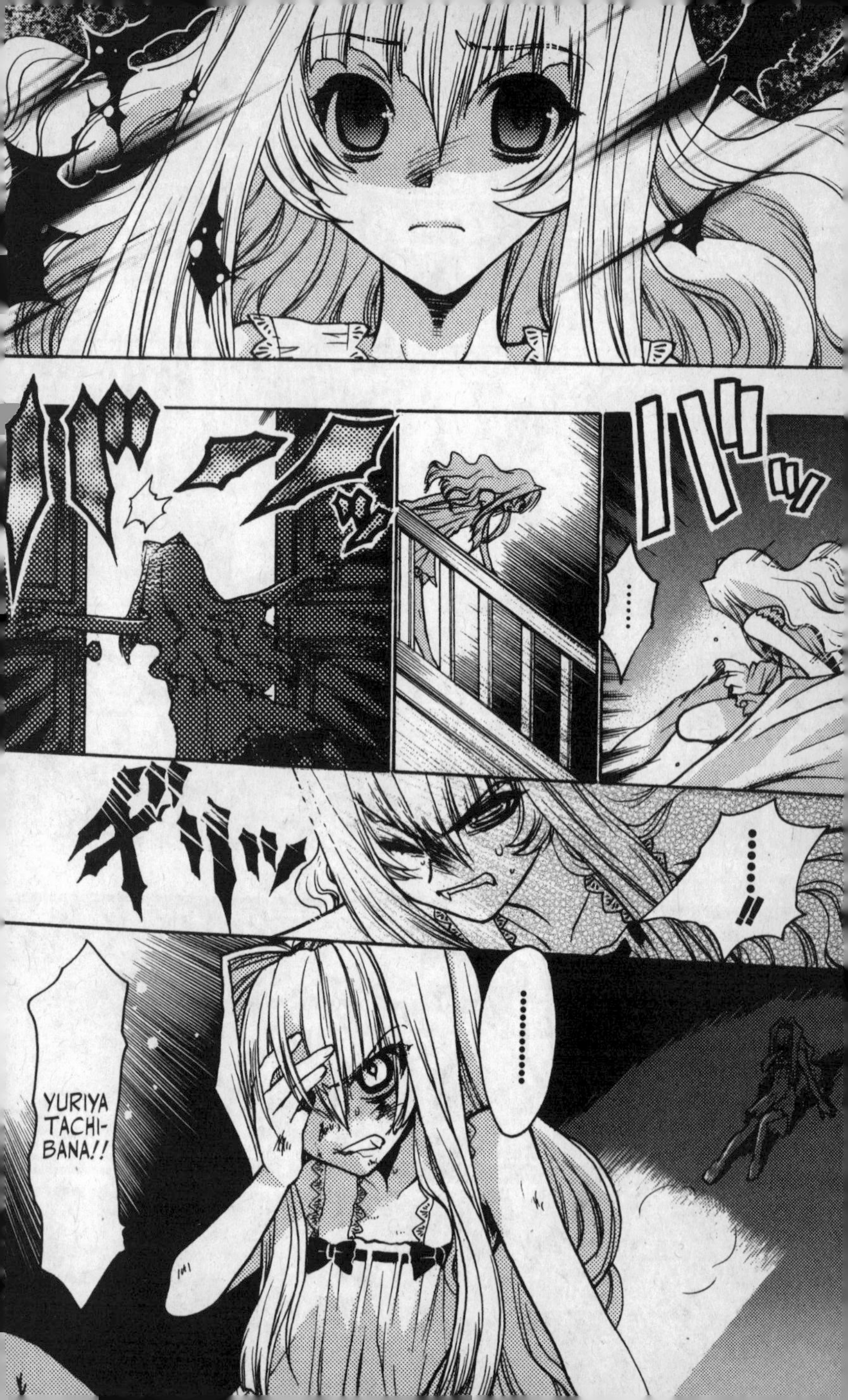
......
......!!
....
YURIYA TACHI-BANA!!

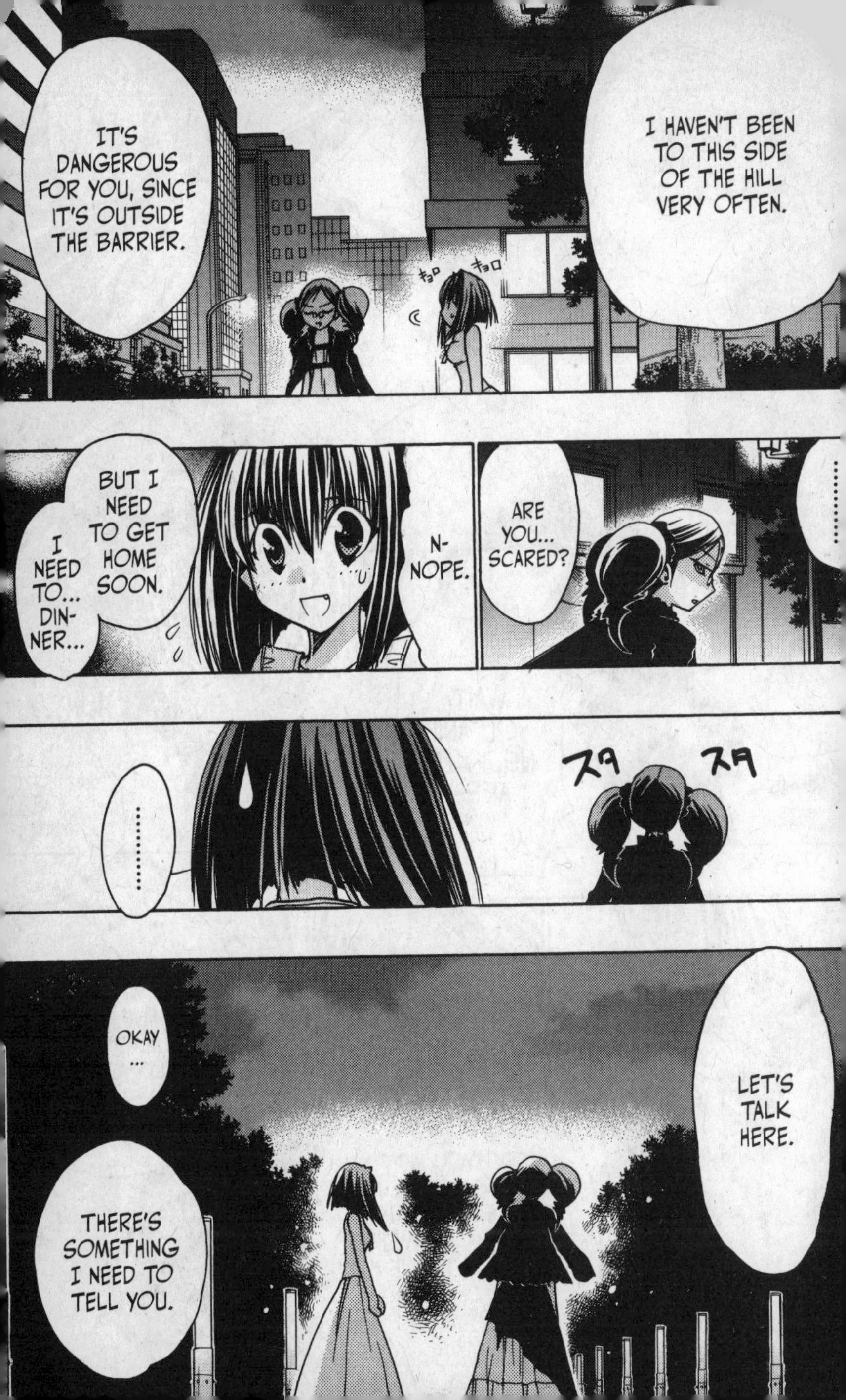
I HAVEN'T BEEN TO THIS SIDE OF THE HILL VERY OFTEN.
キョロ キョロ
IT'S DANGEROUS FOR YOU, SINCE IT'S OUTSIDE THE BARRIER.
......
ARE YOU... SCARED?
N-NOPE.
BUT I NEED TO GET HOME SOON.
I NEED TO... DINNER...
スタ スタ
......
LET'S TALK HERE.
OKAY...
THERE'S SOMETHING I NEED TO TELL YOU.

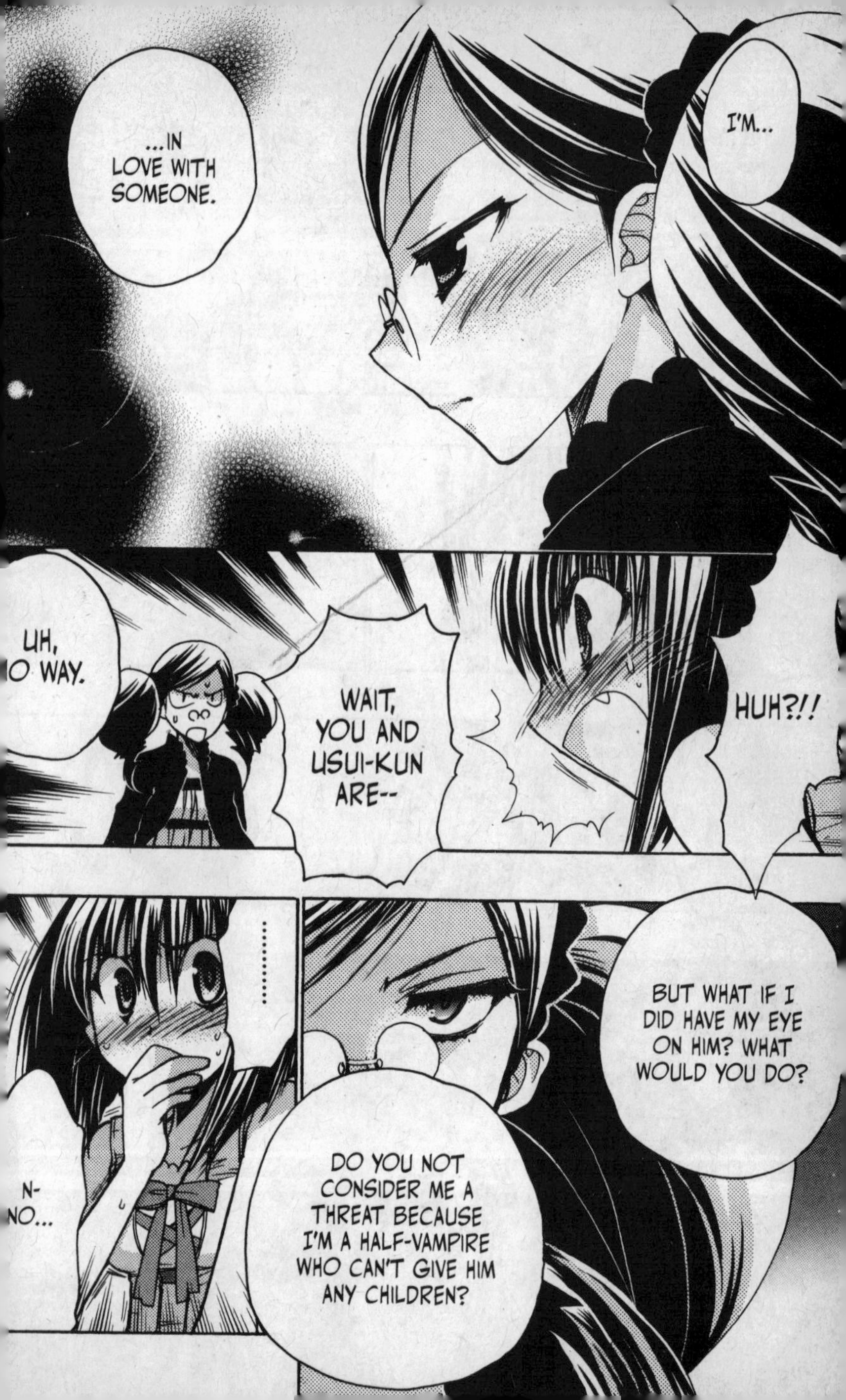
I'M...
...IN LOVE WITH SOMEONE.
HUH?!!
WAIT, YOU AND USUI-KUN ARE--
UH, O WAY.
BUT WHAT IF I DID HAVE MY EYE ON HIM? WHAT WOULD YOU DO?
DO YOU NOT CONSIDER ME A THREAT BECAUSE I'M A HALF-VAMPIRE WHO CAN'T GIVE HIM ANY CHILDREN?
......
N- NO...

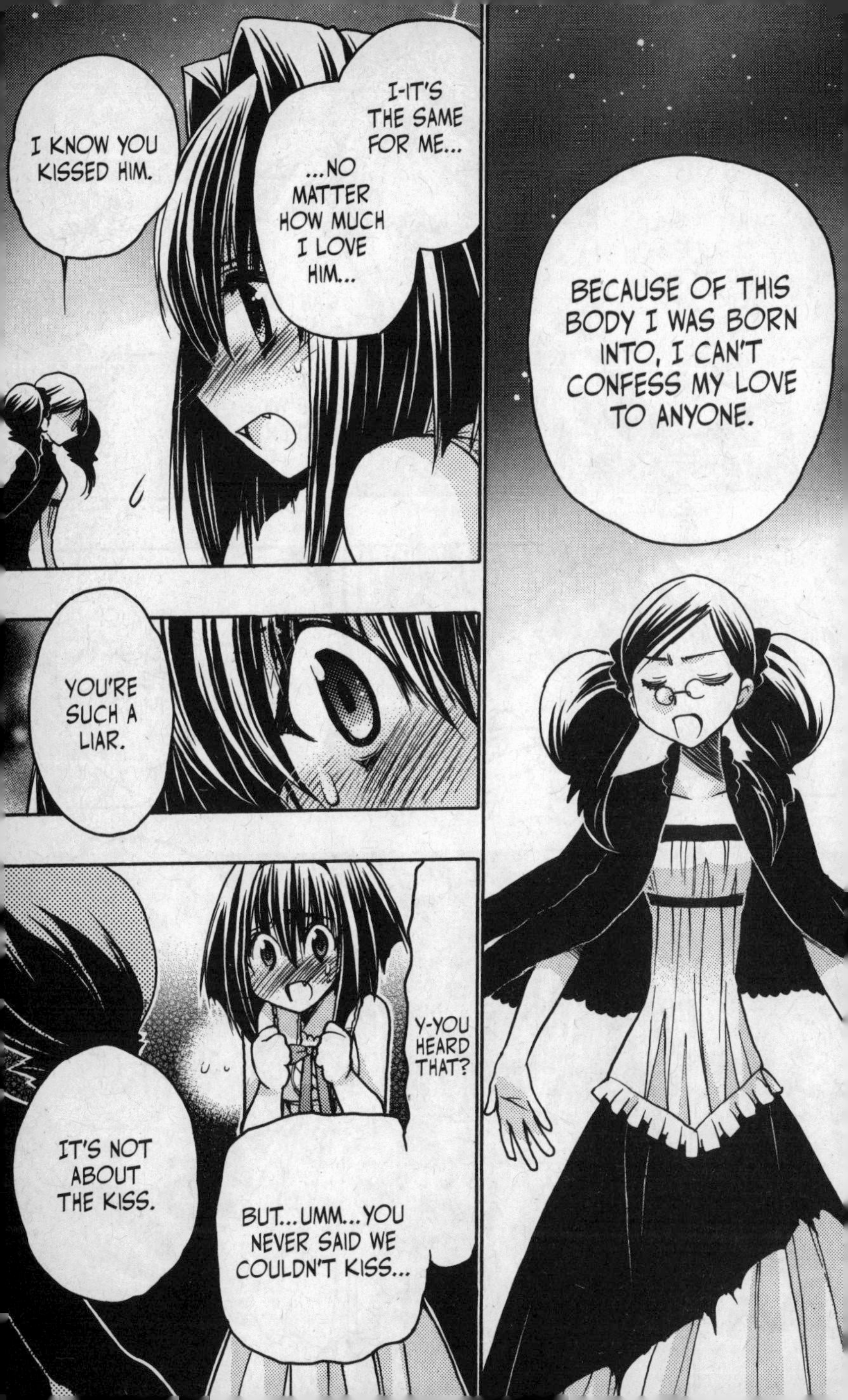
BECAUSE OF THIS BODY I WAS BORN INTO, I CAN'T CONFESS MY LOVE TO ANYONE.
I-IT'S THE SAME FOR ME...
...NO MATTER HOW MUCH I LOVE HIM...
I KNOW YOU KISSED HIM.
YOU'RE SUCH A LIAR.
Y-YOU HEARD THAT?
BUT...UMM...YOU NEVER SAID WE COULDN'T KISS...
IT'S NOT ABOUT THE KISS.

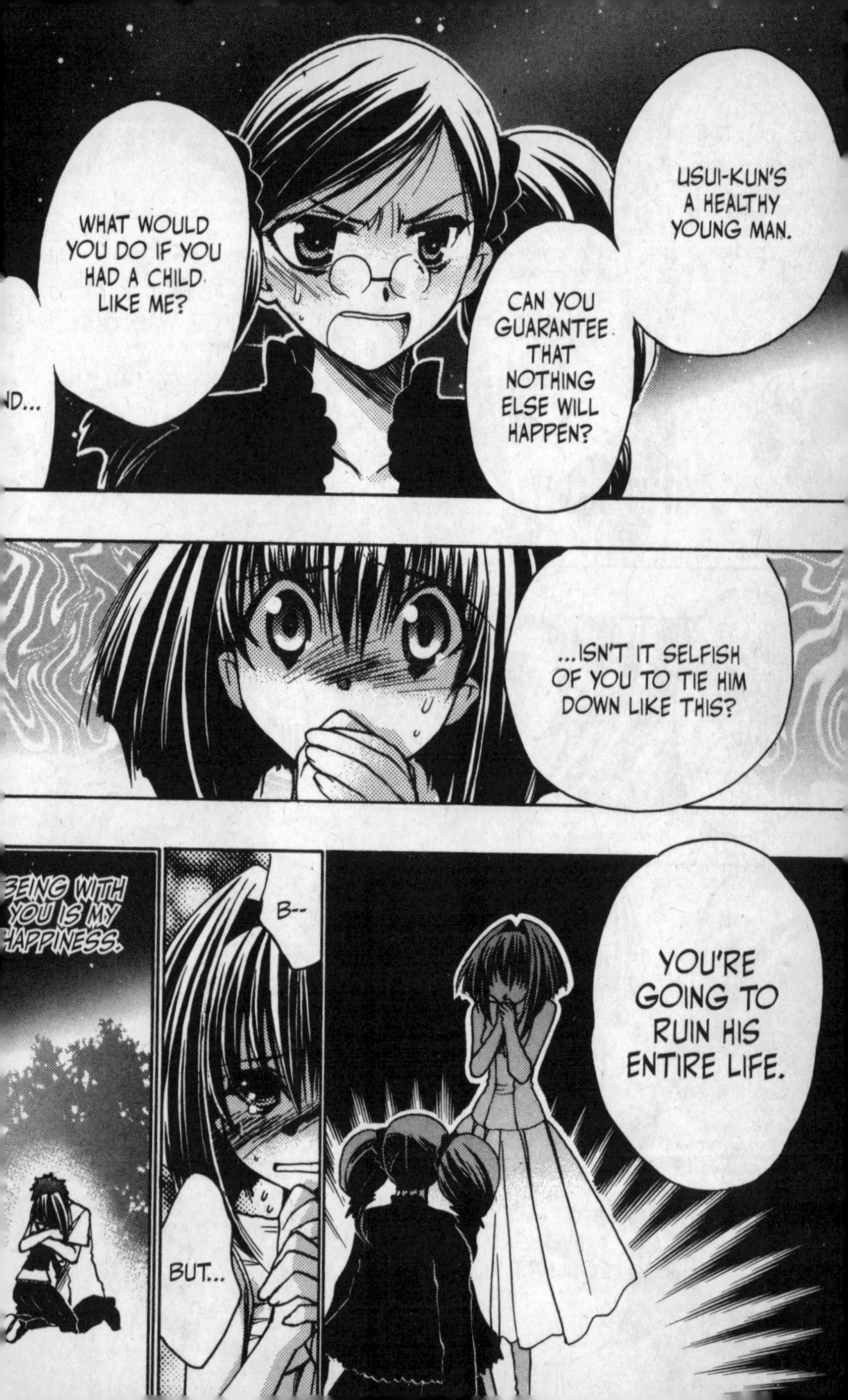
USUI-KUN'S A HEALTHY YOUNG MAN.
CAN YOU GUARANTEE THAT NOTHING ELSE WILL HAPPEN?
WHAT WOULD YOU DO IF YOU HAD A CHILD LIKE ME?
ND...
...ISN'T IT SELFISH OF YOU TO TIE HIM DOWN LIKE THIS?
YOU'RE GOING TO RUIN HIS ENTIRE LIFE.
B--
BUT...
BEING WITH YOU IS MY HAPPINESS.

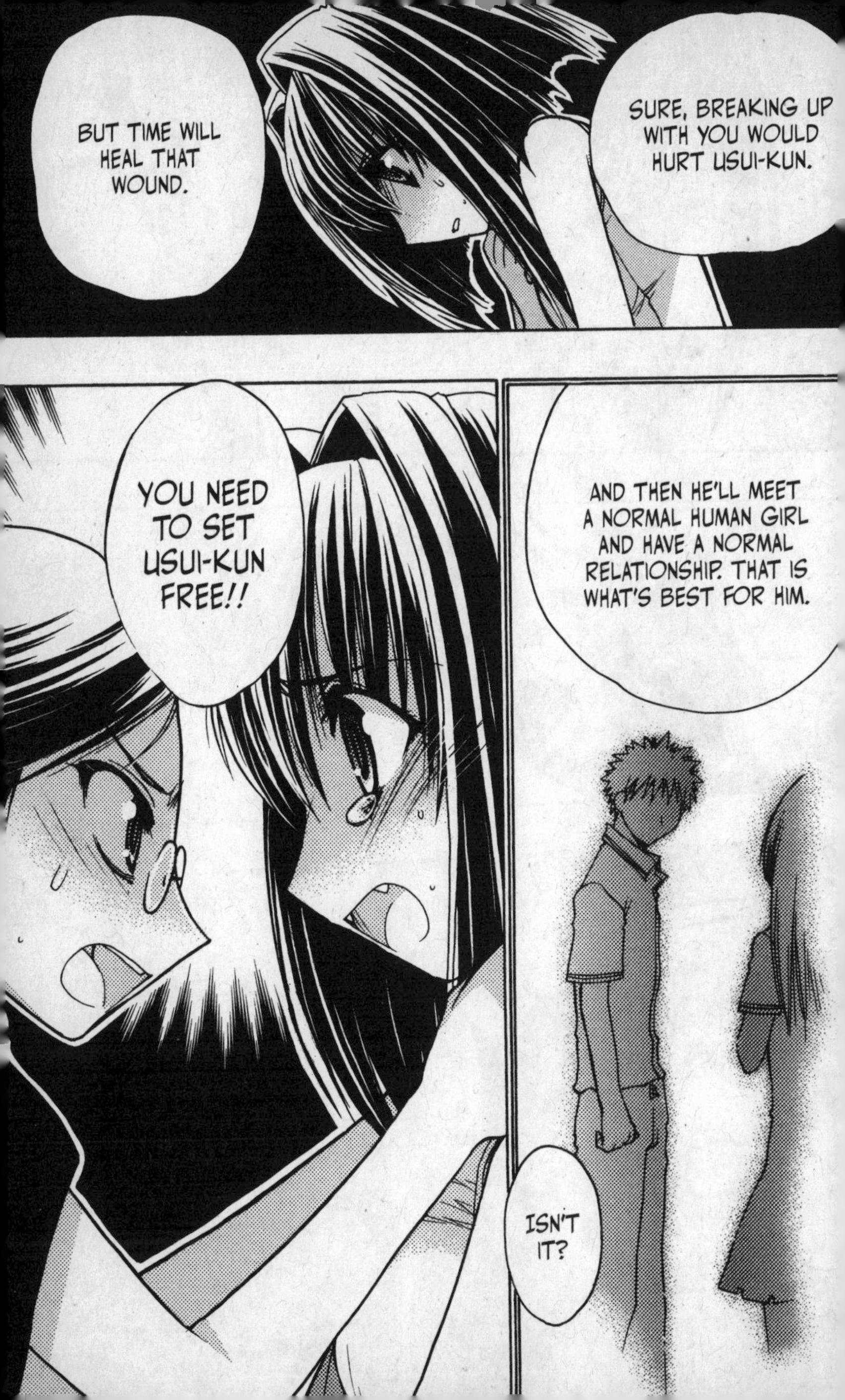
SURE, BREAKING UP WITH YOU WOULD HURT USUI-KUN.
BUT TIME WILL HEAL THAT WOUND.
AND THEN HE'LL MEET A NORMAL HUMAN GIRL AND HAVE A NORMAL RELATIONSHIP. THAT IS WHAT'S BEST FOR HIM.
ISN'T IT?
YOU NEED TO SET USUI-KUN FREE!!

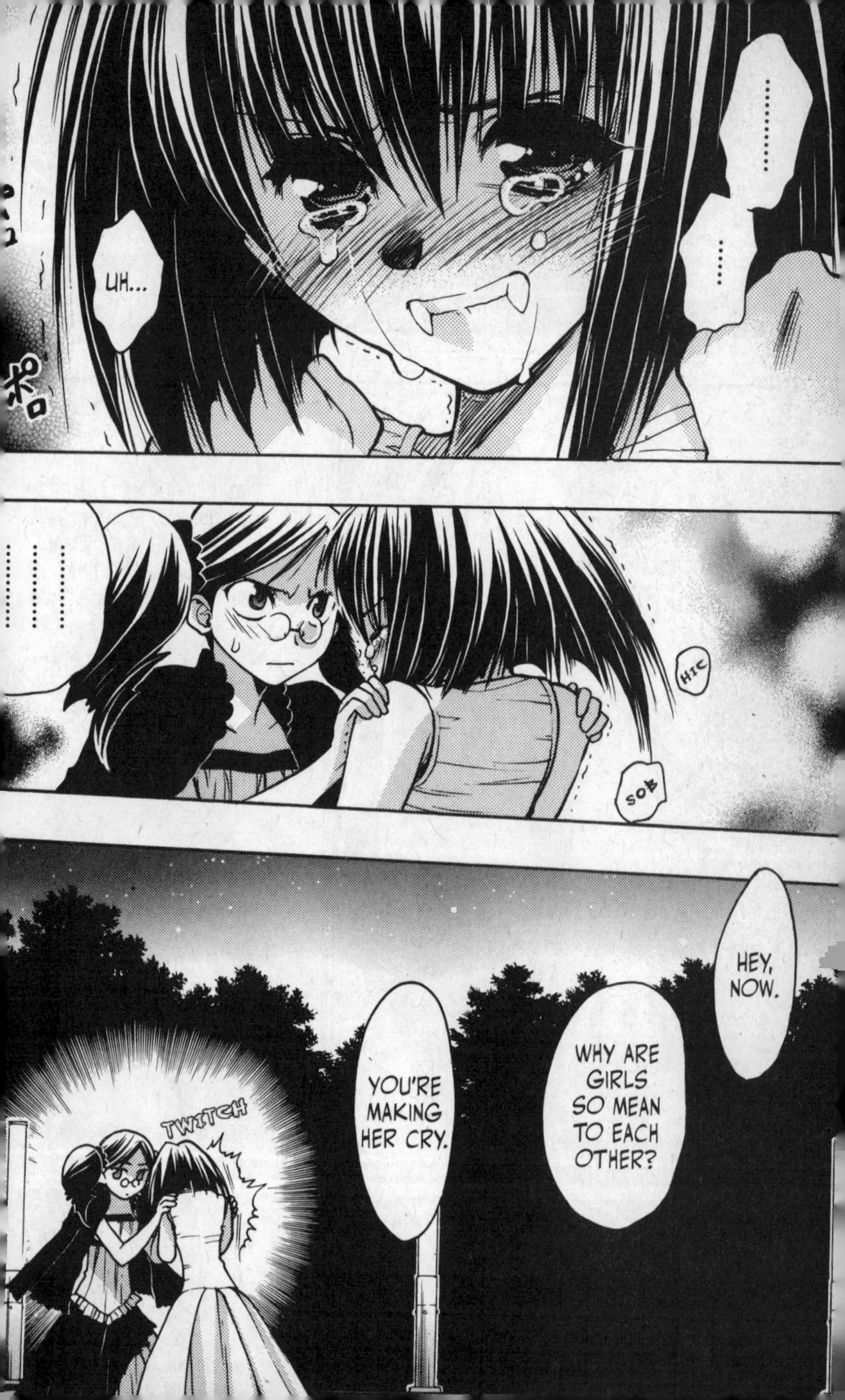
......
......
UH...
ポロ
HIC
SOB
......
HEY, NOW.
WHY ARE GIRLS SO MEAN TO EACH OTHER?
YOU'RE MAKING HER CRY.
TWITCH

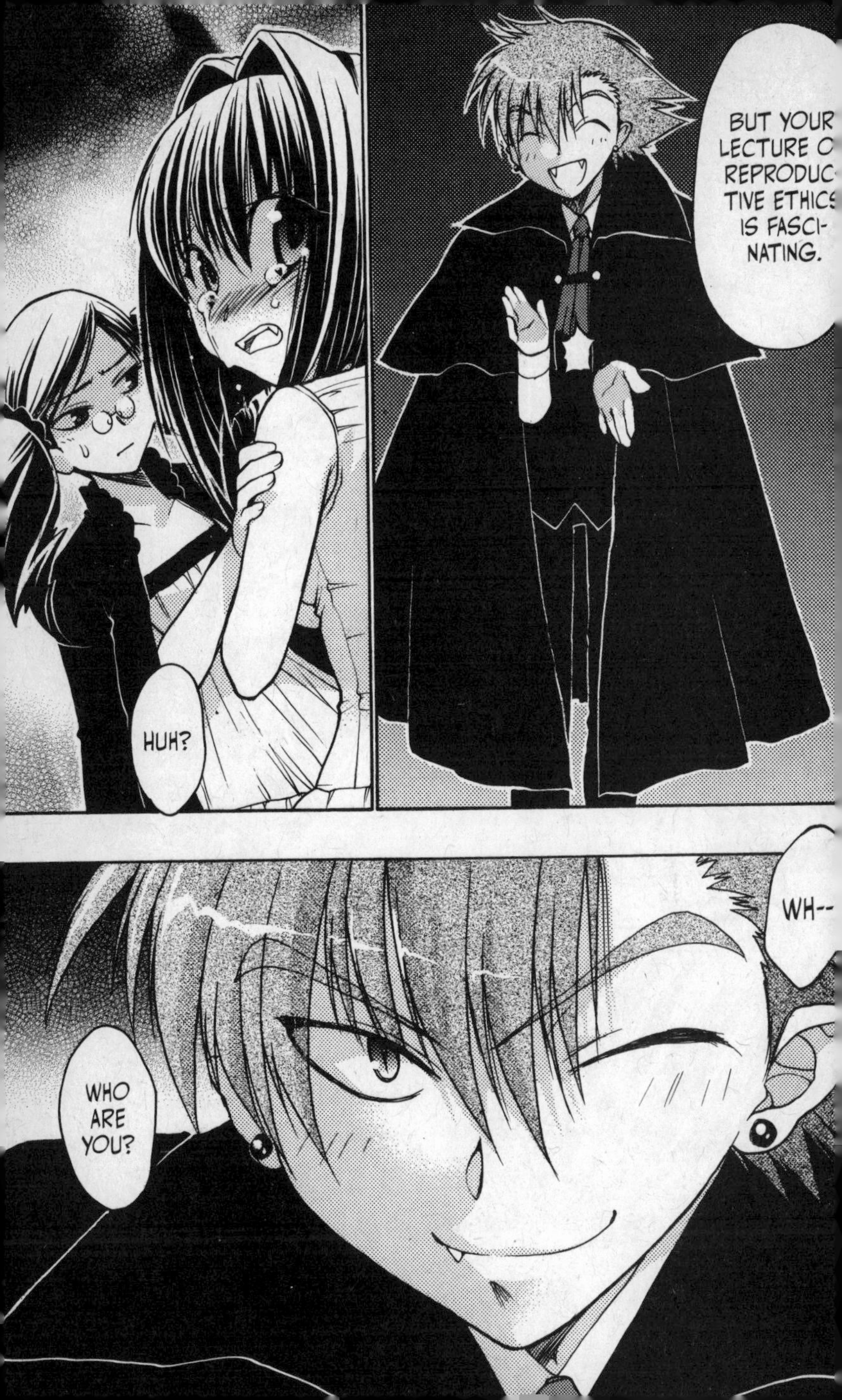
BUT YOUR LECTURE O REPRODUC-TIVE ETHICS IS FASCI-NATING.
HUH?
WH--
WHO ARE YOU?

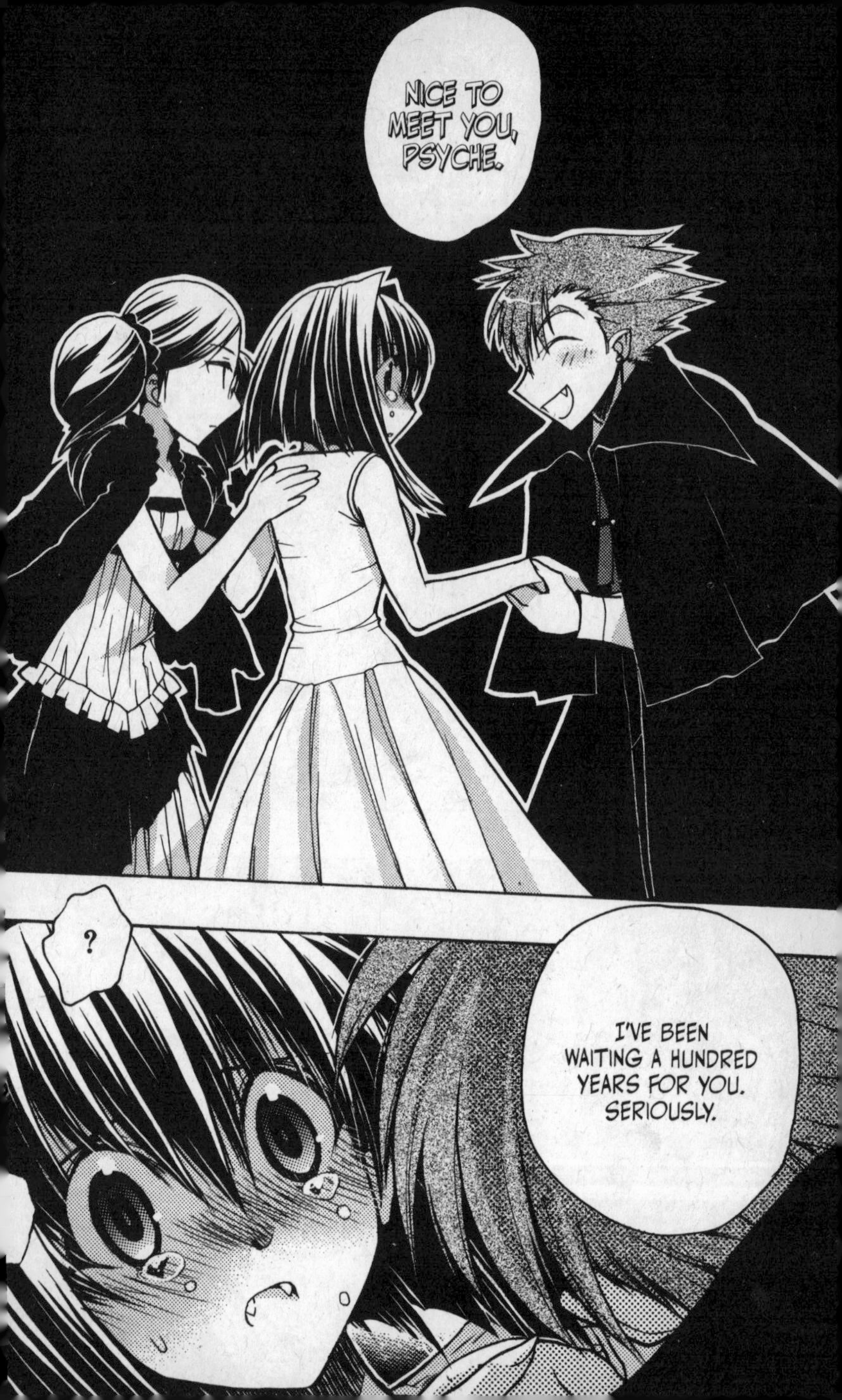
NICE TO MEET YOU, PSYCHE.
I'VE BEEN WAITING A HUNDRED YEARS FOR YOU. SERIOUSLY.
?

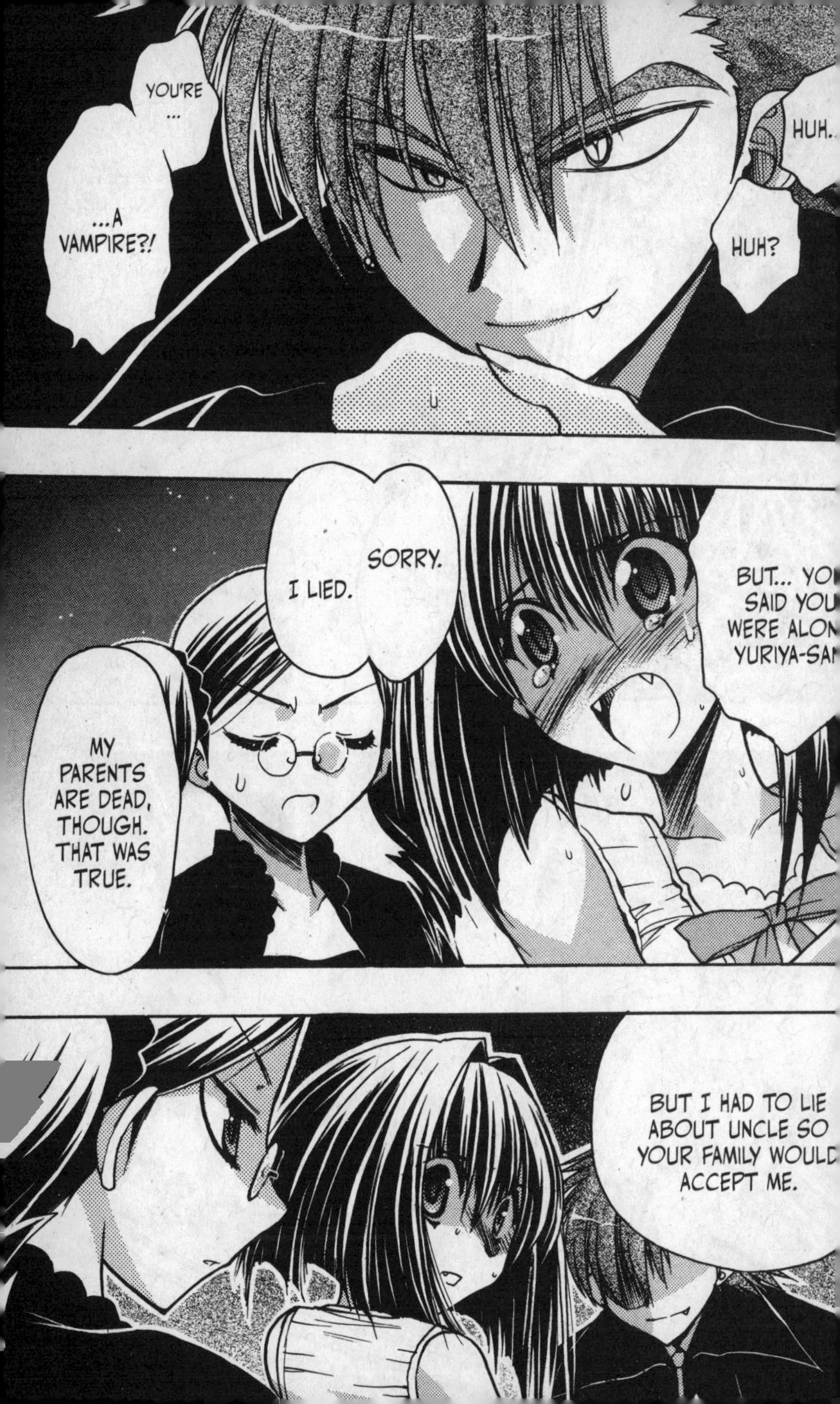
HUH..
HUH?
YOU'RE ...
...A VAMPIRE?!
BUT... YO SAID YOU WERE ALON YURIYA-SA
SORRY. I LIED.
MY PARENTS ARE DEAD, THOUGH. THAT WAS TRUE.
BUT I HAD TO LIE ABOUT UNCLE SO YOUR FAMILY WOULD ACCEPT ME.

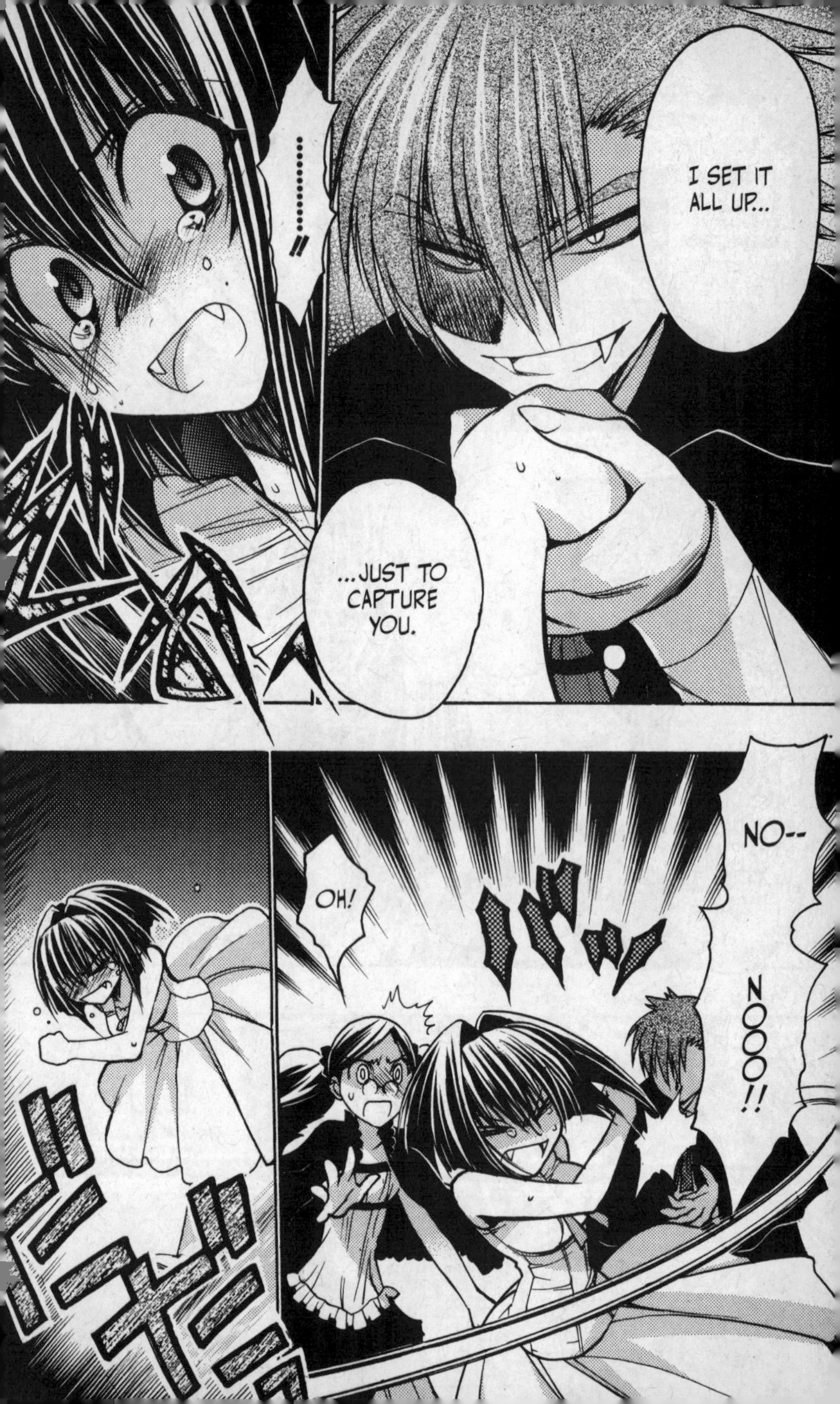
I SET IT ALL UP...
......!!
...JUST TO CAPTURE YOU.
NO--
NOOOO!!
OH!

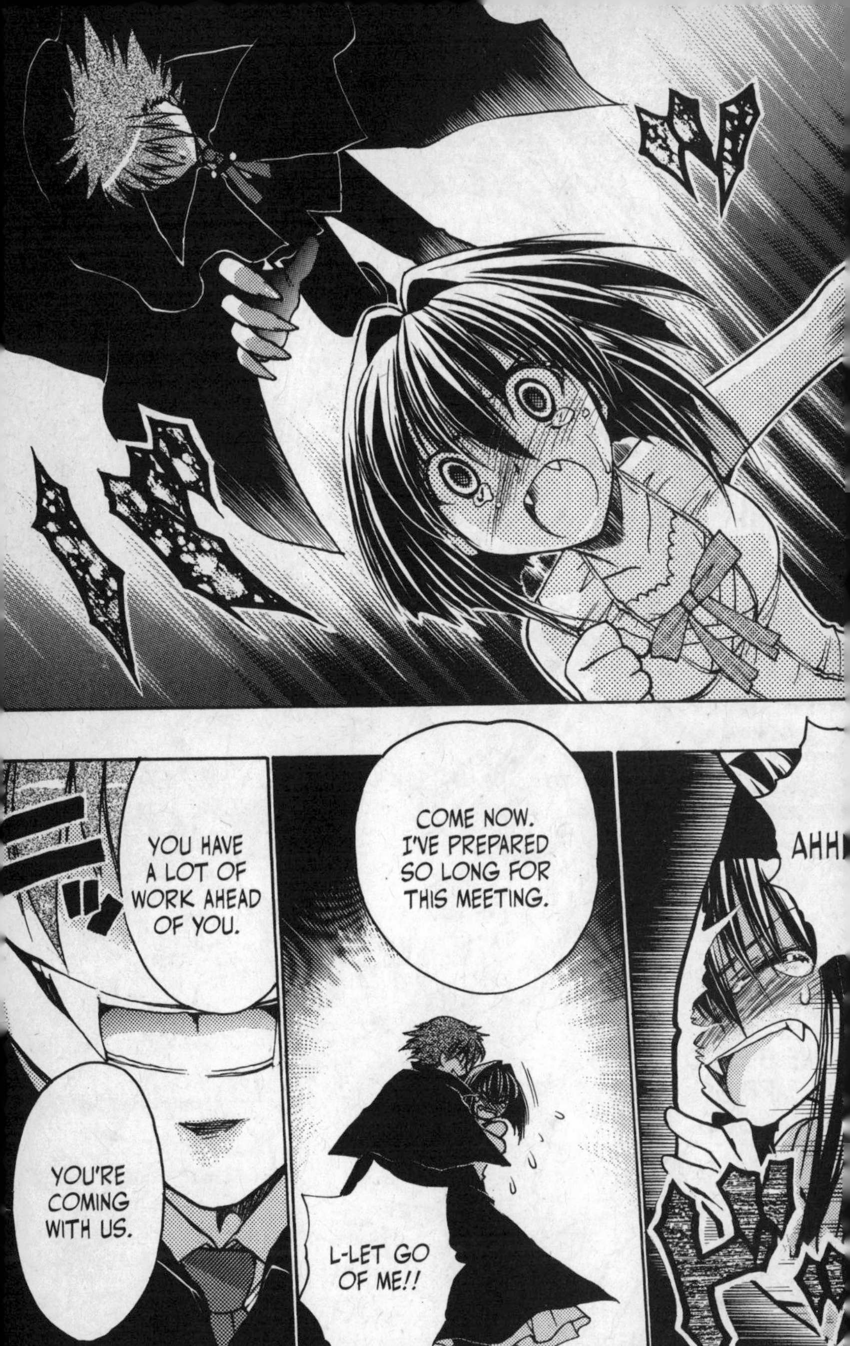
AHH
COME NOW. I'VE PREPARED SO LONG FOR THIS MEETING.
L-LET GO OF ME!!
YOU HAVE A LOT OF WORK AHEAD OF YOU.
YOU'RE COMING WITH US.

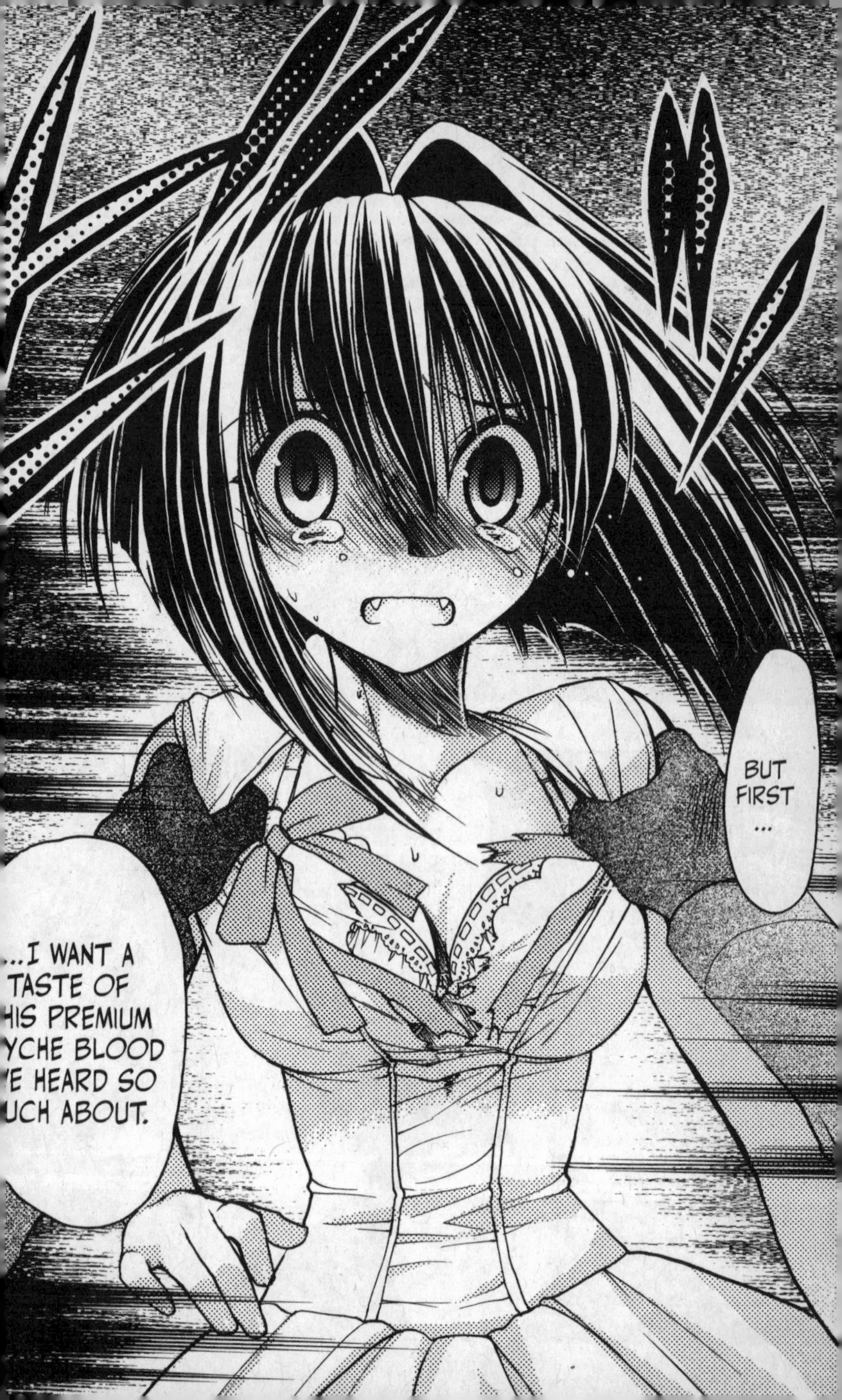

BUT FIRST ...
...I WANT A TASTE OF HIS PREMIUM YCHE BLOOD 'E HEARD SO UCH ABOUT.

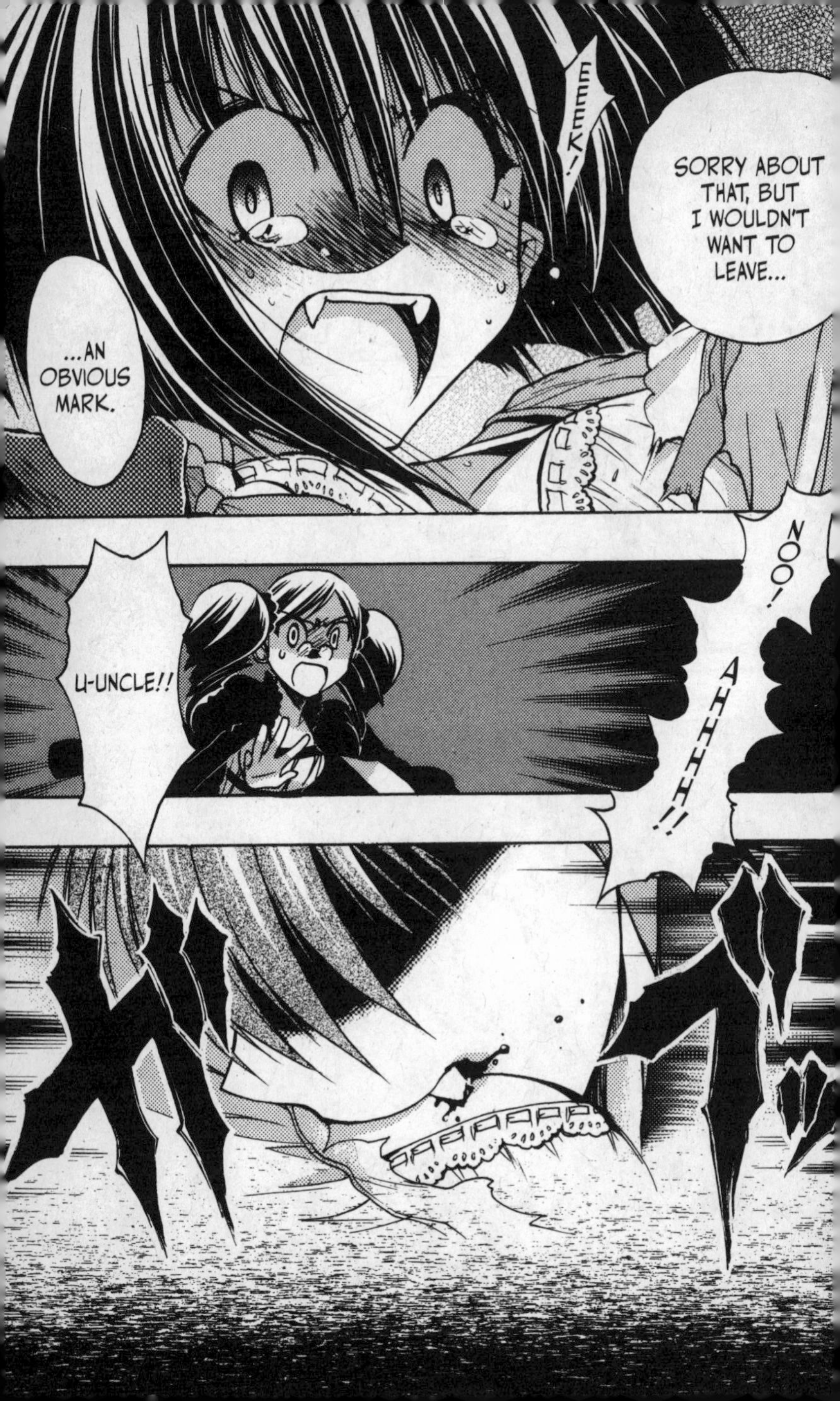
SORRY ABOUT THAT, BUT I WOULDN'T WANT TO LEAVE...
EEEK!
...AN OBVIOUS MARK.
NOO! AHHHHH!!
U-UNCLE!!

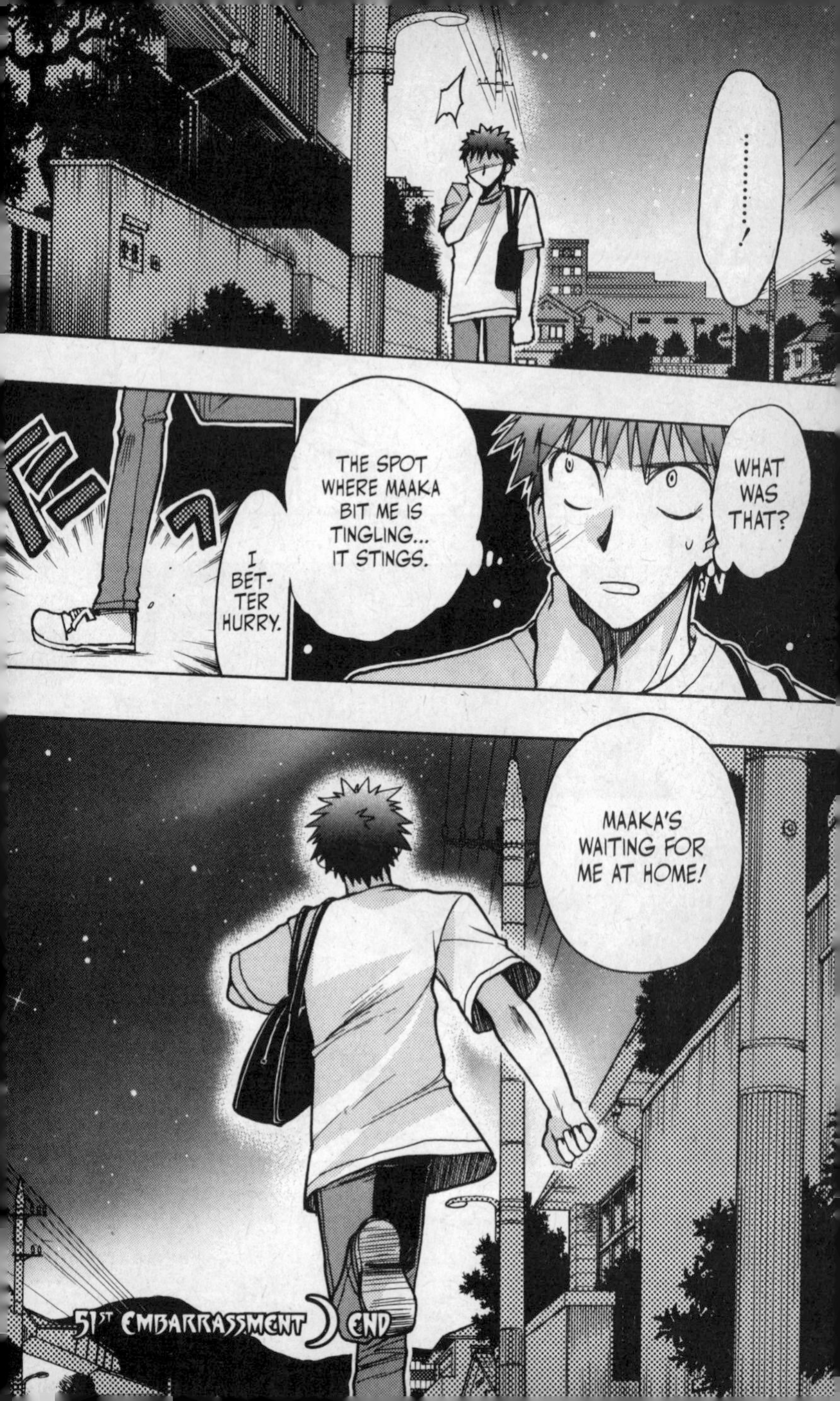
......!
WHAT WAS THAT?
THE SPOT WHERE MAAKA BIT ME IS TINGLING... IT STINGS.
I BET-TER HURRY.
MAAKA'S WAITING FOR ME AT HOME!
51ST EMBARRASSMENT END

52ND EMBARRASSMENT THE MARKERS' SEARCH AND KENTA'S GUIDANCE

~SEARCH~

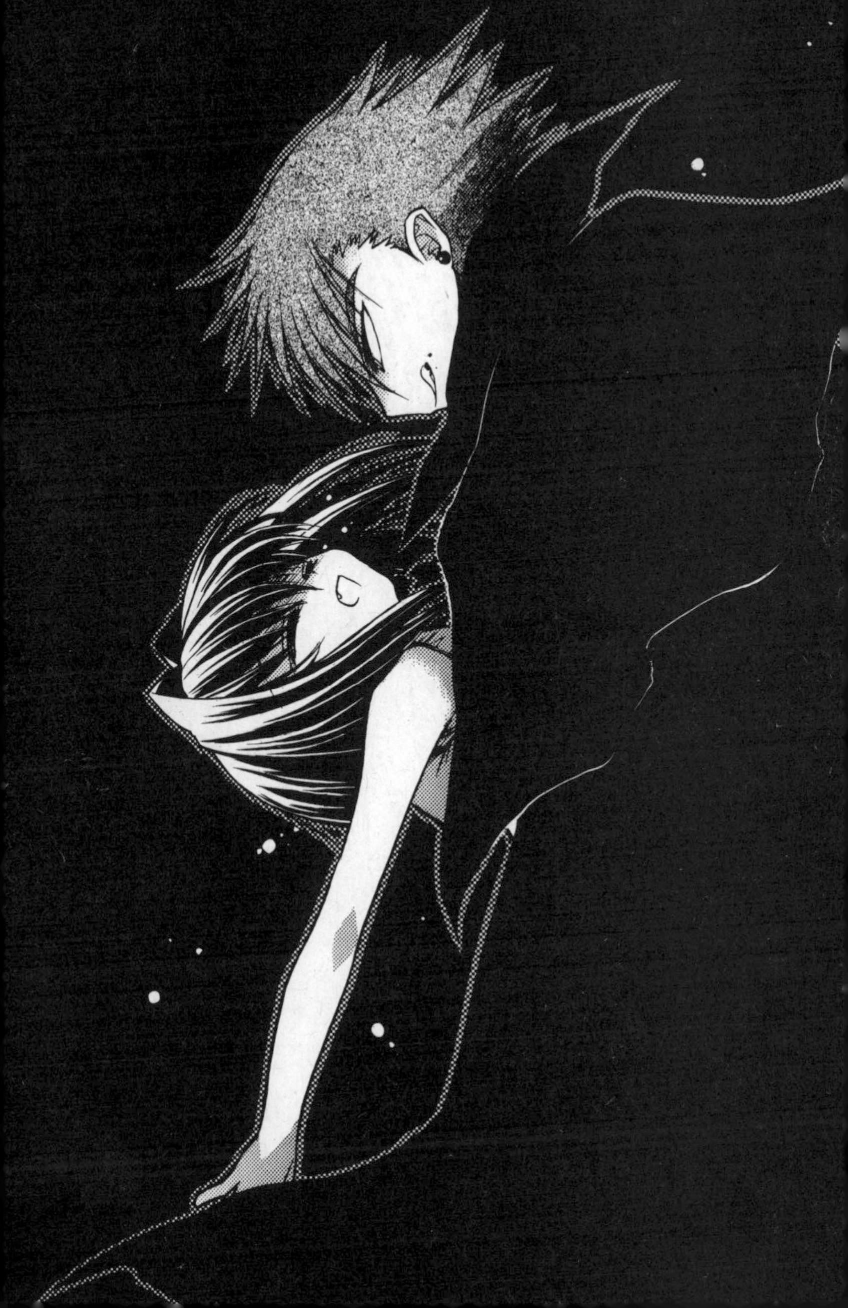

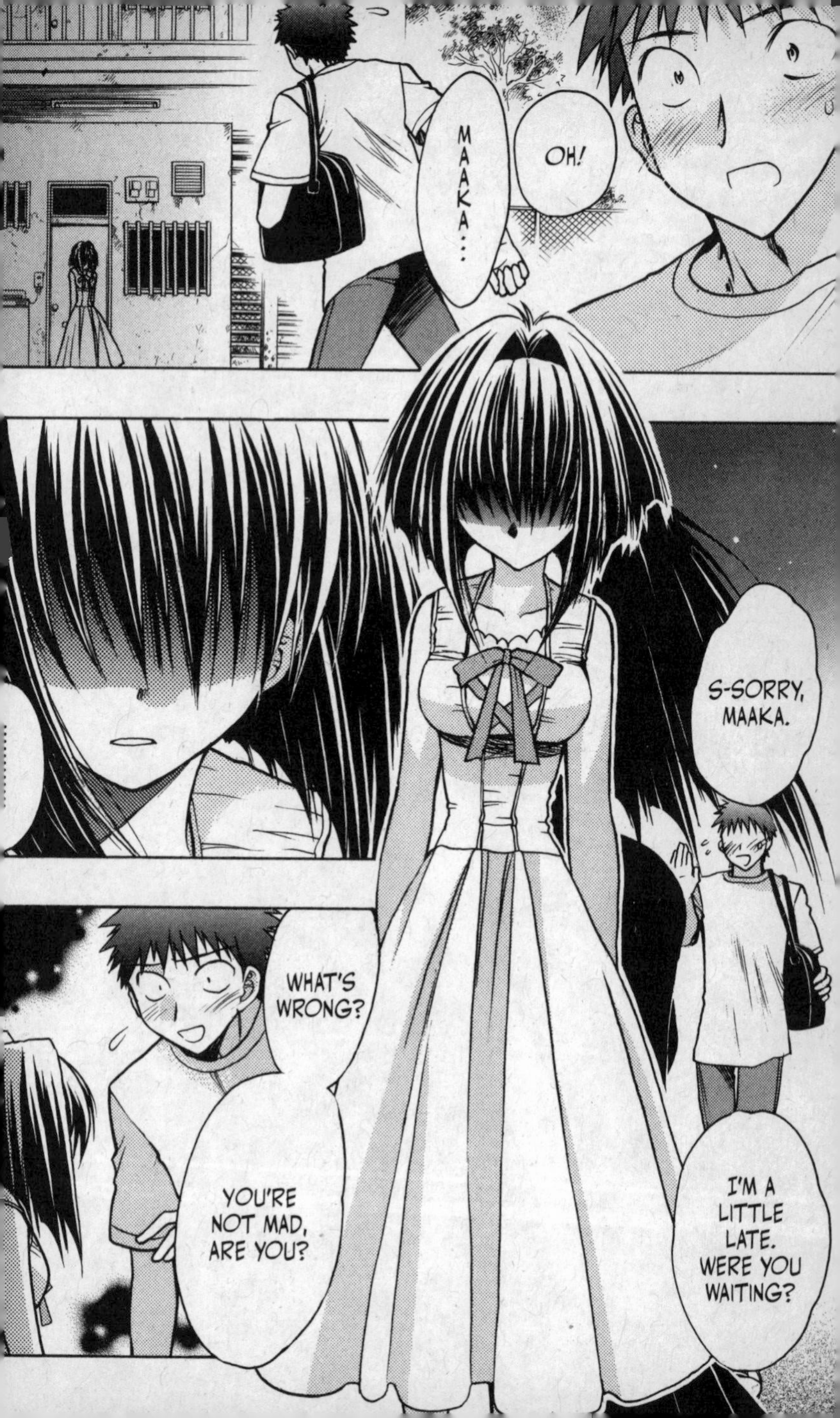
OH!
MAAKA...
S-SORRY, MAAKA.
I'M A LITTLE LATE. WERE YOU WAITING?
WHAT'S WRONG?
YOU'RE NOT MAD, ARE YOU?

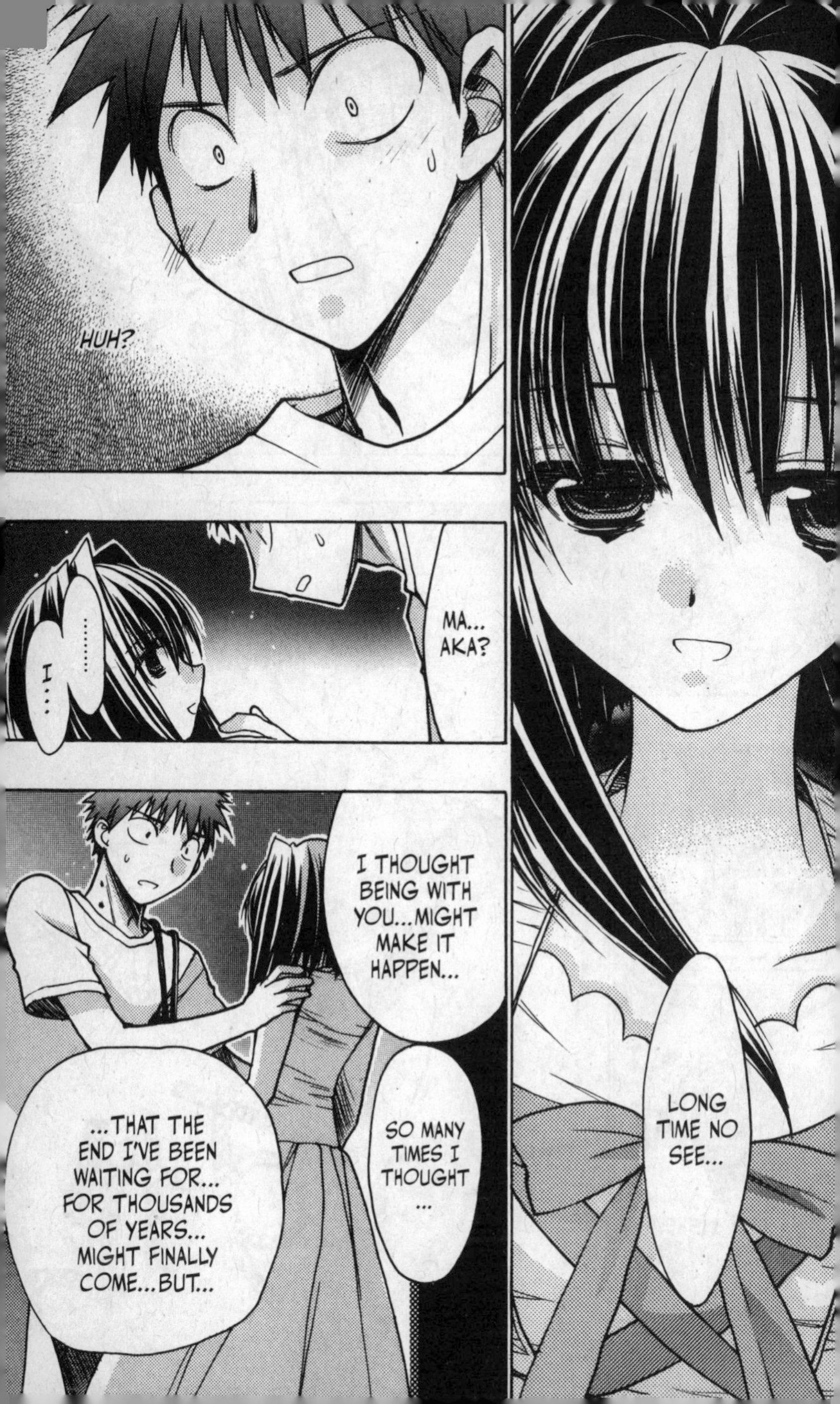
LONG TIME NO SEE...
HUH?
MA... AKA?
...... I...
I THOUGHT BEING WITH YOU...MIGHT MAKE IT HAPPEN...
SO MANY TIMES I THOUGHT ...
...THAT THE END I'VE BEEN WAITING FOR... FOR THOUSANDS OF YEARS... MIGHT FINALLY COME...BUT...

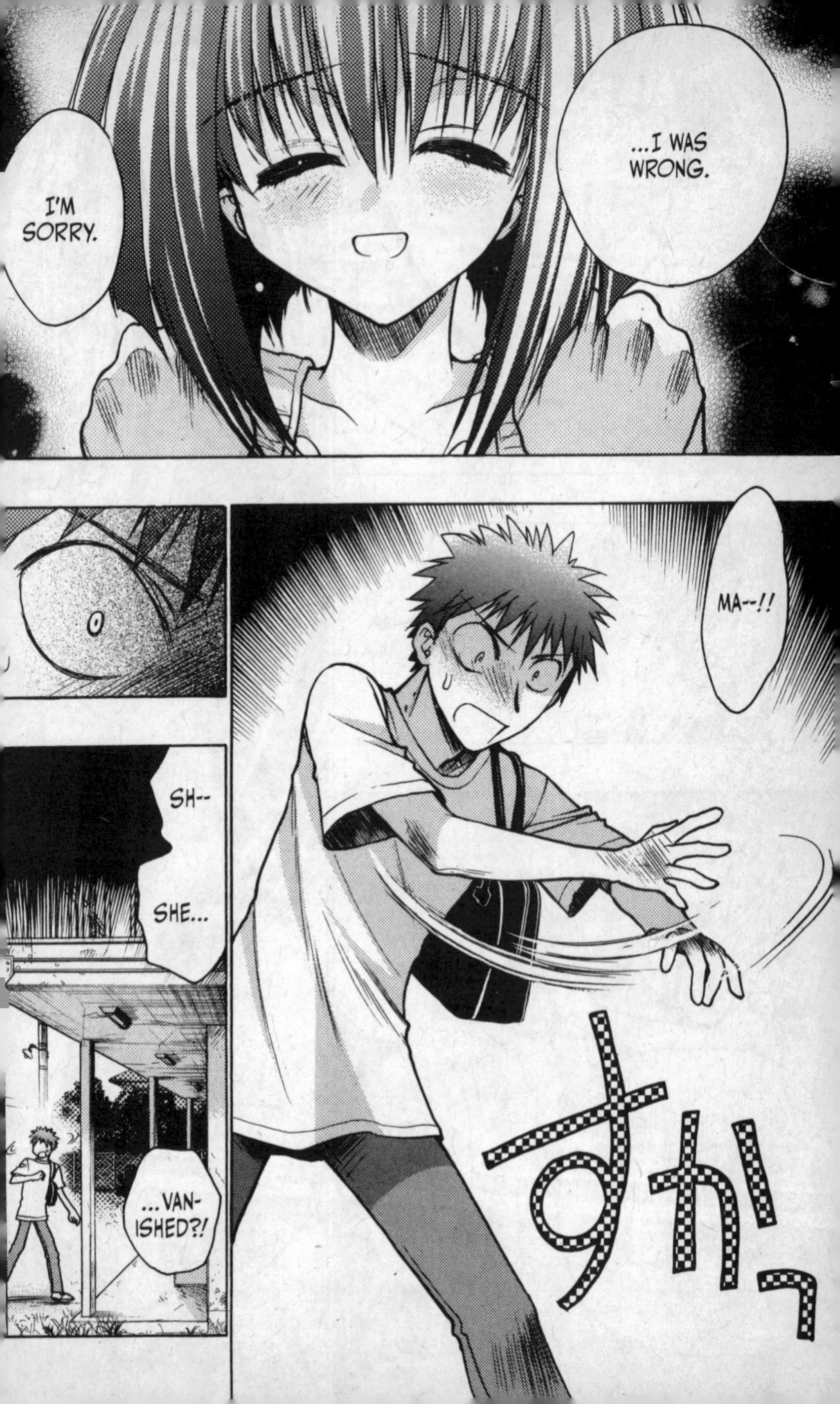
...I WAS WRONG.
I'M SORRY.
MA--!!
すかっ
SH--
SHE...
...VAN-ISHED?!

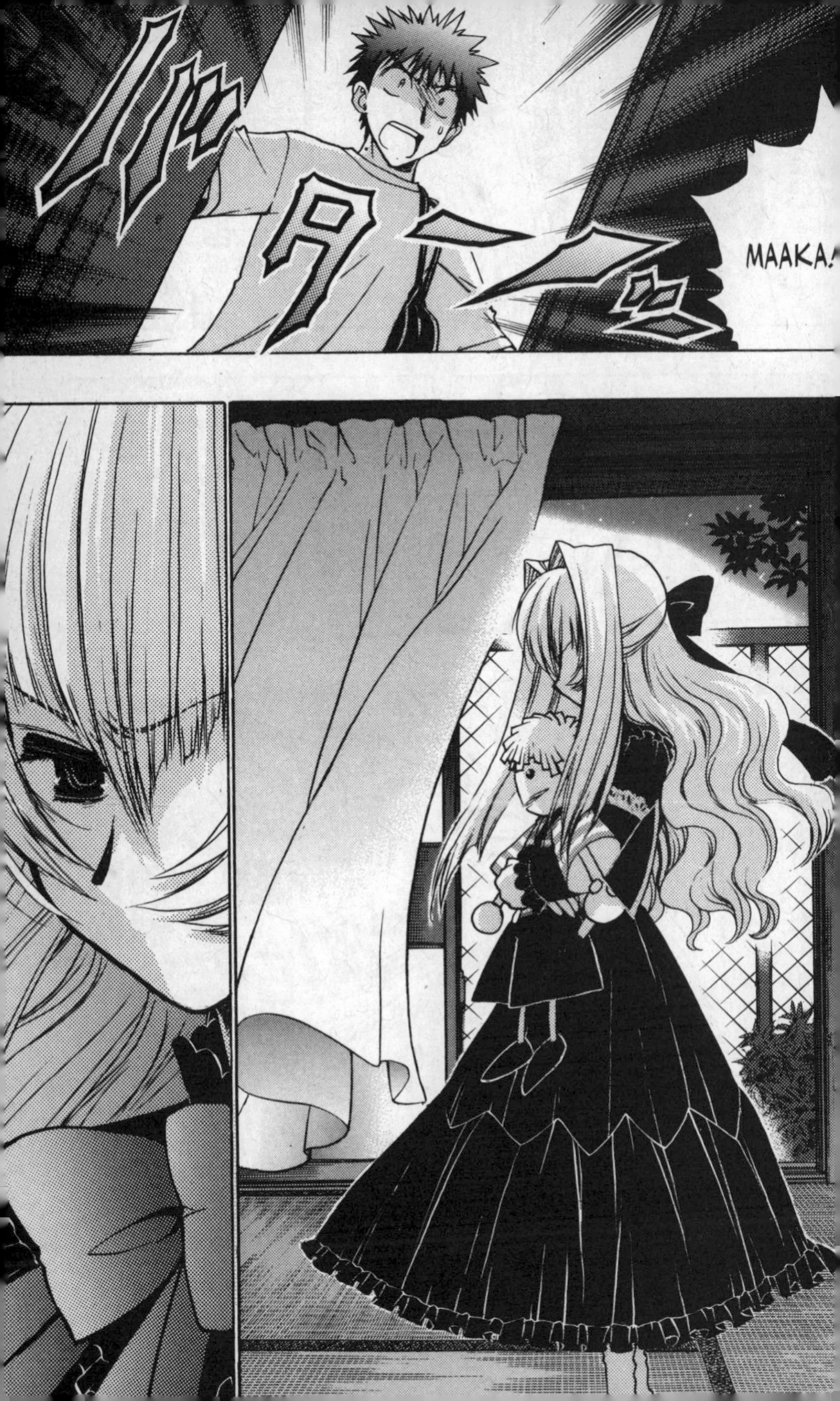
MAAKA!

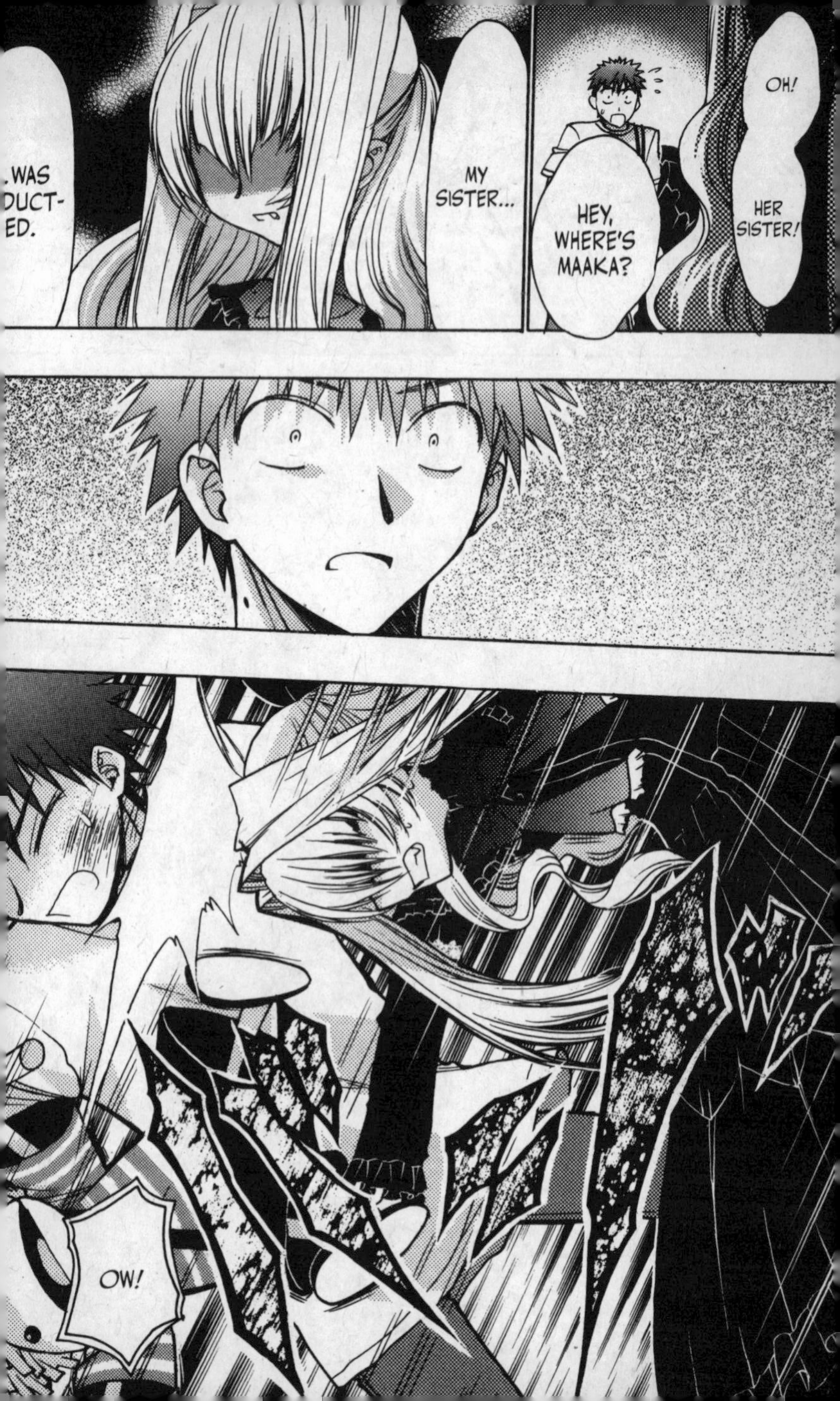
OH!
HER SISTER!
HEY, WHERE'S MAAKA?
MY SISTER...
.WAS DUCT- ED.
OW!

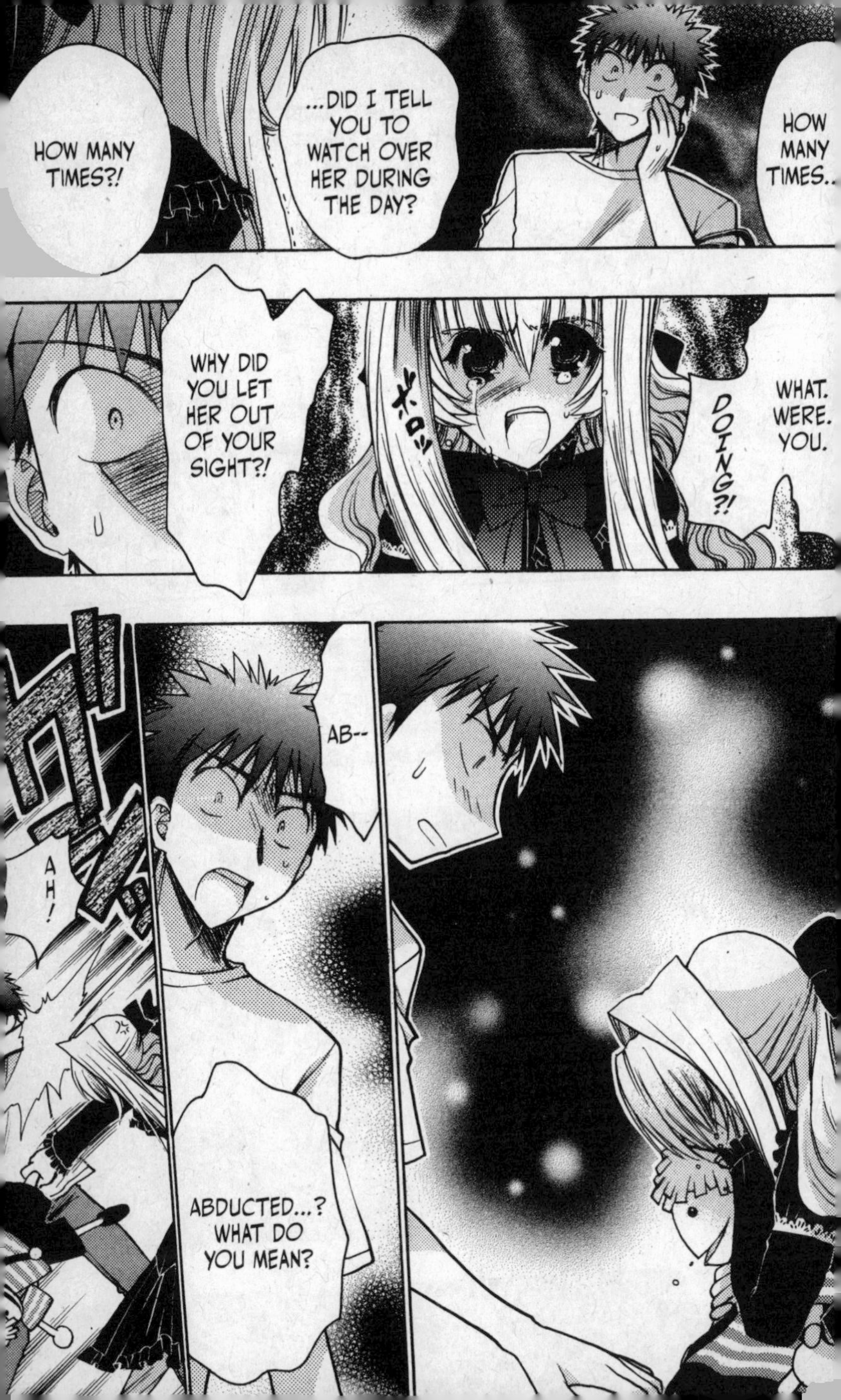
HOW MANY TIMES...
...DID I TELL YOU TO WATCH OVER HER DURING THE DAY?
HOW MANY TIMES?!
WHAT. WERE. YOU.
DOING?!
WHY DID YOU LET HER OUT OF YOUR SIGHT?!
AB--
ABDUCTED...? WHAT DO YOU MEAN?
AH!

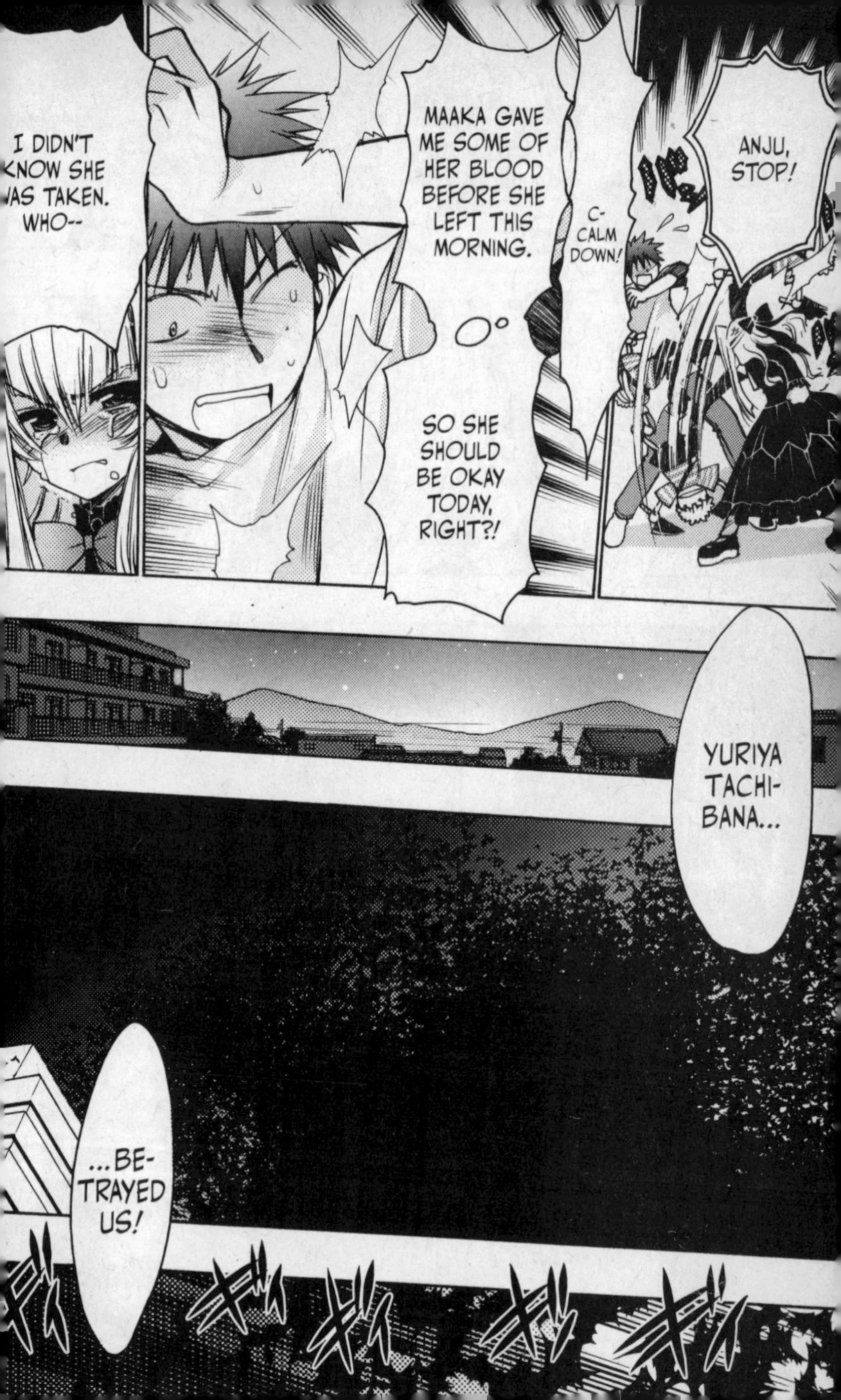
ANJU, STOP!
C-CALM DOWN!
MAAKA GAVE ME SOME OF HER BLOOD BEFORE SHE LEFT THIS MORNING.
SO SHE SHOULD BE OKAY TODAY, RIGHT?!
I DIDN'T KNOW SHE WAS TAKEN. WHO--
YURIYA TACHI-BANA...
...BE-TRAYED US!

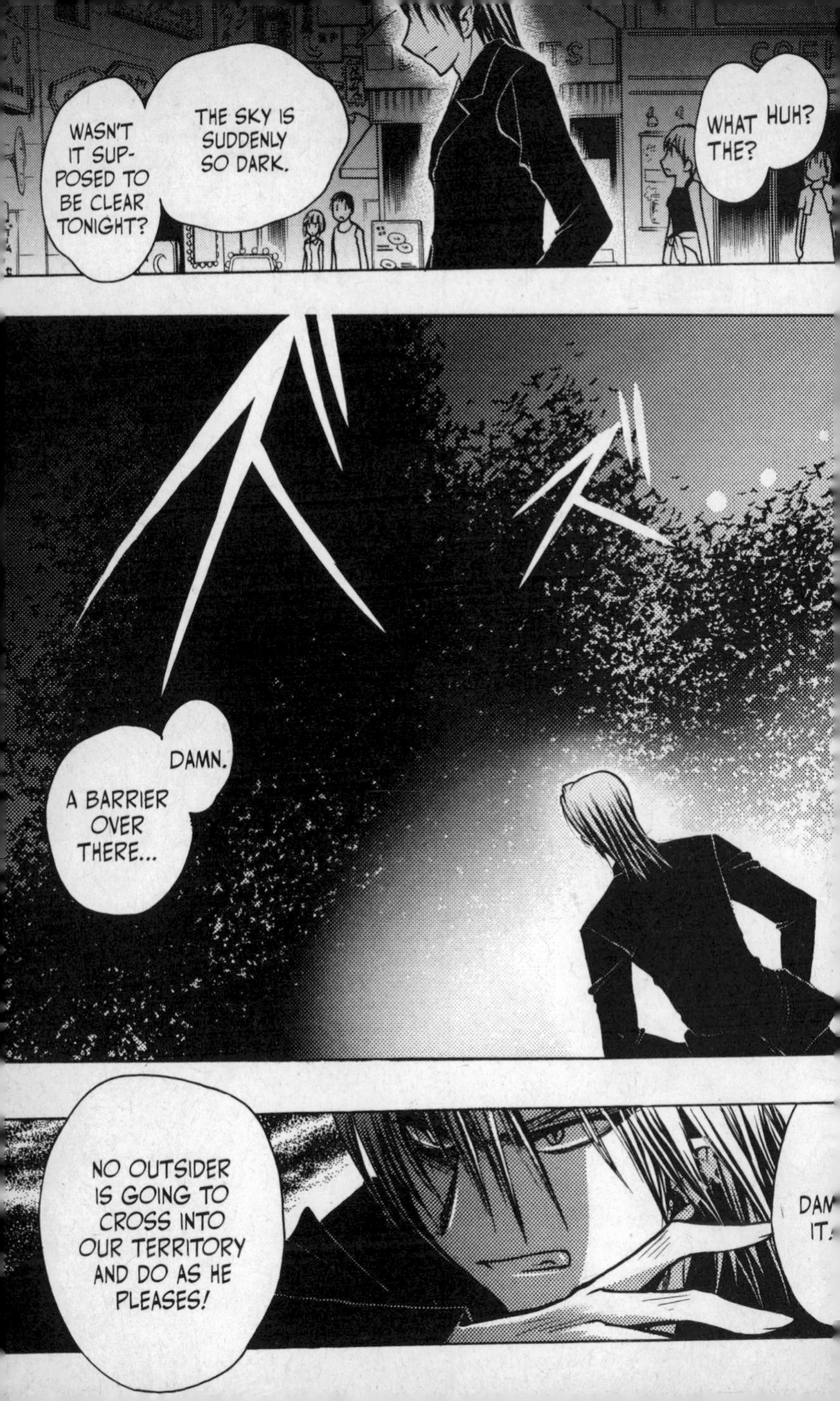
HUH? WHAT THE?
THE SKY IS SUDDENLY SO DARK.
WASN'T IT SUP-POSED TO BE CLEAR TONIGHT?
DAMN. A BARRIER OVER THERE...
DAM IT.
NO OUTSIDER IS GOING TO CROSS INTO OUR TERRITORY AND DO AS HE PLEASES!

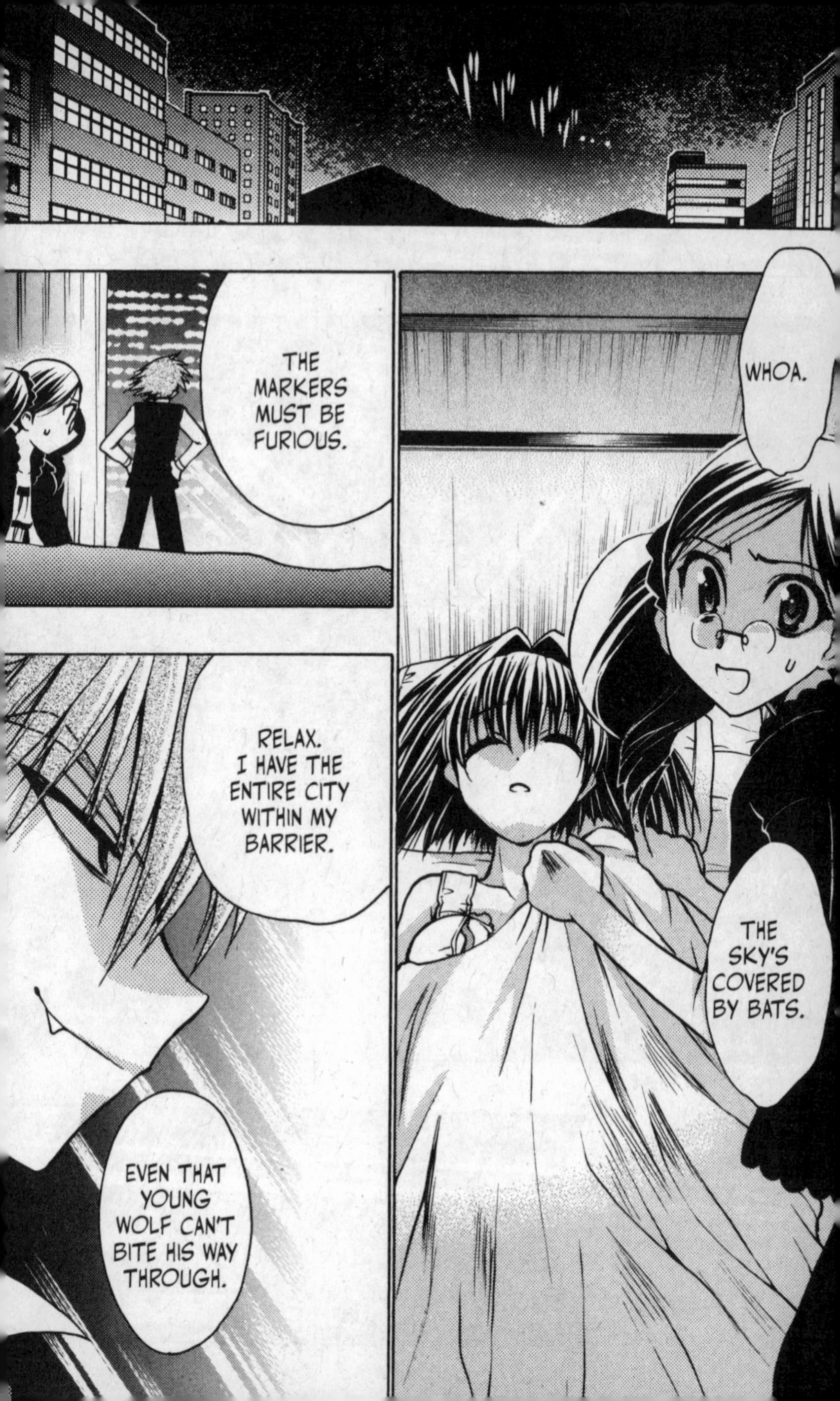
WHOA.
THE SKY'S COVERED BY BATS.
THE MARKERS MUST BE FURIOUS.
RELAX. I HAVE THE ENTIRE CITY WITHIN MY BARRIER.
EVEN THAT YOUNG WOLF CAN'T BITE HIS WAY THROUGH.

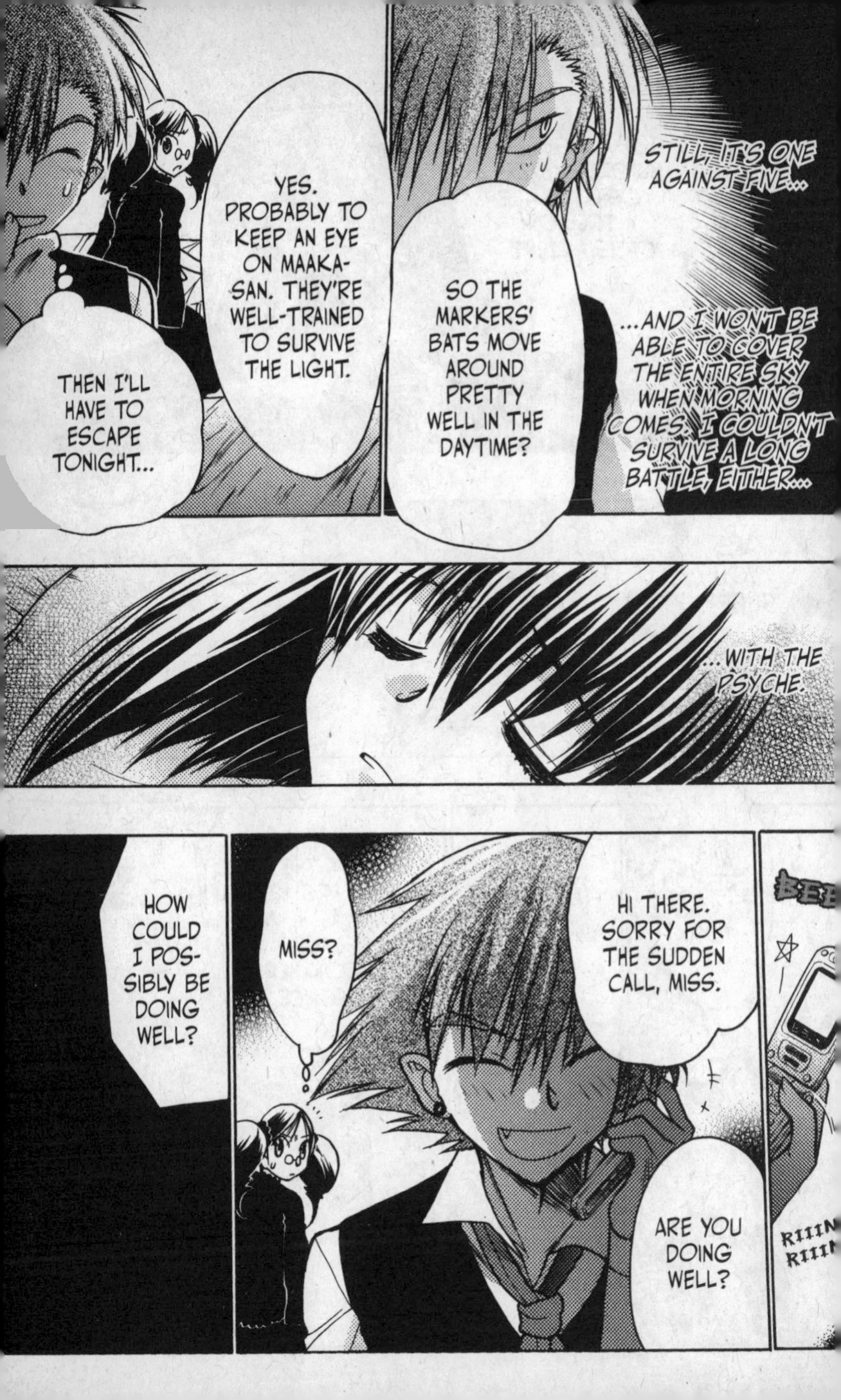
STILL, IT'S ONE AGAINST FIVE...
SO THE MARKERS' BATS MOVE AROUND PRETTY WELL IN THE DAYTIME?
...AND I WON'T BE ABLE TO COVER THE ENTIRE SKY WHEN MORNING COMES. I COULDN'T SURVIVE A LONG BATTLE, EITHER...
YES. PROBABLY TO KEEP AN EYE ON MAAKA-SAN. THEY'RE WELL-TRAINED TO SURVIVE THE LIGHT.
THEN I'LL HAVE TO ESCAPE TONIGHT...
...WITH THE PSYCHE.
HI THERE. SORRY FOR THE SUDDEN CALL, MISS.
ARE YOU DOING WELL?
MISS?
HOW COULD I POS-SIBLY BE DOING WELL?

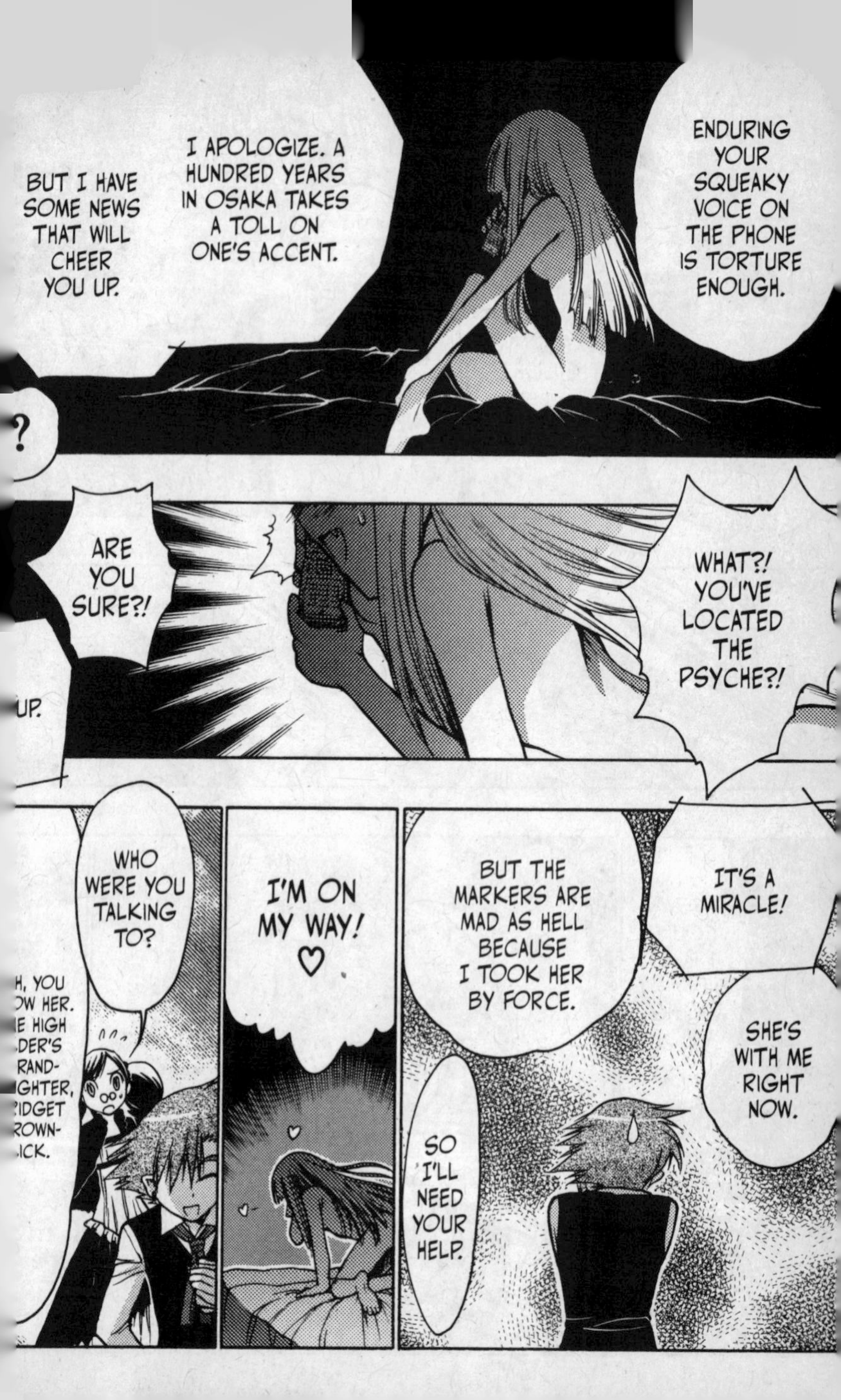
ENDURING YOUR SQUEAKY VOICE ON THE PHONE IS TORTURE ENOUGH.
I APOLOGIZE. A HUNDRED YEARS IN OSAKA TAKES A TOLL ON ONE'S ACCENT.
BUT I HAVE SOME NEWS THAT WILL CHEER YOU UP.
?
WHAT?! YOU'VE LOCATED THE PSYCHE?!
ARE YOU SURE?!
IT'S A MIRACLE!
SHE'S WITH ME RIGHT NOW.
BUT THE MARKERS ARE MAD AS HELL BECAUSE I TOOK HER BY FORCE.
SO I'LL NEED YOUR HELP.
I'M ON MY WAY! ♡
WHO WERE YOU TALKING TO?

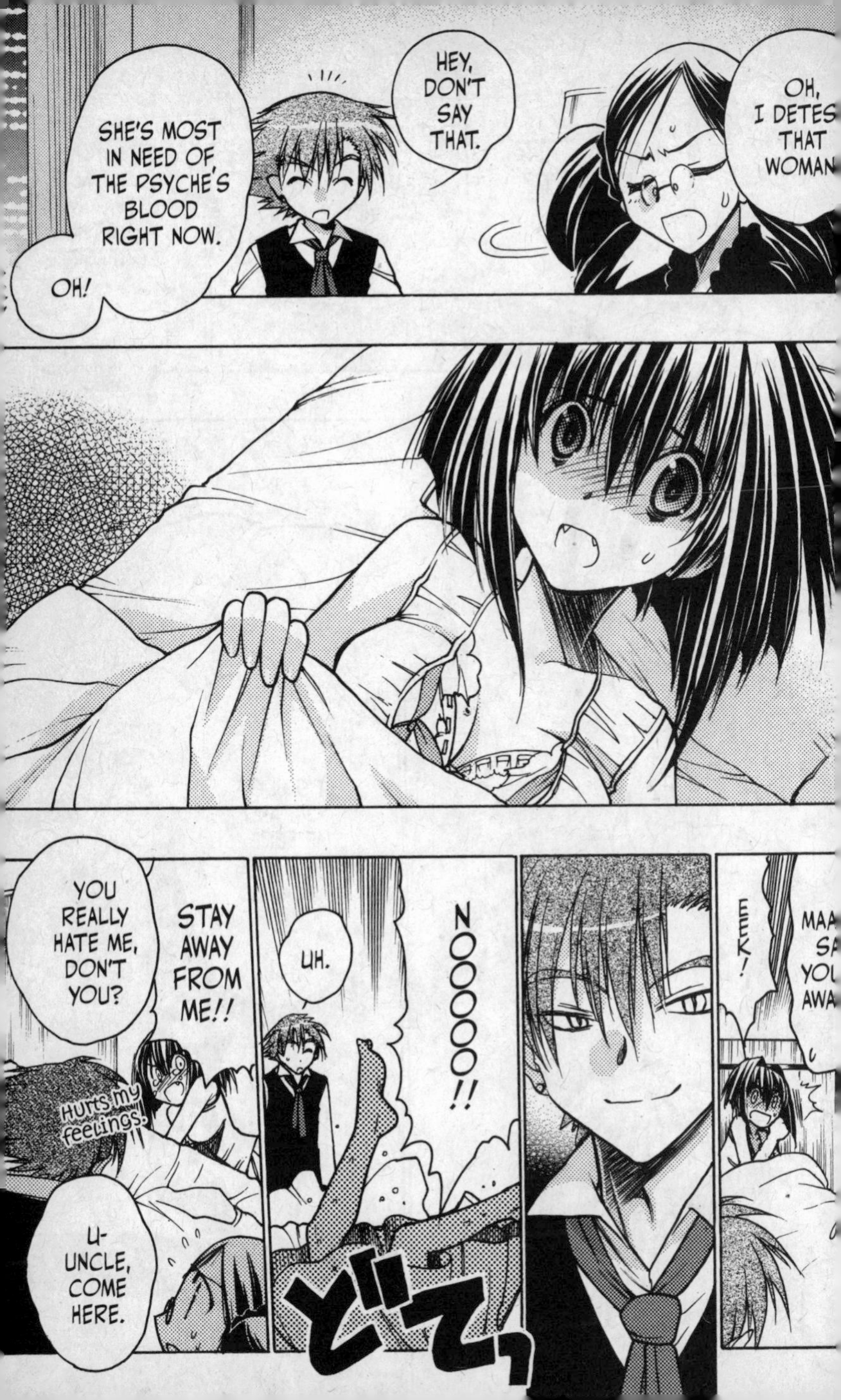
OH, I DETES THAT WOMAN
HEY, DON'T SAY THAT.
SHE'S MOST IN NEED OF THE PSYCHE'S BLOOD RIGHT NOW.
OH!
MAA SA YOU AWA
EEK!
NOOOOOO!!
UH.
STAY AWAY FROM ME!!
YOU REALLY HATE ME, DON'T YOU?
Hurts my feelings.
U-UNCLE, COME HERE.

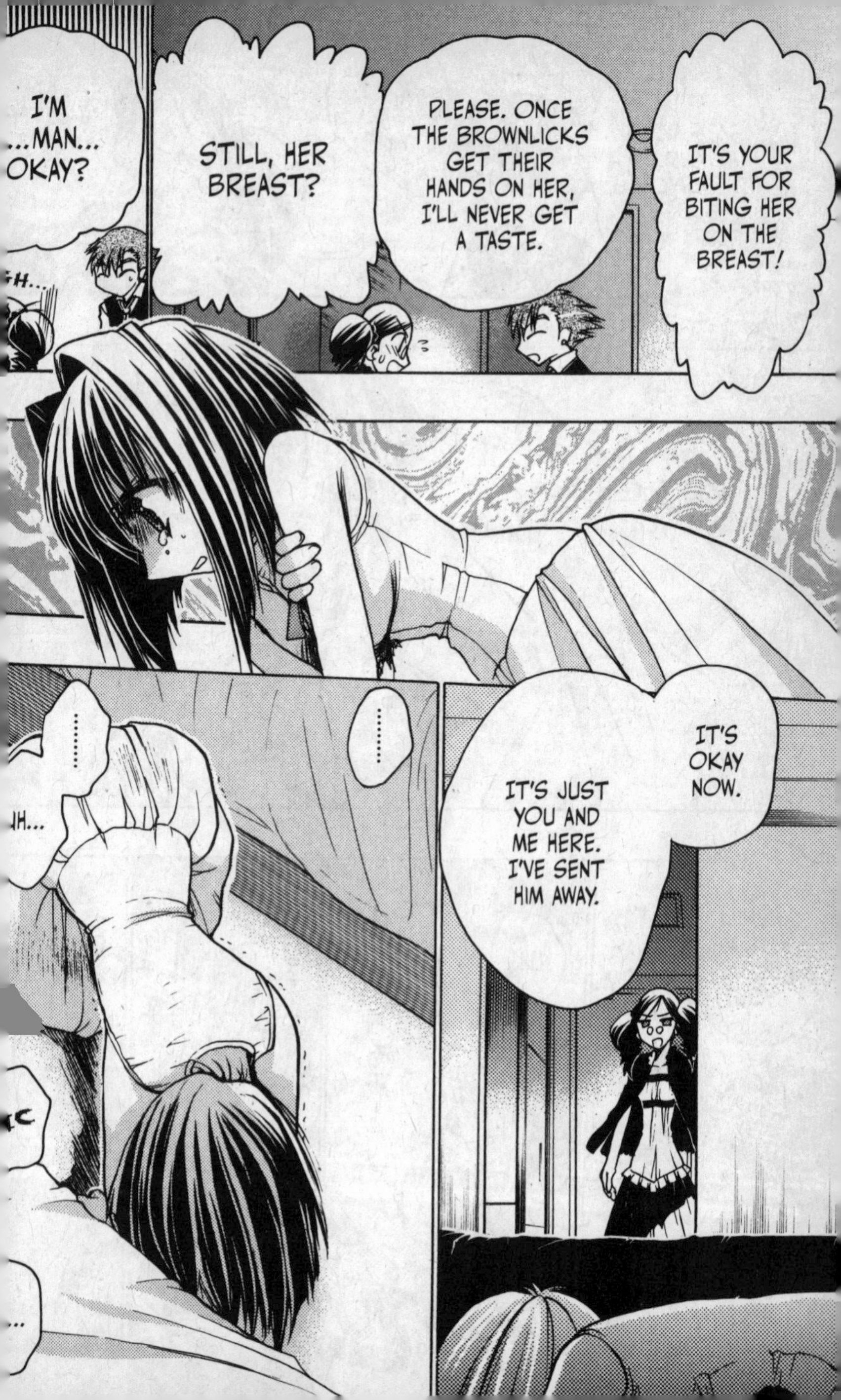
IT'S YOUR FAULT FOR BITING HER ON THE BREAST!
PLEASE. ONCE THE BROWNLICKS GET THEIR HANDS ON HER, I'LL NEVER GET A TASTE.
STILL, HER BREAST?
I'M ...MAN... OKAY?
IT'S OKAY NOW.
IT'S JUST YOU AND ME HERE. I'VE SENT HIM AWAY.
......
......

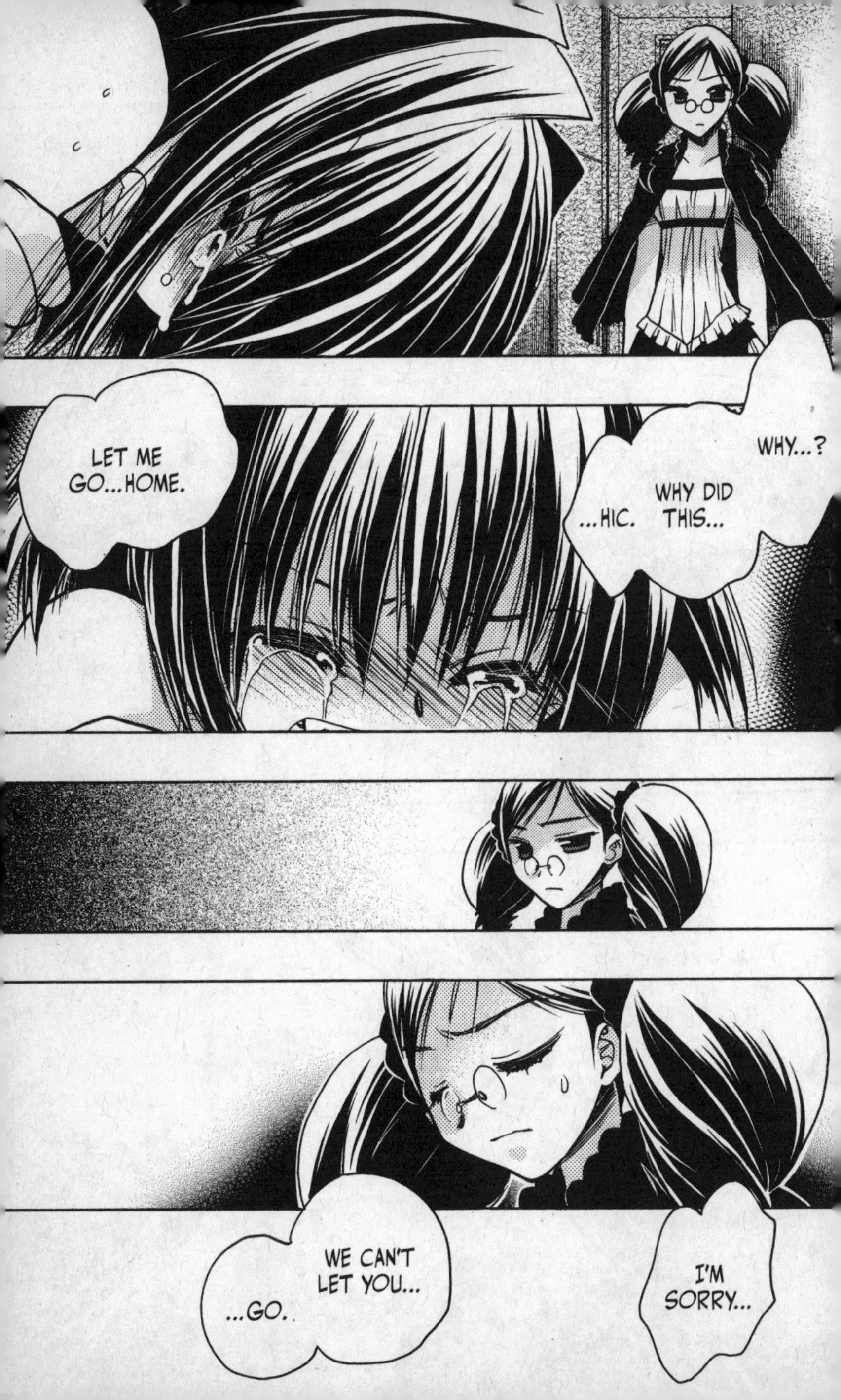
WHY...? WHY DID THIS... ...HIC.
LET ME GO...HOME.
I'M SORRY...
WE CAN'T LET YOU... ...GO.

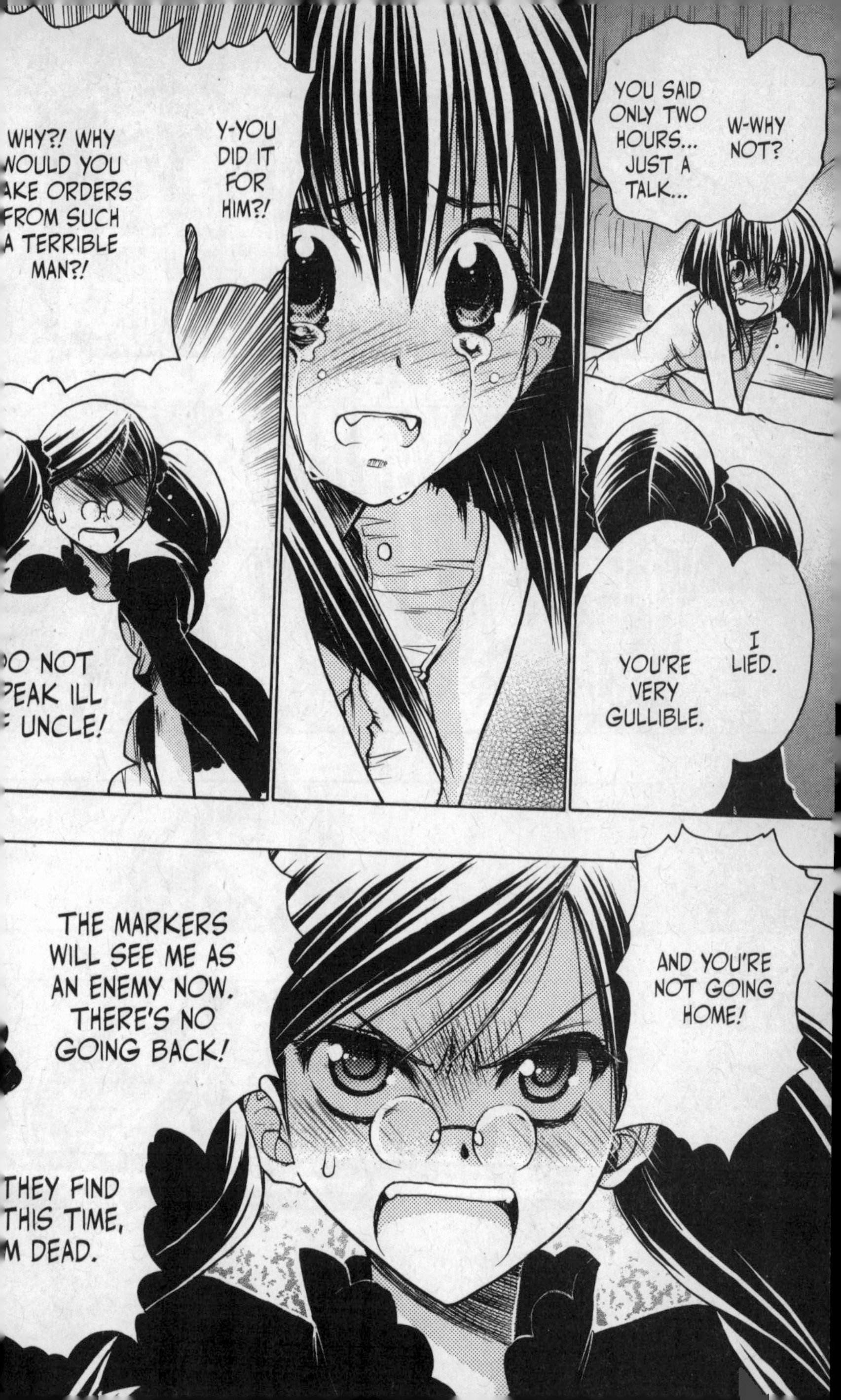
W-WHY NOT?
YOU SAID ONLY TWO HOURS... JUST A TALK...
I LIED.
YOU'RE VERY GULLIBLE.
Y-YOU DID IT FOR HIM?!
WHY?! WHY WOULD YOU AKE ORDERS FROM SUCH A TERRIBLE MAN?!
O NOT PEAK ILL UNCLE!
AND YOU'RE NOT GOING HOME!
THE MARKERS WILL SEE ME AS AN ENEMY NOW. THERE'S NO GOING BACK!
THEY FIND THIS TIME, M DEAD.

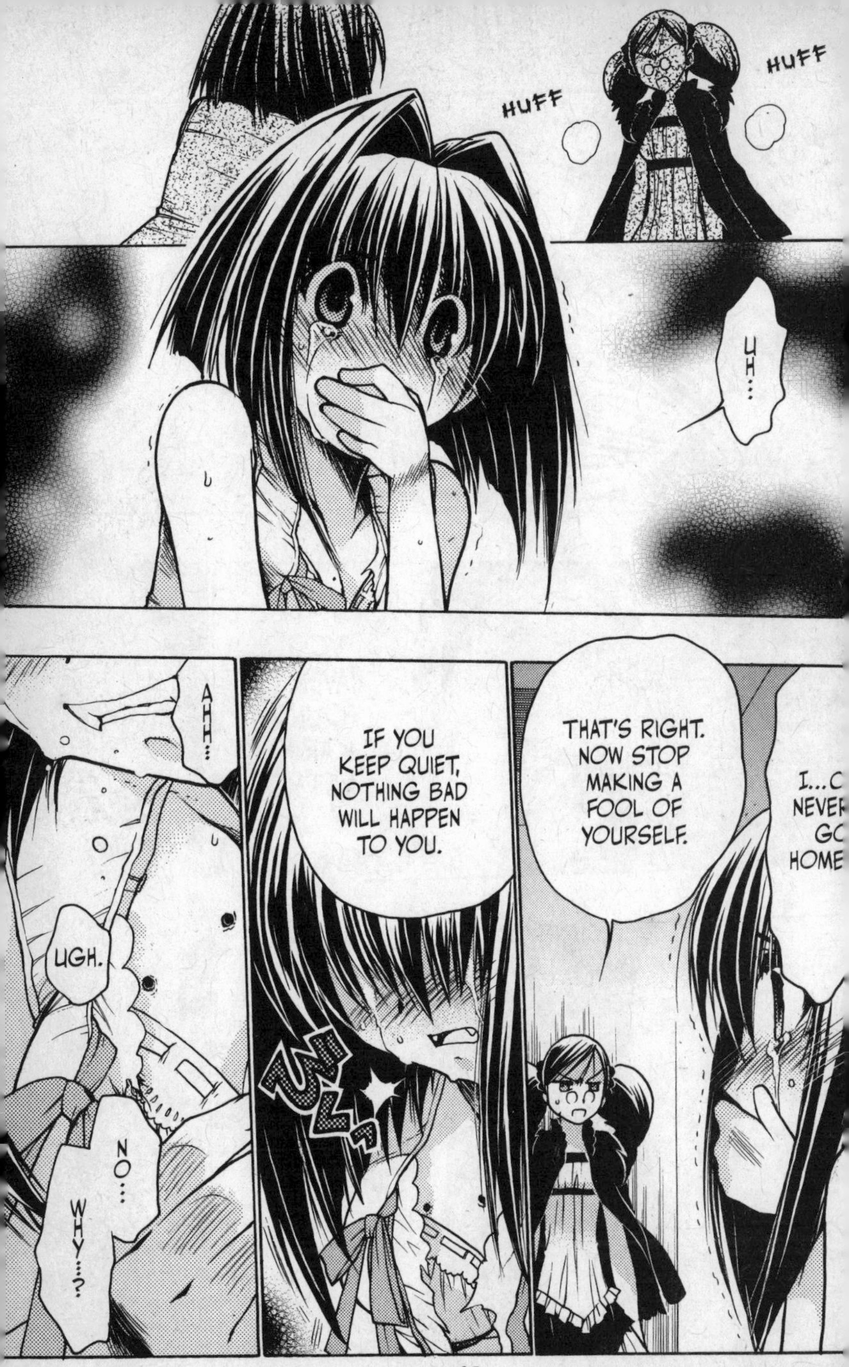
HUFF
HUFF
UH...
THAT'S RIGHT. NOW STOP MAKING A FOOL OF YOURSELF.
IF YOU KEEP QUIET, NOTHING BAD WILL HAPPEN TO YOU.
AHH...
UGH.
NO...
WHY...?

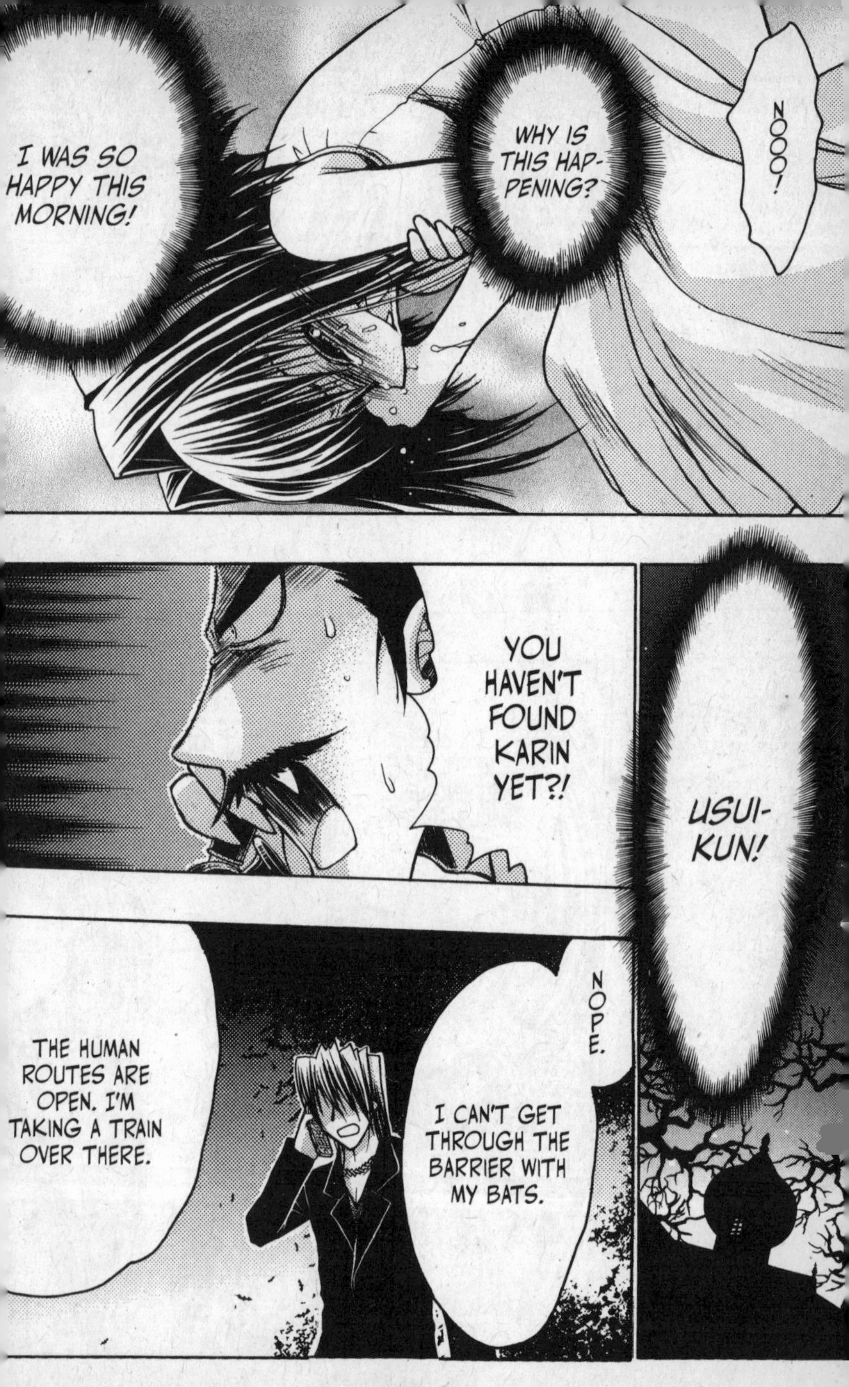
NOOO!
WHY IS THIS HAP-PENING?
I WAS SO HAPPY THIS MORNING!
USUI-KUN!
YOU HAVEN'T FOUND KARIN YET?!
NOPE.
I CAN'T GET THROUGH THE BARRIER WITH MY BATS.
THE HUMAN ROUTES ARE OPEN. I'M TAKING A TRAIN OVER THERE.

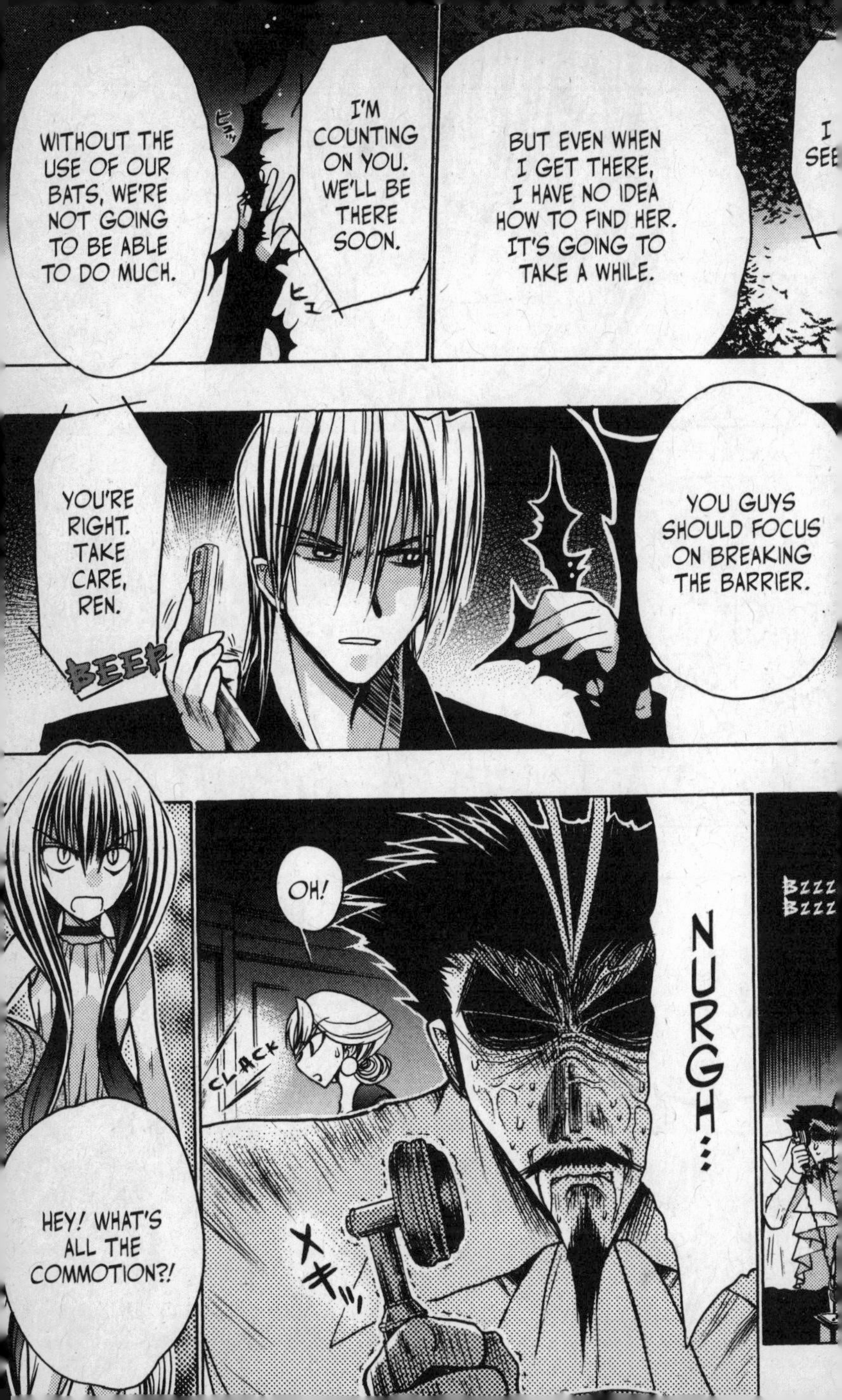
I SEE
BUT EVEN WHEN I GET THERE, I HAVE NO IDEA HOW TO FIND HER. IT'S GOING TO TAKE A WHILE.
I'M COUNTING ON YOU. WE'LL BE THERE SOON.
WITHOUT THE USE OF OUR BATS, WE'RE NOT GOING TO BE ABLE TO DO MUCH.
YOU GUYS SHOULD FOCUS ON BREAKING THE BARRIER.
YOU'RE RIGHT. TAKE CARE, REN.
BEEP
BZZZ BZZZ
NURGH..
OH!
CLACK
メキッ
HEY! WHAT'S ALL THE COMMOTION?!

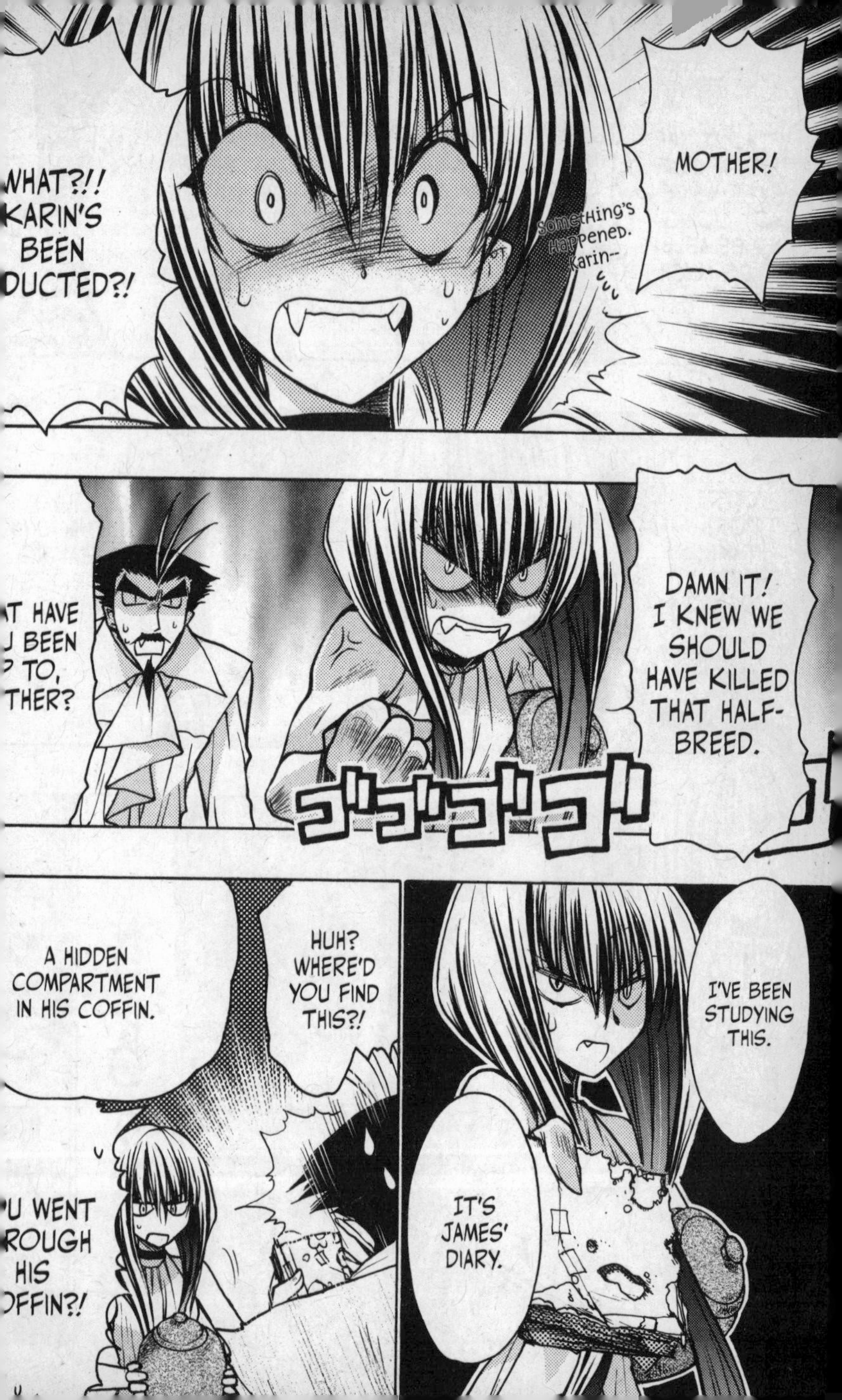
MOTHER!
Something's Happened. Karin--
WHAT?!! KARIN'S BEEN DUCTED?!
DAMN IT! I KNEW WE SHOULD HAVE KILLED THAT HALF-BREED.
ゴゴゴゴ
T HAVE U BEEN TO, THER?
I'VE BEEN STUDYING THIS.
IT'S JAMES' DIARY.
HUH? WHERE'D YOU FIND THIS?!
A HIDDEN COMPARTMENT IN HIS COFFIN.
U WENT ROUGH HIS OFFIN?!

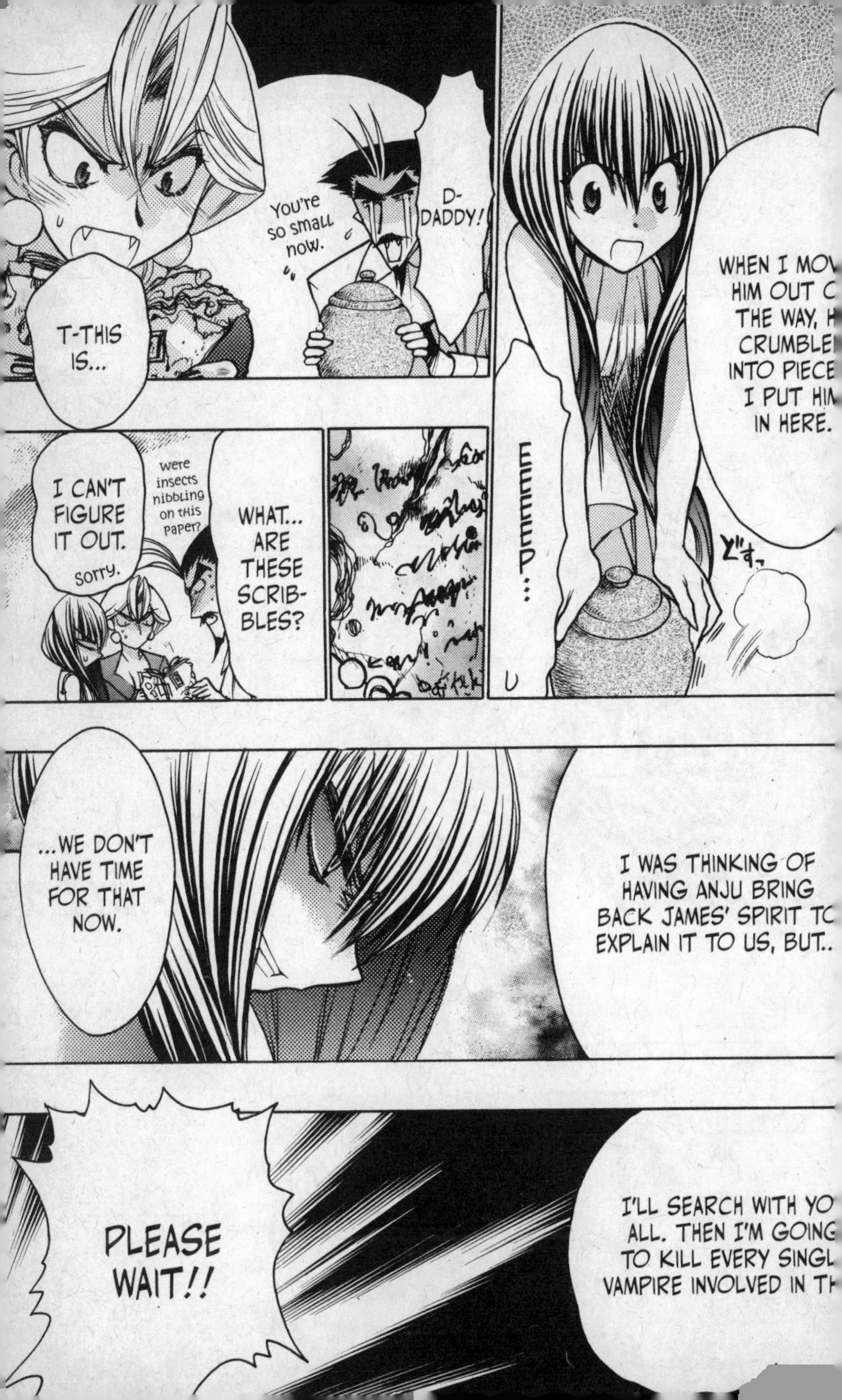
WHEN I MOV HIM OUT O THE WAY, H CRUMBLE INTO PIECE I PUT HIM IN HERE.
EEEEP...
どすっ
D-DADDY!
You're so small now.
T-THIS IS...
WHAT... ARE THESE SCRIB-BLES?
were insects nibbling on this paper?
I CAN'T FIGURE IT OUT.
Sorry.
I WAS THINKING OF HAVING ANJU BRING BACK JAMES' SPIRIT TO EXPLAIN IT TO US, BUT..
...WE DON'T HAVE TIME FOR THAT NOW.
I'LL SEARCH WITH YO ALL. THEN I'M GOING TO KILL EVERY SINGL VAMPIRE INVOLVED IN TH
PLEASE WAIT!!

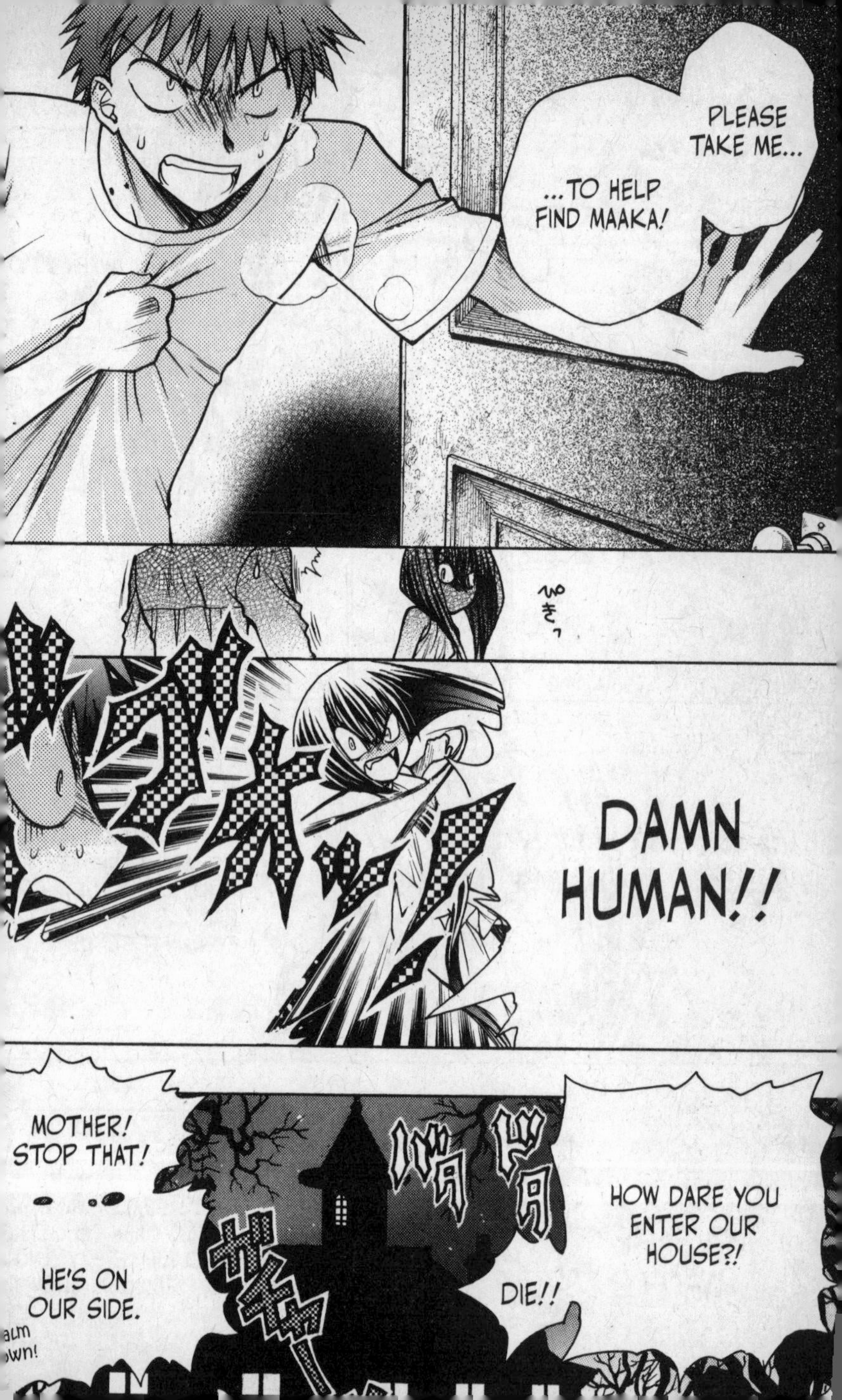
PLEASE TAKE ME...
...TO HELP FIND MAAKA!
DAMN HUMAN!!
HOW DARE YOU ENTER OUR HOUSE?!
DIE!!
MOTHER! STOP THAT!
HE'S ON OUR SIDE.

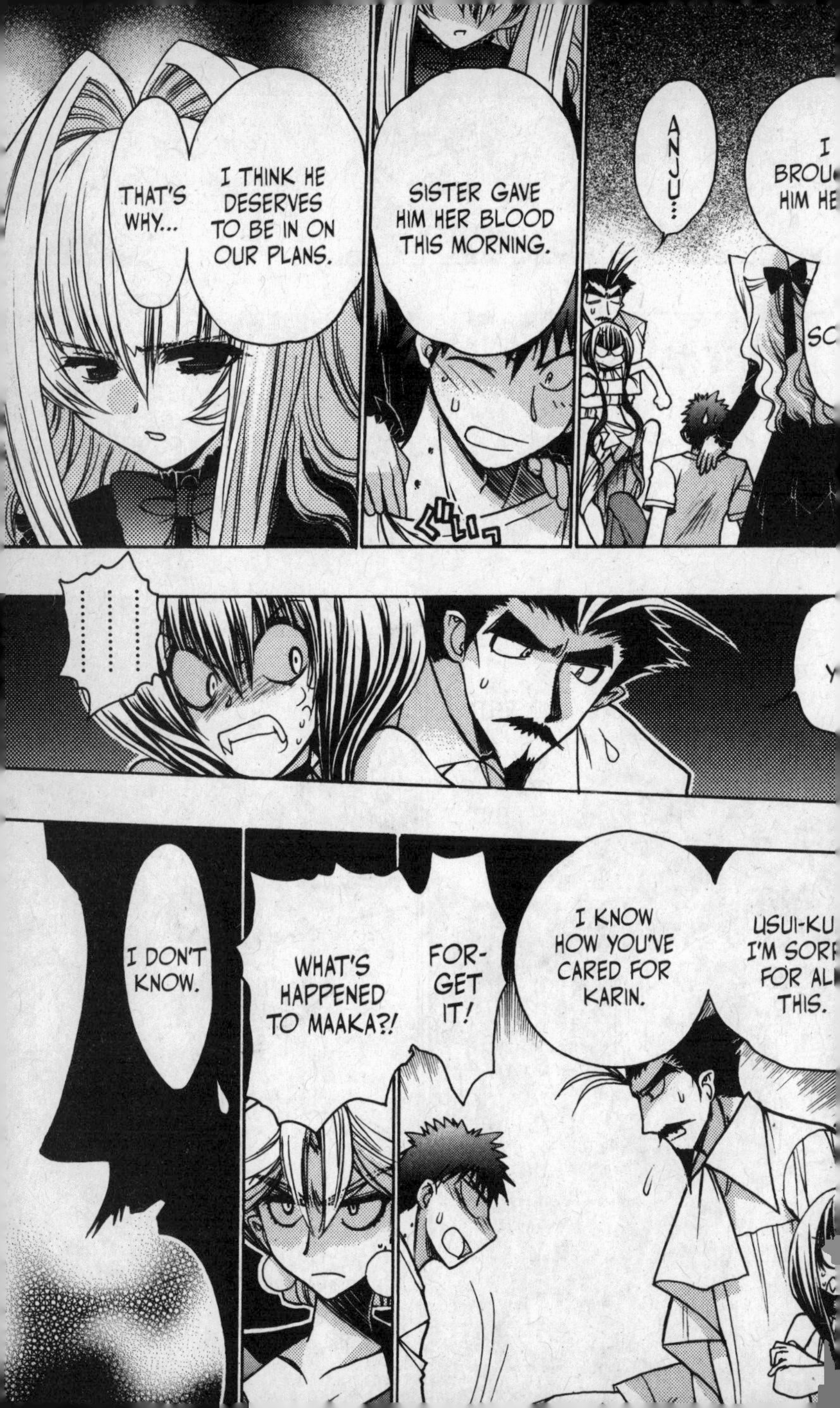
I BROU HIM HE
SC
ANJU...
SISTER GAVE HIM HER BLOOD THIS MORNING.
I THINK HE DESERVES TO BE IN ON OUR PLANS.
THAT'S WHY...
Y
......
USUI-KU I'M SORR FOR AL THIS.
I KNOW HOW YOU'VE CARED FOR KARIN.
FOR-GET IT!
WHAT'S HAPPENED TO MAAKA?!
I DON'T KNOW.

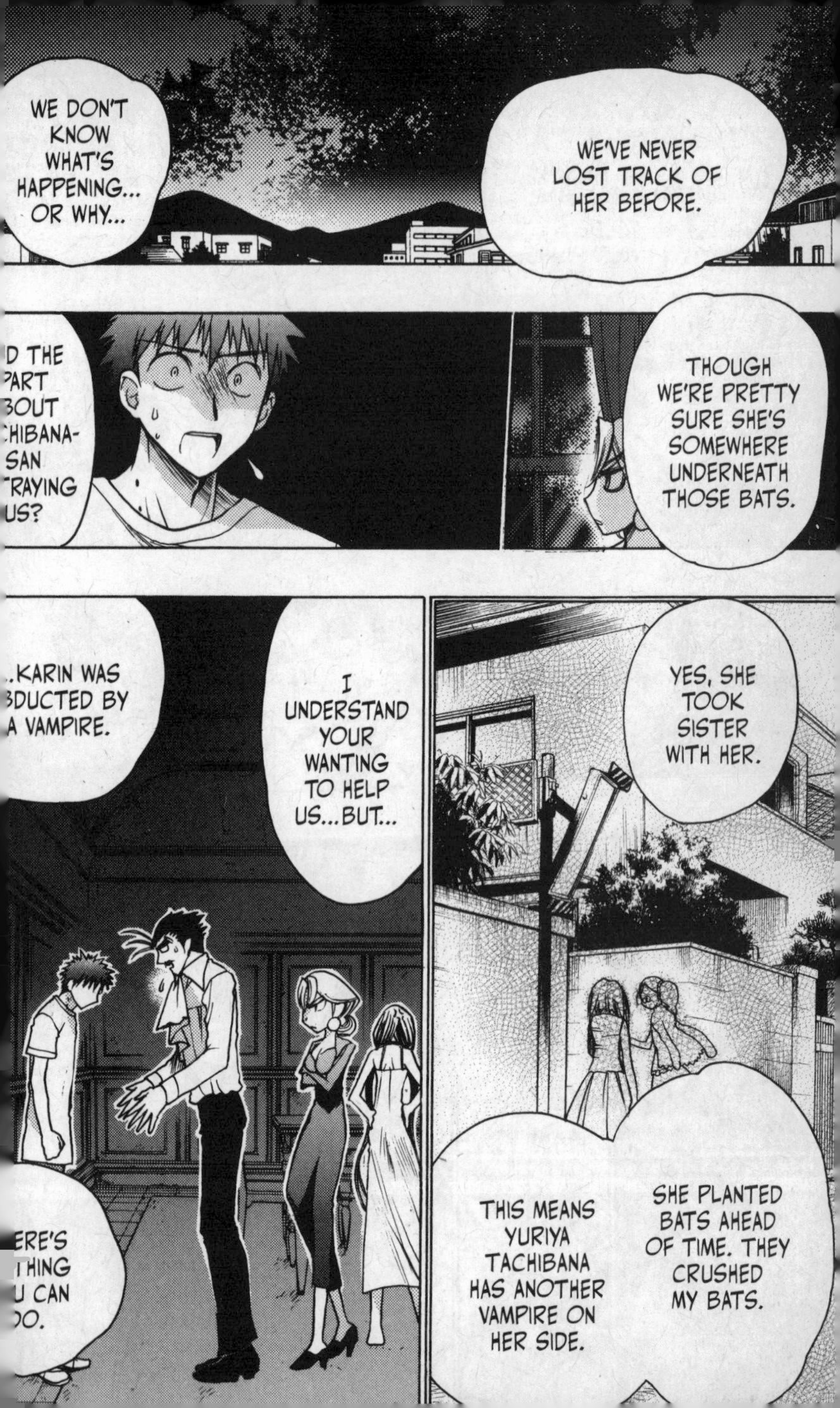
WE'VE NEVER LOST TRACK OF HER BEFORE.
WE DON'T KNOW WHAT'S HAPPENING... OR WHY...
THOUGH WE'RE PRETTY SURE SHE'S SOMEWHERE UNDERNEATH THOSE BATS.
D THE PART BOUT CHIBANA-SAN TRAYING US?
YES, SHE TOOK SISTER WITH HER.
SHE PLANTED BATS AHEAD OF TIME. THEY CRUSHED MY BATS.
THIS MEANS YURIYA TACHIBANA HAS ANOTHER VAMPIRE ON HER SIDE.
I UNDERSTAND YOUR WANTING TO HELP US...BUT...
..KARIN WAS BDUCTED BY A VAMPIRE.
ERE'S THING U CAN DO.

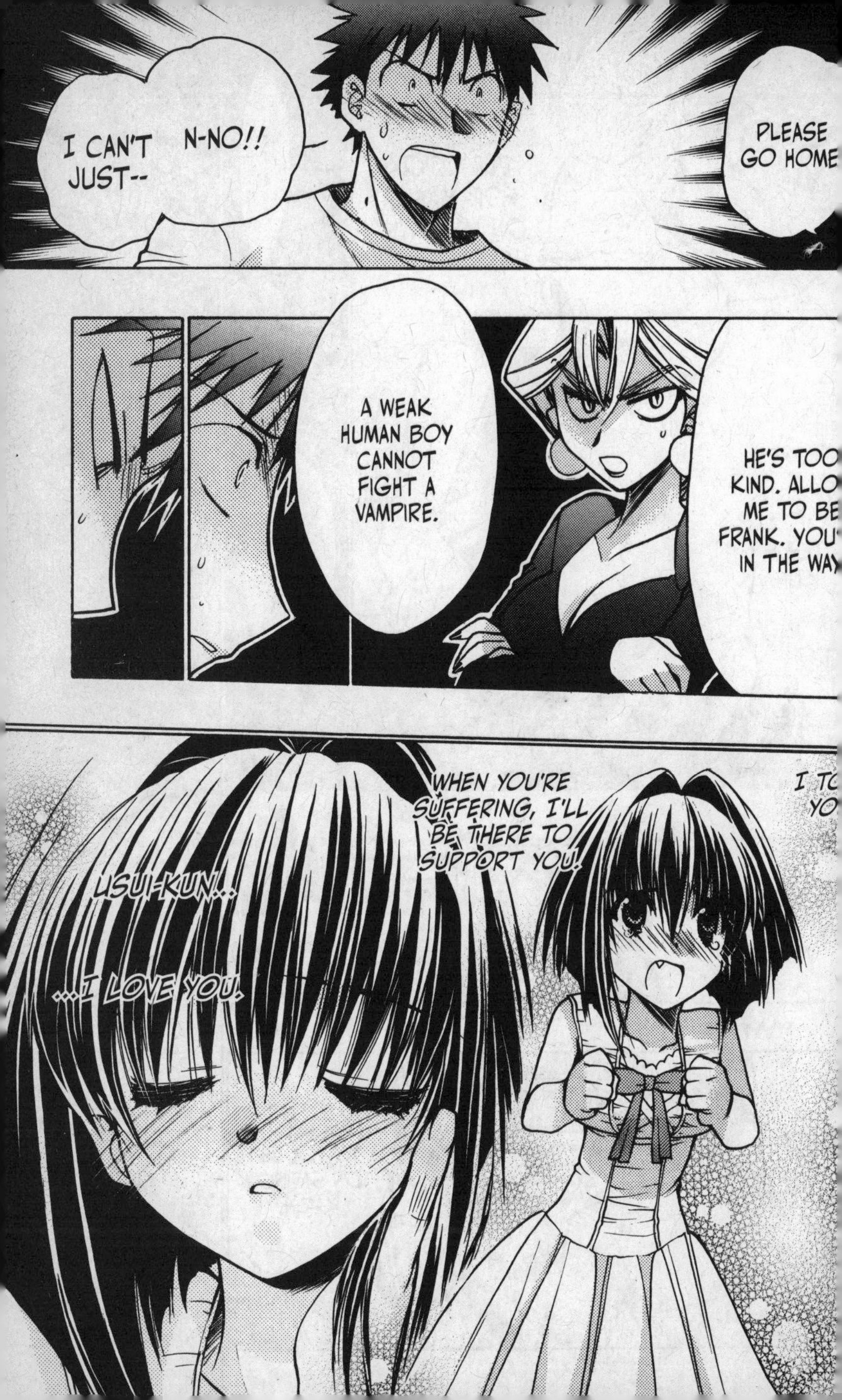
PLEASE GO HOME
N-NO!!
I CAN'T JUST--
HE'S TOO KIND. ALLO ME TO BE FRANK. YOU IN THE WAY
A WEAK HUMAN BOY CANNOT FIGHT A VAMPIRE.
I TO YO
WHEN YOU'RE SUFFERING, I'LL BE THERE TO SUPPORT YOU.
USUI-KUN...
...I LOVE YOU.

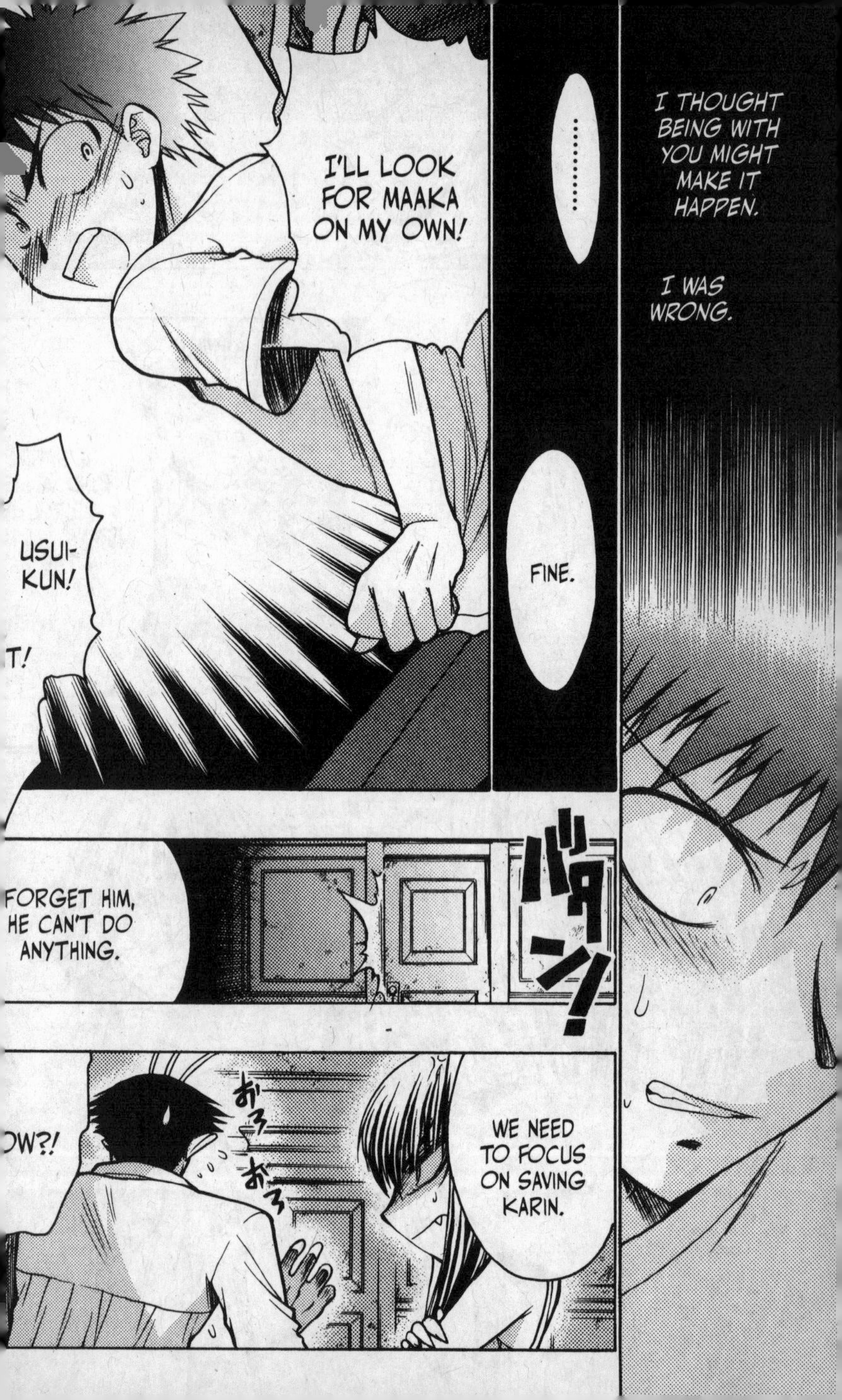
I THOUGHT BEING WITH YOU MIGHT MAKE IT HAPPEN.
I WAS WRONG.
......
FINE.
I'LL LOOK FOR MAAKA ON MY OWN!
USUI-KUN!
T!
バターン!
FORGET HIM, HE CAN'T DO ANYTHING.
WE NEED TO FOCUS ON SAVING KARIN.
おろ
おろ
OW?!

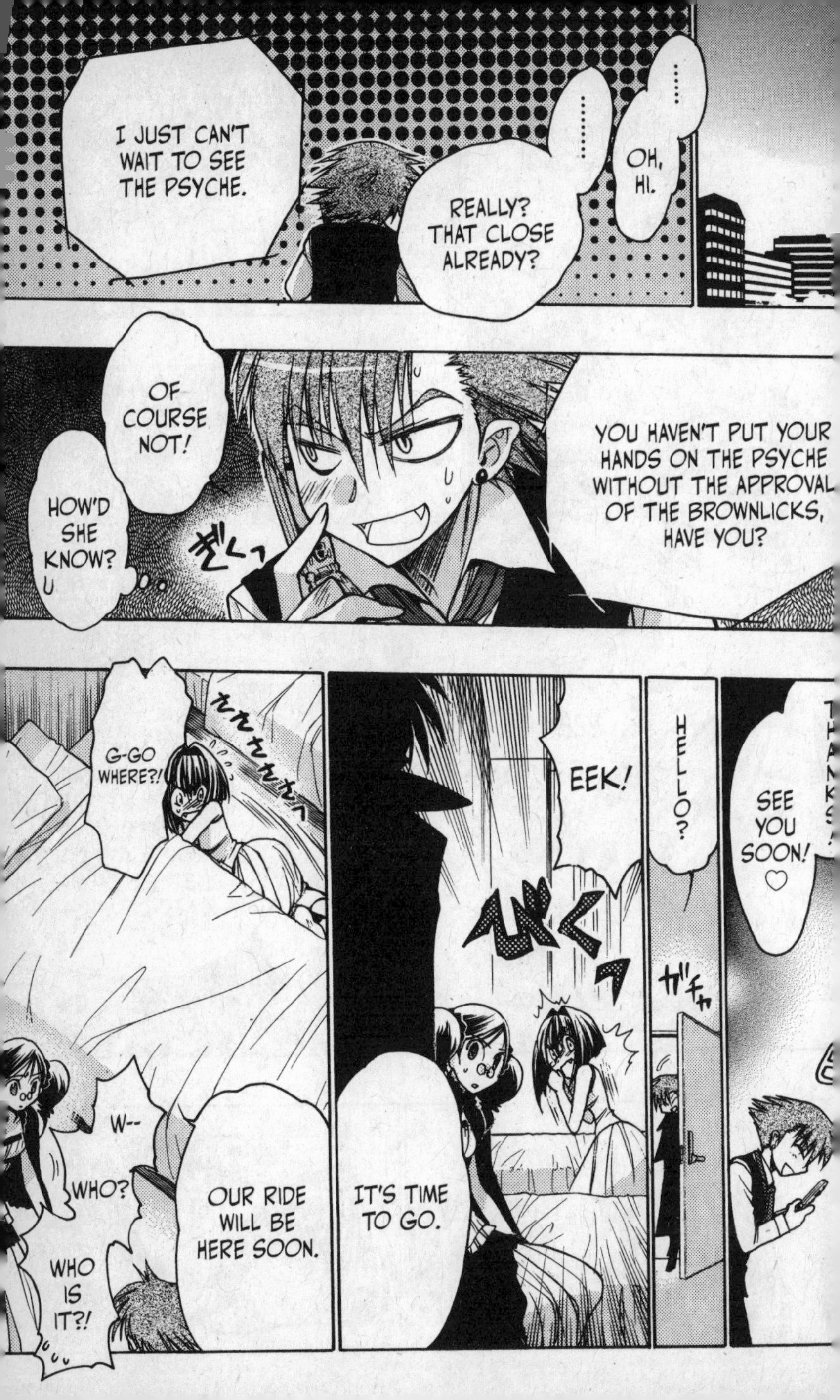
......
OH, HI.
......
REALLY? THAT CLOSE ALREADY?
I JUST CAN'T WAIT TO SEE THE PSYCHE.
YOU HAVEN'T PUT YOUR HANDS ON THE PSYCHE WITHOUT THE APPROVAL OF THE BROWNLICKS, HAVE YOU?
OF COURSE NOT!
ぎくっ
HOW'D SHE KNOW?
THANKS!
SEE YOU SOON! ♡
HELLO?
ガチャ
EEK!
びくっ
IT'S TIME TO GO.
OUR RIDE WILL BE HERE SOON.
G-GO WHERE?!
W--
WHO?
WHO IS IT?!

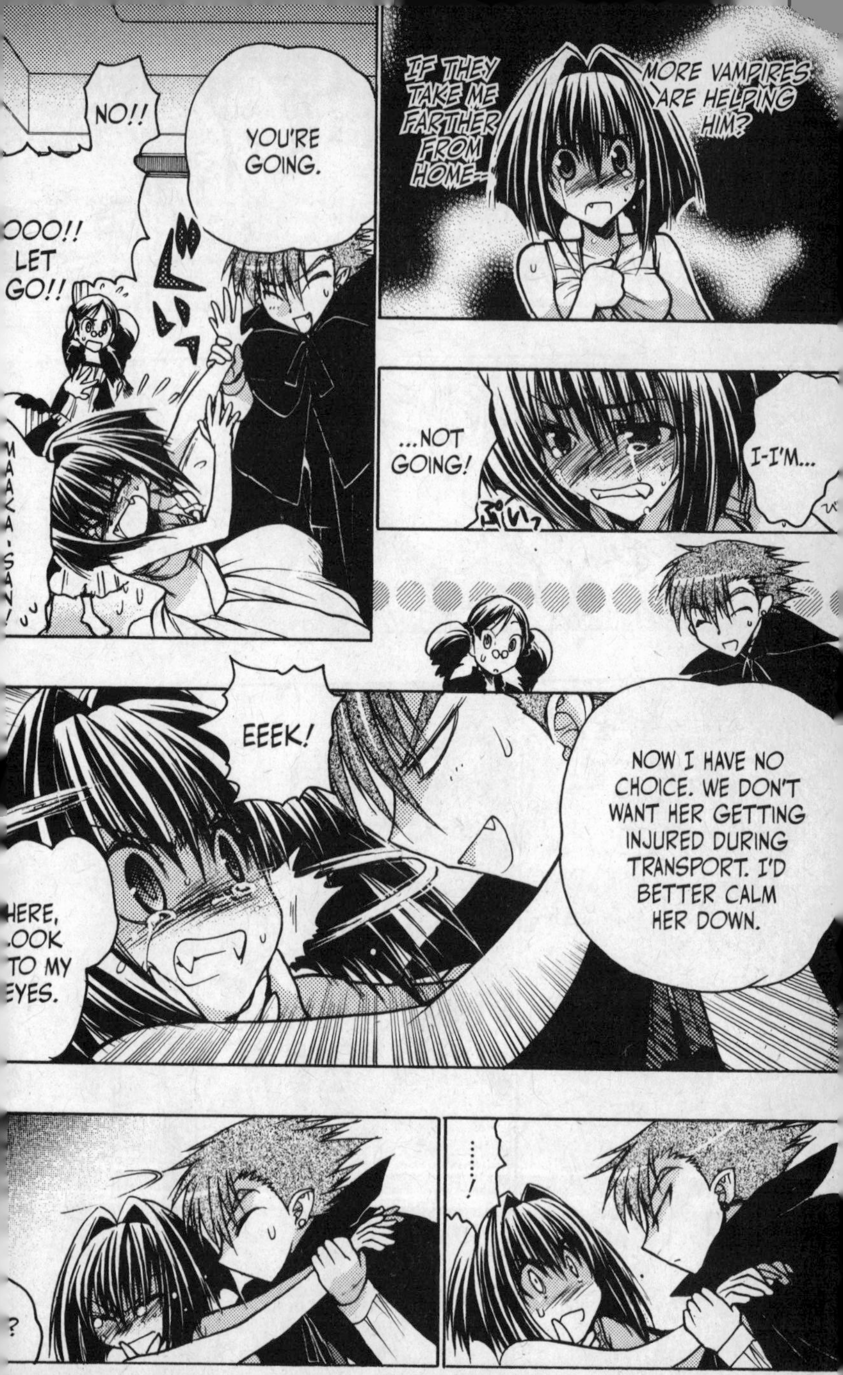
MORE VAMPIRES ARE HELPING HIM?
IF THEY TAKE ME FARTHER FROM HOME...
I-I'M...
...NOT GOING!
YOU'RE GOING.
NO!!
OOO!! LET GO!!
MAAKA-SAN!
NOW I HAVE NO CHOICE. WE DON'T WANT HER GETTING INJURED DURING TRANSPORT. I'D BETTER CALM HER DOWN.
EEEK!
HERE, OOK TO MY EYES.
......!
?

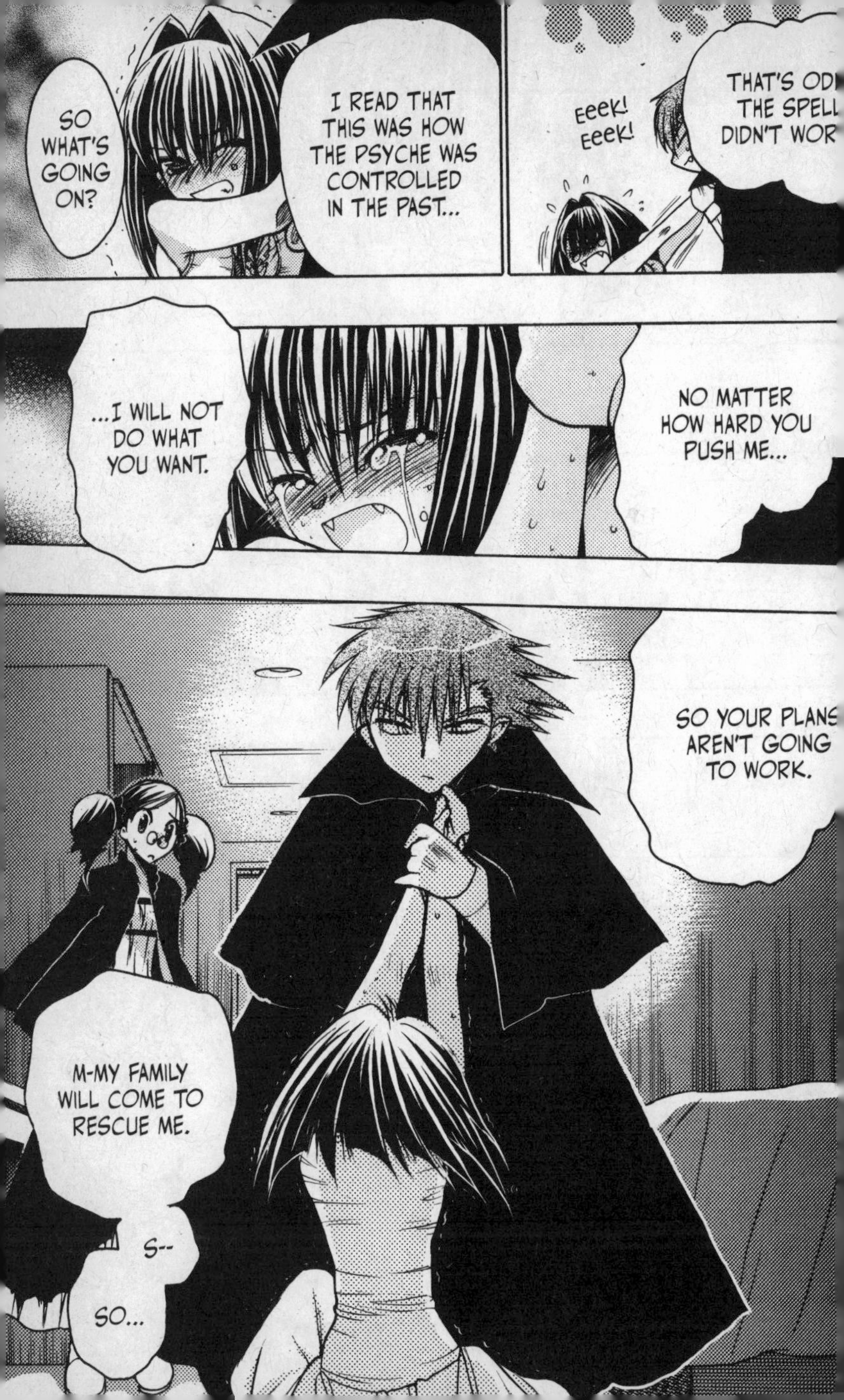
THAT'S OD
THE SPELL
DIDN'T WOR
Eeek! Eeek!
I READ THAT THIS WAS HOW THE PSYCHE WAS CONTROLLED IN THE PAST...
SO WHAT'S GOING ON?
NO MATTER HOW HARD YOU PUSH ME...
...I WILL NOT DO WHAT YOU WANT.
SO YOUR PLANS AREN'T GOING TO WORK.
M-MY FAMILY WILL COME TO RESCUE ME.
S--
SO...

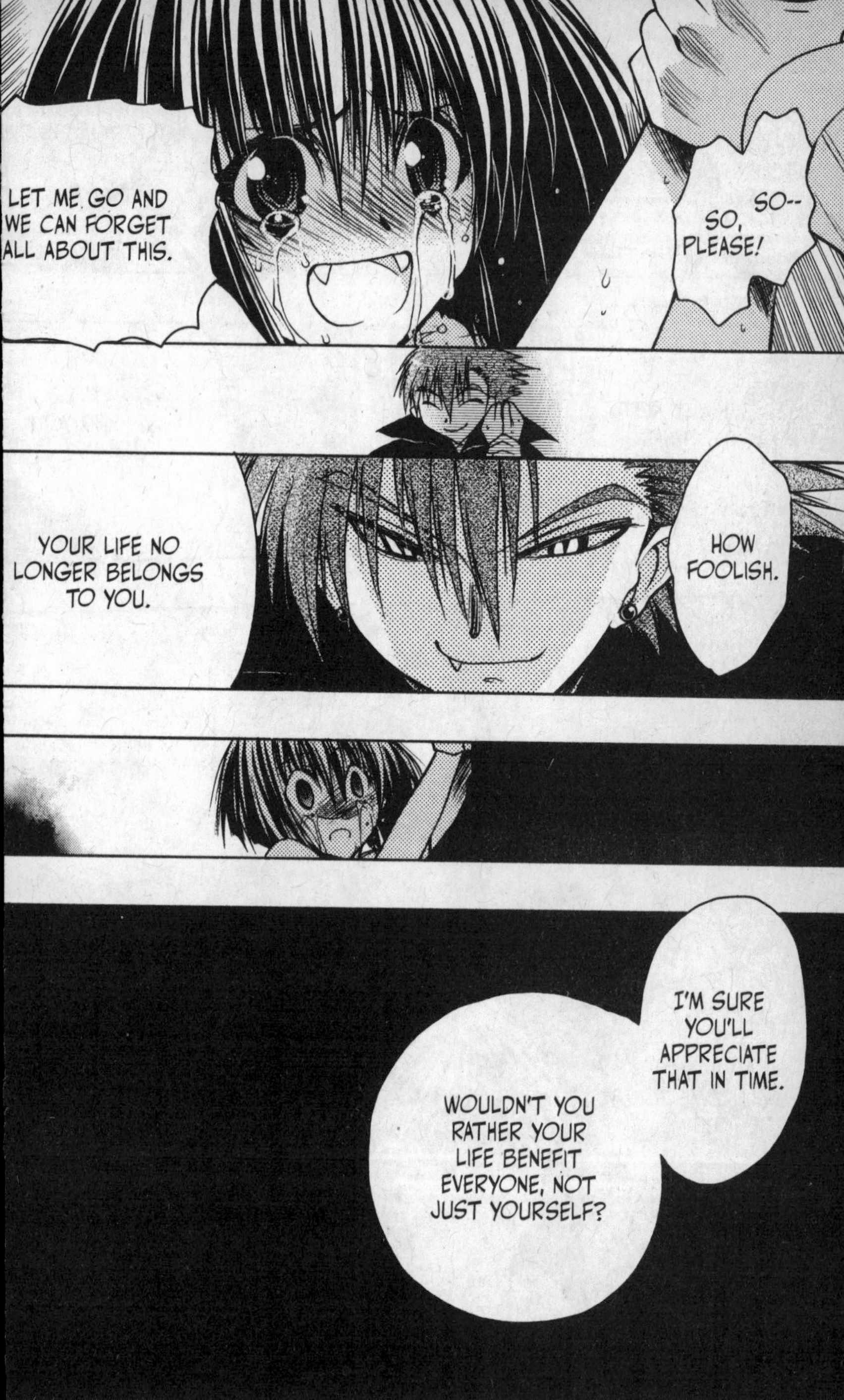
SO-- SO, PLEASE!
LET ME GO AND WE CAN FORGET ALL ABOUT THIS.
HOW FOOLISH.
YOUR LIFE NO LONGER BELONGS TO YOU.
I'M SURE YOU'LL APPRECIATE THAT IN TIME.
WOULDN'T YOU RATHER YOUR LIFE BENEFIT EVERYONE, NOT JUST YOURSELF?

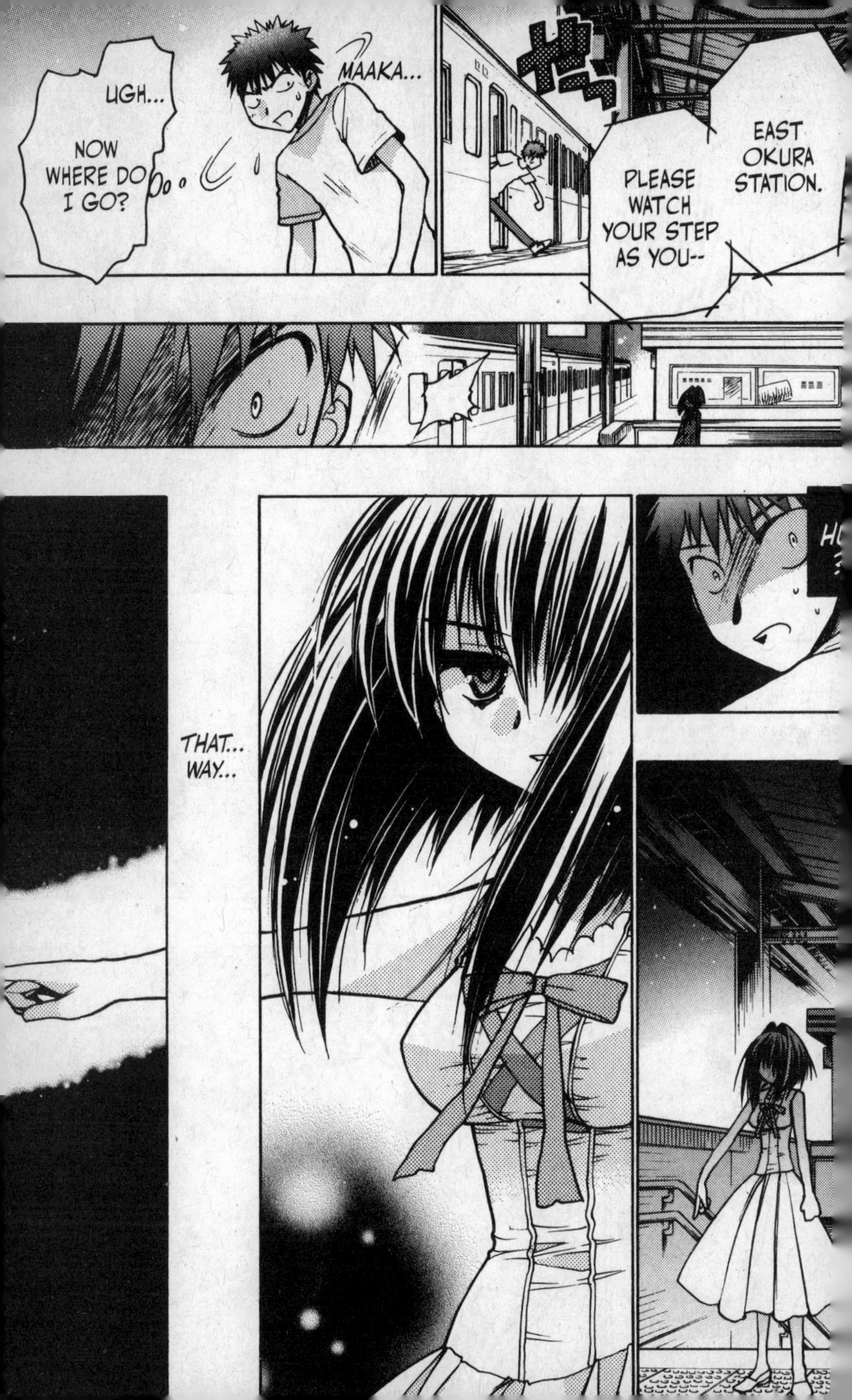
EAST OKURA STATION.
PLEASE WATCH YOUR STEP AS YOU--
MAAKA...
UGH... NOW WHERE DO I GO?
THAT... WAY...

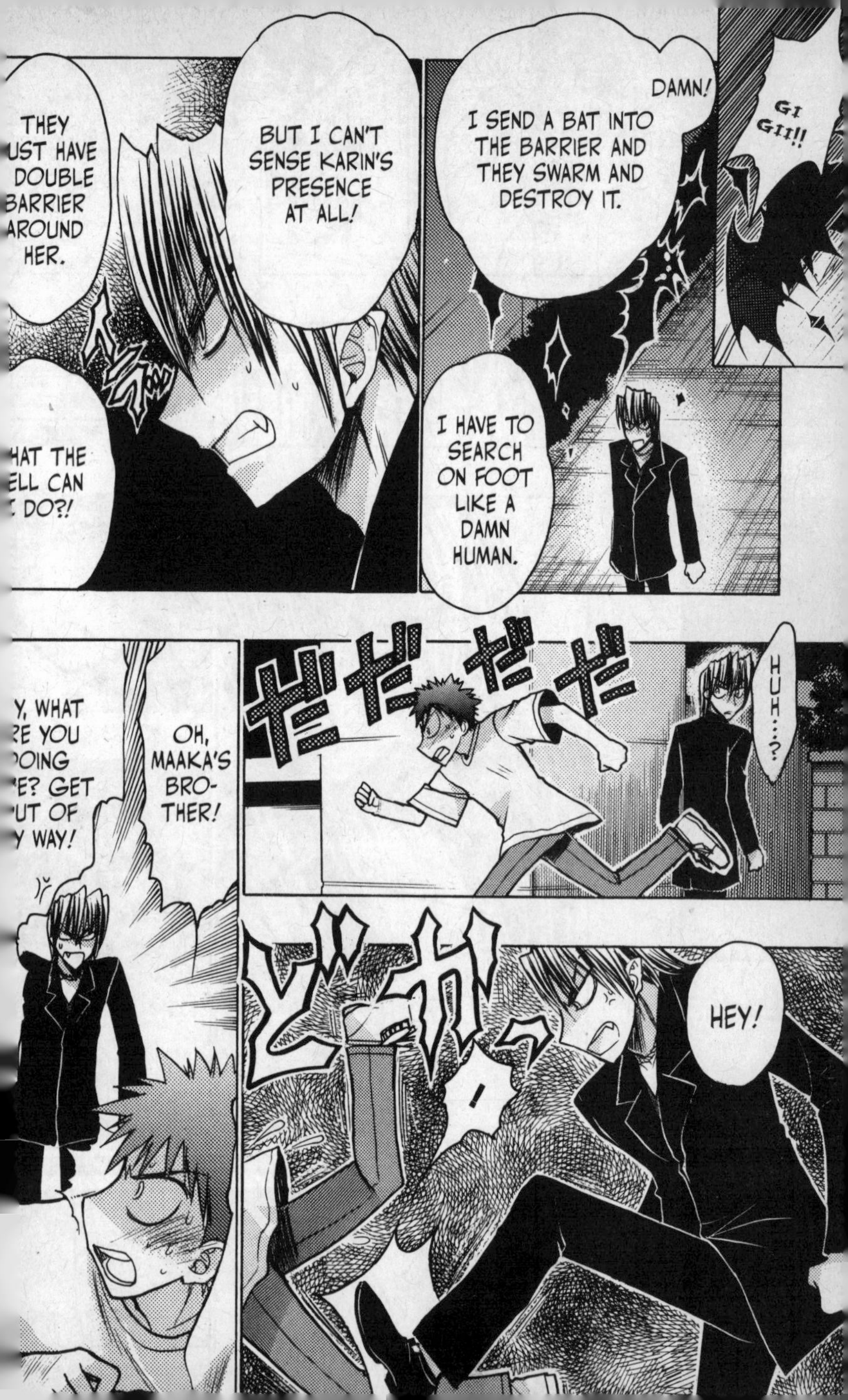
GI GII!!
DAMN!
I SEND A BAT INTO THE BARRIER AND THEY SWARM AND DESTROY IT.
I HAVE TO SEARCH ON FOOT LIKE A DAMN HUMAN.
BUT I CAN'T SENSE KARIN'S PRESENCE AT ALL!
THEY UST HAVE DOUBLE BARRIER AROUND HER.
HAT THE ELL CAN DO?!
HUH...?
だだだだ
OH, MAAKA'S BRO-THER!
Y, WHAT RE YOU OING E? GET UT OF WAY!
HEY!
どかっ
!

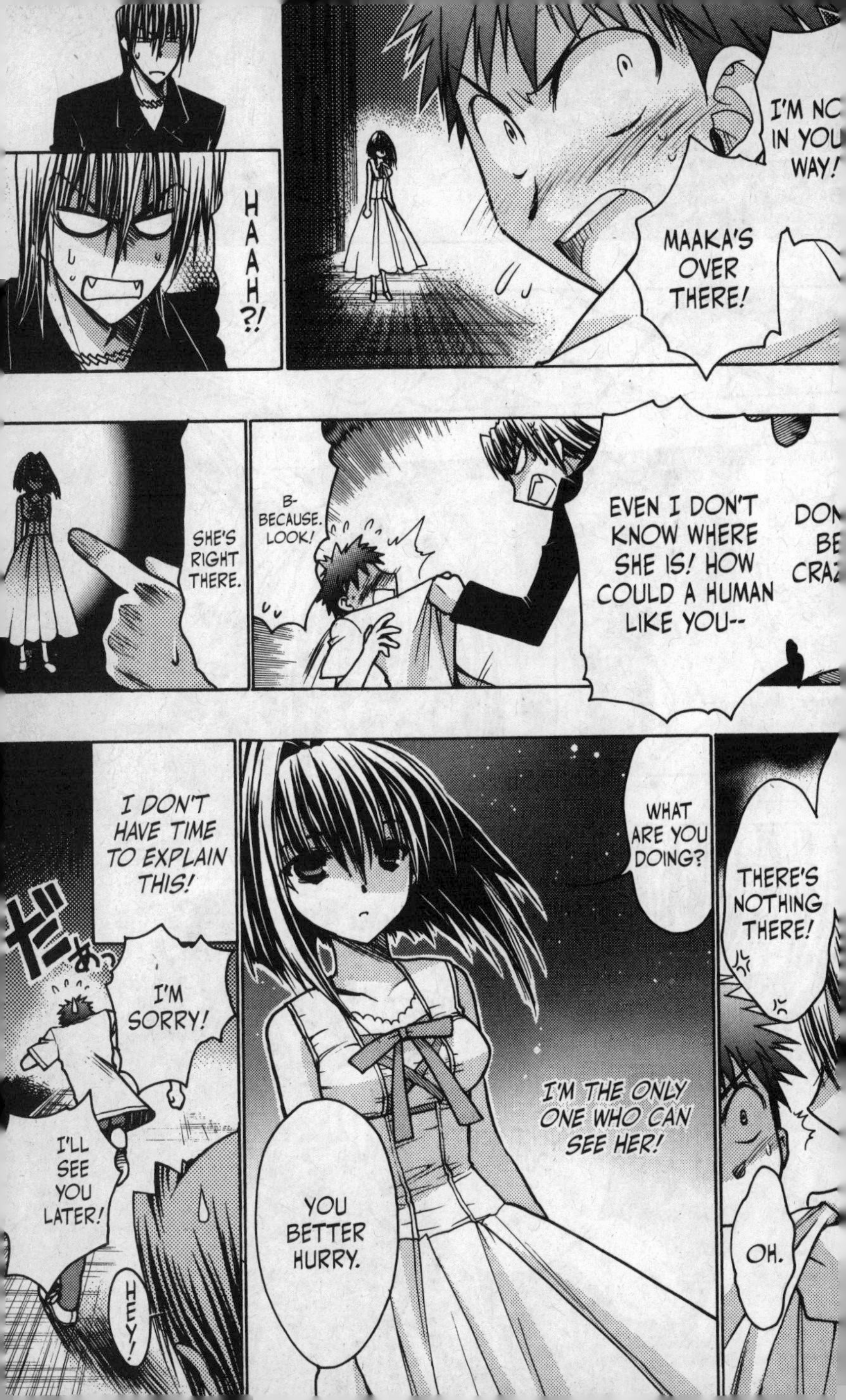
I'M NC IN YOU WAY!
MAAKA'S OVER THERE!
HAAAH?!
DON BE CRAZ
EVEN I DON'T KNOW WHERE SHE IS! HOW COULD A HUMAN LIKE YOU--
B-BECAUSE. LOOK!
SHE'S RIGHT THERE.
THERE'S NOTHING THERE!
OH.
WHAT ARE YOU DOING?
I'M THE ONLY ONE WHO CAN SEE HER!
YOU BETTER HURRY.
I DON'T HAVE TIME TO EXPLAIN THIS!
I'M SORRY!
I'LL SEE YOU LATER!
HEY!

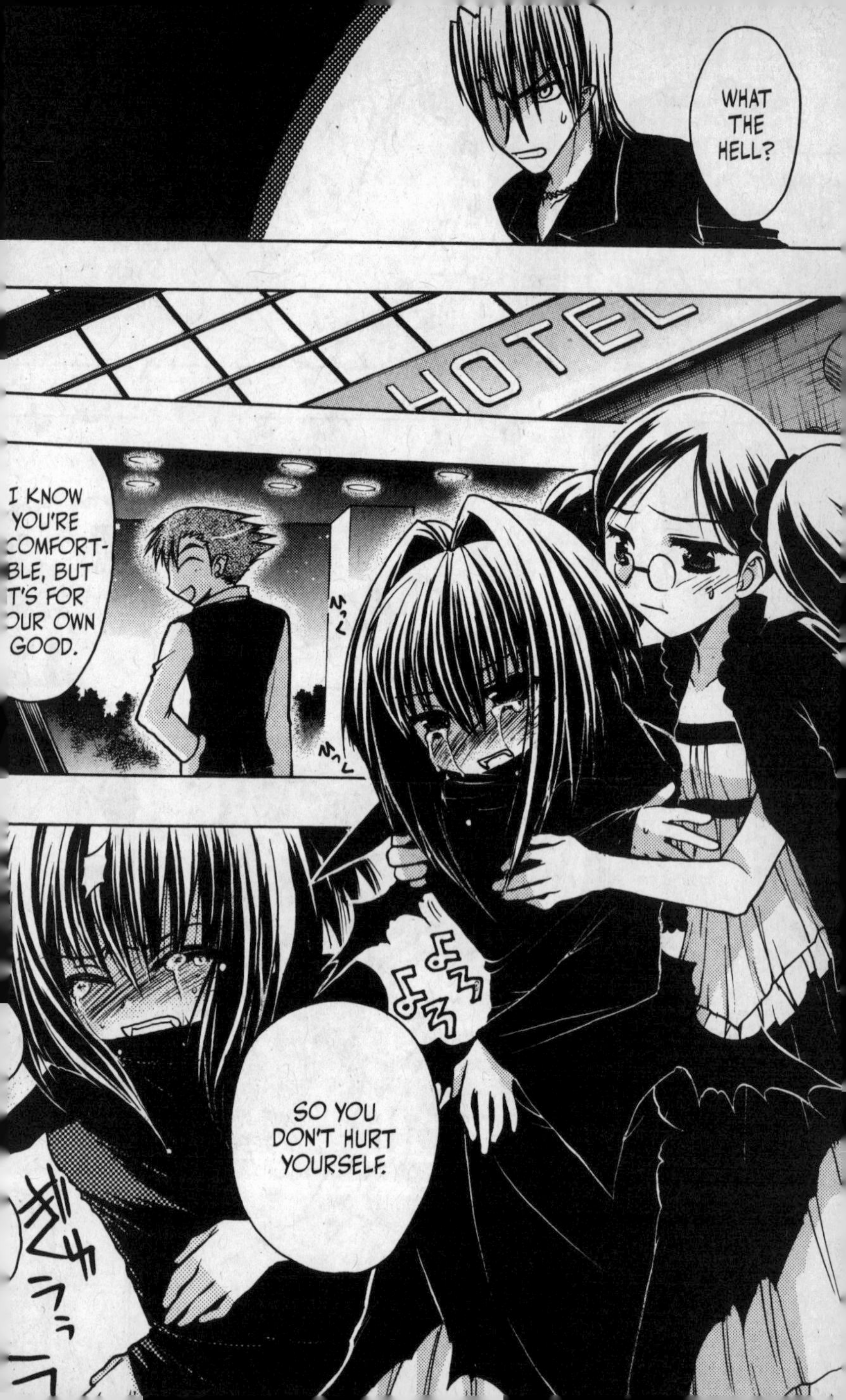
WHAT THE HELL?
HOTEL
I KNOW YOU'RE COMFORT- BLE, BUT T'S FOR OUR OWN GOOD.
よろよろ
SO YOU DON'T HURT YOURSELF.

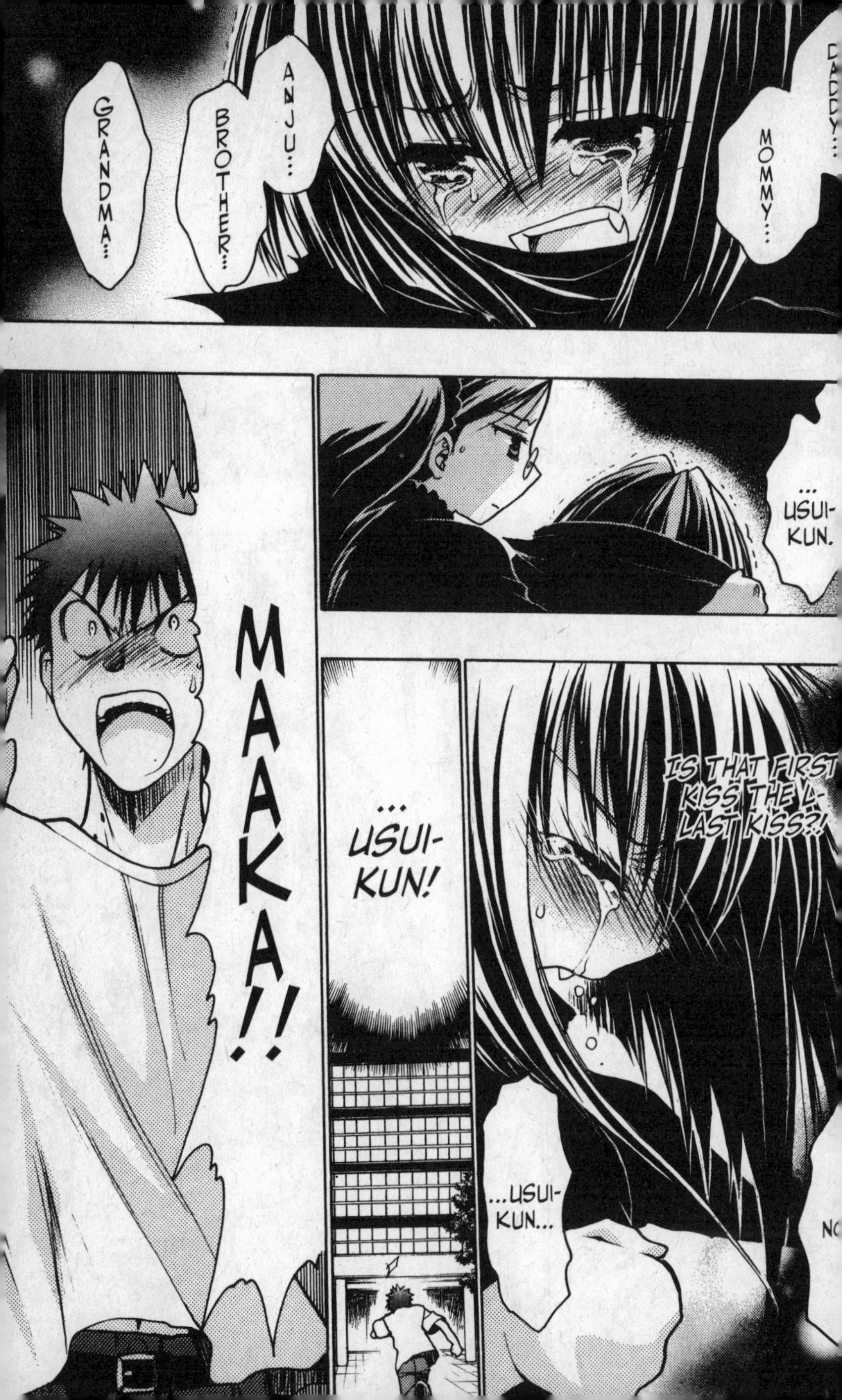
DADDY...
MOMMY...
ANJU...
BROTHER...
GRANDMA...
...USUI-KUN.
IS THAT FIRST KISS THE L-LAST KISS?!
...USUI-KUN...
...USUI-KUN!
MAAKA!!

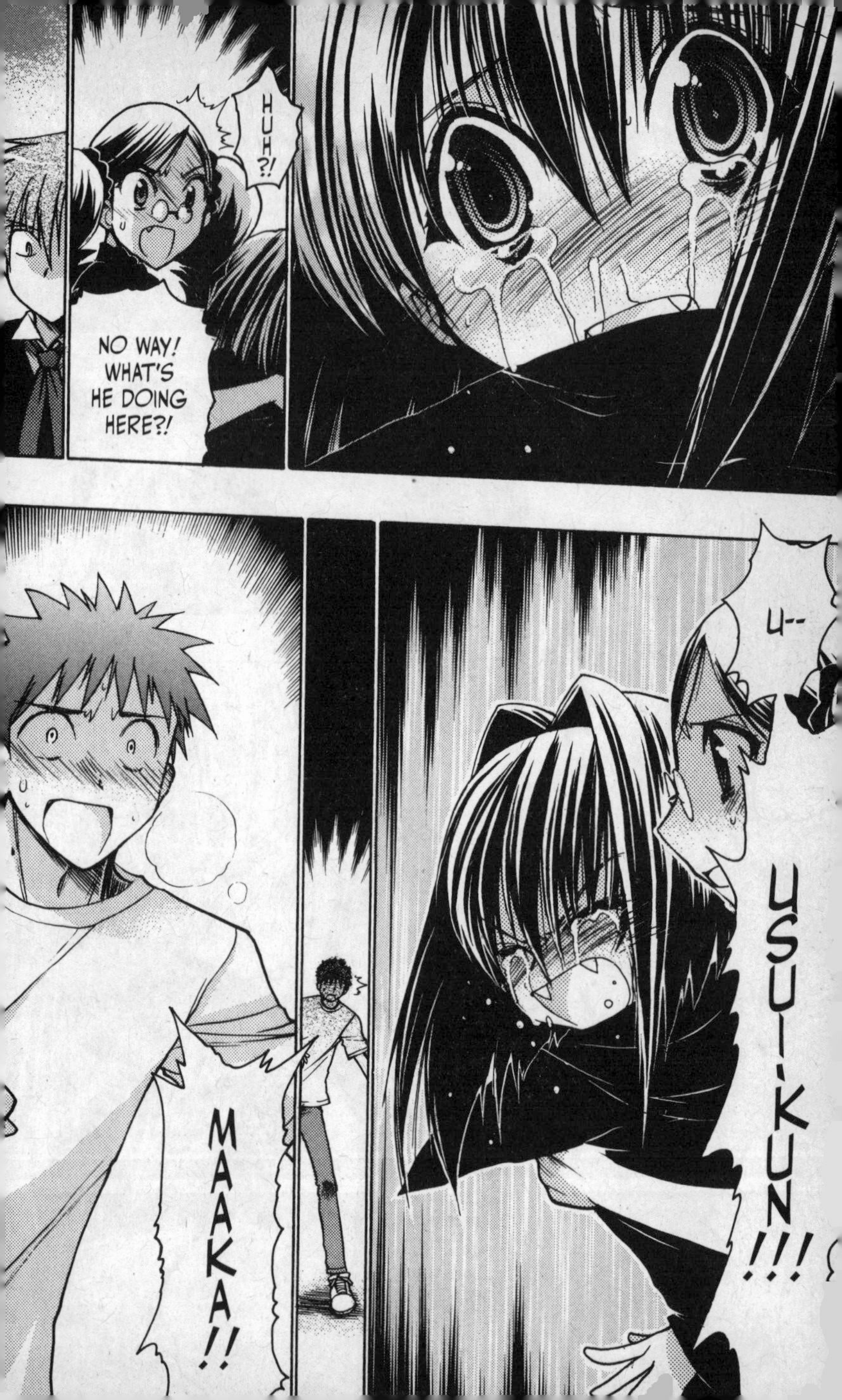
HUH?!
NO WAY! WHAT'S HE DOING HERE?!
U--
USUI-KUN!!!
MAAKA!!

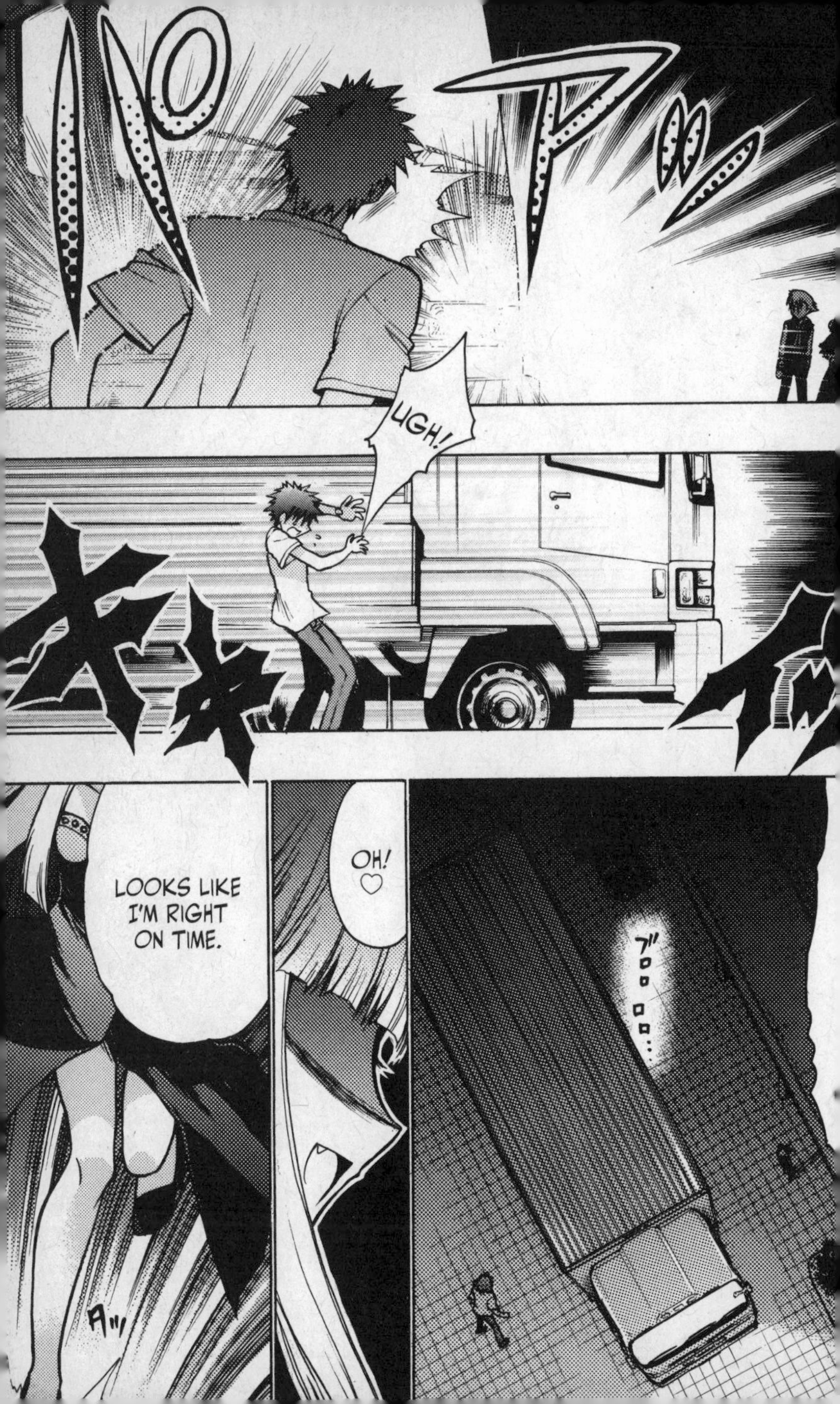
UGH!
OH! ♡
LOOKS LIKE I'M RIGHT ON TIME.

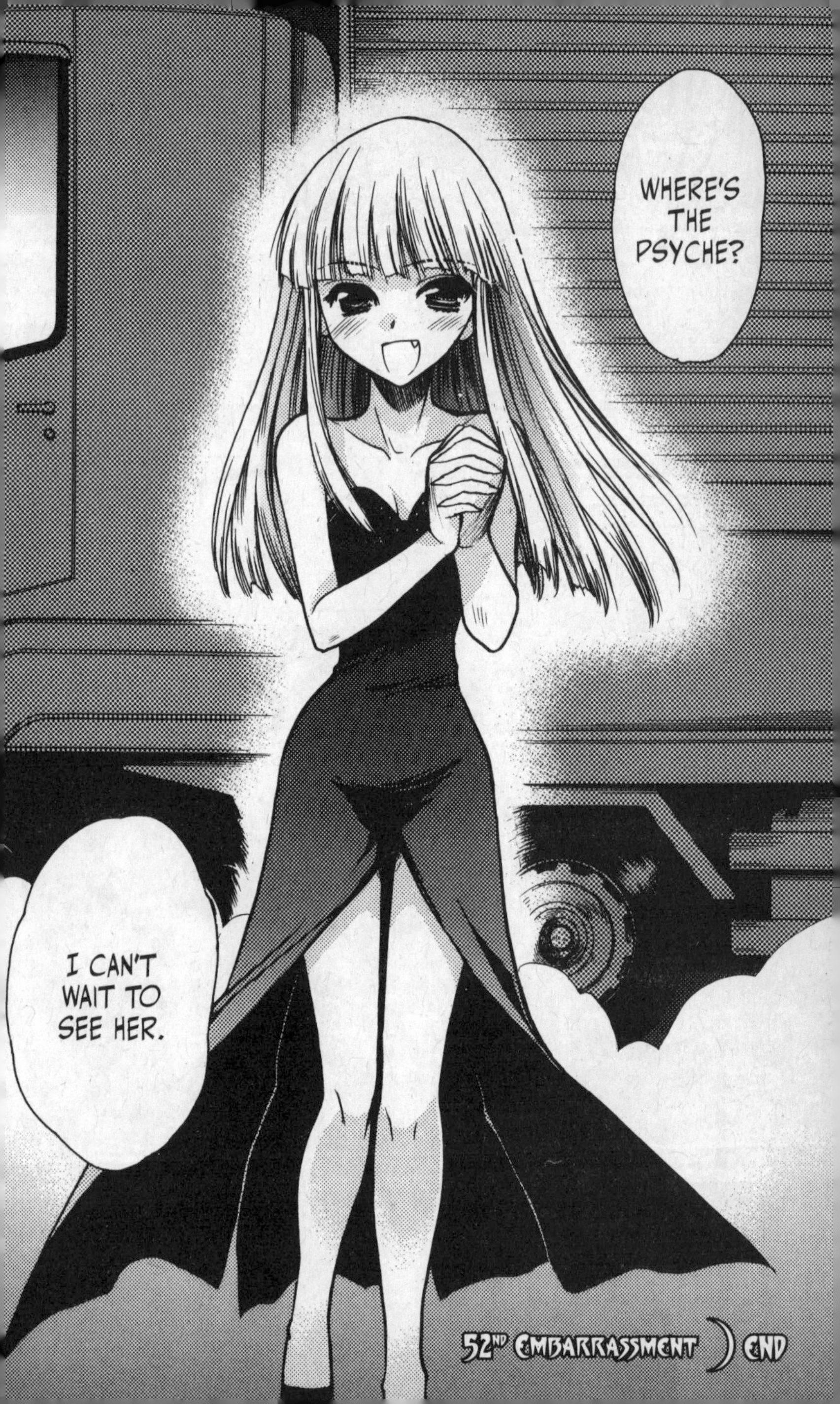
WHERE'S THE PSYCHE?
I CAN'T WAIT TO SEE HER.
52ND EMBARRASSMENT) END

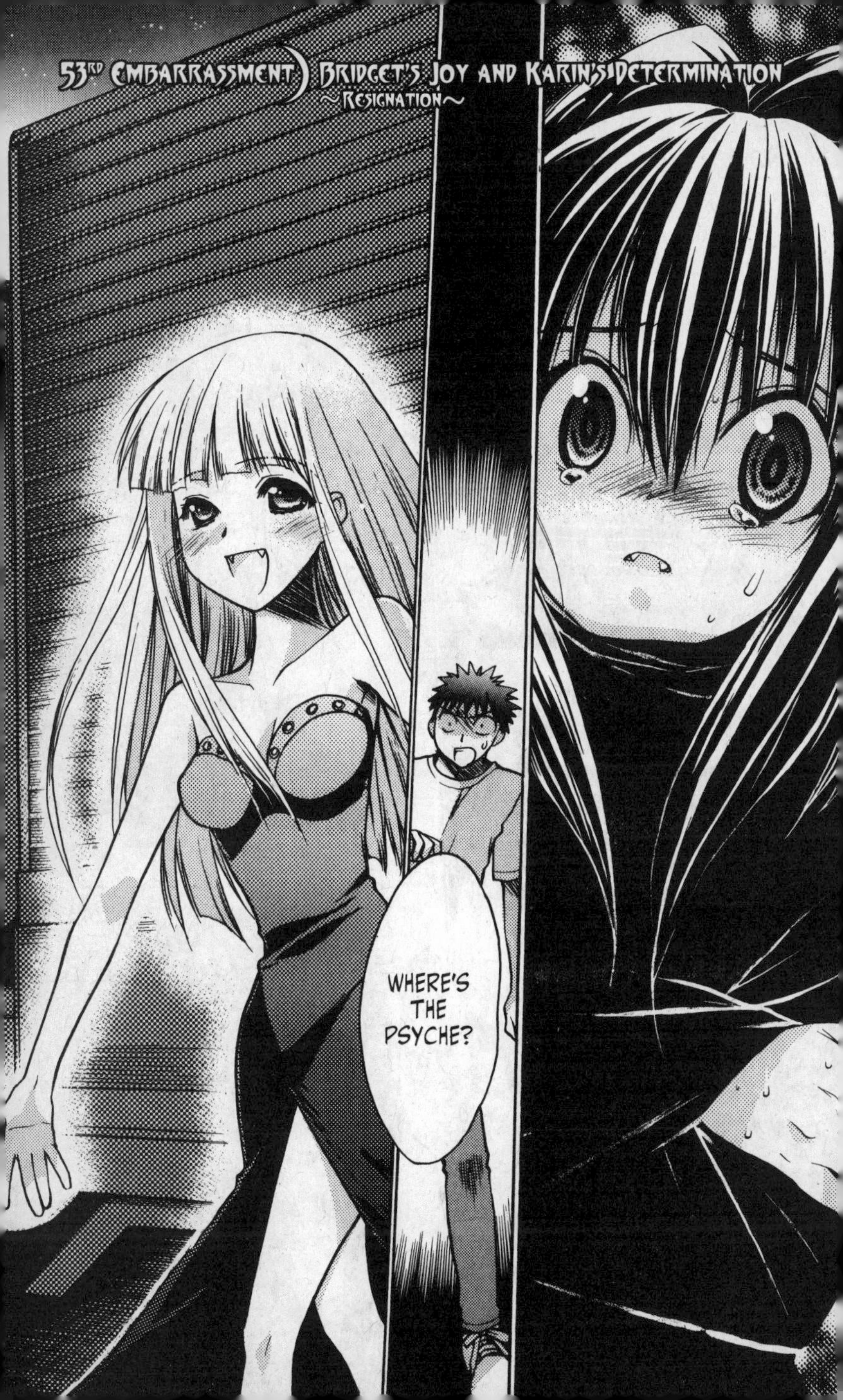
53RD EMBARRASSMENT BRIDGET'S JOY AND KARIN'S DETERMINATION
~RESIGNATION~
WHERE'S THE PSYCHE?

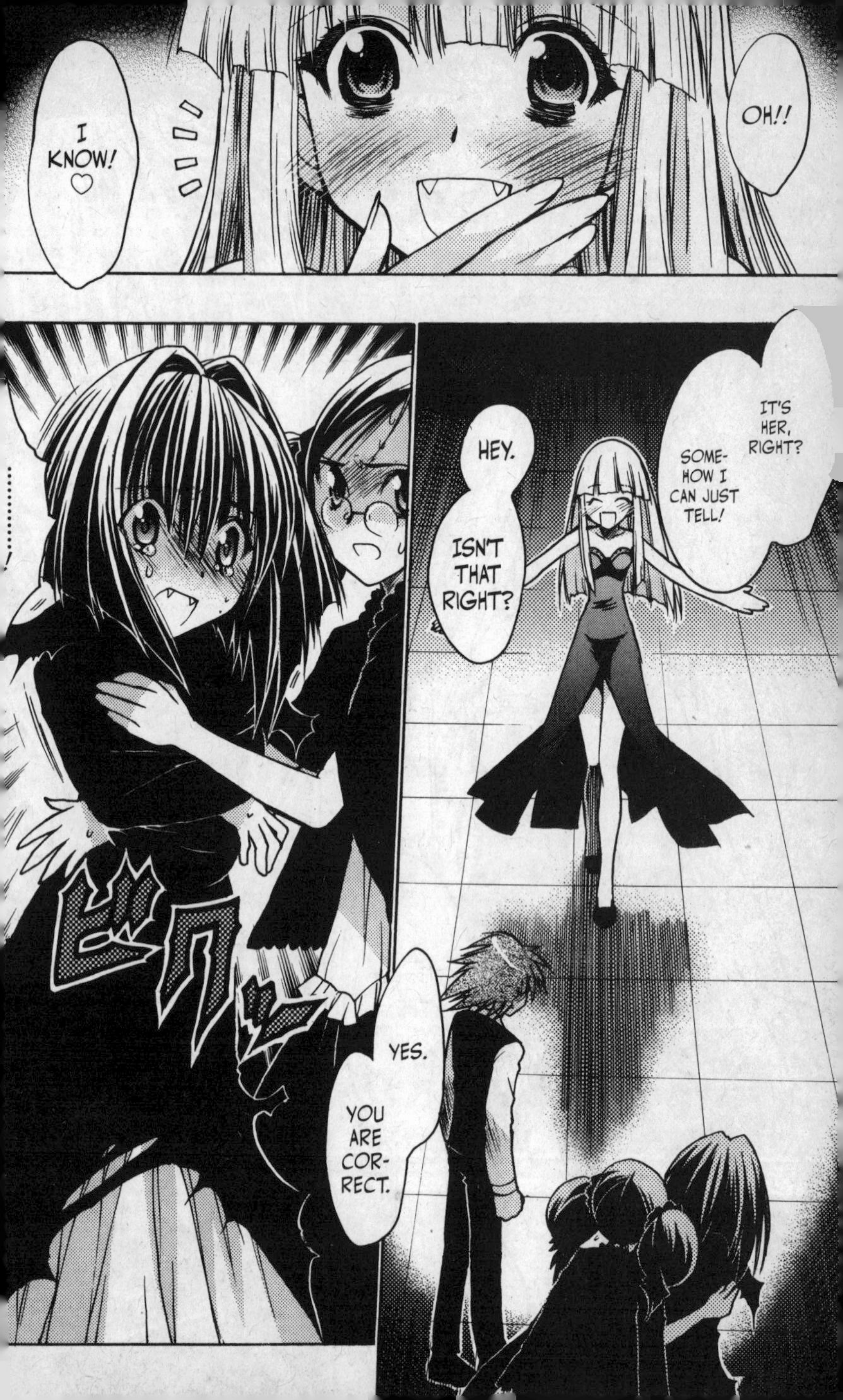
OH!!
I KNOW! ♡
IT'S HER, RIGHT?
SOME-HOW I CAN JUST TELL!
HEY.
ISN'T THAT RIGHT?
YES.
YOU ARE COR-RECT.
ビクッ

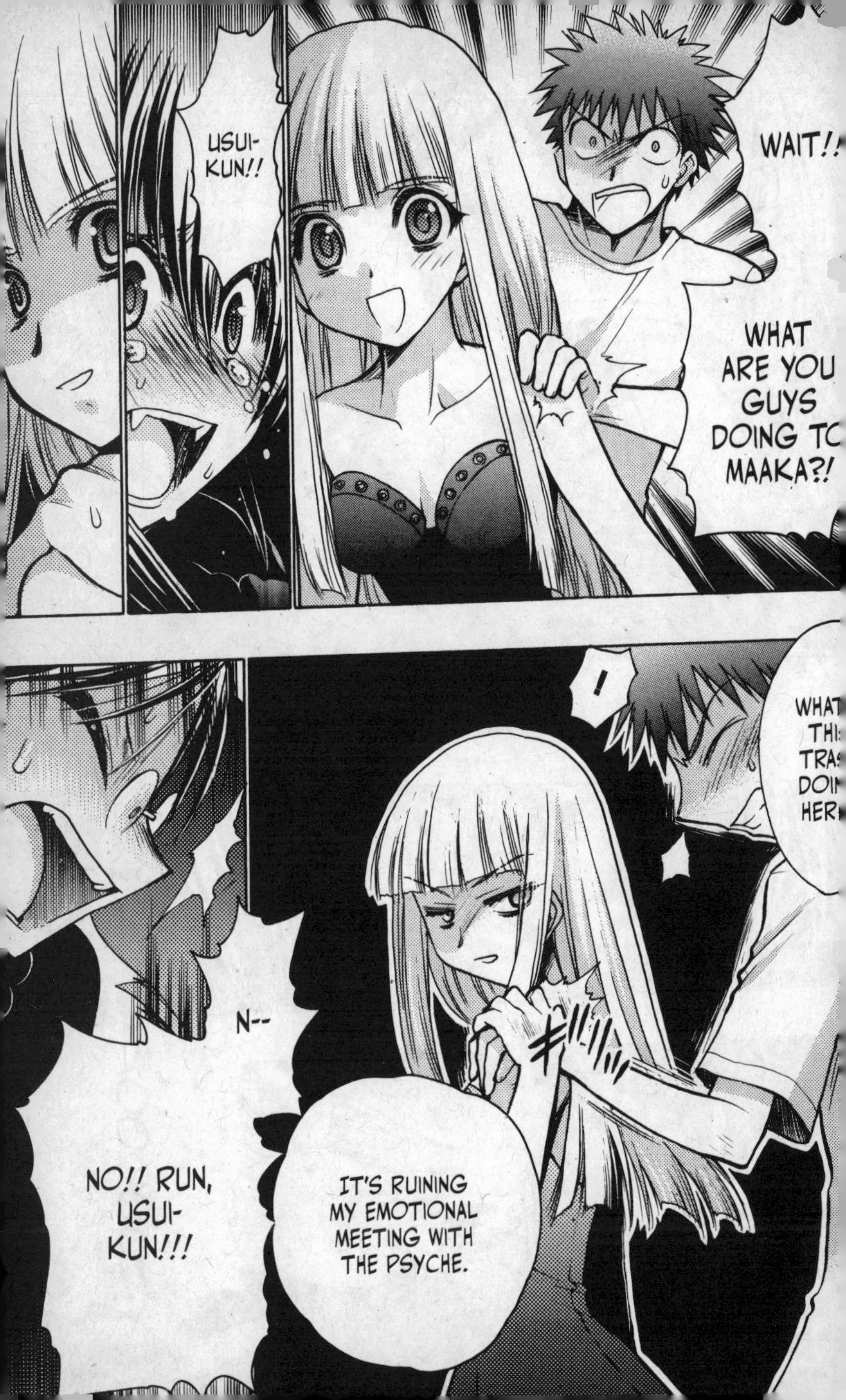
WAIT!!
WHAT ARE YOU GUYS DOING TO MAAKA?!
USUI-KUN!!
!
WHAT THI TRAS DOIN HER
IT'S RUINING MY EMOTIONAL MEETING WITH THE PSYCHE.
N--
NO!! RUN, USUI-KUN!!!

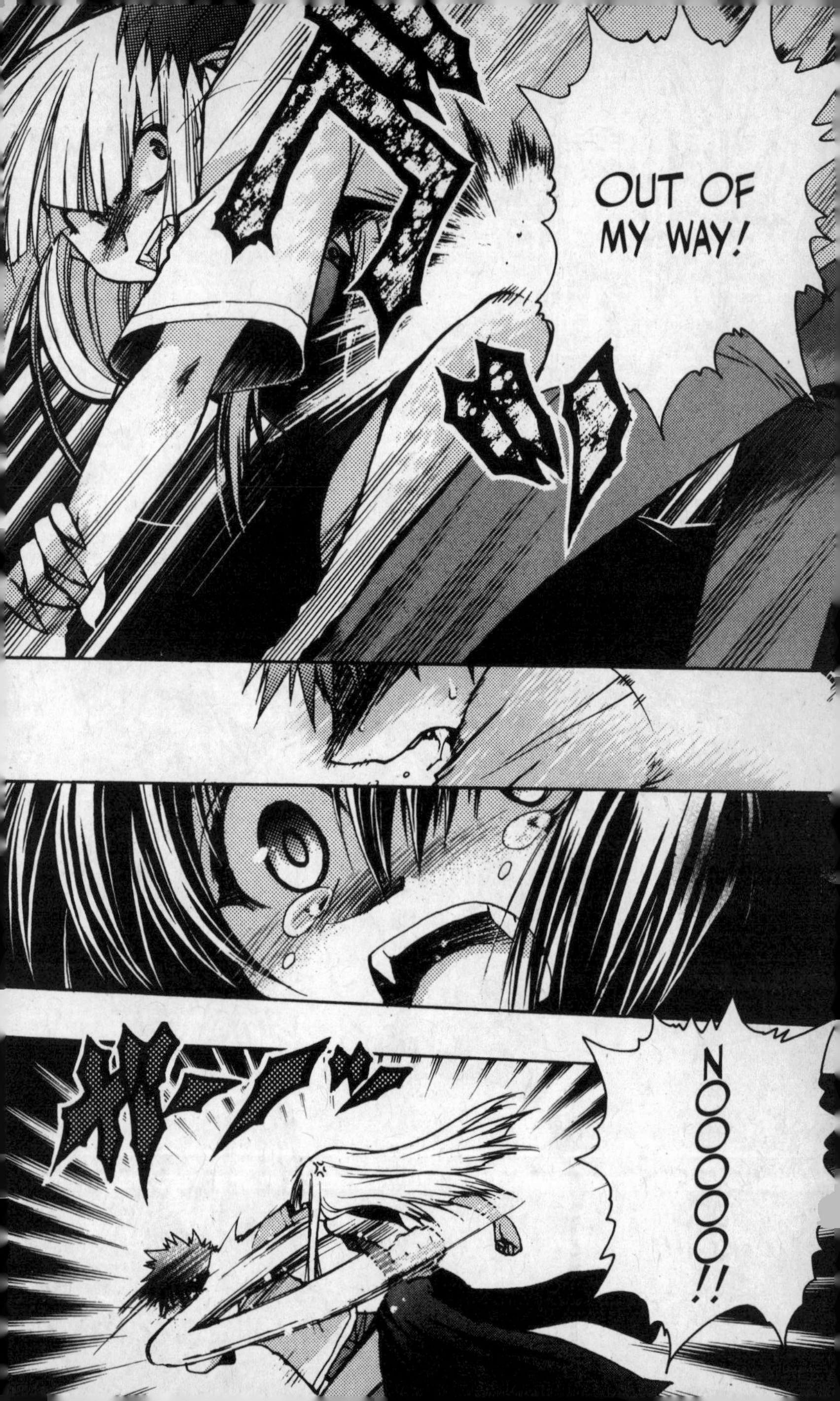
OUT OF MY WAY!
NOOOOOO!!

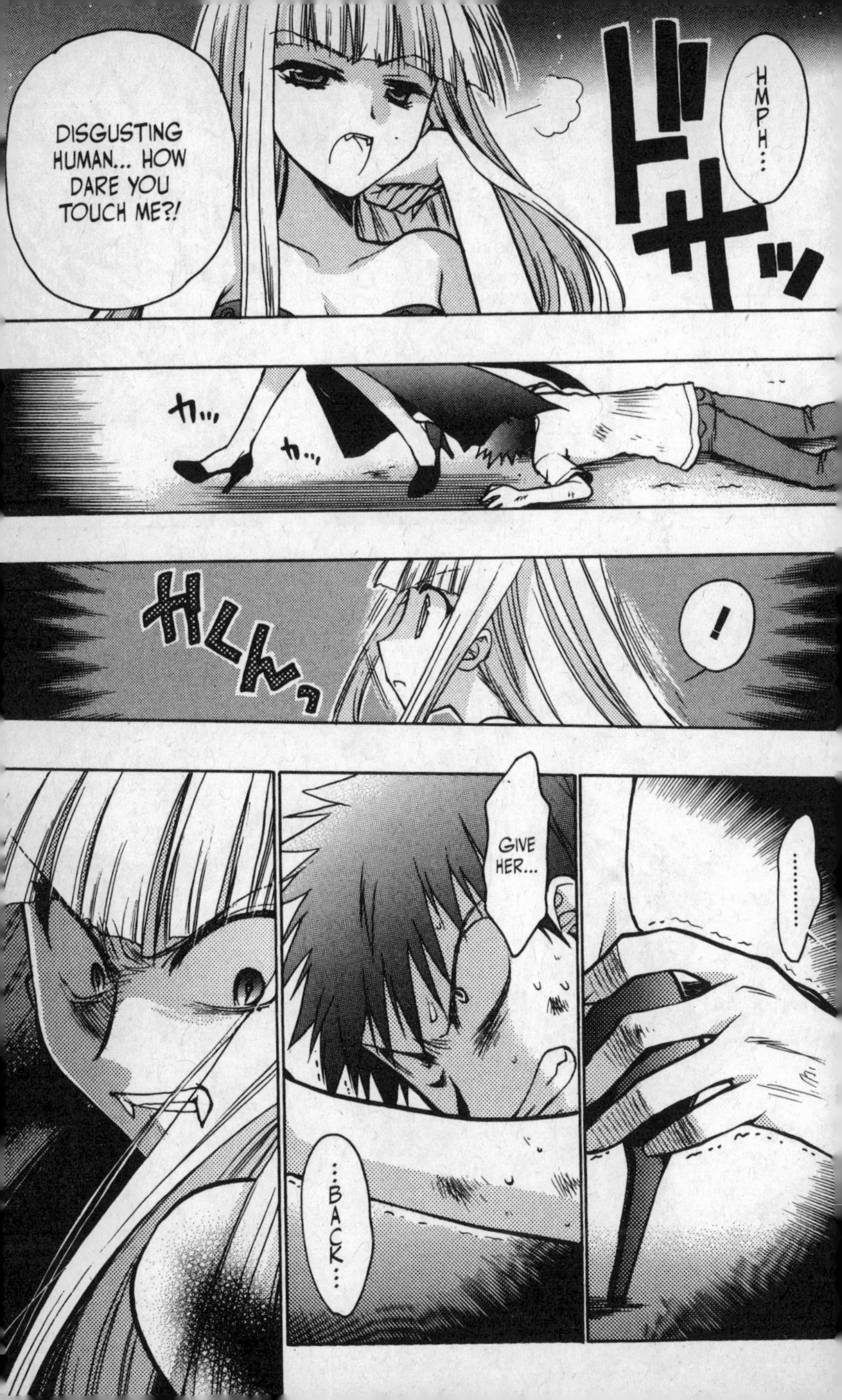

ドサッ
HMPH...
DISGUSTING HUMAN... HOW DARE YOU TOUCH ME?!
!
....
GIVE HER...
...BACK...

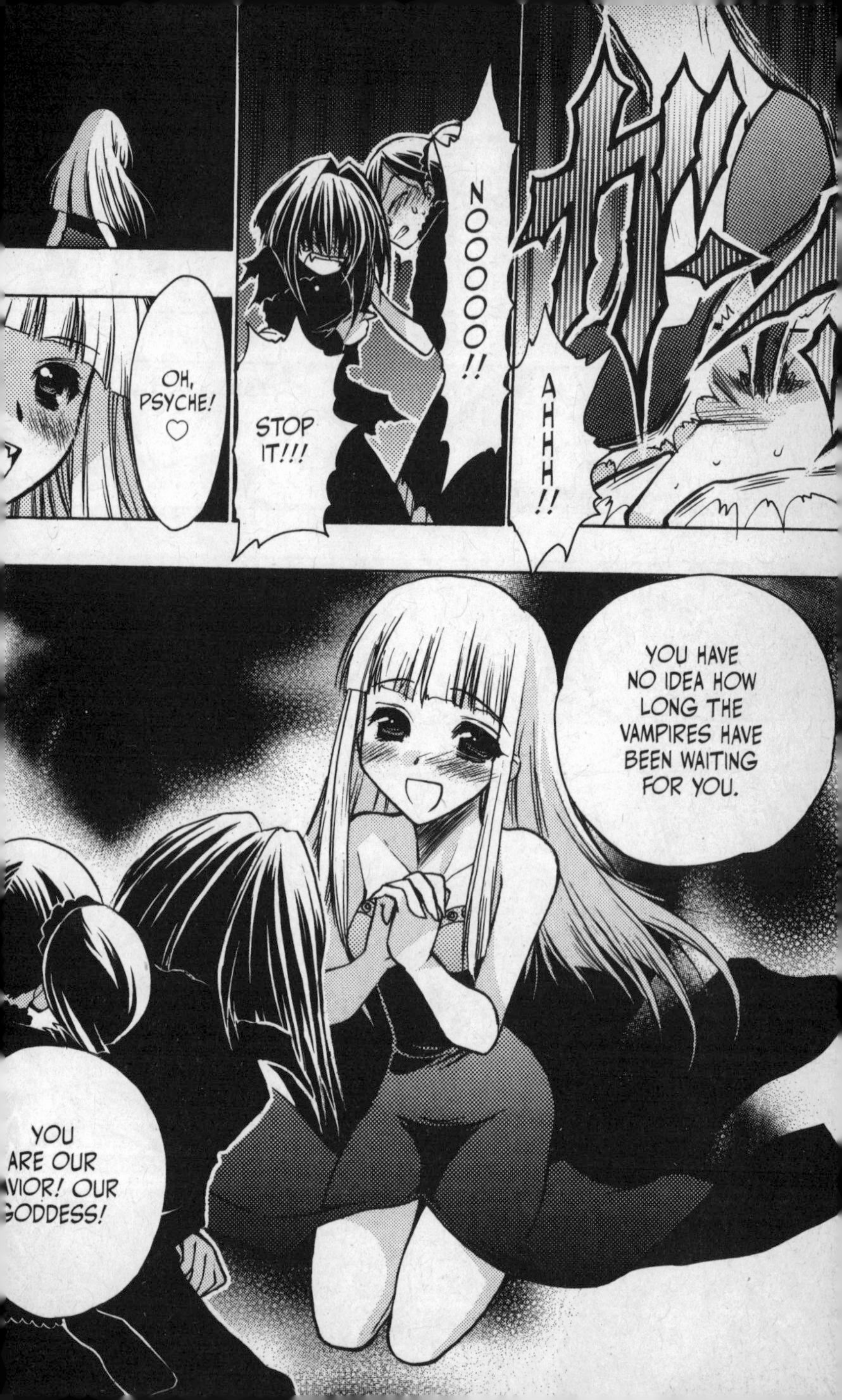
AHHHH!!
NOOOOOO!!
STOP IT!!!
OH, PSYCHE! ♡
YOU HAVE NO IDEA HOW LONG THE VAMPIRES HAVE BEEN WAITING FOR YOU.
YOU ARE OUR AVIOR! OUR GODDESS!

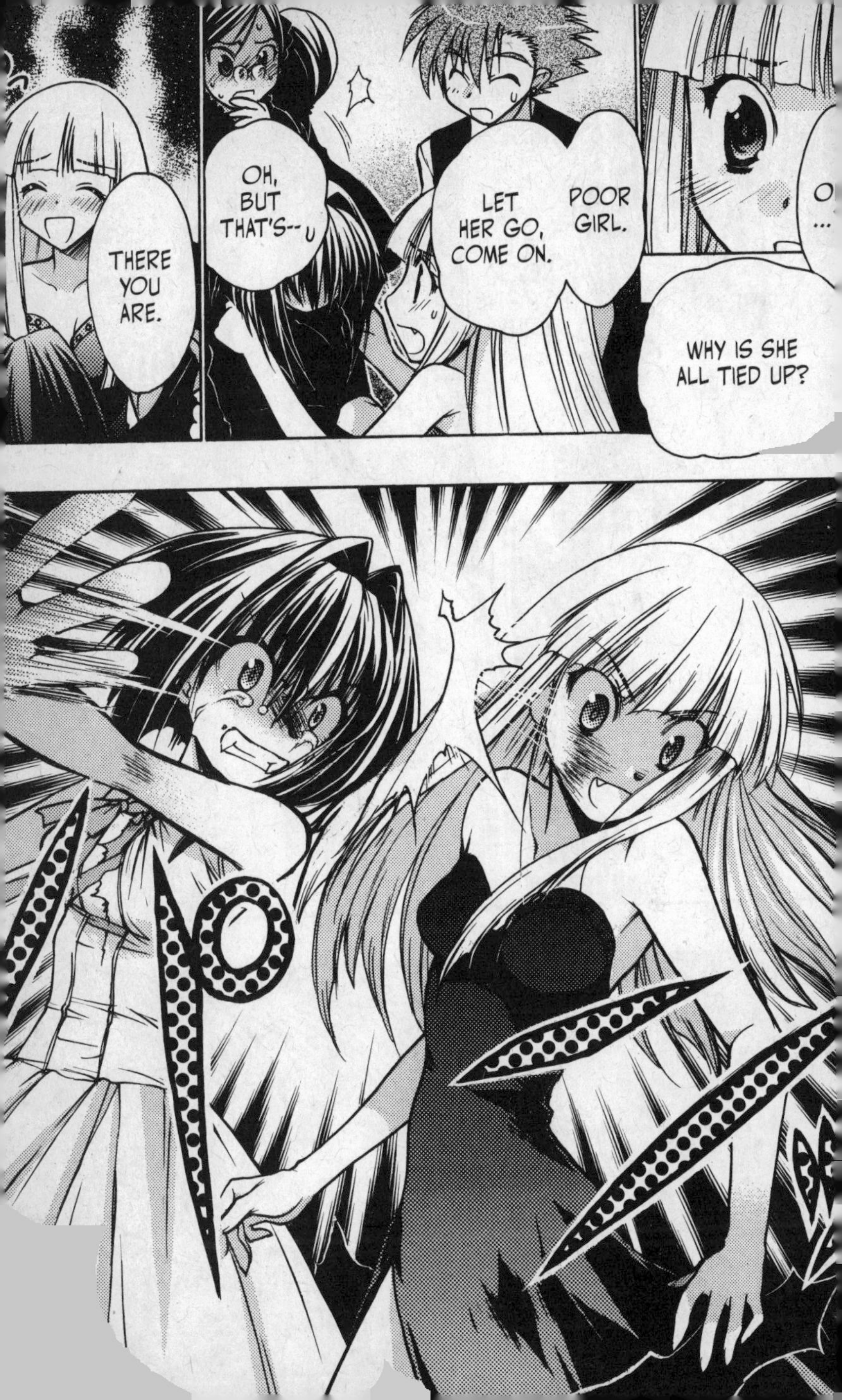
O
...
WHY IS SHE ALL TIED UP?
POOR GIRL.
LET HER GO, COME ON.
OH, BUT THAT'S--
THERE YOU ARE.

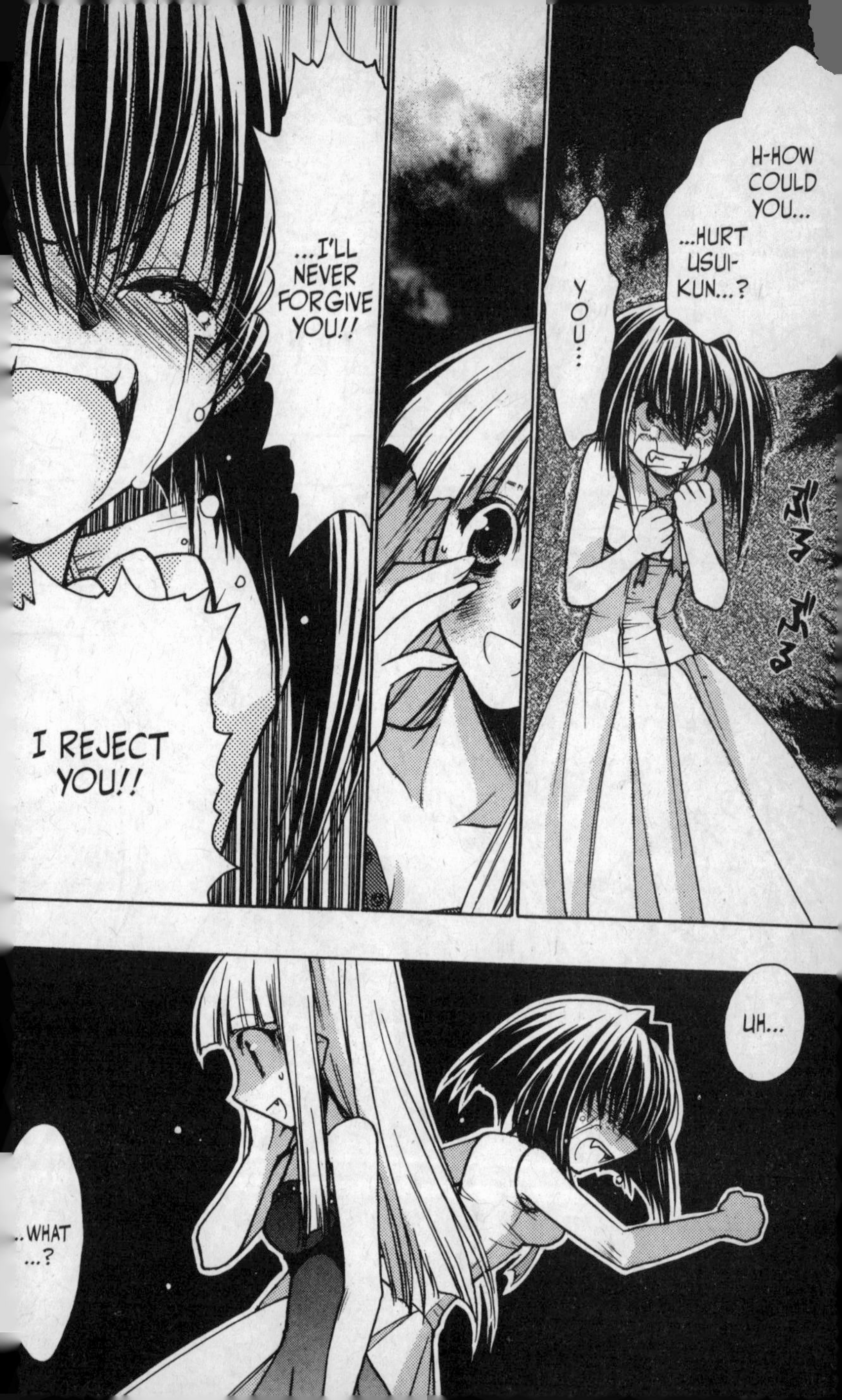
H-HOW COULD YOU...
...HURT USUI-KUN...?
YOU...
...I'LL NEVER FORGIVE YOU!!
I REJECT YOU!!
UH...
...WHAT ...?

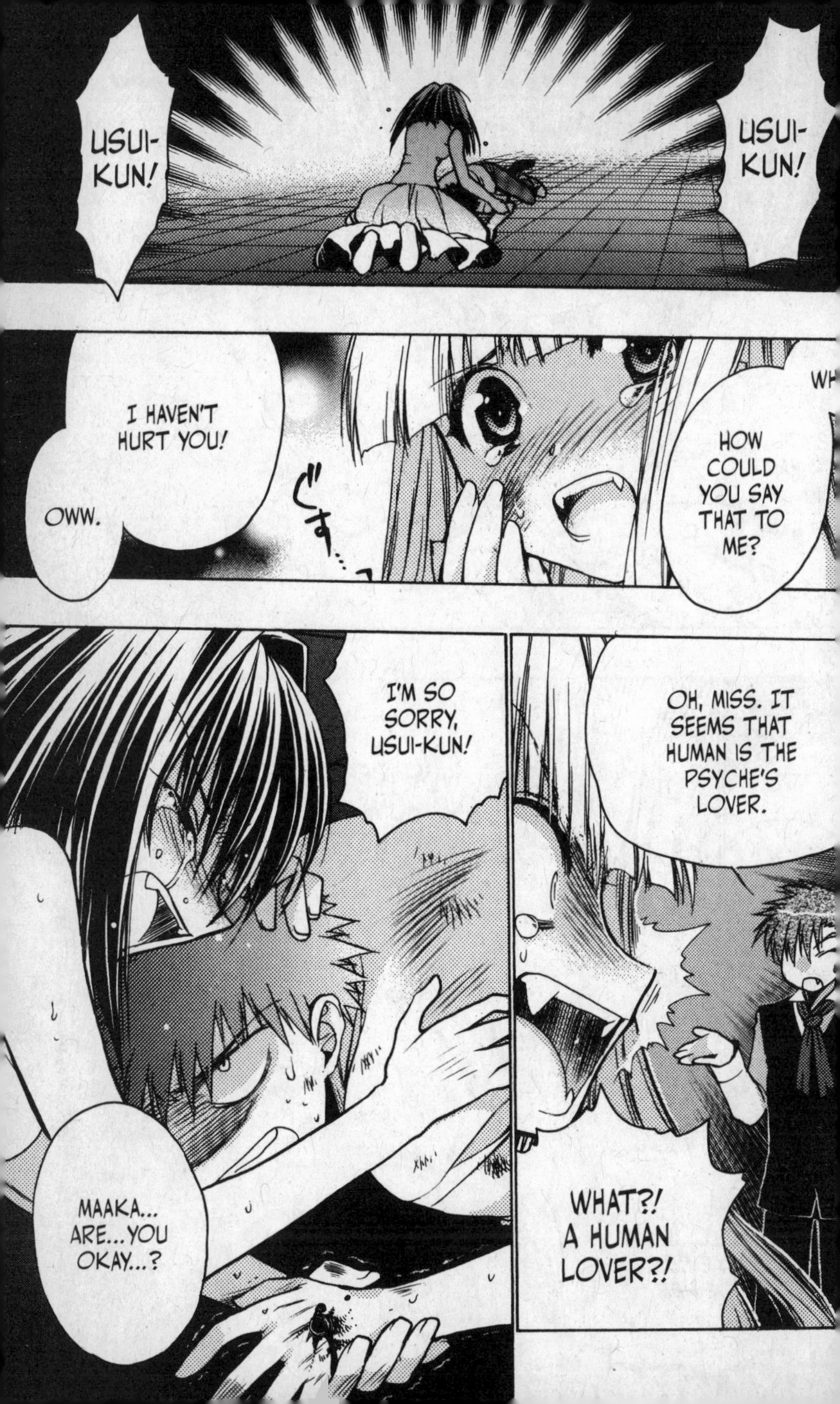
USUI-KUN!
USUI-KUN!
HOW COULD YOU SAY THAT TO ME?
ぐす…
I HAVEN'T HURT YOU!
OWW.
OH, MISS. IT SEEMS THAT HUMAN IS THE PSYCHE'S LOVER.
WHAT?! A HUMAN LOVER?!
I'M SO SORRY, USUI-KUN!
MAAKA... ARE...YOU OKAY...?

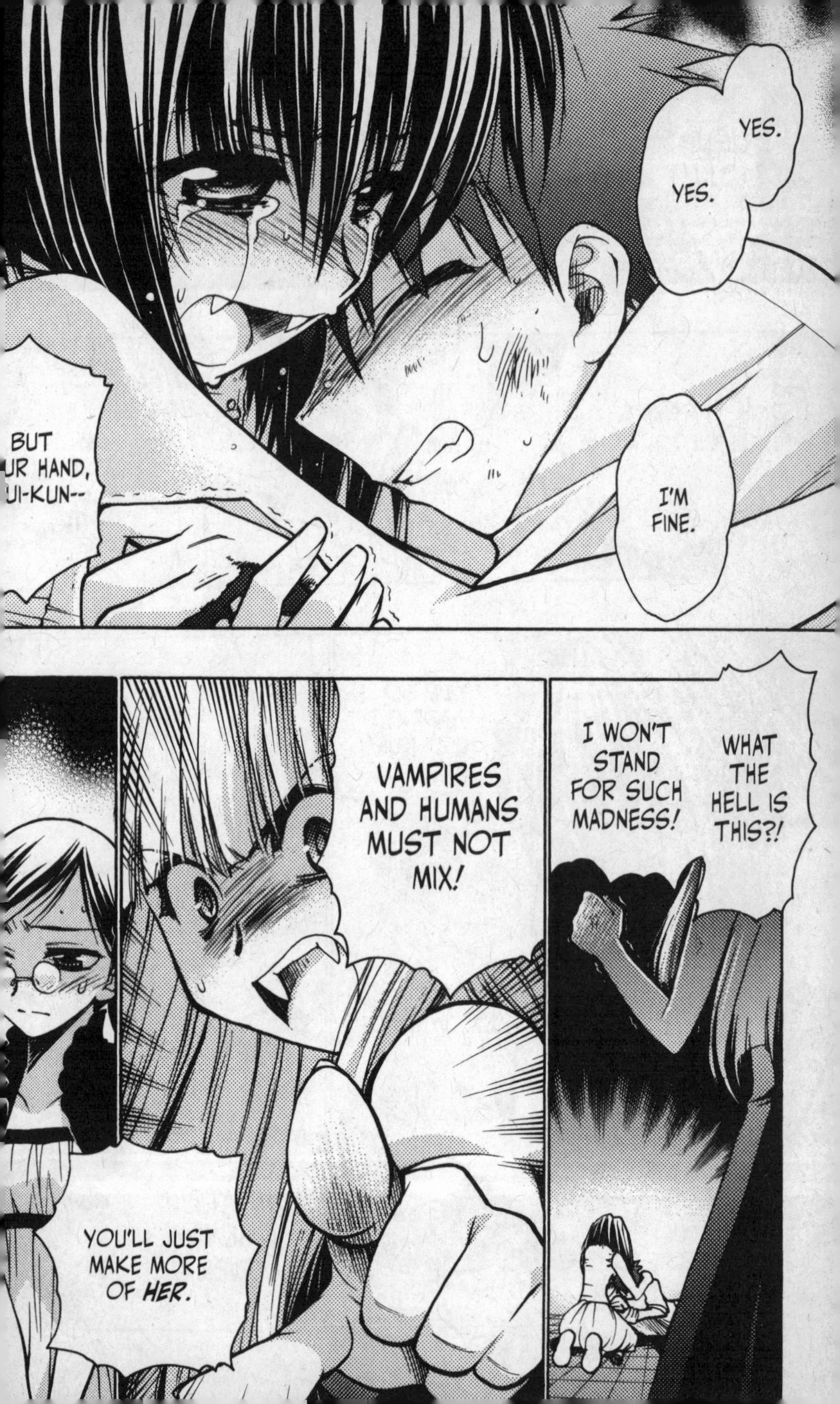
YES. YES.
I'M FINE.
BUT UR HAND, UI-KUN--
WHAT THE HELL IS THIS?!
I WON'T STAND FOR SUCH MADNESS!
VAMPIRES AND HUMANS MUST NOT MIX!
YOU'LL JUST MAKE MORE OF *HER*.

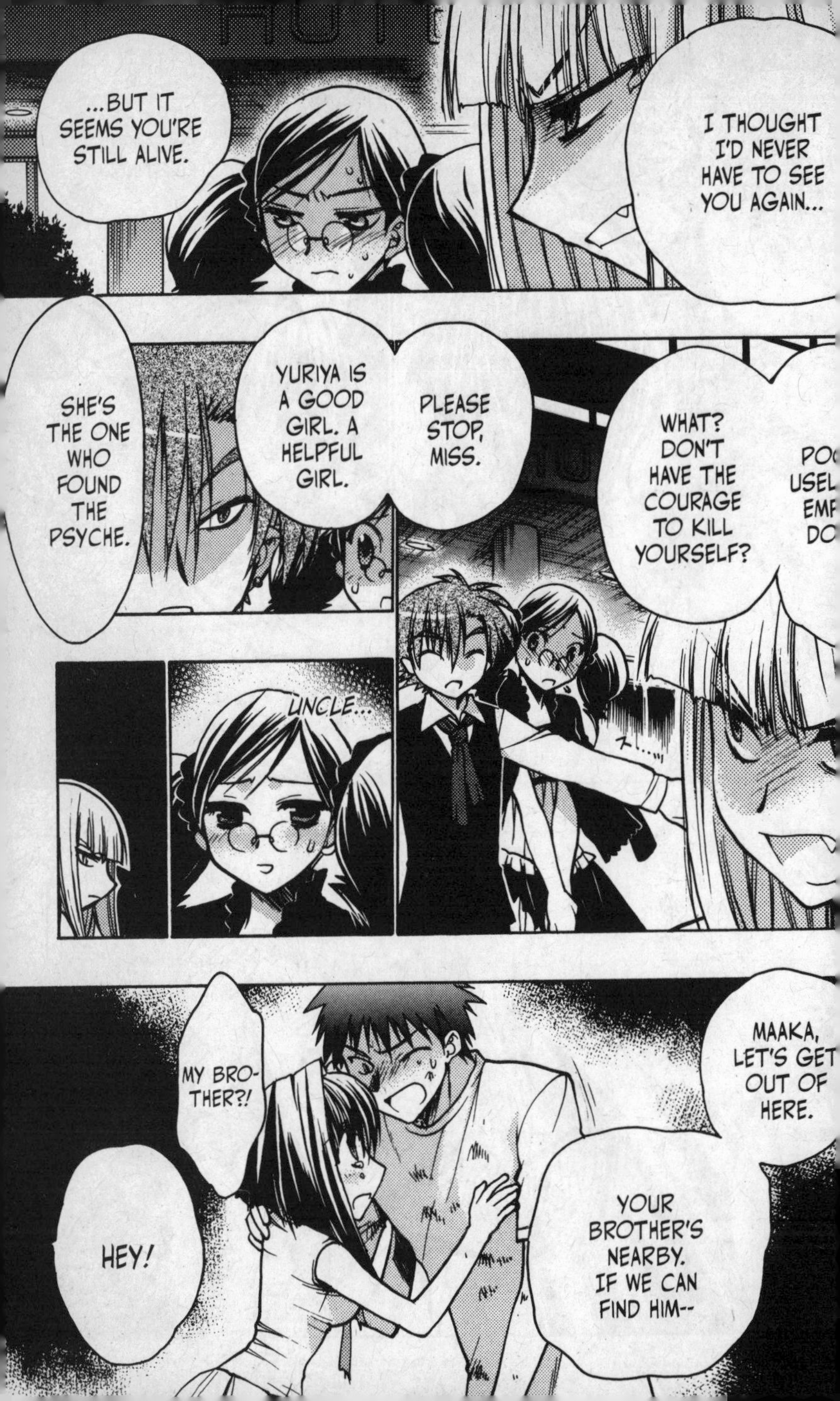
I THOUGHT I'D NEVER HAVE TO SEE YOU AGAIN...
...BUT IT SEEMS YOU'RE STILL ALIVE.
WHAT? DON'T HAVE THE COURAGE TO KILL YOURSELF?
PLEASE STOP, MISS.
YURIYA IS A GOOD GIRL. A HELPFUL GIRL.
SHE'S THE ONE WHO FOUND THE PSYCHE.
UNCLE...
MAAKA, LET'S GET OUT OF HERE.
YOUR BROTHER'S NEARBY. IF WE CAN FIND HIM--
MY BRO-THER?!
HEY!

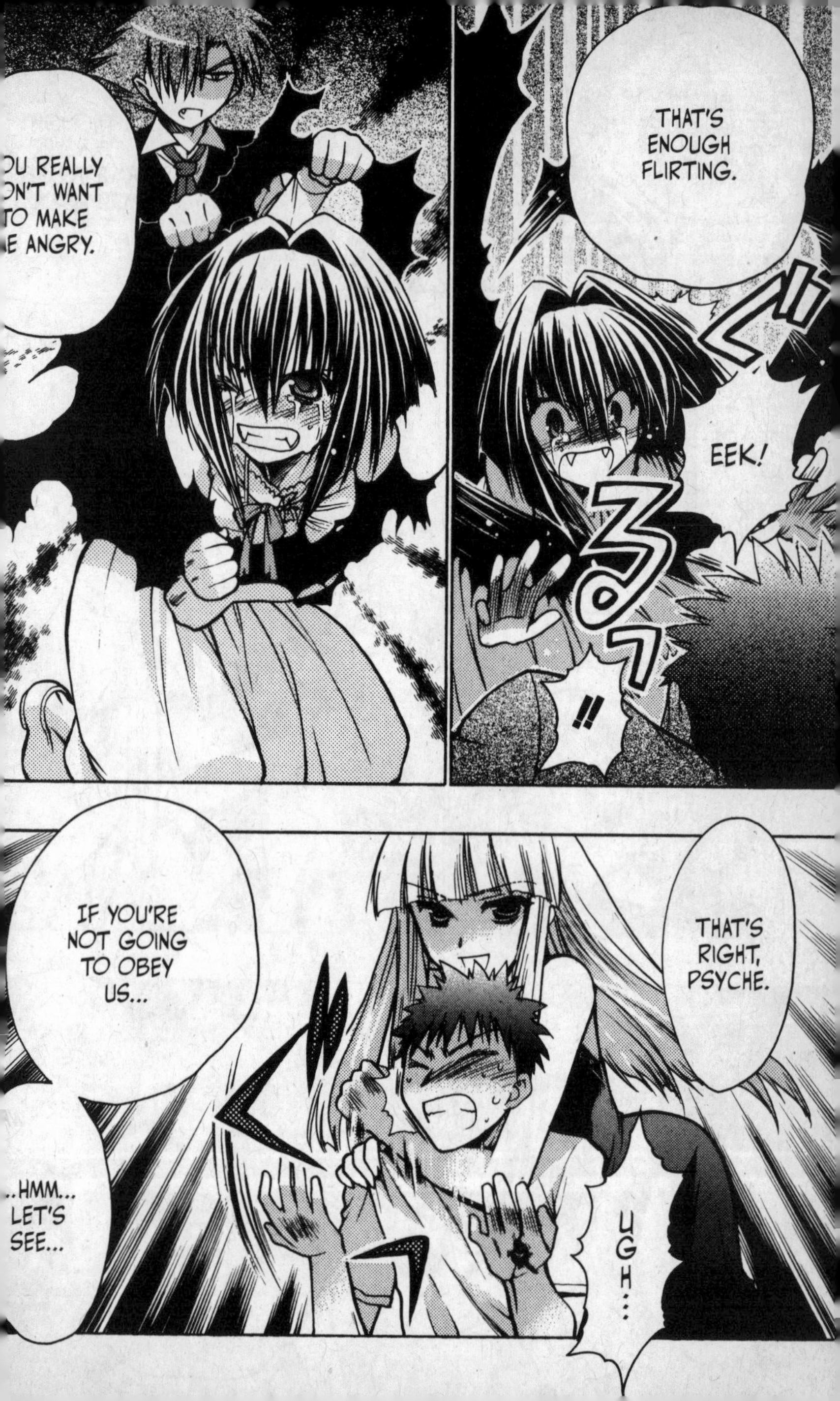
THAT'S ENOUGH FLIRTING.
EEK!
!!
OU REALLY ON'T WANT TO MAKE E ANGRY.
THAT'S RIGHT, PSYCHE.
IF YOU'RE NOT GOING TO OBEY US...
UGH...
..HMM... LET'S SEE...

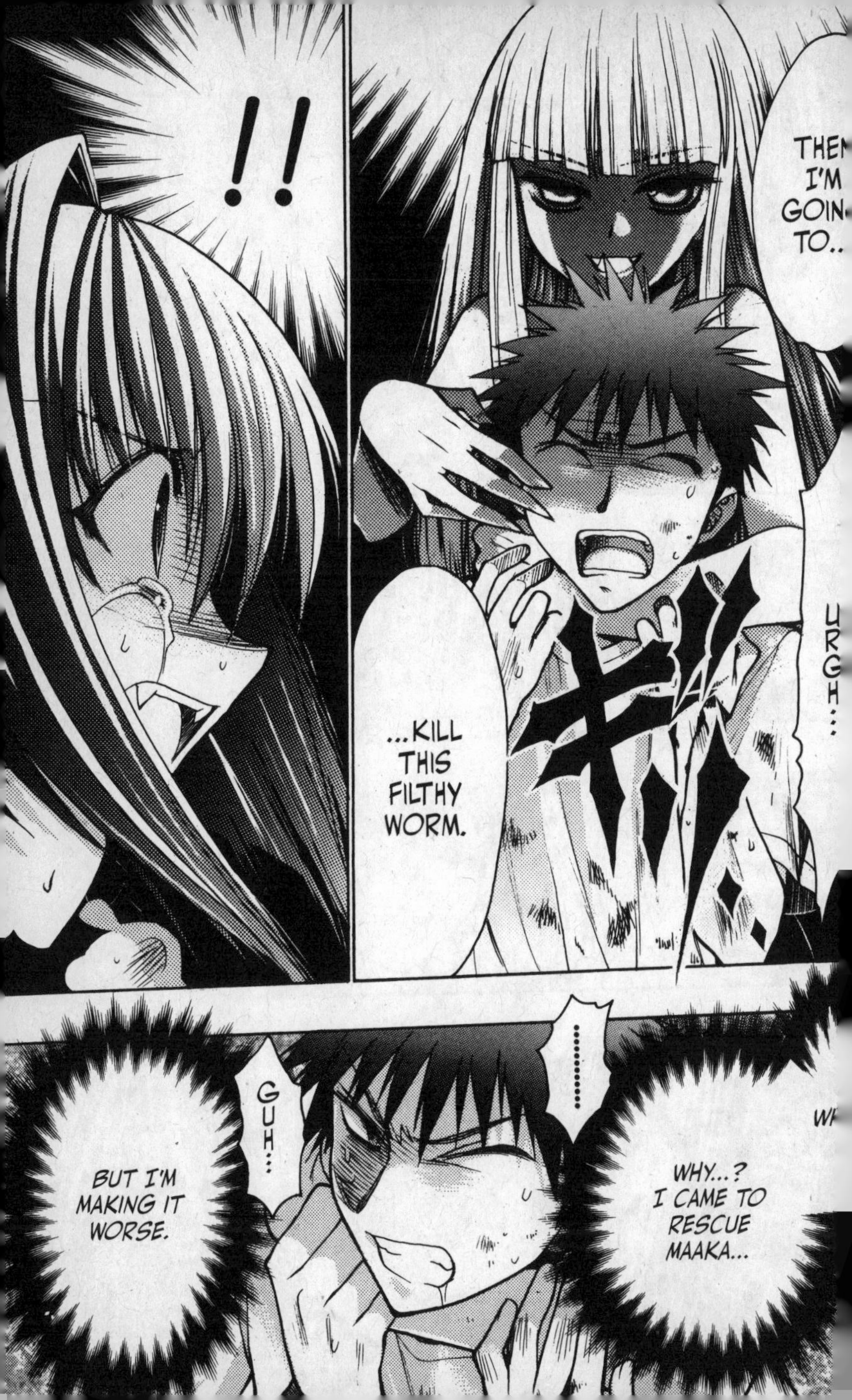
THEN I'M GOIN TO...
URGH...
...KILL THIS FILTHY WORM.
!!
WH
WHY...? I CAME TO RESCUE MAAKA...
......
GUH...
BUT I'M MAKING IT WORSE.

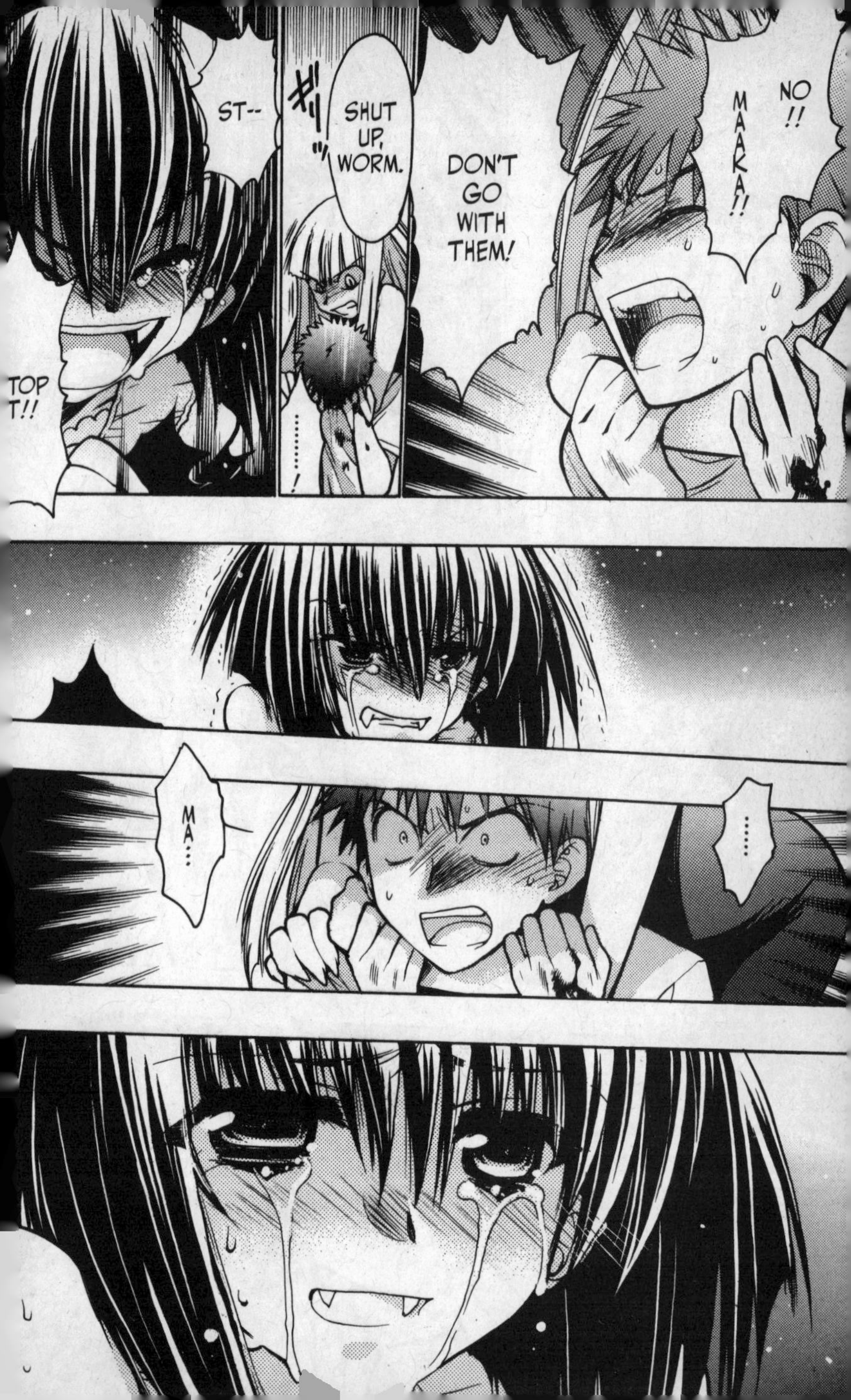
NO!!
MAAKA!!
DON'T GO WITH THEM!
SHUT UP, WORM.
......!
ST--
TOP T!!
......
MA...

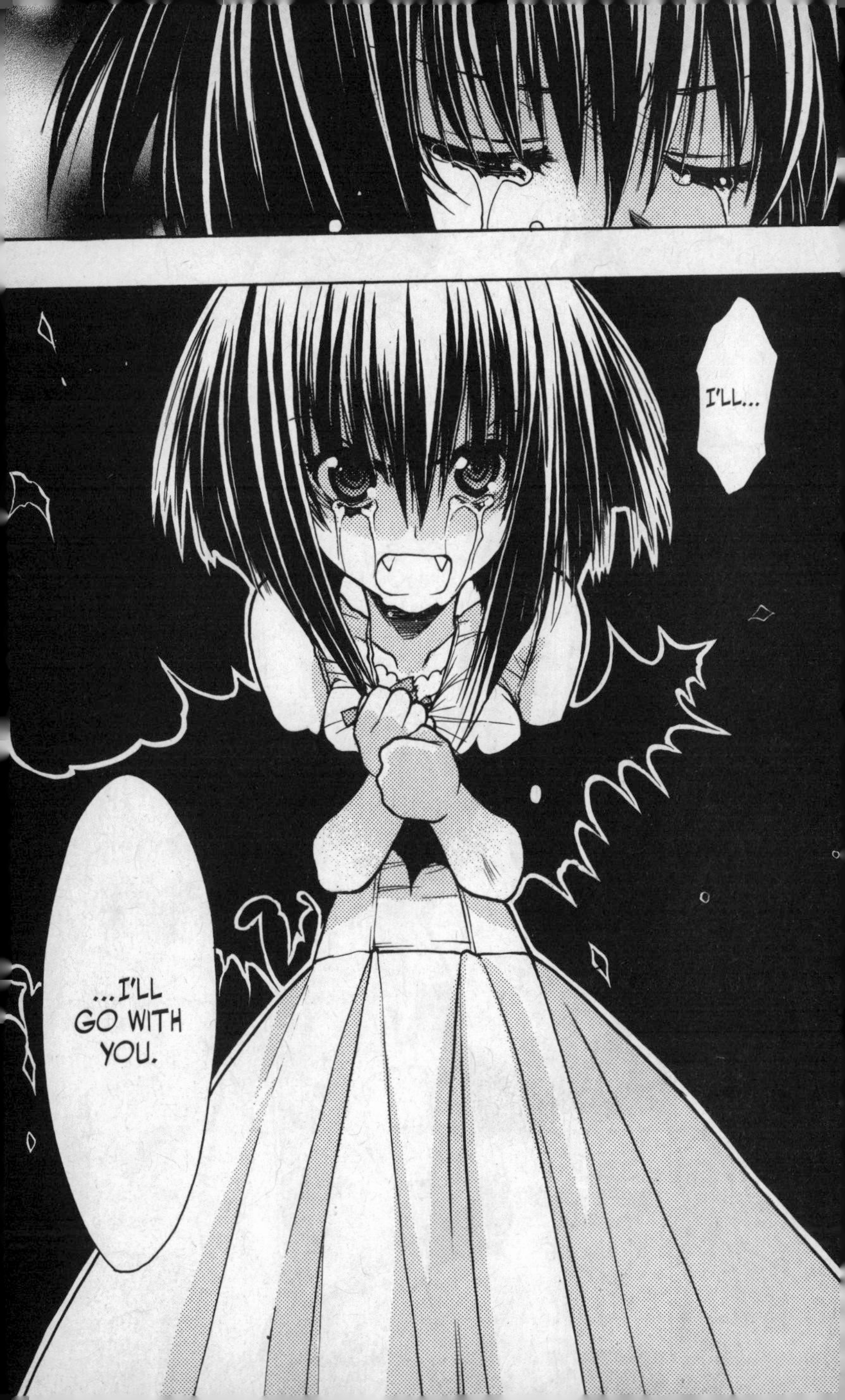
I'LL...
...I'LL GO WITH YOU.

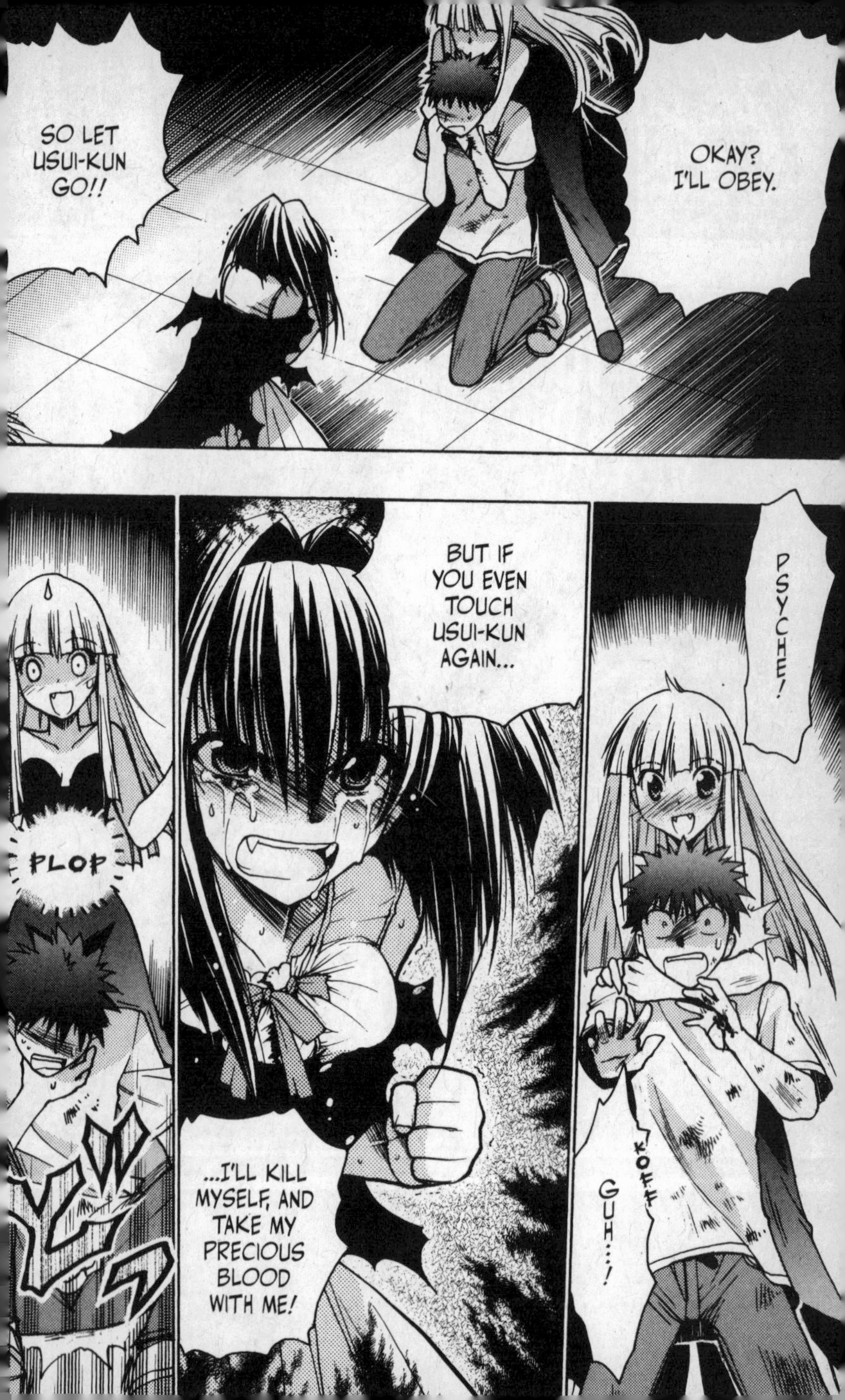

OKAY? I'LL OBEY.
SO LET USUI-KUN GO!!
PSYCHE!
KOFF
GUH...!
BUT IF YOU EVEN TOUCH USUI-KUN AGAIN...
...I'LL KILL MYSELF, AND TAKE MY PRECIOUS BLOOD WITH ME!
PLOP

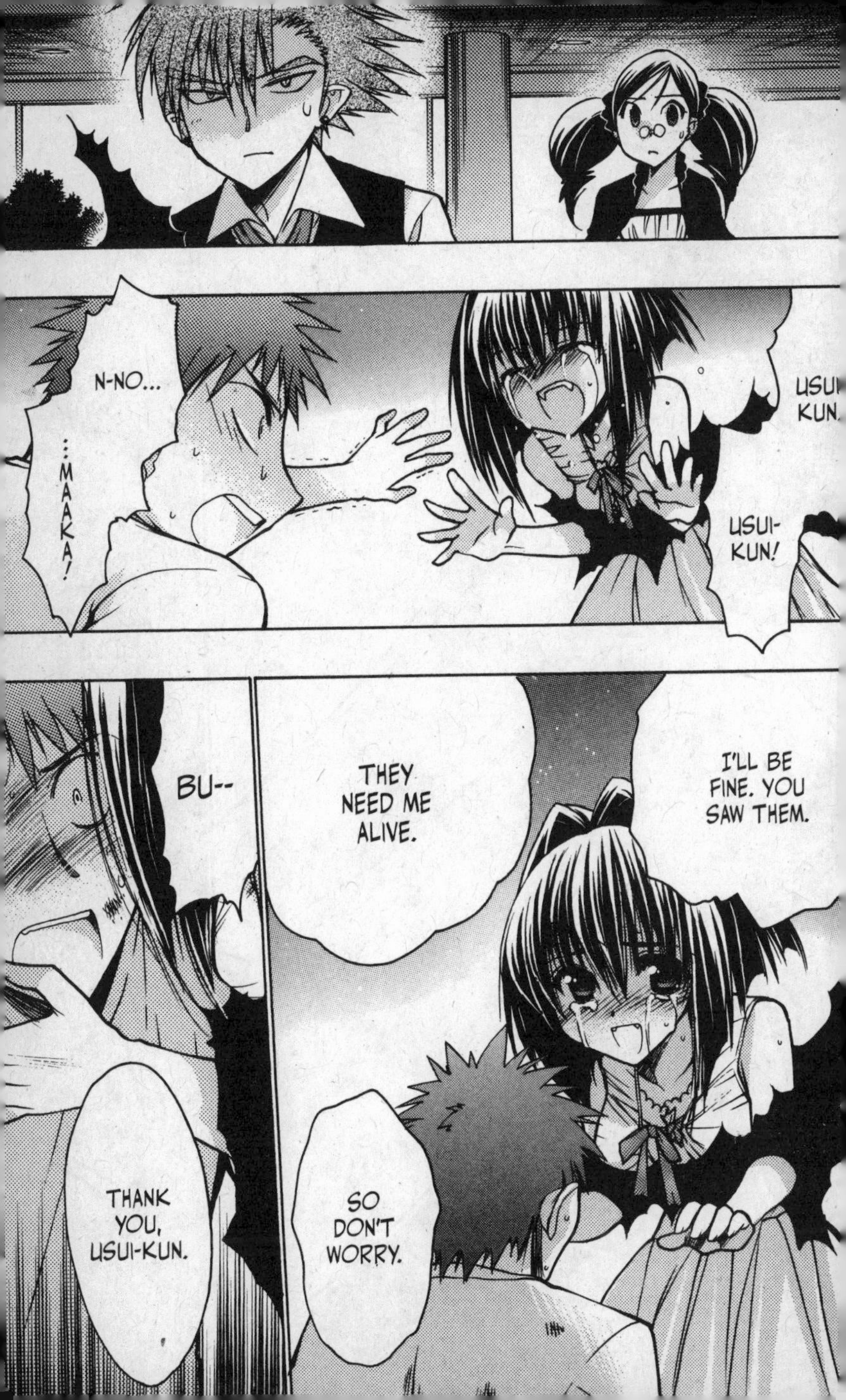
USUI KUN.
USUI-KUN!
N-NO...
...MAAKA!
I'LL BE FINE. YOU SAW THEM.
THEY NEED ME ALIVE.
SO DON'T WORRY.
BU--
THANK YOU, USUI-KUN.

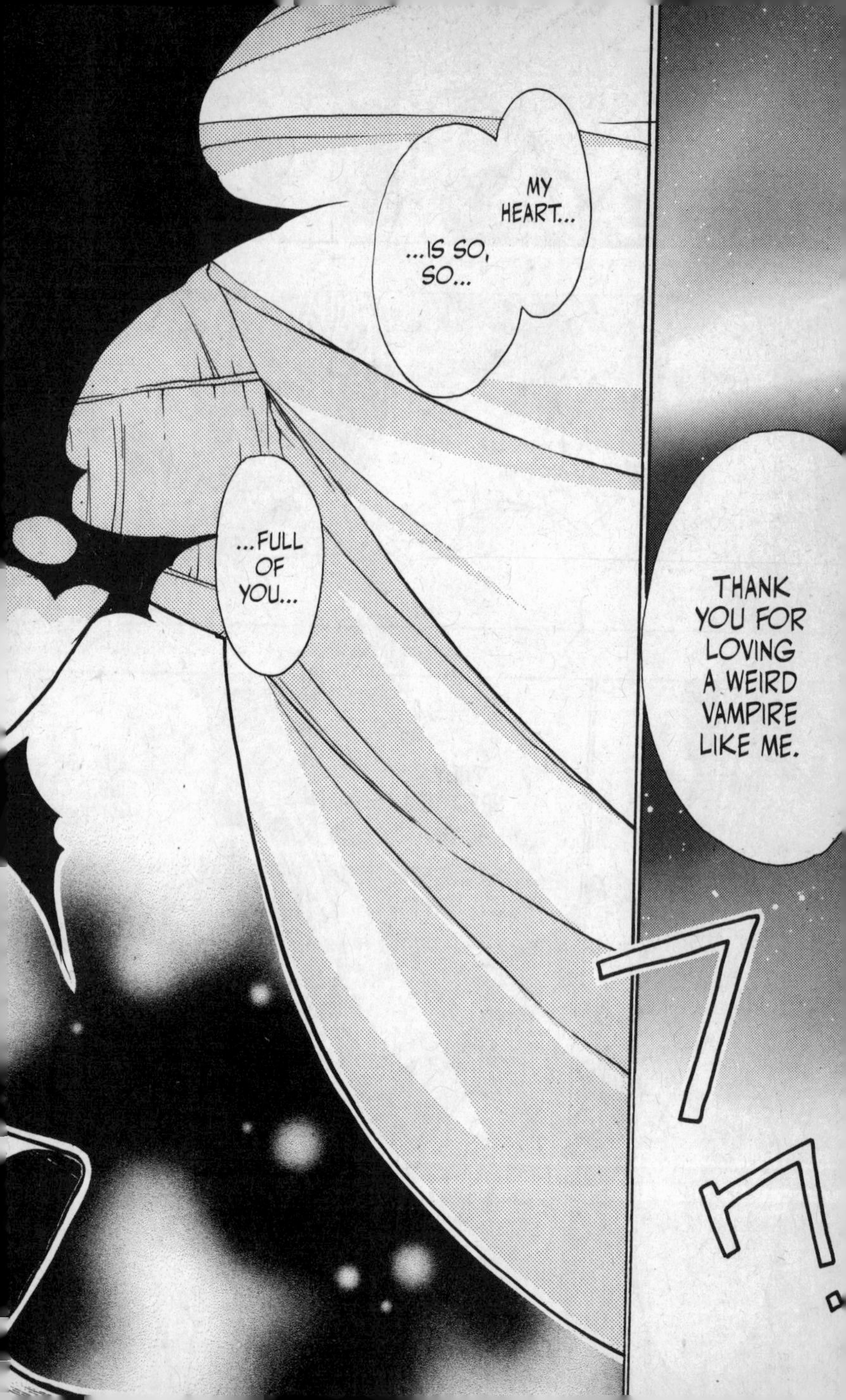
THANK YOU FOR LOVING A WEIRD VAMPIRE LIKE ME.
MY HEART...
...IS SO, SO...
...FULL OF YOU...

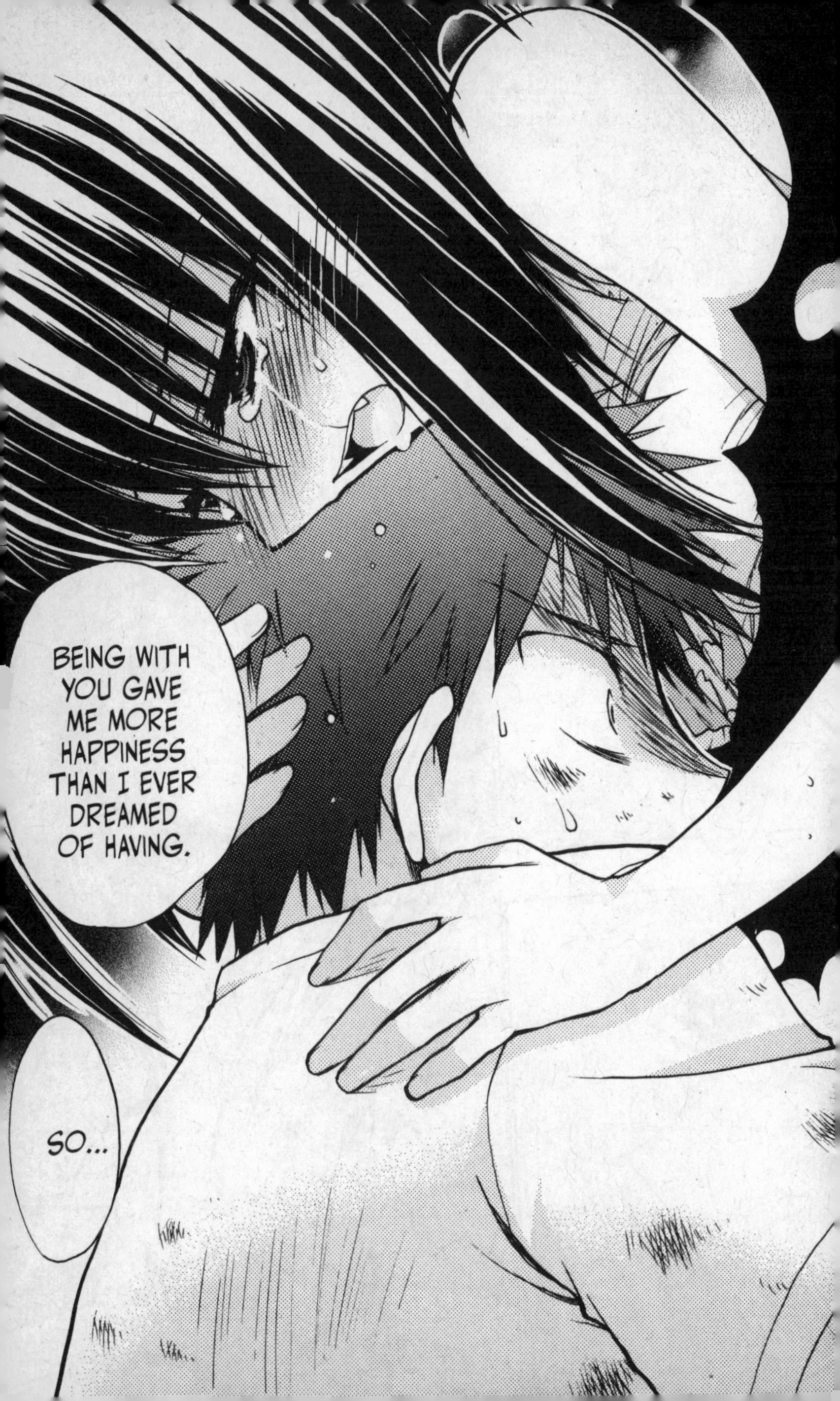
BEING WITH YOU GAVE ME MORE HAPPINESS THAN I EVER DREAMED OF HAVING.
SO...

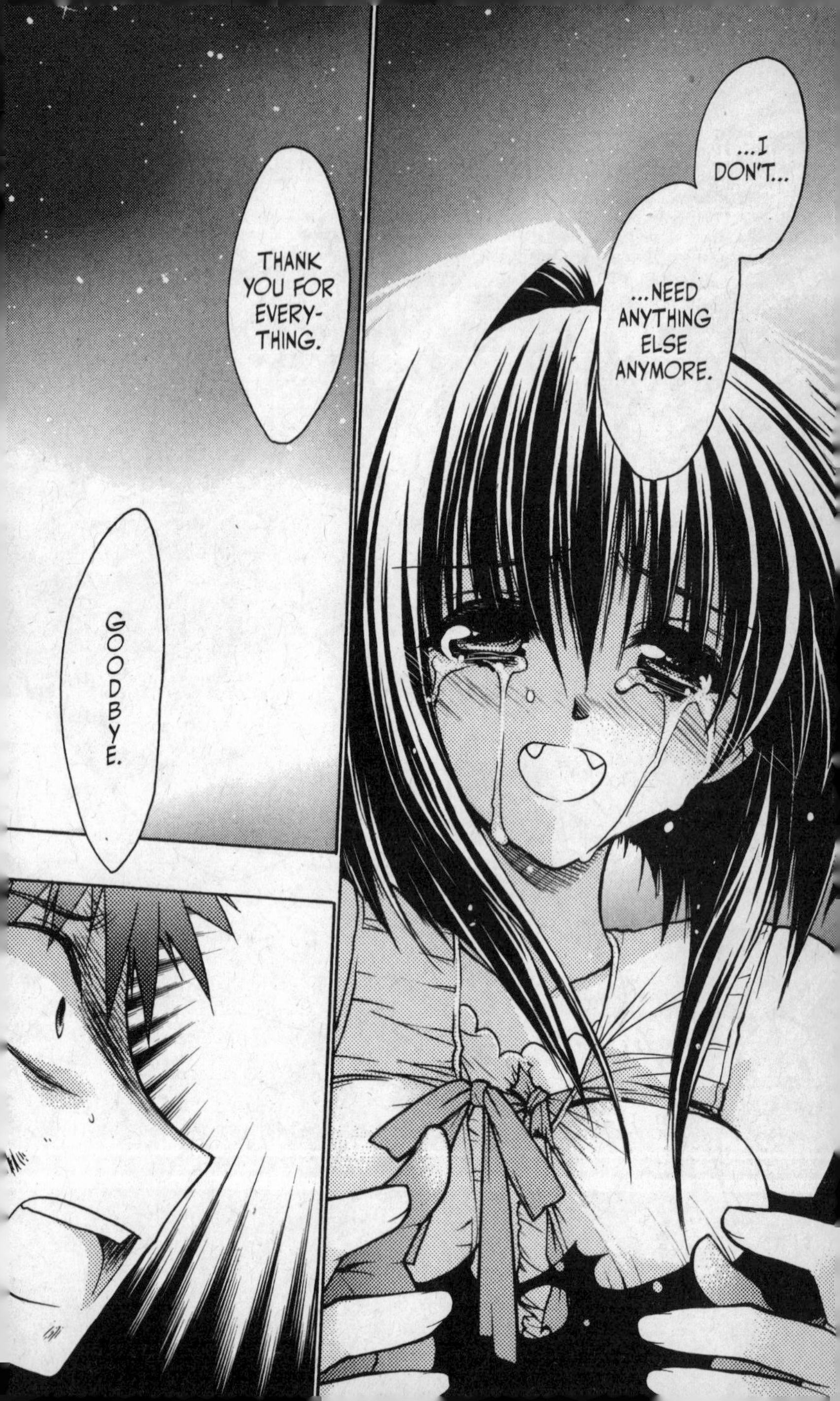
...I DON'T...
...NEED ANYTHING ELSE ANYMORE.
THANK YOU FOR EVERY-THING.
GOODBYE.

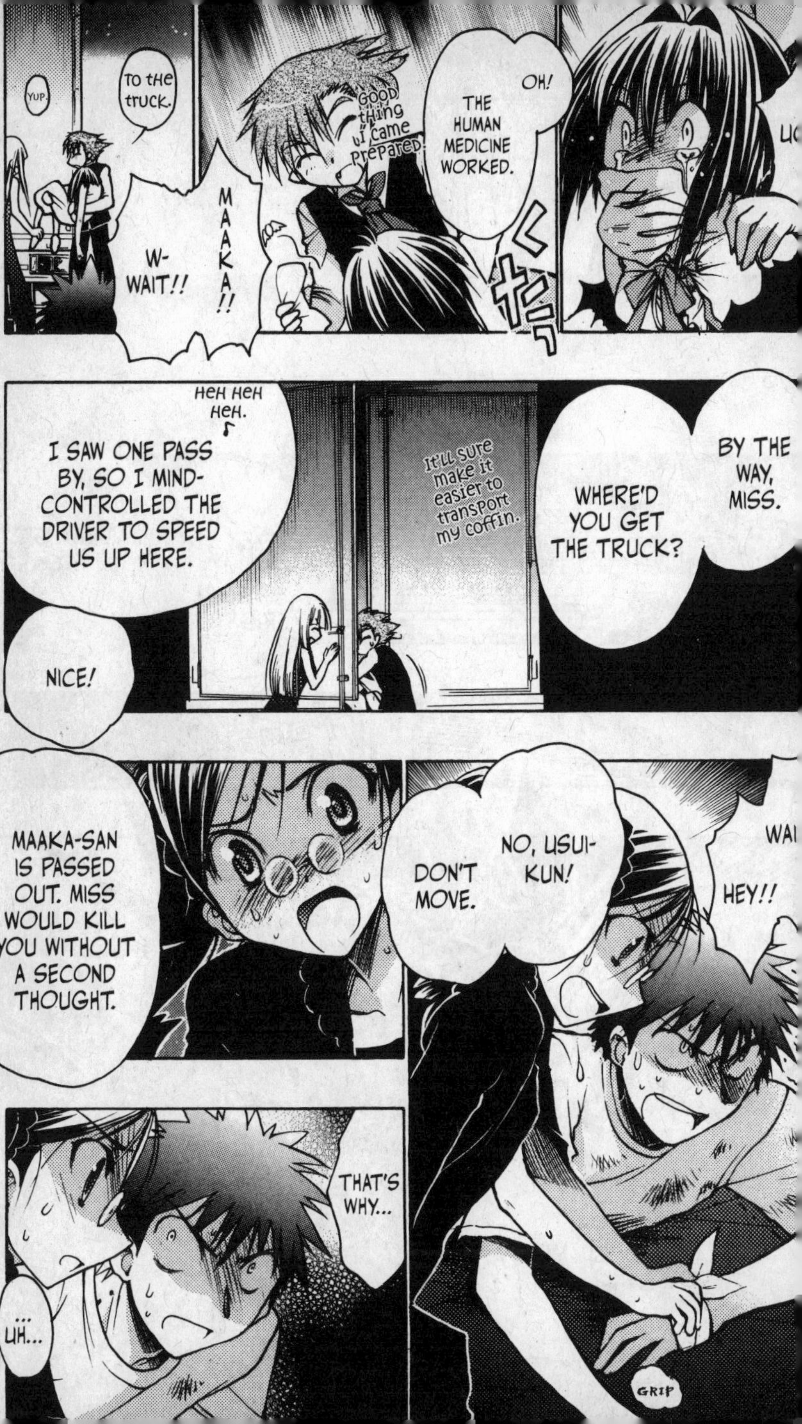
UG
OH!
THE HUMAN MEDICINE WORKED.
Good thing I came prepared!
MAAKA!!
W-WAIT!!
To the truck.
YUP.
BY THE WAY, MISS.
WHERE'D YOU GET THE TRUCK?
It'll sure make it easier to transport my coffin.
HEH HEH HEH.
I SAW ONE PASS BY, SO I MIND-CONTROLLED THE DRIVER TO SPEED US UP HERE.
NICE!
WAI
HEY!!
NO, USUI-KUN!
DON'T MOVE.
GRIP
MAAKA-SAN IS PASSED OUT. MISS WOULD KILL YOU WITHOUT A SECOND THOUGHT.
THAT'S WHY...
... UH...

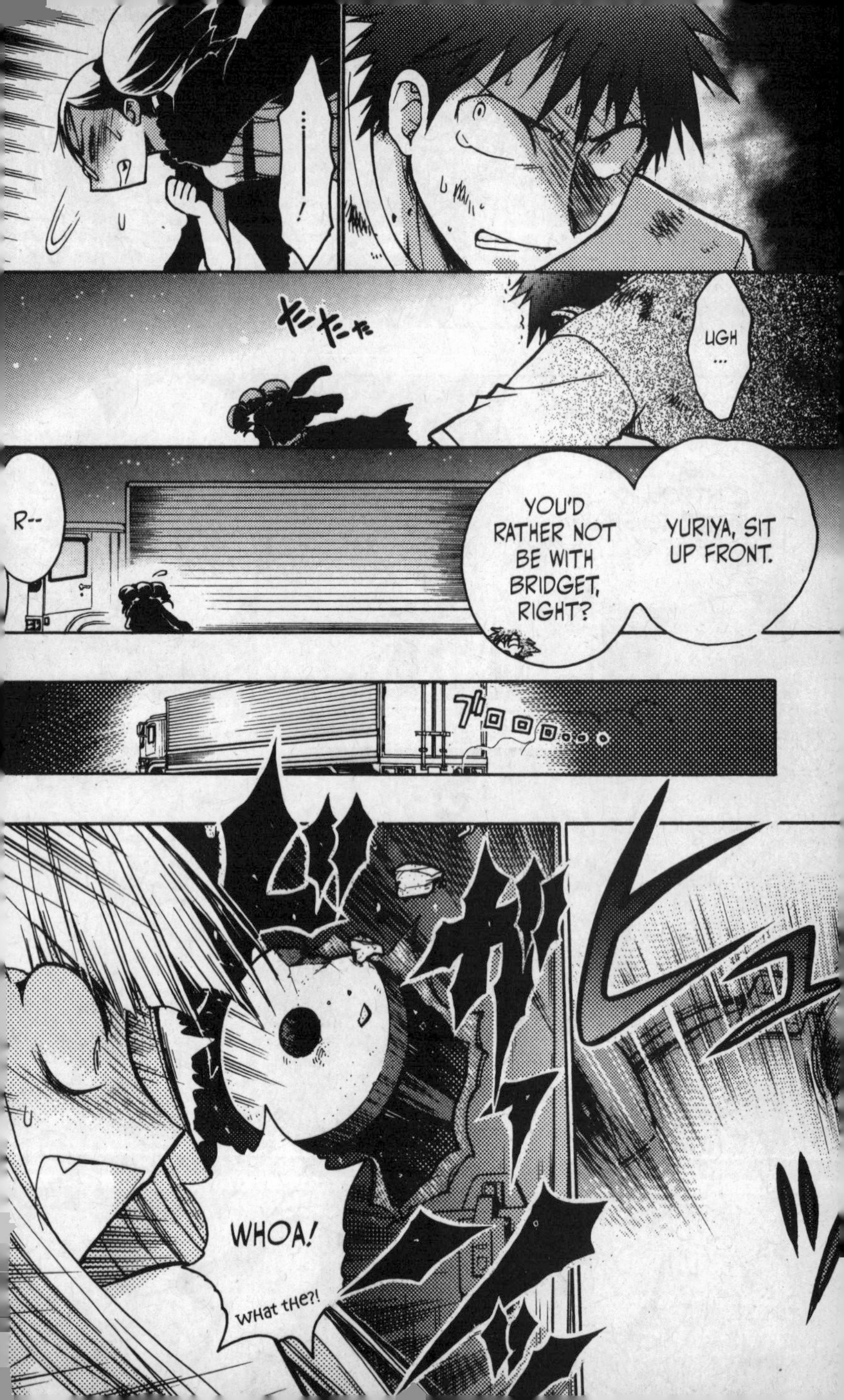
......!
UGH ...
YURIYA, SIT UP FRONT.
YOU'D RATHER NOT BE WITH BRIDGET, RIGHT?
R--
ブロロロ...
WHOA!
WHAT THE?!

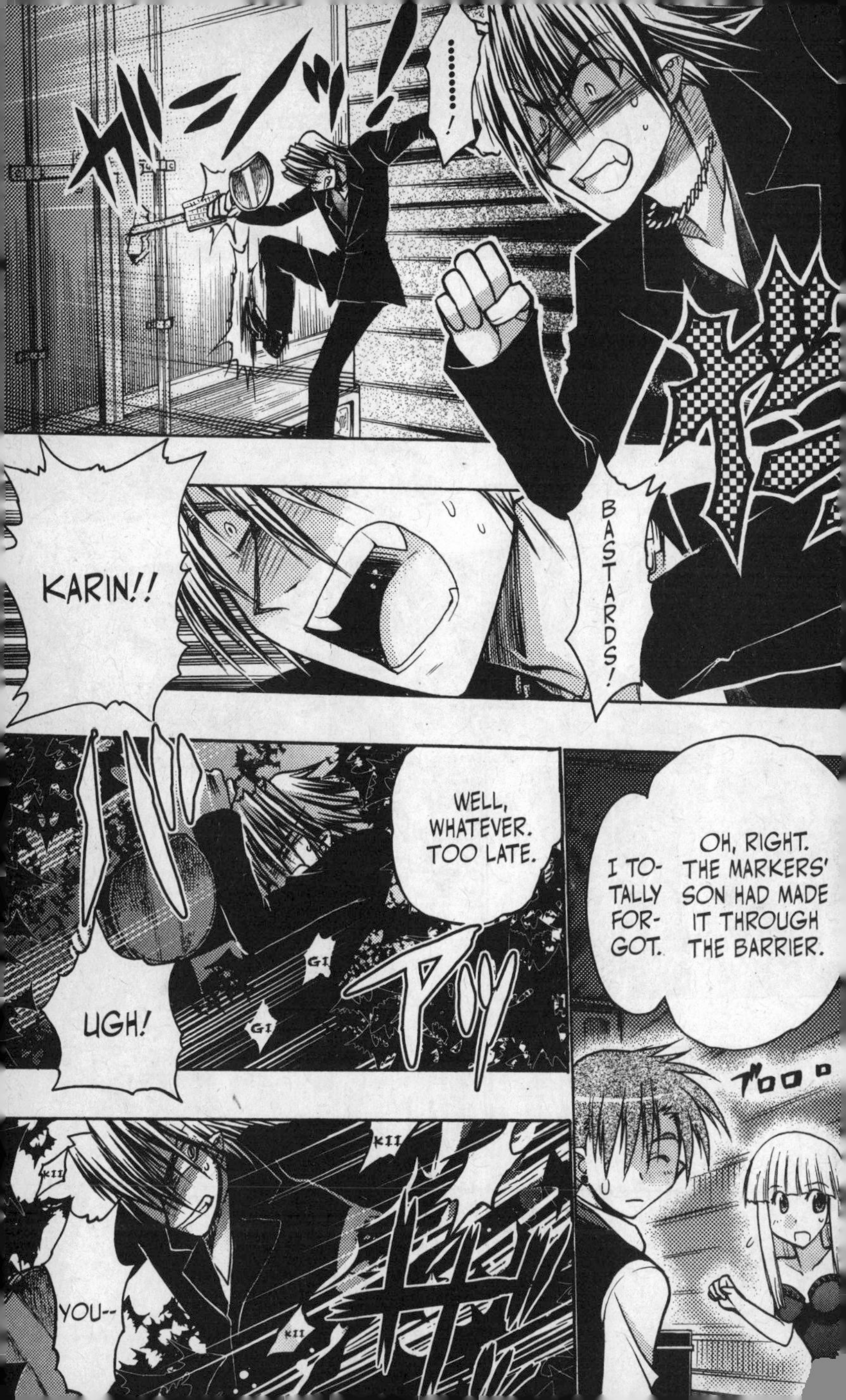

......!
BASTARDS!
KARIN!!
OH, RIGHT. THE MARKERS' SON HAD MADE IT THROUGH THE BARRIER.
I TOTALLY FORGOT.
WELL, WHATEVER. TOO LATE.
GI
GI
UGH!
KII
KII
YOU--
KII

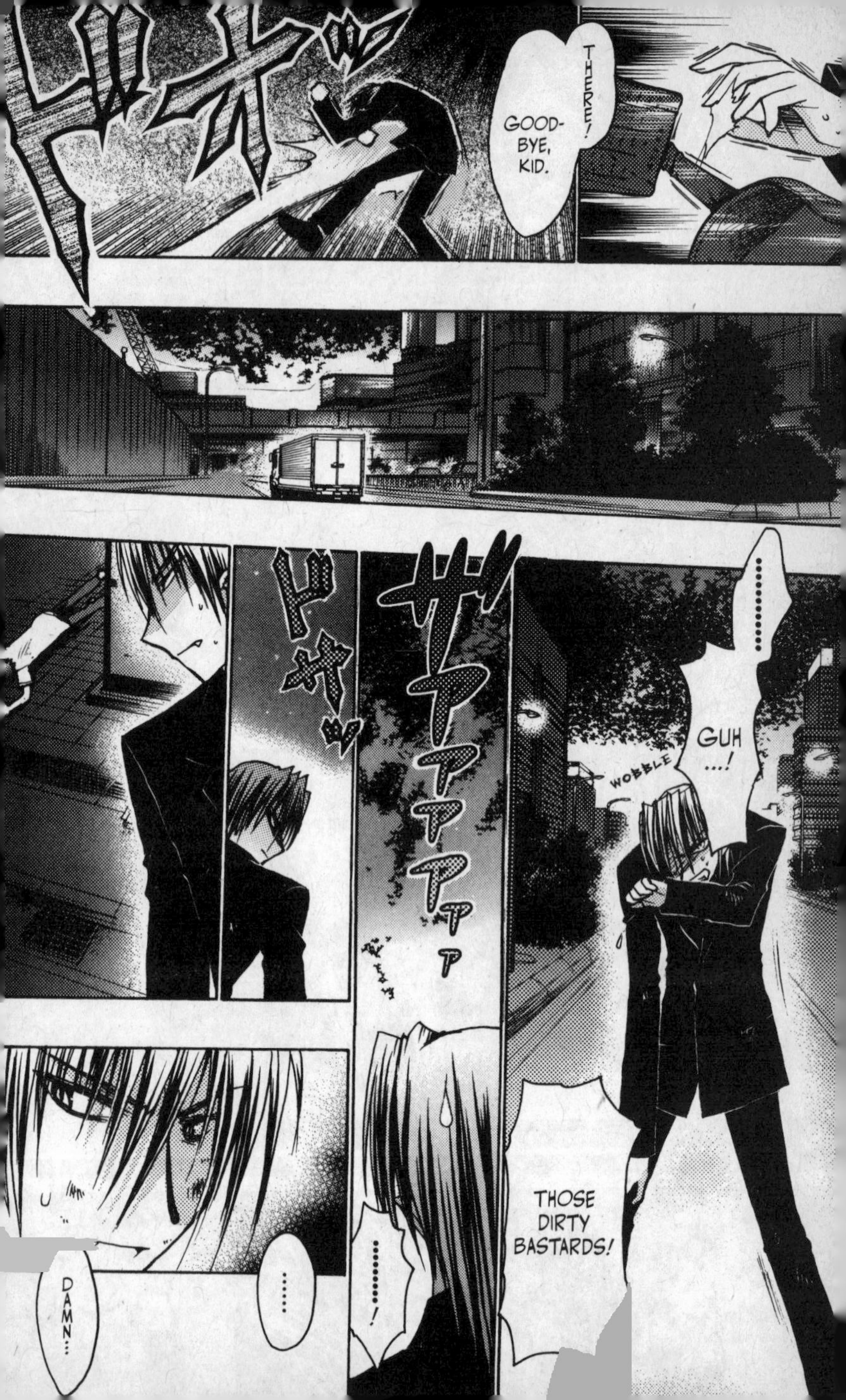
THERE!
GOOD-BYE, KID.
......
WOBBLE
GUH ...!
THOSE DIRTY BASTARDS!
......!
......
DAMN...

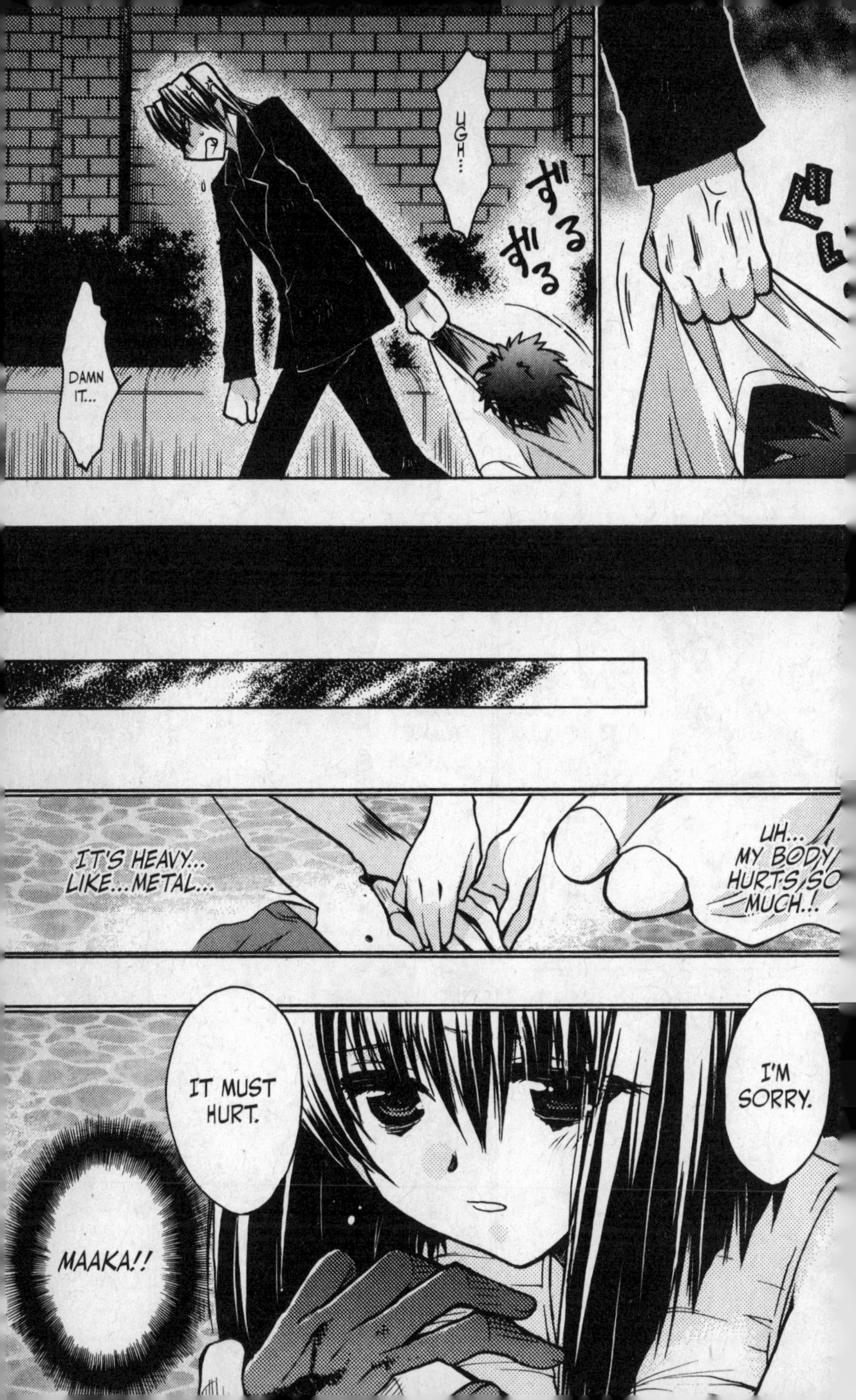
ずるずる
UGH...
DAMN IT...
UH... MY BODY HURTS SO MUCH..!
IT'S HEAVY... LIKE...METAL...
I'M SORRY.
IT MUST HURT.
MAAKA!!

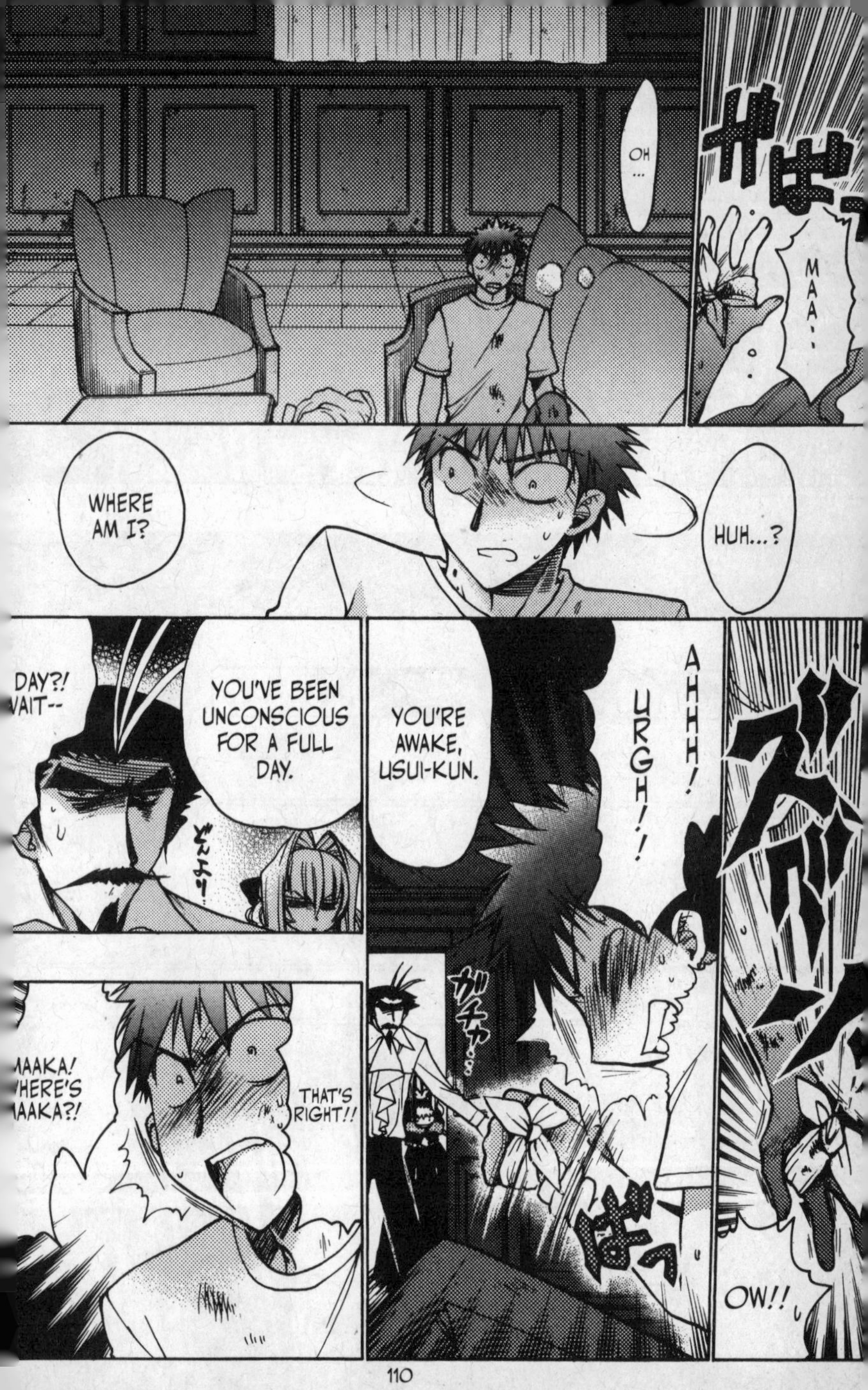
がばっ
MAA-
OH...
HUH...?
WHERE AM I?
OW!!
ぱっ
AHHH! URGH!!
ガチャ
YOU'RE AWAKE, USUI-KUN.
YOU'VE BEEN UNCONSCIOUS FOR A FULL DAY.
どんより
DAY?! WAIT--
THAT'S RIGHT!!
MAAKA! WHERE'S MAAKA?!

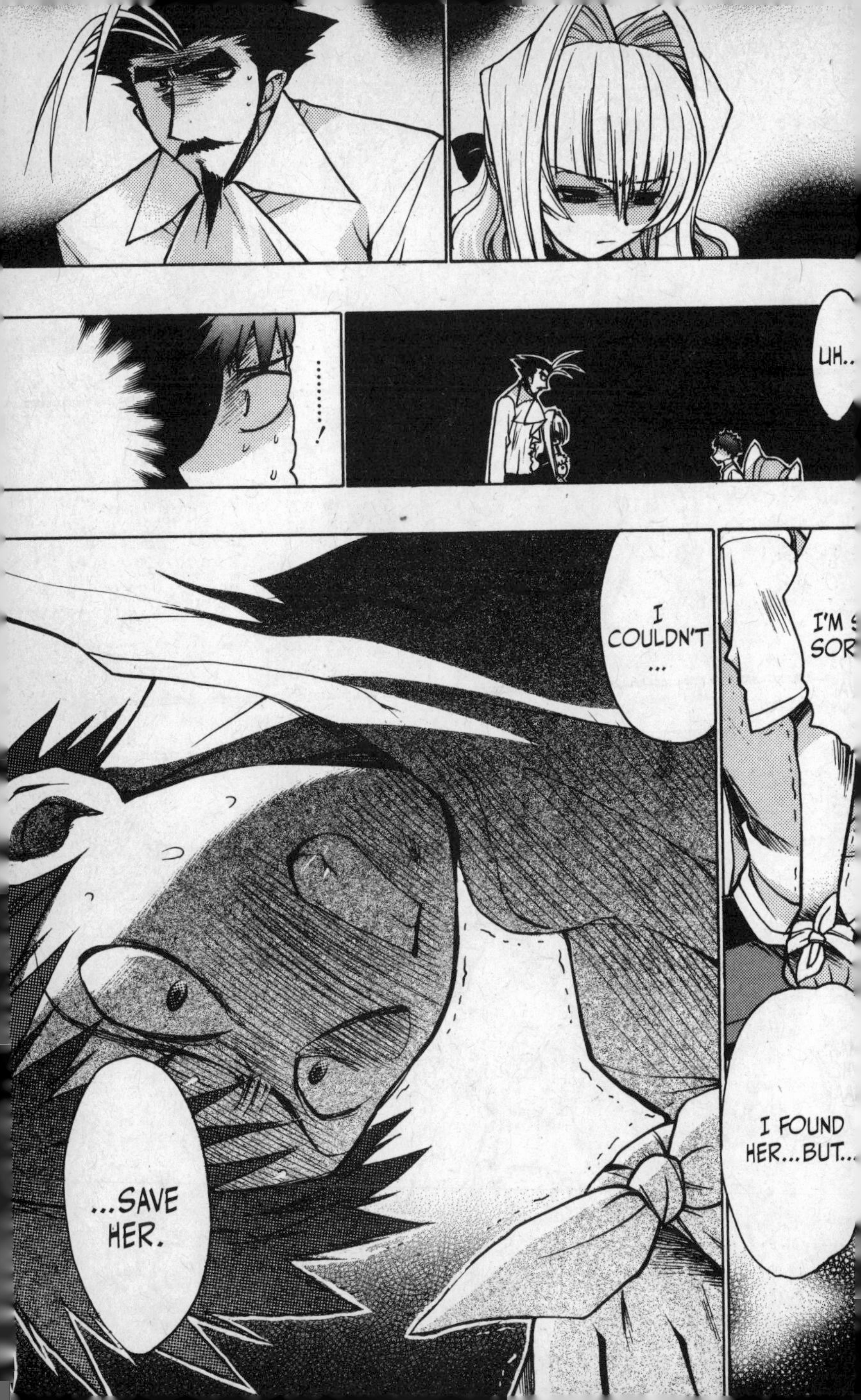
UH..
......!
I'M S
SOR
I FOUND HER...BUT...
I COULDN'T ...
...SAVE HER.

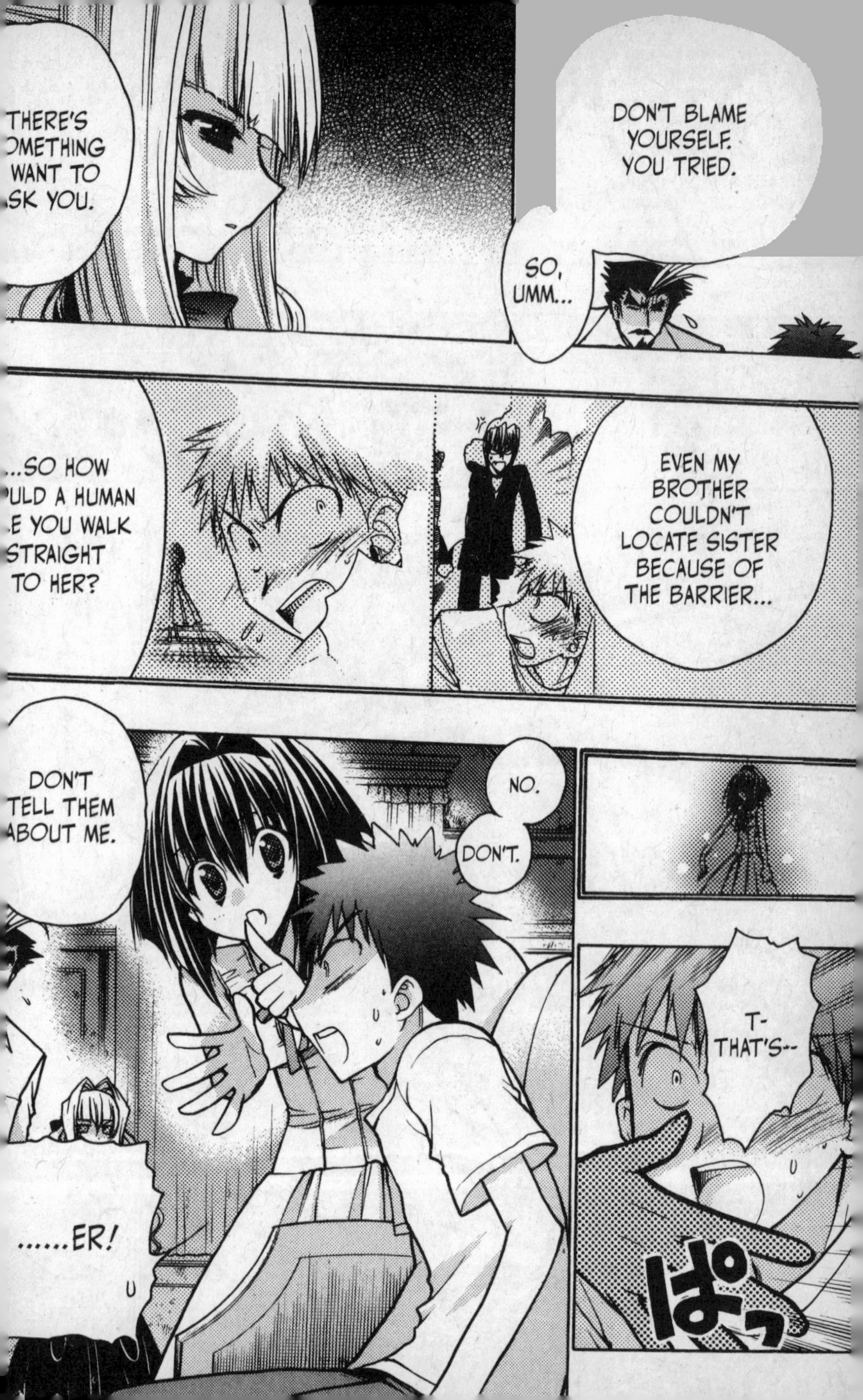
DON'T BLAME YOURSELF. YOU TRIED.
SO, UMM...
THERE'S OMETHING WANT TO SK YOU.
EVEN MY BROTHER COULDN'T LOCATE SISTER BECAUSE OF THE BARRIER...
...SO HOW ULD A HUMAN E YOU WALK STRAIGHT TO HER?
T- THAT'S--
ぱっ
NO.
DON'T.
DON'T TELL THEM ABOUT ME.
......ER!

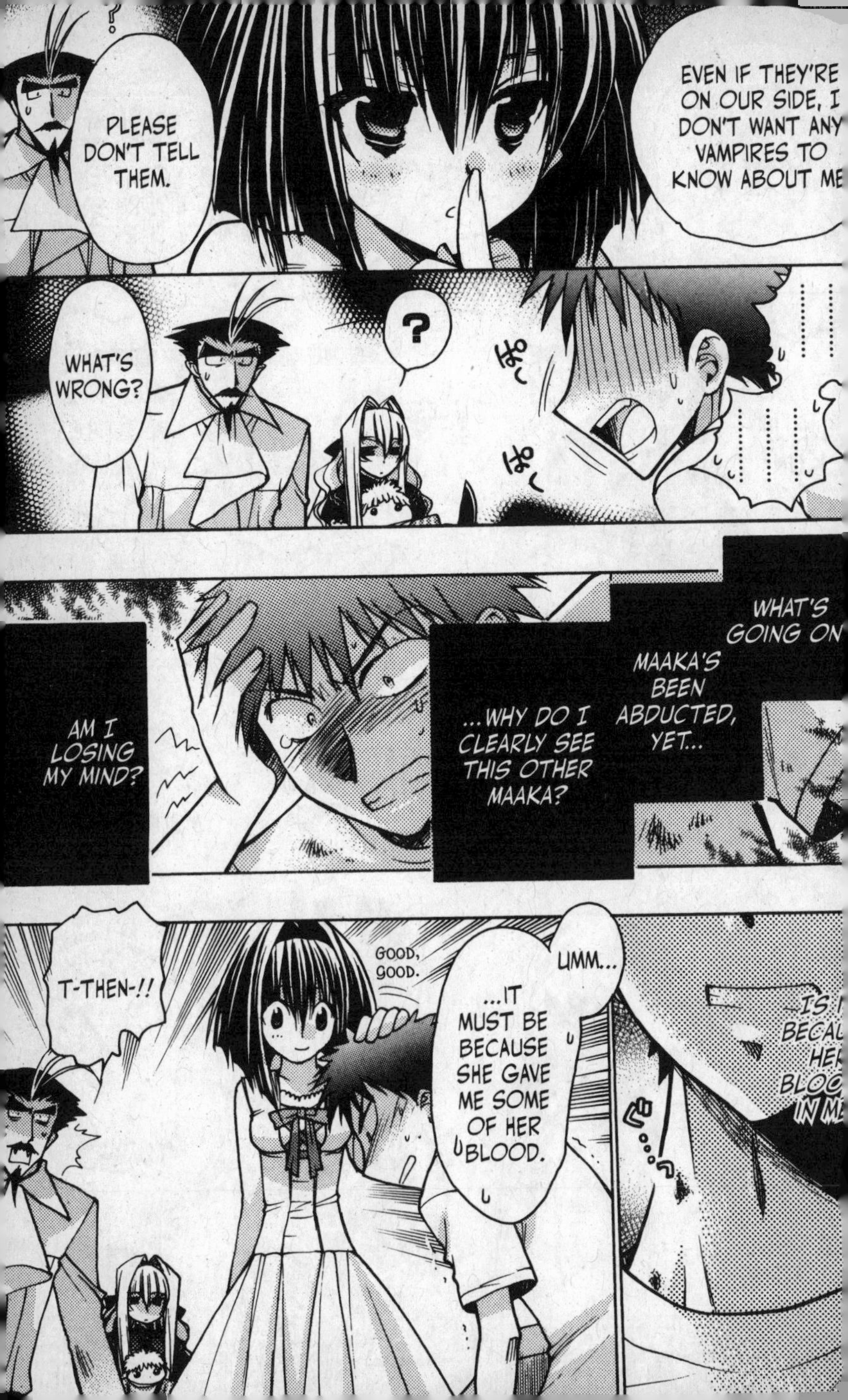

EVEN IF THEY'RE ON OUR SIDE, I DON'T WANT ANY VAMPIRES TO KNOW ABOUT ME
PLEASE DON'T TELL THEM.
?
ぱく ぱく
?
WHAT'S WRONG?
WHAT'S GOING ON
MAAKA'S BEEN ABDUCTED, YET...
...WHY DO I CLEARLY SEE THIS OTHER MAAKA?
AM I LOSING MY MIND?
UMM...
...IT MUST BE BECAUSE SHE GAVE ME SOME OF HER BLOOD.
GOOD, GOOD.
T-THEN-!!

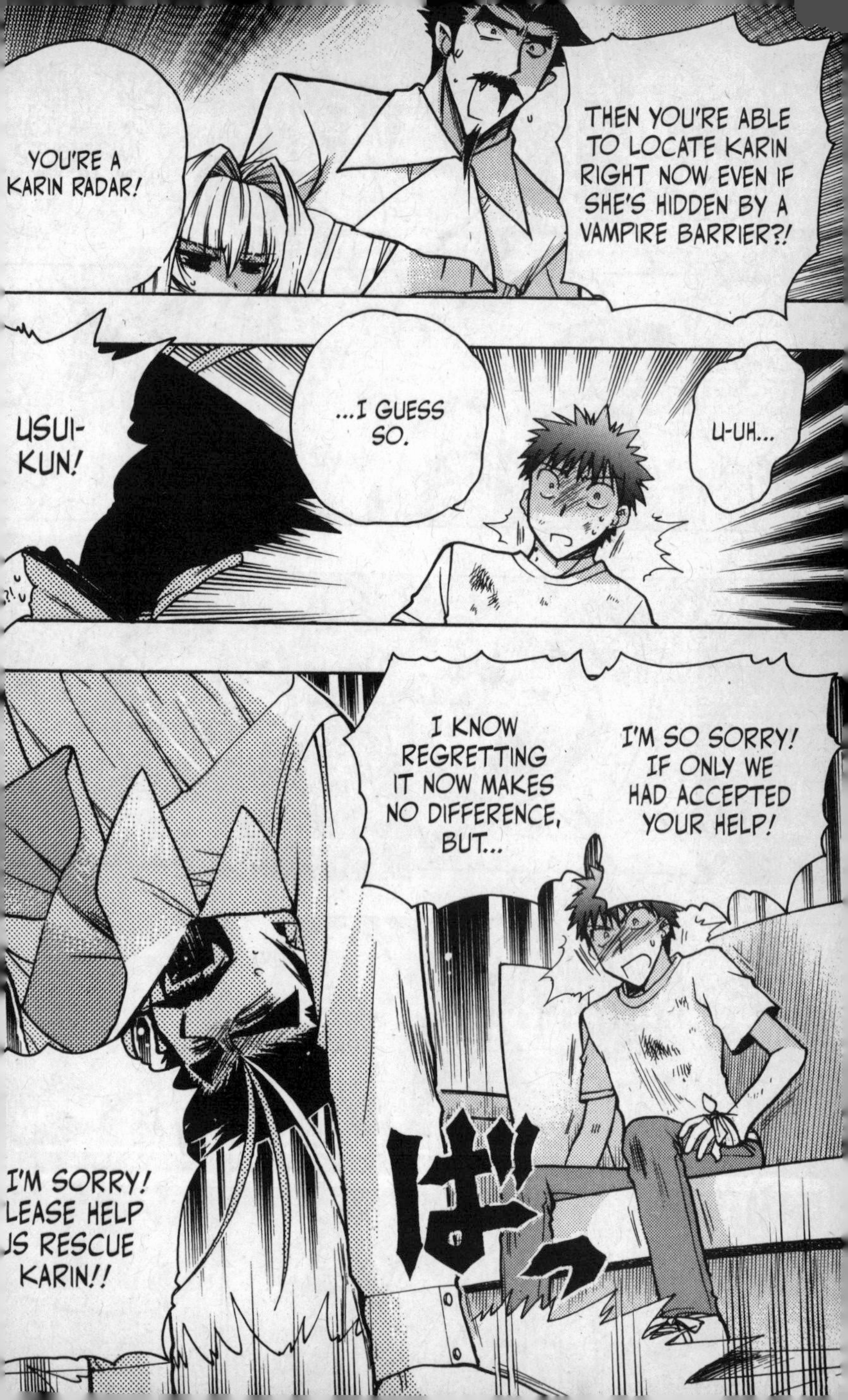
THEN YOU'RE ABLE TO LOCATE KARIN RIGHT NOW EVEN IF SHE'S HIDDEN BY A VAMPIRE BARRIER?!
YOU'RE A KARIN RADAR!
U-UH...
...I GUESS SO.
USUI-KUN!
I'M SO SORRY! IF ONLY WE HAD ACCEPTED YOUR HELP!
I KNOW REGRETTING IT NOW MAKES NO DIFFERENCE, BUT...
ばっ
I'M SORRY! LEASE HELP JS RESCUE KARIN!!

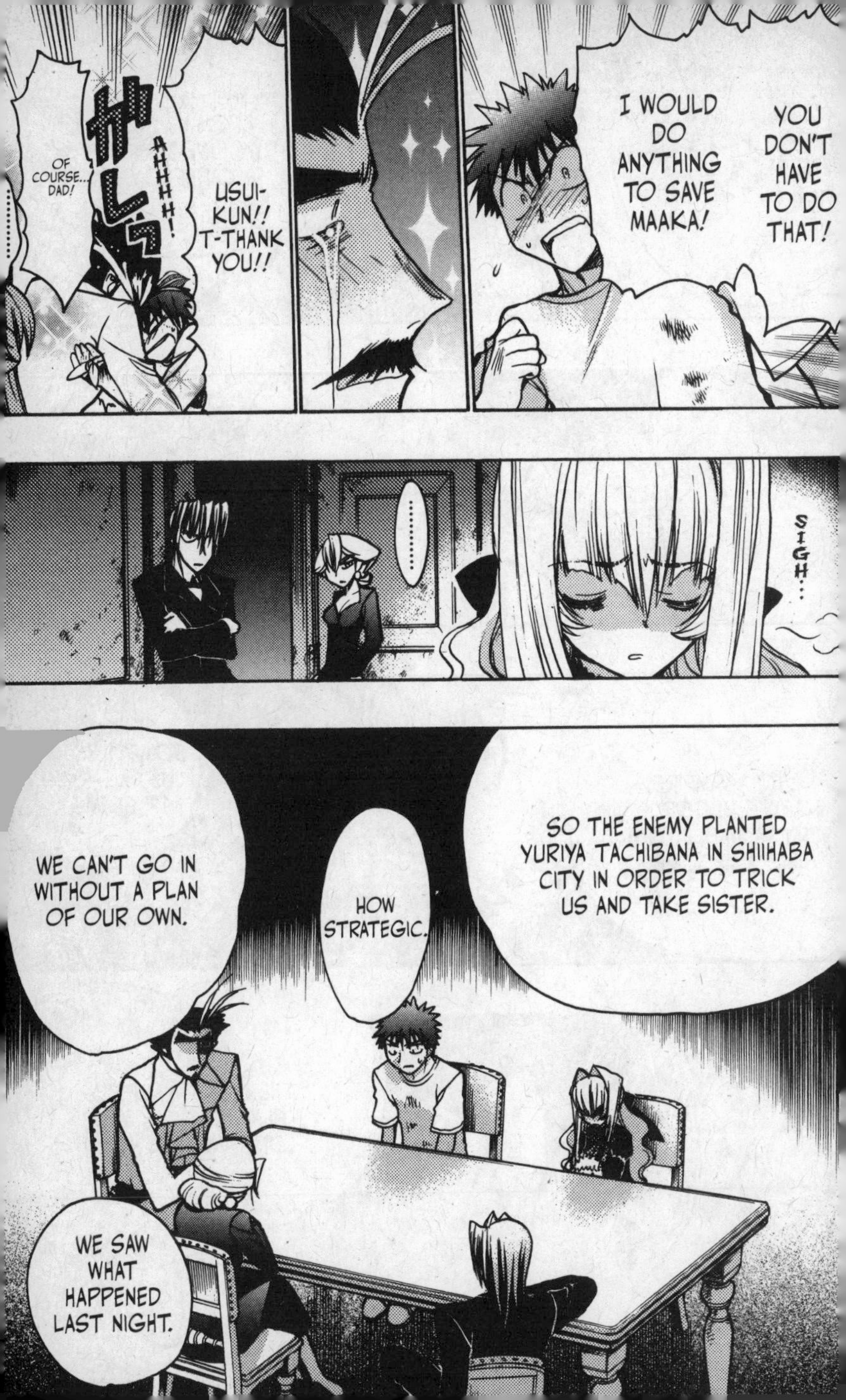
YOU DON'T HAVE TO DO THAT!
I WOULD DO ANYTHING TO SAVE MAAKA!
USUI-KUN!! T-THANK YOU!!
AHHHH!
OF COURSE... DAD!
SIGH...
....
SO THE ENEMY PLANTED YURIYA TACHIBANA IN SHIIHABA CITY IN ORDER TO TRICK US AND TAKE SISTER.
HOW STRATEGIC.
WE CAN'T GO IN WITHOUT A PLAN OF OUR OWN.
WE SAW WHAT HAPPENED LAST NIGHT.

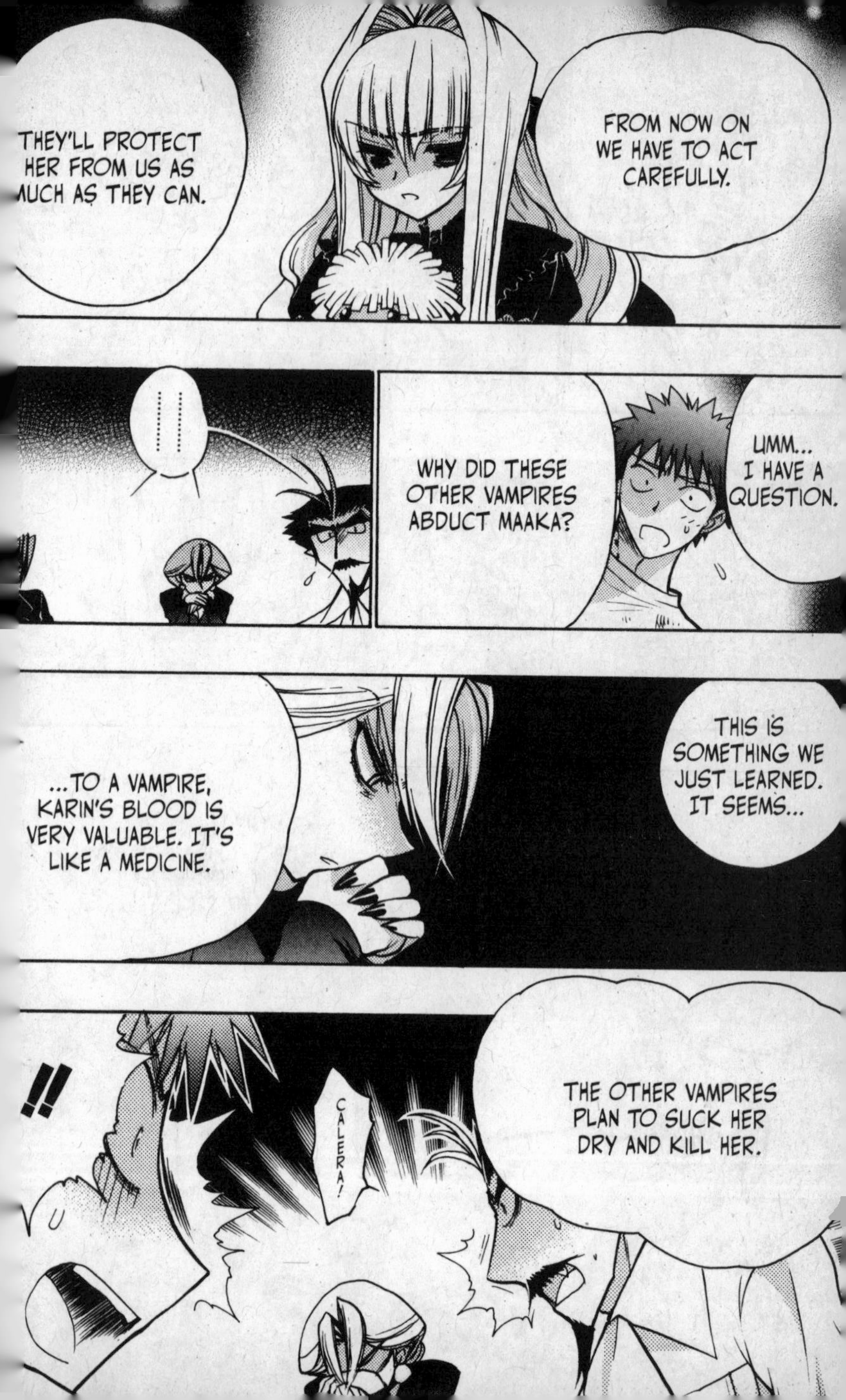
FROM NOW ON WE HAVE TO ACT CAREFULLY.
THEY'LL PROTECT HER FROM US AS MUCH AS THEY CAN.
UMM... I HAVE A QUESTION.
WHY DID THESE OTHER VAMPIRES ABDUCT MAAKA?
......
THIS IS SOMETHING WE JUST LEARNED. IT SEEMS...
...TO A VAMPIRE, KARIN'S BLOOD IS VERY VALUABLE. IT'S LIKE A MEDICINE.
THE OTHER VAMPIRES PLAN TO SUCK HER DRY AND KILL HER.
CALERA!
!!

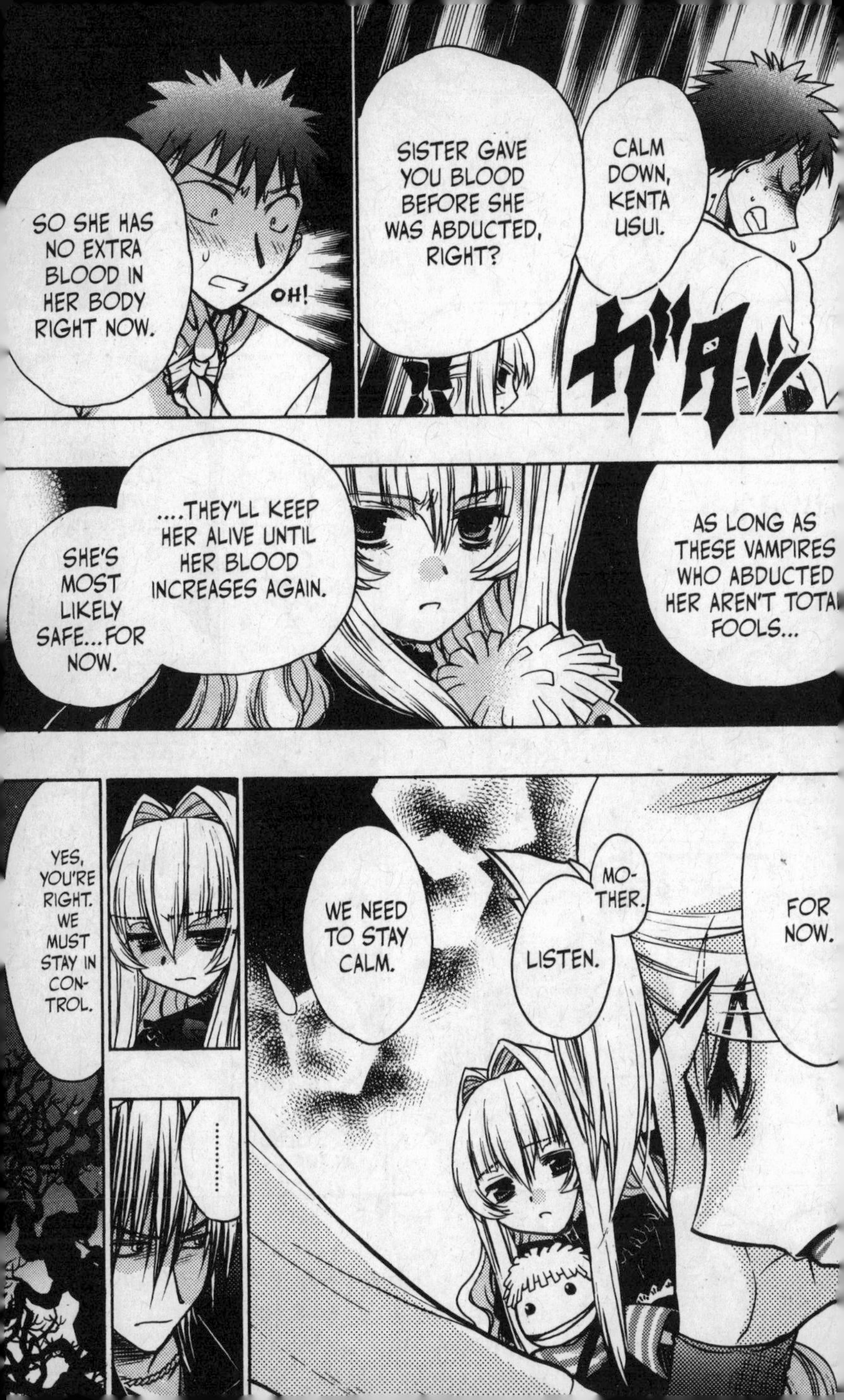
CALM DOWN, KENTA USUI.
SISTER GAVE YOU BLOOD BEFORE SHE WAS ABDUCTED, RIGHT?
ガタッ!!
OH!
SO SHE HAS NO EXTRA BLOOD IN HER BODY RIGHT NOW.
AS LONG AS THESE VAMPIRES WHO ABDUCTED HER AREN'T TOTA FOOLS...
....THEY'LL KEEP HER ALIVE UNTIL HER BLOOD INCREASES AGAIN.
SHE'S MOST LIKELY SAFE...FOR NOW.
FOR NOW.
MOTHER.
LISTEN.
WE NEED TO STAY CALM.
YES, YOU'RE RIGHT. WE MUST STAY IN CONTROL.
....

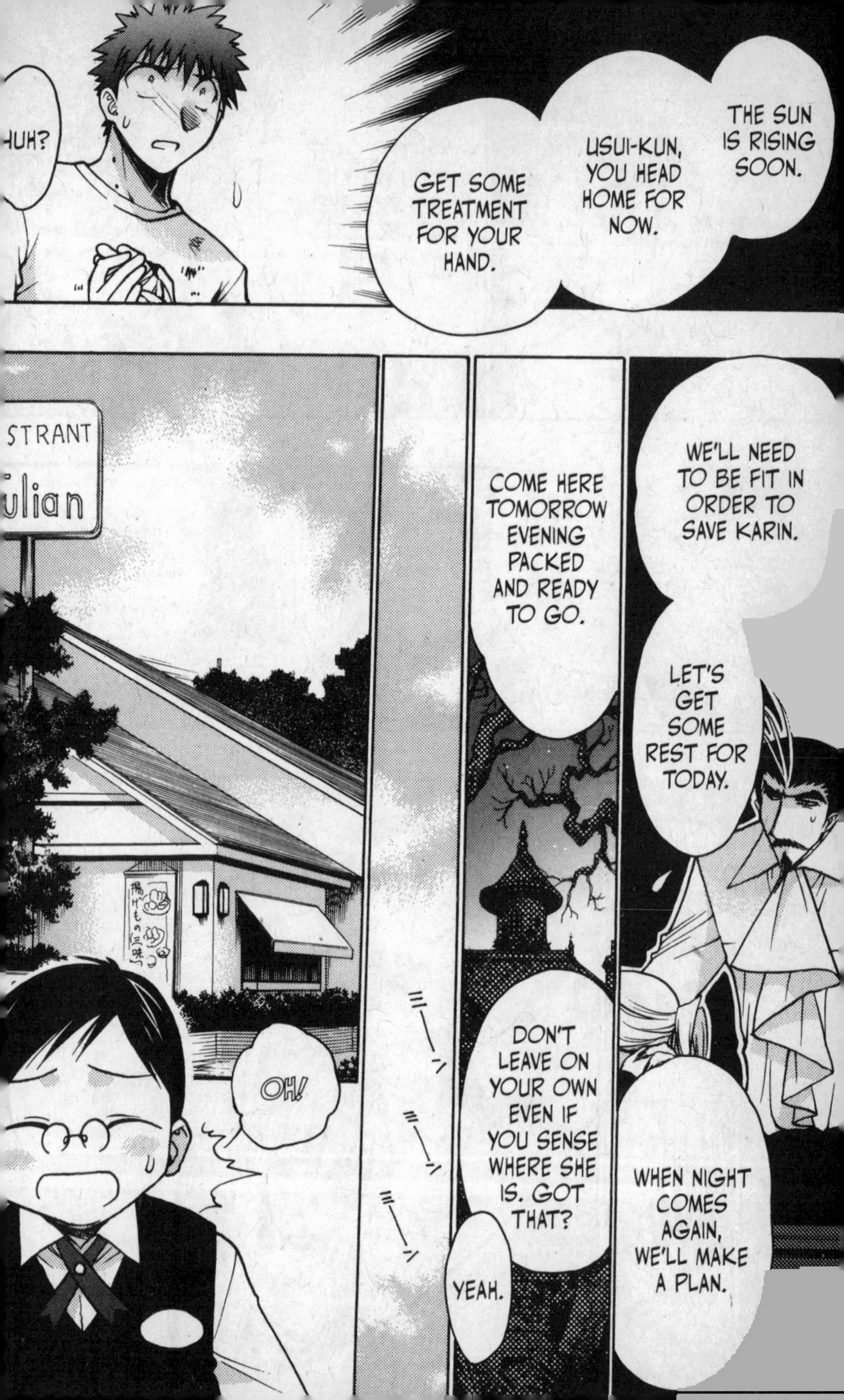

THE SUN IS RISING SOON.
USUI-KUN, YOU HEAD HOME FOR NOW.
GET SOME TREATMENT FOR YOUR HAND.
HUH?
WE'LL NEED TO BE FIT IN ORDER TO SAVE KARIN.
LET'S GET SOME REST FOR TODAY.
WHEN NIGHT COMES AGAIN, WE'LL MAKE A PLAN.
COME HERE TOMORROW EVENING PACKED AND READY TO GO.
DON'T LEAVE ON YOUR OWN EVEN IF YOU SENSE WHERE SHE IS. GOT THAT?
YEAH.
STRANT
ulian
OH!

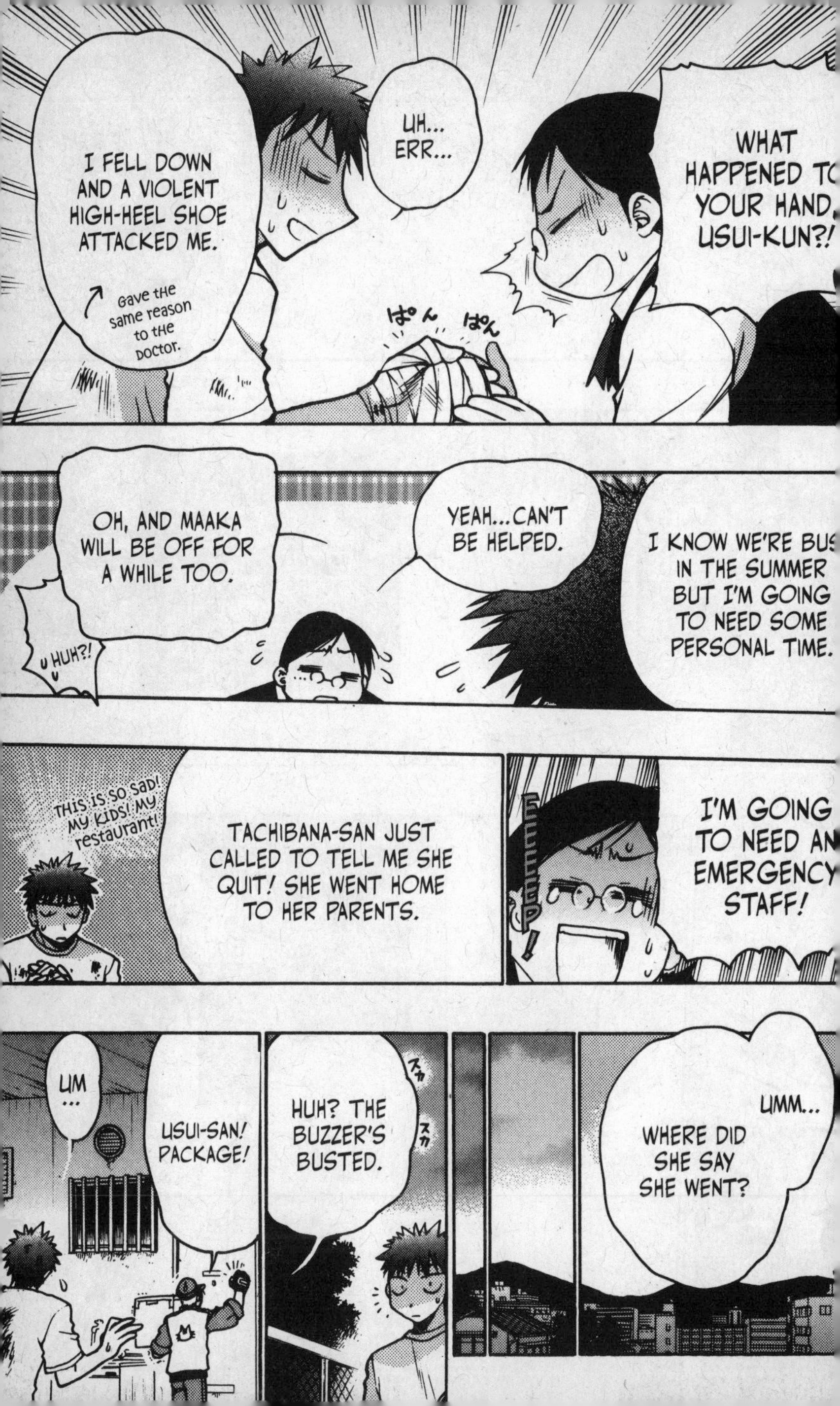

WHAT HAPPENED TO YOUR HAND, USUI-KUN?!
UH... ERR...
ぱん ぱん
I FELL DOWN AND A VIOLENT HIGH-HEEL SHOE ATTACKED ME.
Gave the same reason to the doctor.
I KNOW WE'RE BUSY IN THE SUMMER BUT I'M GOING TO NEED SOME PERSONAL TIME.
YEAH...CAN'T BE HELPED.
OH, AND MAAKA WILL BE OFF FOR A WHILE TOO.
HUH?!
I'M GOING TO NEED AN EMERGENCY STAFF!
TACHIBANA-SAN JUST CALLED TO TELL ME SHE QUIT! SHE WENT HOME TO HER PARENTS.
THIS IS SO SAD! MY KIDS! MY restaurant!
UMM...
WHERE DID SHE SAY SHE WENT?
スカ
スカ
HUH? THE BUZZER'S BUSTED.
USUI-SAN! PACKAGE!
UM ...

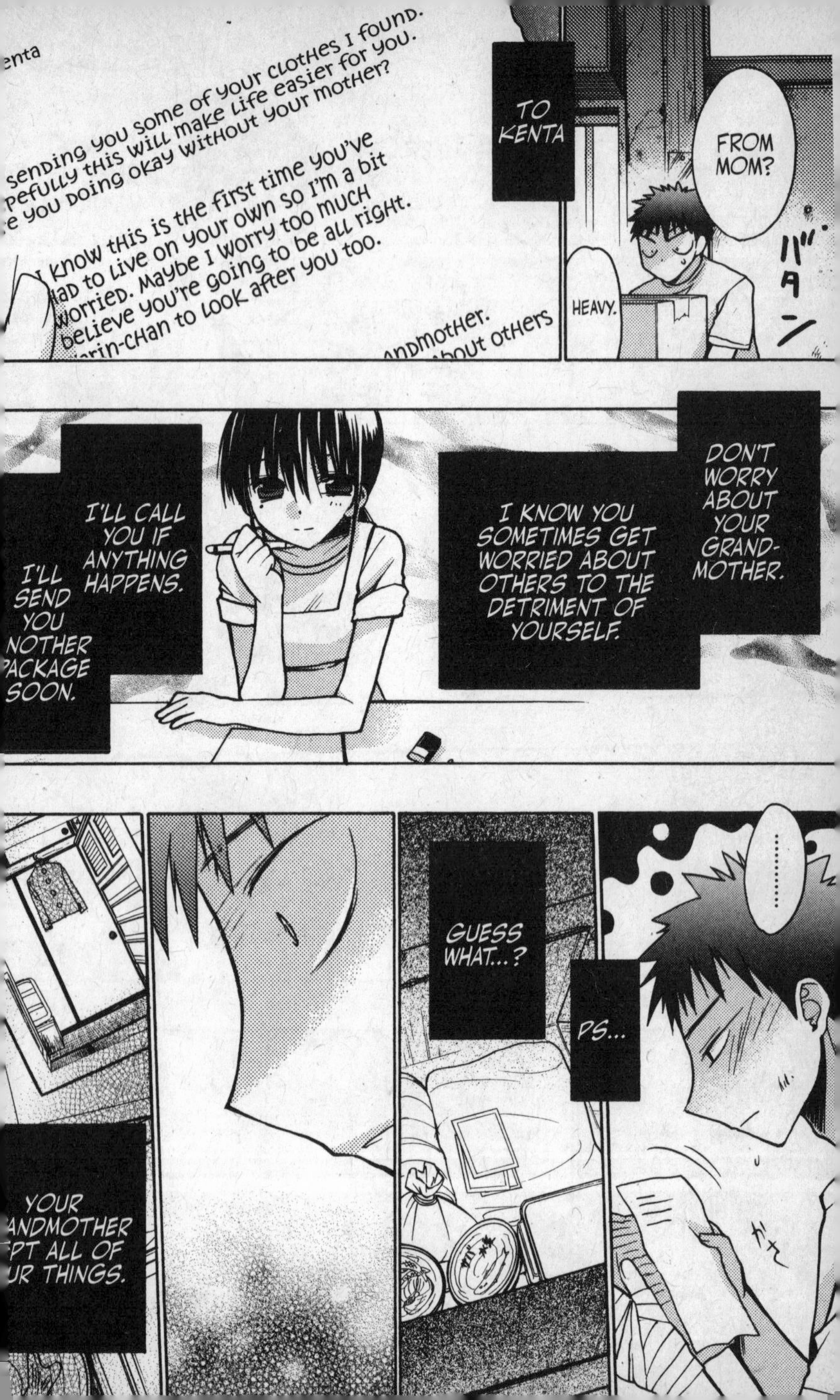

TO KENTA
FROM MOM?
HEAVY.
バタン
enta
sending you some of your clothes I found.
pefully this will make life easier for you.
e you doing okay without your mother?
I know this is the first time you've
had to live on your own so I'm a bit
worried. Maybe I worry too much
believe you're going to be all right.
arin-chan to look after you too.
andmother.
about others
DON'T WORRY ABOUT YOUR GRAND-MOTHER.
I KNOW YOU SOMETIMES GET WORRIED ABOUT OTHERS TO THE DETRIMENT OF YOURSELF.
I'LL CALL YOU IF ANYTHING HAPPENS.
I'LL SEND YOU NOTHER PACKAGE SOON.
......
PS...
GUESS WHAT...?
YOUR ANDMOTHER EPT ALL OF UR THINGS.

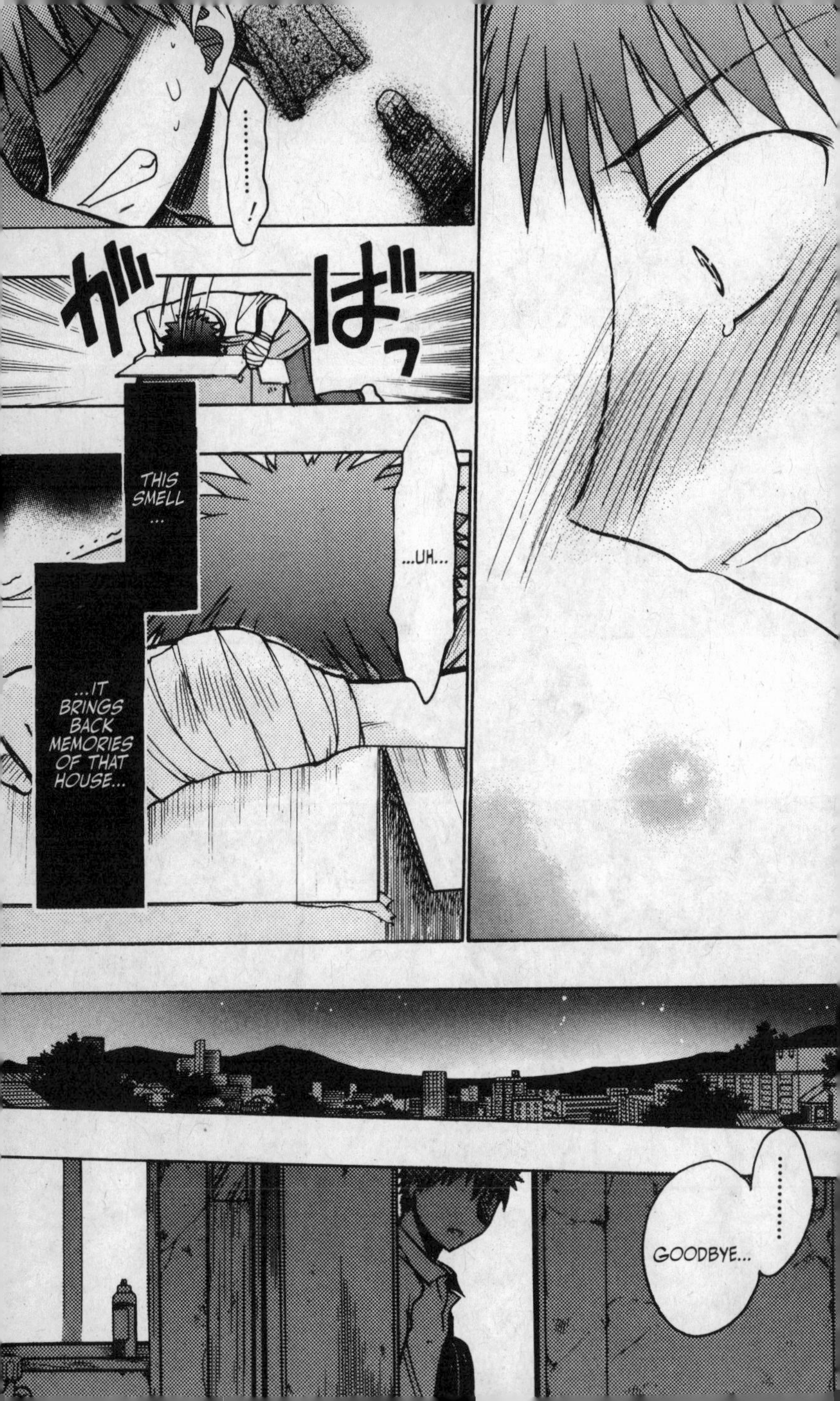
......!
がばっ
THIS SMELL...
...UH...
...IT BRINGS BACK MEMORIES OF THAT HOUSE...
......
GOODBYE...

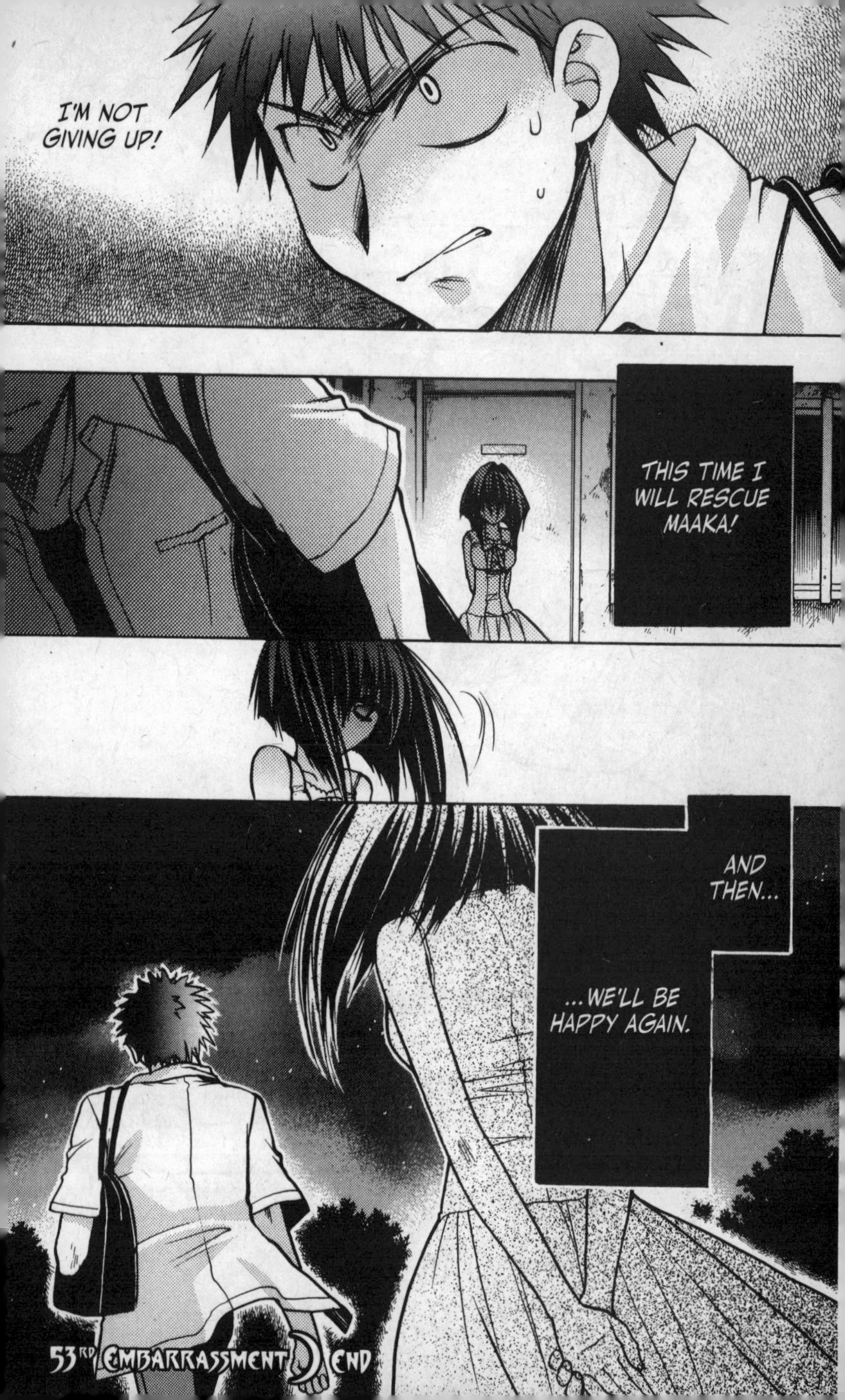
I'M NOT GIVING UP!
THIS TIME I WILL RESCUE MAAKA!
AND THEN...
...WE'LL BE HAPPY AGAIN.
53RD EMBARRASSMENT END

54th Embarrassment) Karin Captured and Kenta's Rescue Party
~A Prisoner~

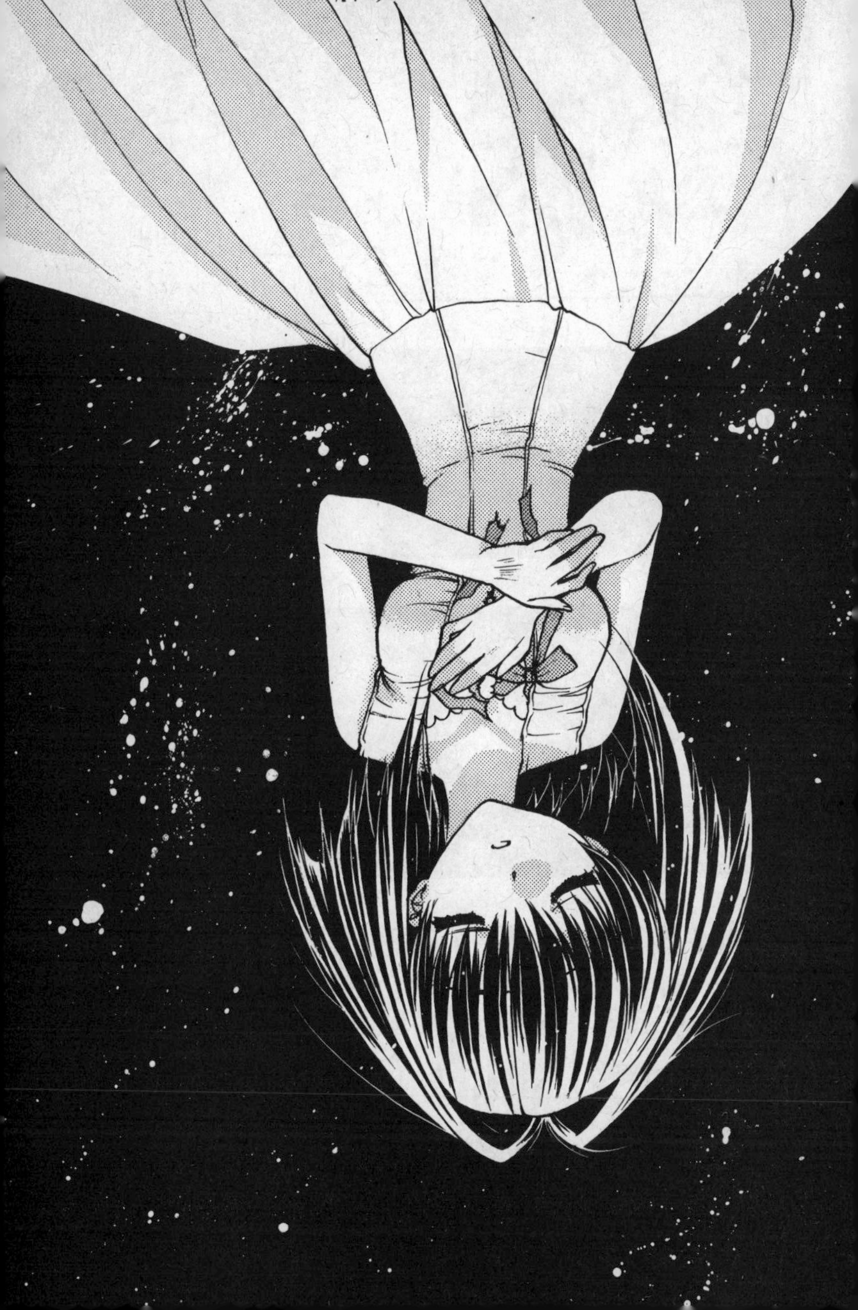

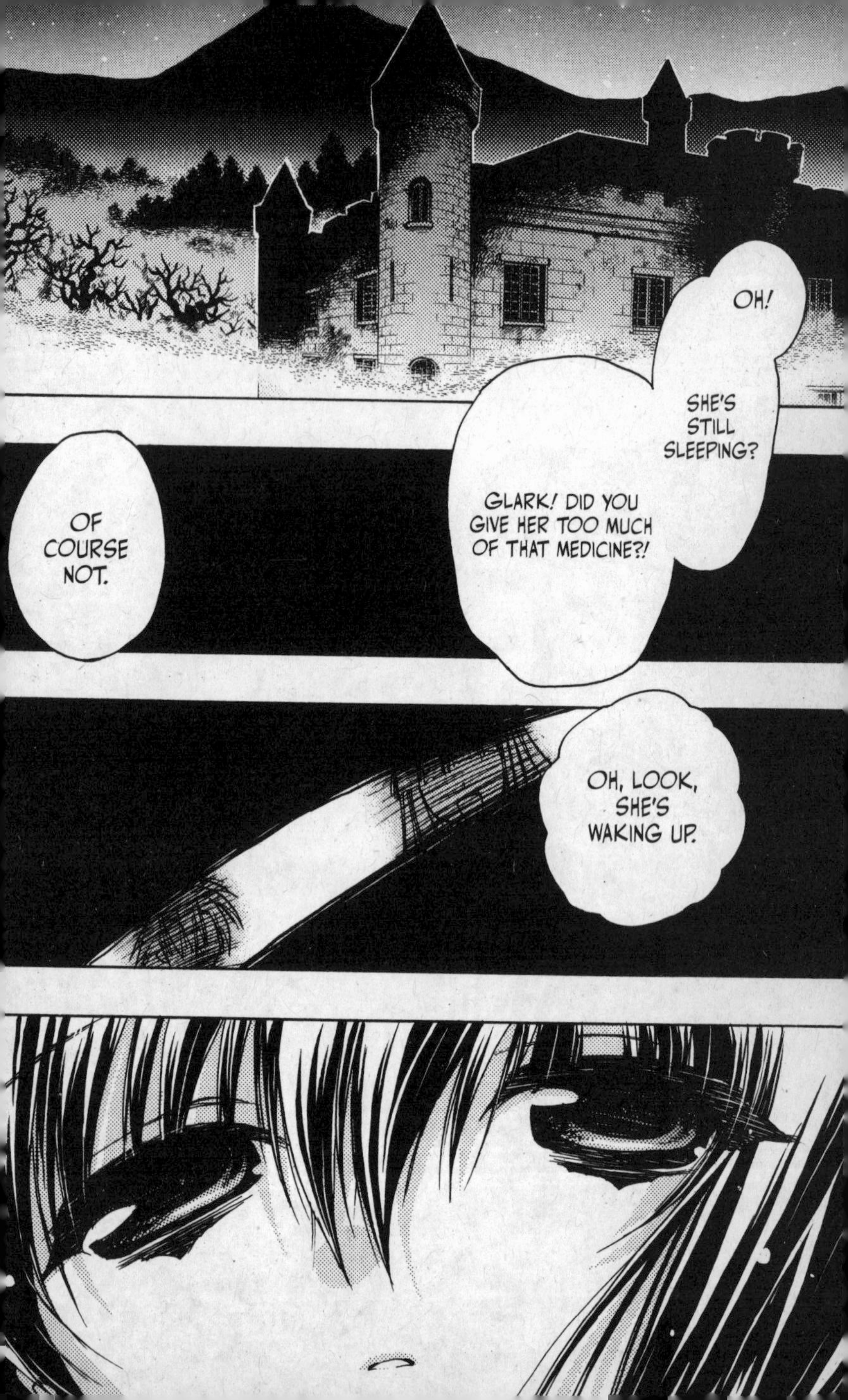
OH!
SHE'S STILL SLEEPING?
GLARK! DID YOU GIVE HER TOO MUCH OF THAT MEDICINE?!
OF COURSE NOT.
OH, LOOK, SHE'S WAKING UP.

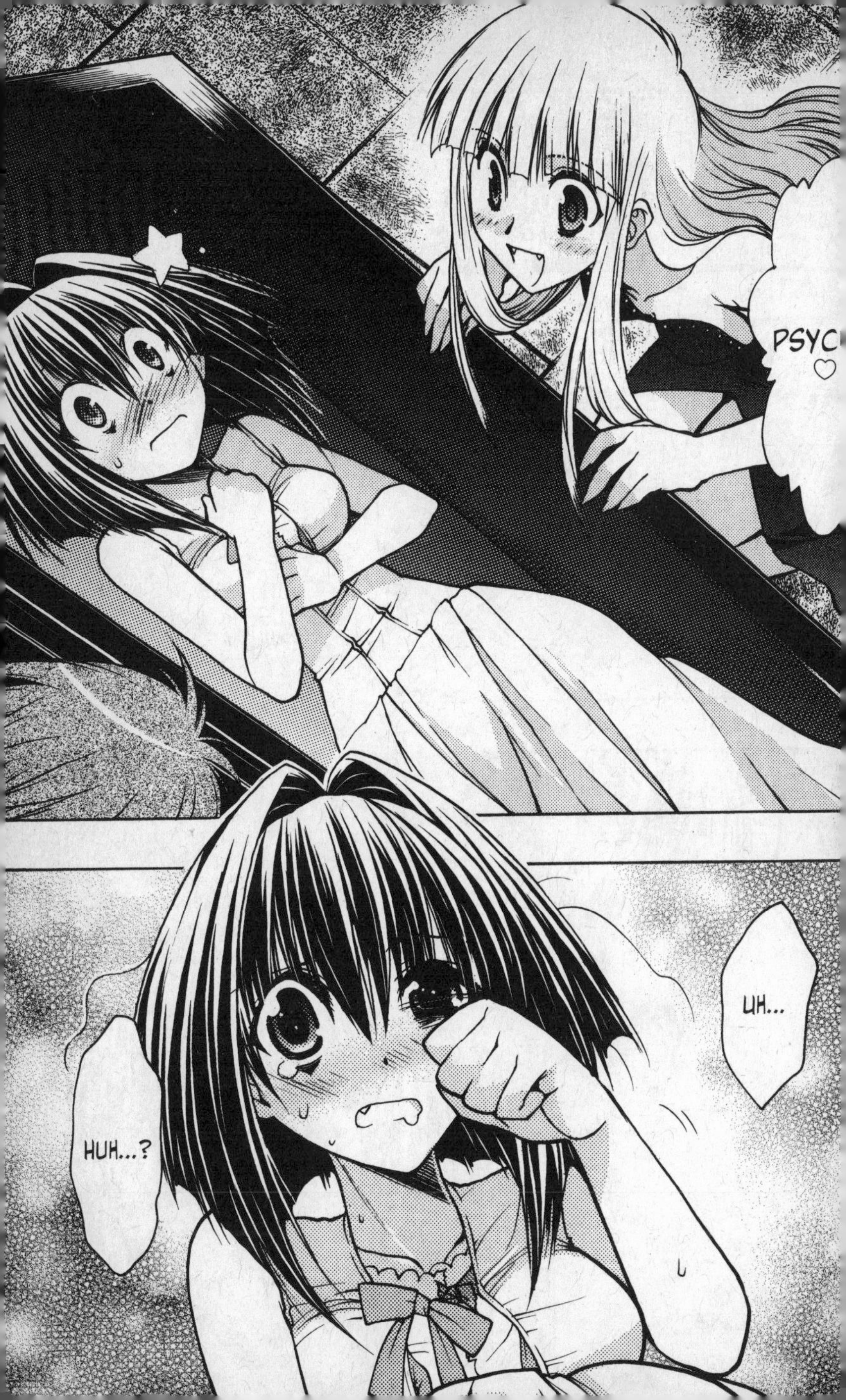
PSYC ♡
UH...
HUH...?

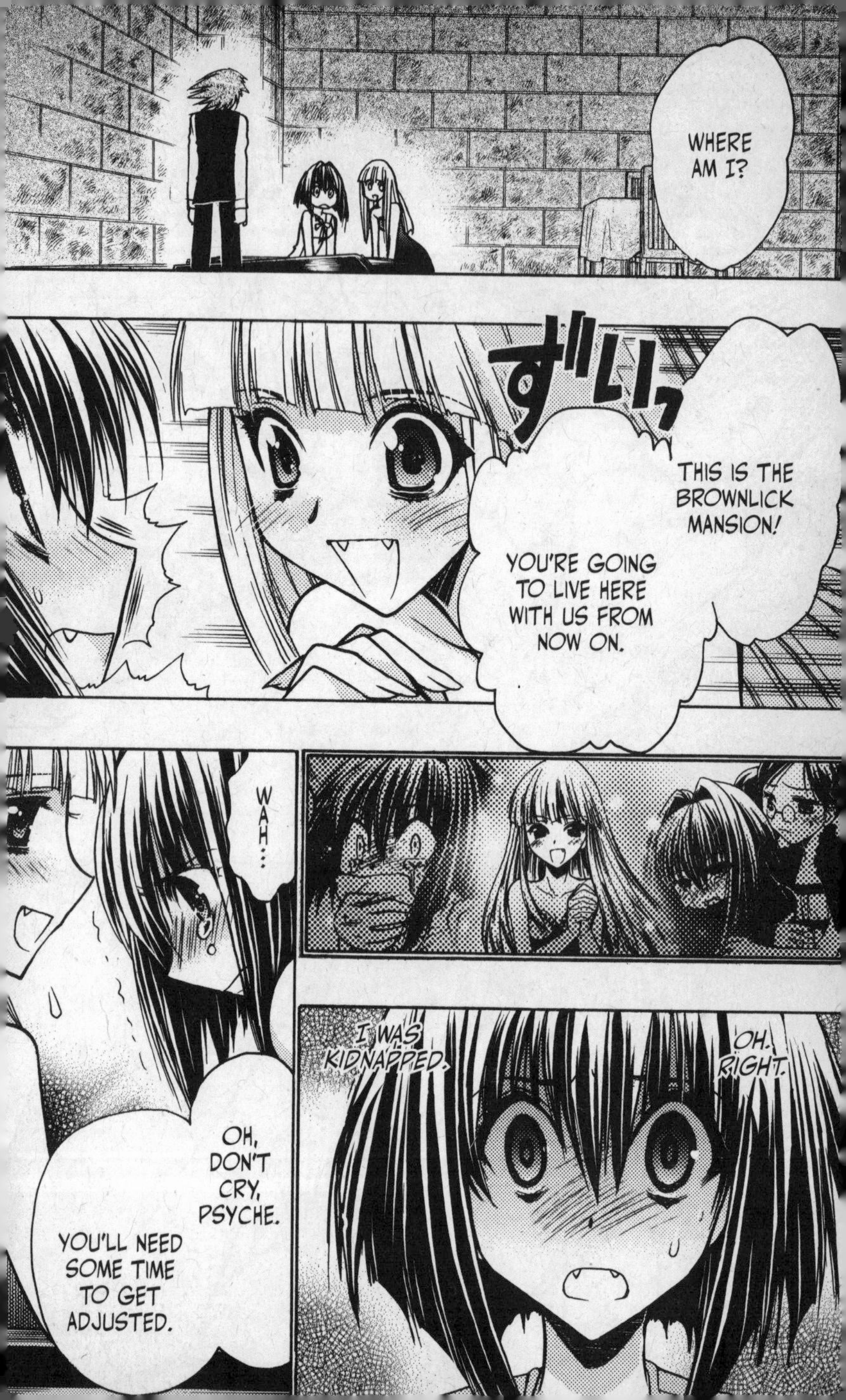
WHERE AM I?
ずいっ
THIS IS THE BROWNLICK MANSION!
YOU'RE GOING TO LIVE HERE WITH US FROM NOW ON.
OH. RIGHT.
I WAS KIDNAPPED.
WAH...
OH, DON'T CRY, PSYCHE.
YOU'LL NEED SOME TIME TO GET ADJUSTED.

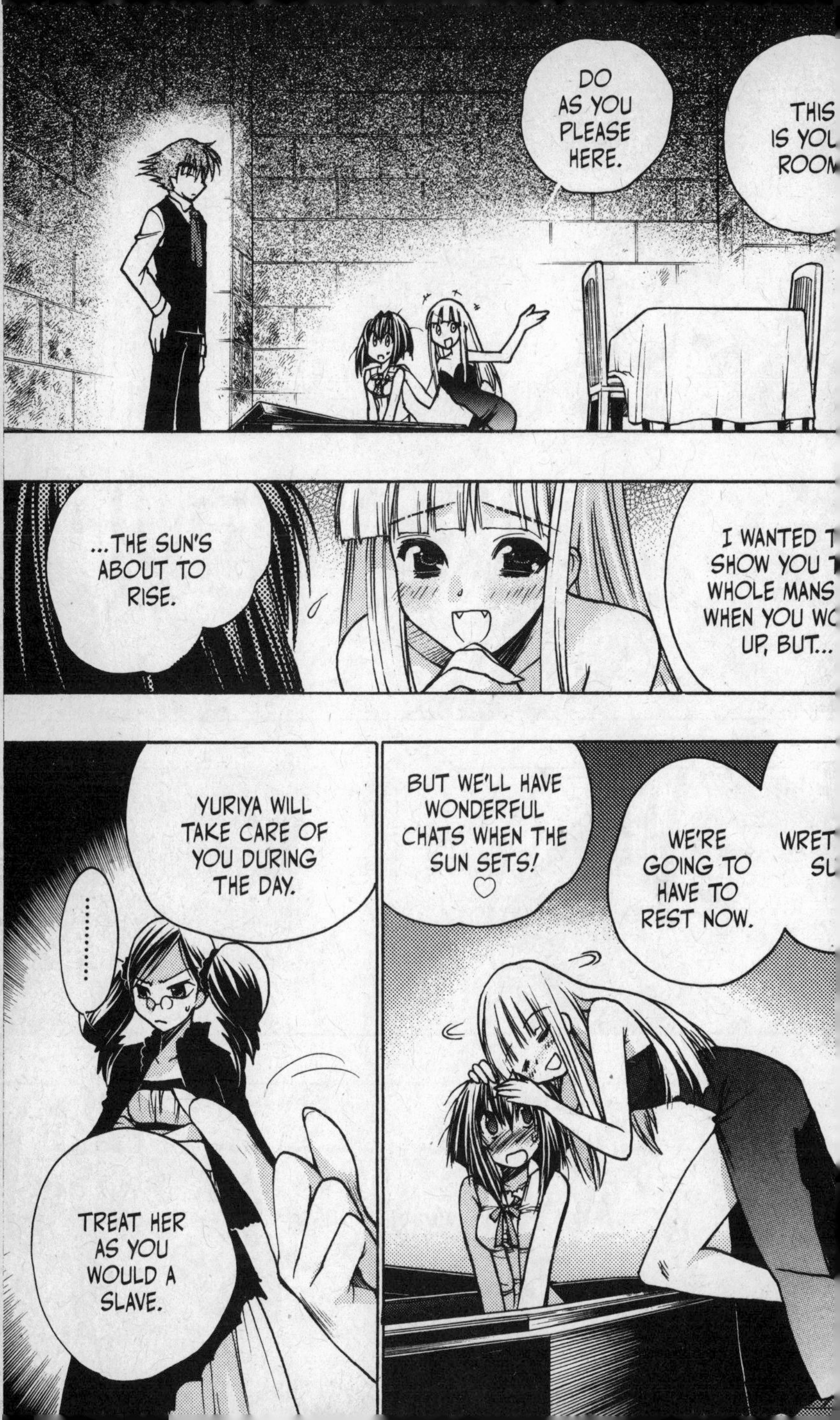
THIS IS YOU ROOM
DO AS YOU PLEASE HERE.
I WANTED T SHOW YOU T WHOLE MANS WHEN YOU WO UP, BUT...
...THE SUN'S ABOUT TO RISE.
WRET SL
WE'RE GOING TO HAVE TO REST NOW.
BUT WE'LL HAVE WONDERFUL CHATS WHEN THE SUN SETS! ♡
YURIYA WILL TAKE CARE OF YOU DURING THE DAY.
....
TREAT HER AS YOU WOULD A SLAVE.

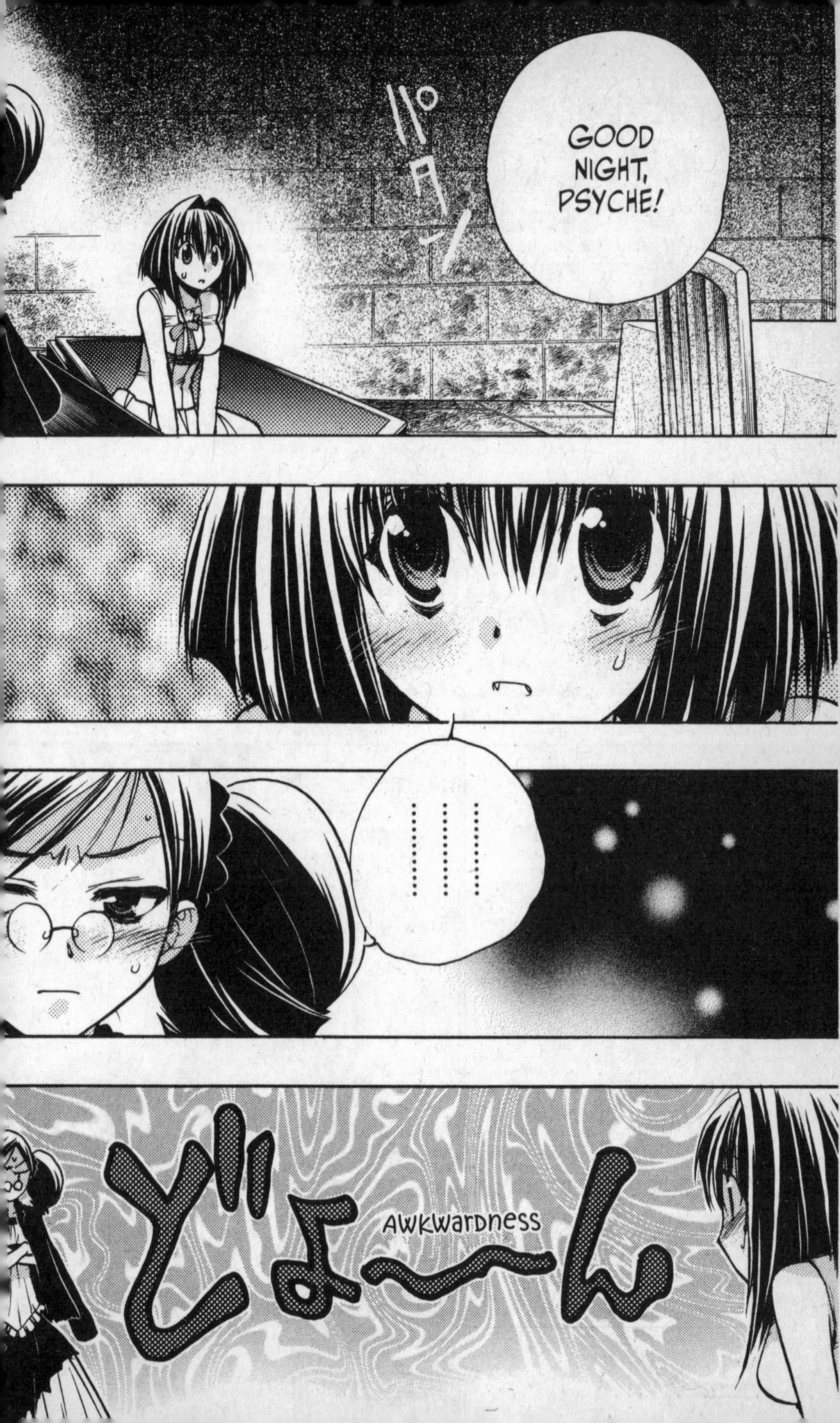

GOOD NIGHT, PSYCHE!
パタン
...
どよ～ん
AWKWARDNESS

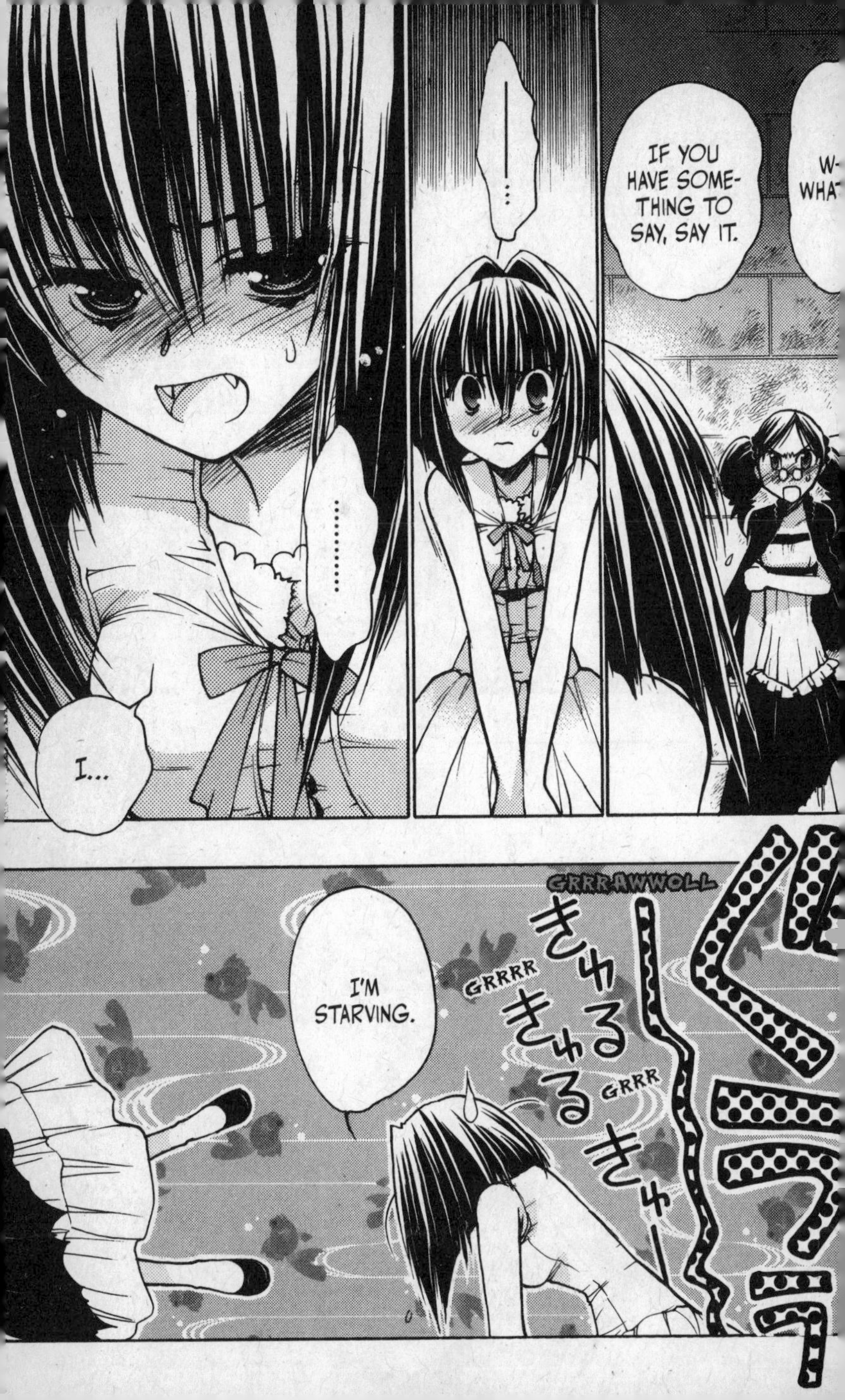
W-
WHA
IF YOU HAVE SOME-THING TO SAY, SAY IT.
...
......
I...
GRRRAWWOLL
きゅるきゅるきゅ
GRRRR
GRRR
I'M STARVING.

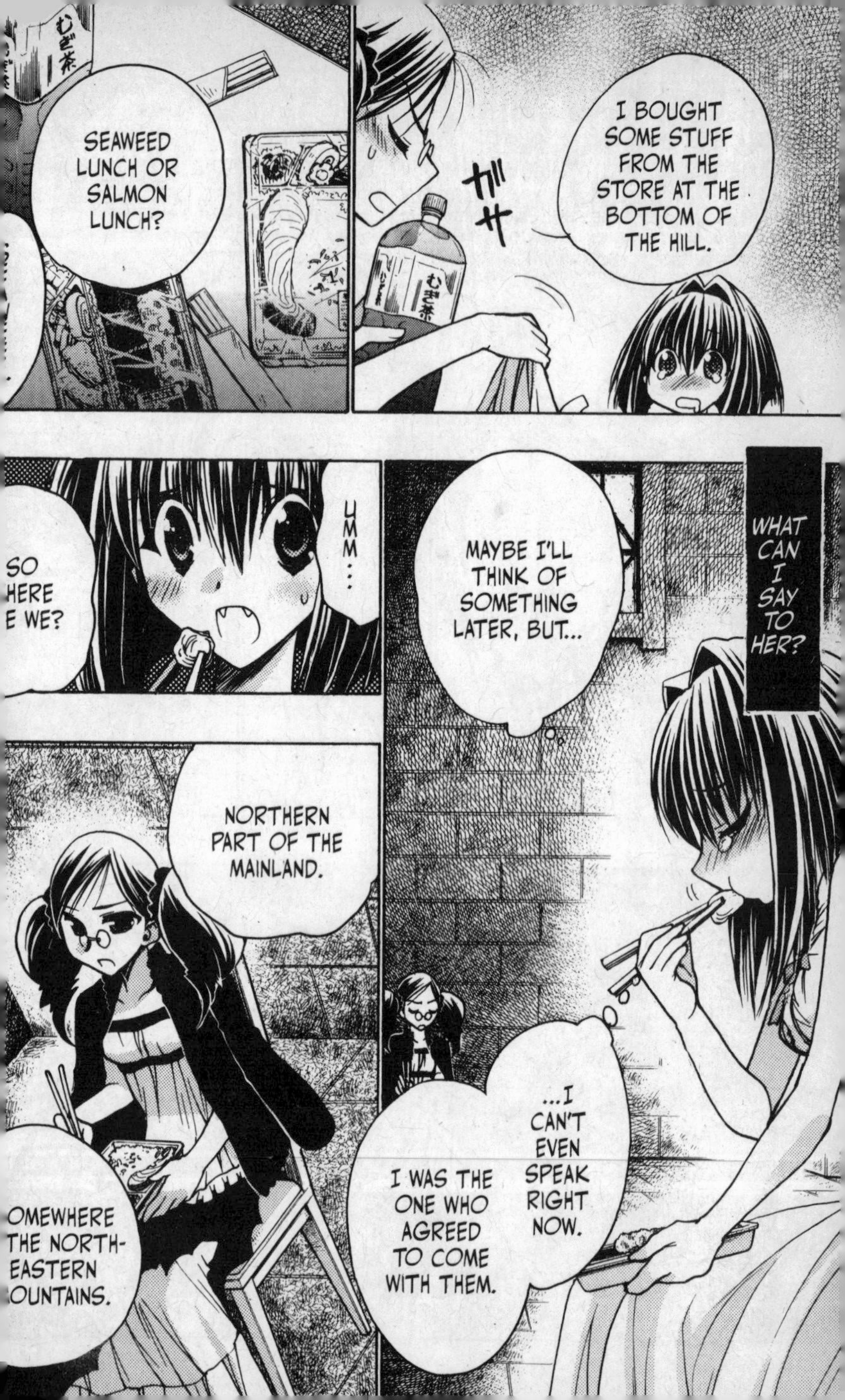
I BOUGHT SOME STUFF FROM THE STORE AT THE BOTTOM OF THE HILL.
ガサ
むぎ茶
SEAWEED LUNCH OR SALMON LUNCH?
むぎ茶
WHAT CAN I SAY TO HER?
MAYBE I'LL THINK OF SOMETHING LATER, BUT...
...I CAN'T EVEN SPEAK RIGHT NOW.
I WAS THE ONE WHO AGREED TO COME WITH THEM.
UMM...
SO
HERE
E WE?
NORTHERN PART OF THE MAINLAND.
OMEWHERE
THE NORTH-
EASTERN
OUNTAINS.

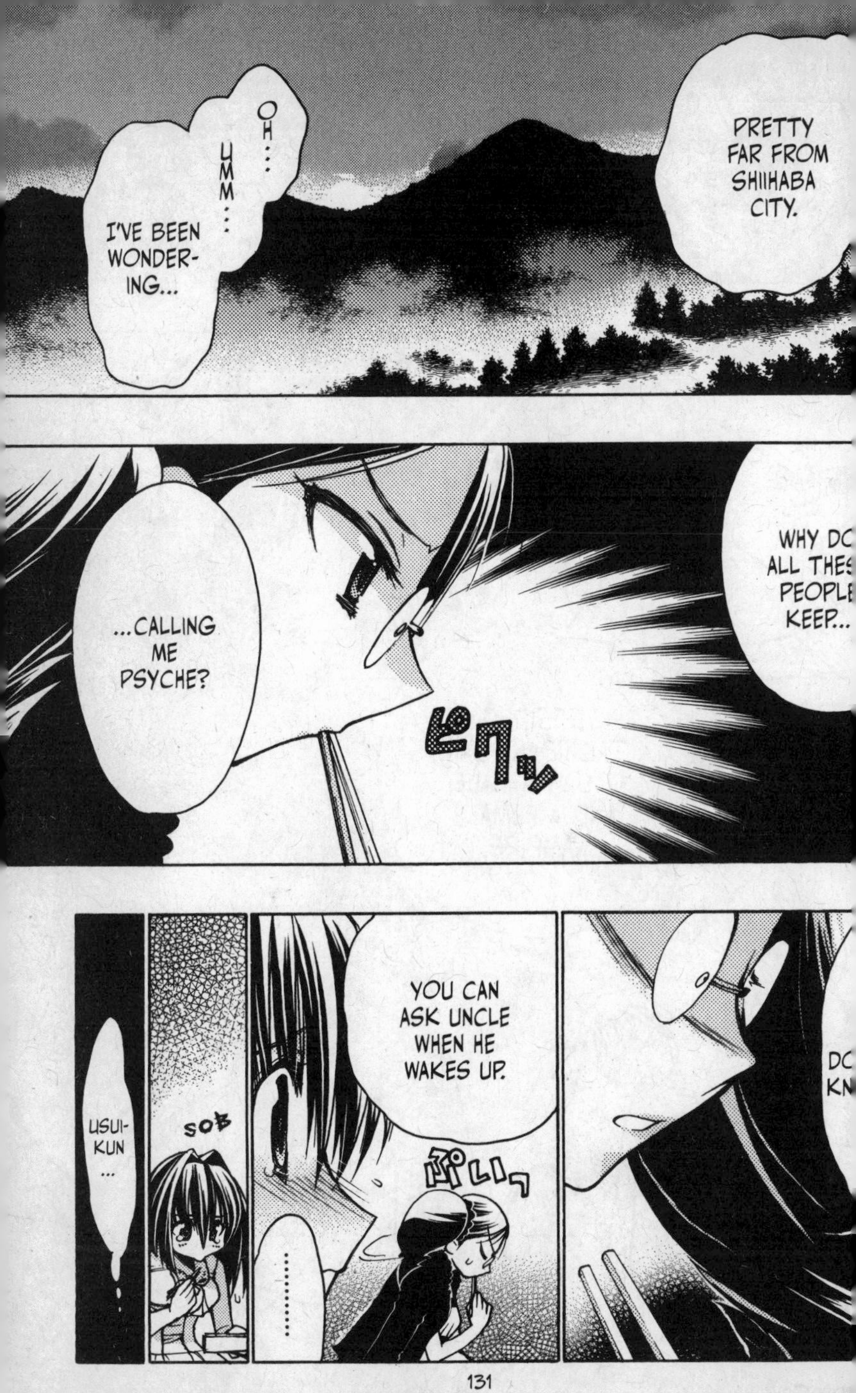

PRETTY FAR FROM SHIIHABA CITY.
OH... UMM... I'VE BEEN WONDERING...
WHY DO ALL THES PEOPLE KEEP...
...CALLING ME PSYCHE?
ピクッ
DO KN
YOU CAN ASK UNCLE WHEN HE WAKES UP.
ぷいっ
......
SOB
USUI-KUN ...

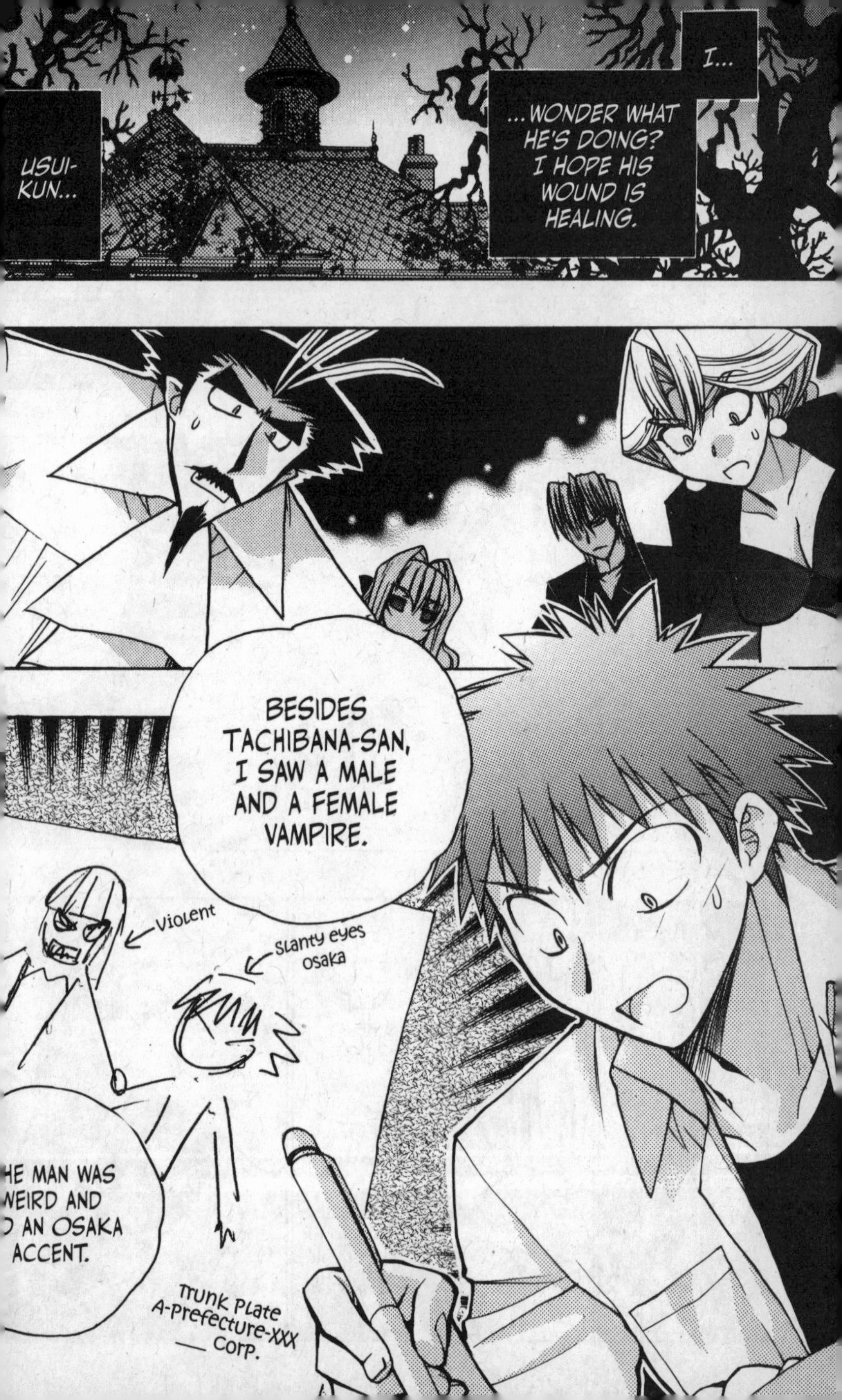
I...
...WONDER WHAT HE'S DOING? I HOPE HIS WOUND IS HEALING.
USUI-KUN...
BESIDES TACHIBANA-SAN, I SAW A MALE AND A FEMALE VAMPIRE.
Violent
Slanty eyes osaka
HE MAN WAS NEIRD AND D AN OSAKA ACCENT.
Trunk Plate A-Prefecture-XXX — Corp.

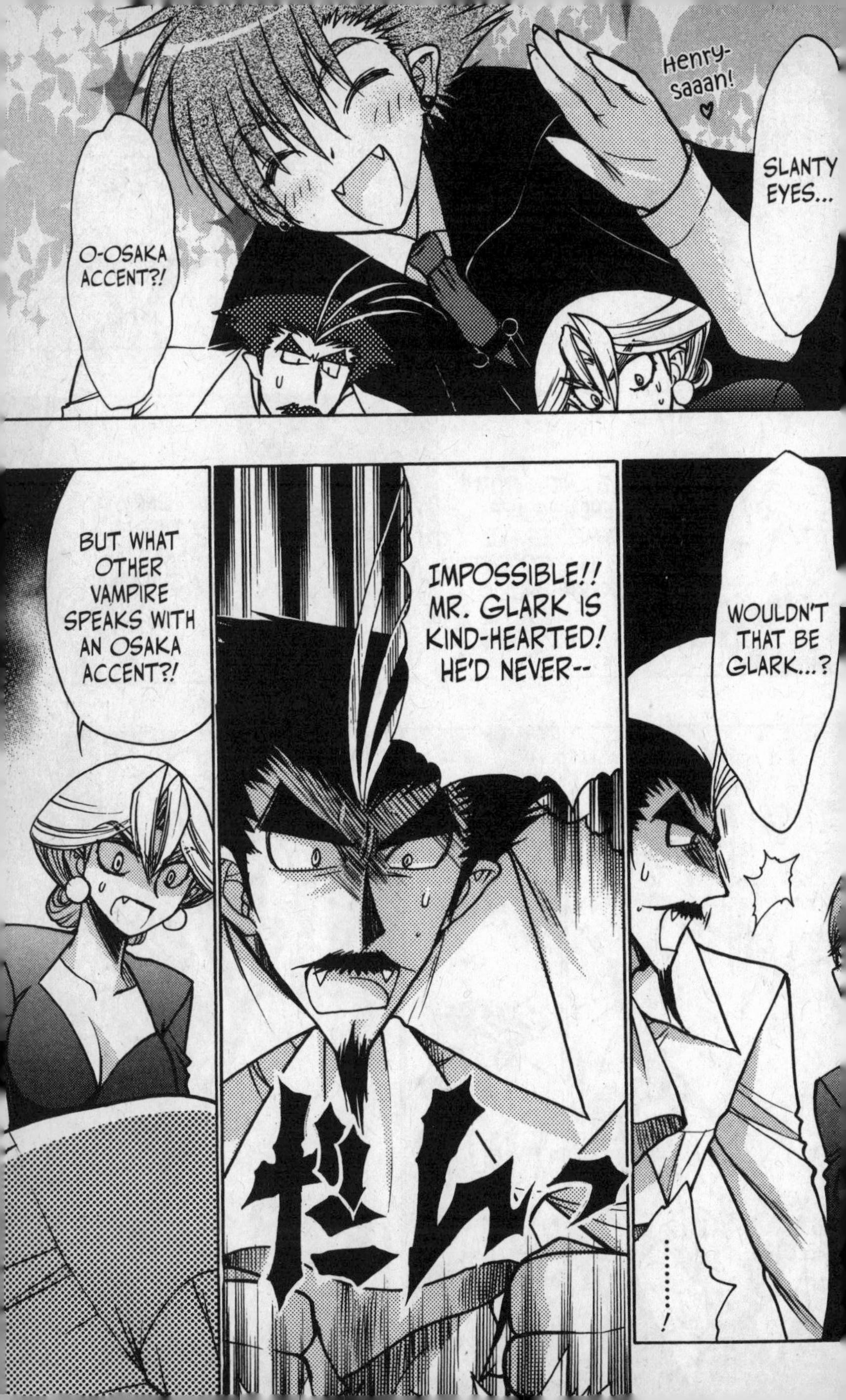
Henry-saaan! ♥
SLANTY EYES...
O-OSAKA ACCENT?!
WOULDN'T THAT BE GLARK...?
......!
IMPOSSIBLE!! MR. GLARK IS KIND-HEARTED! HE'D NEVER--
BUT WHAT OTHER VAMPIRE SPEAKS WITH AN OSAKA ACCENT?!

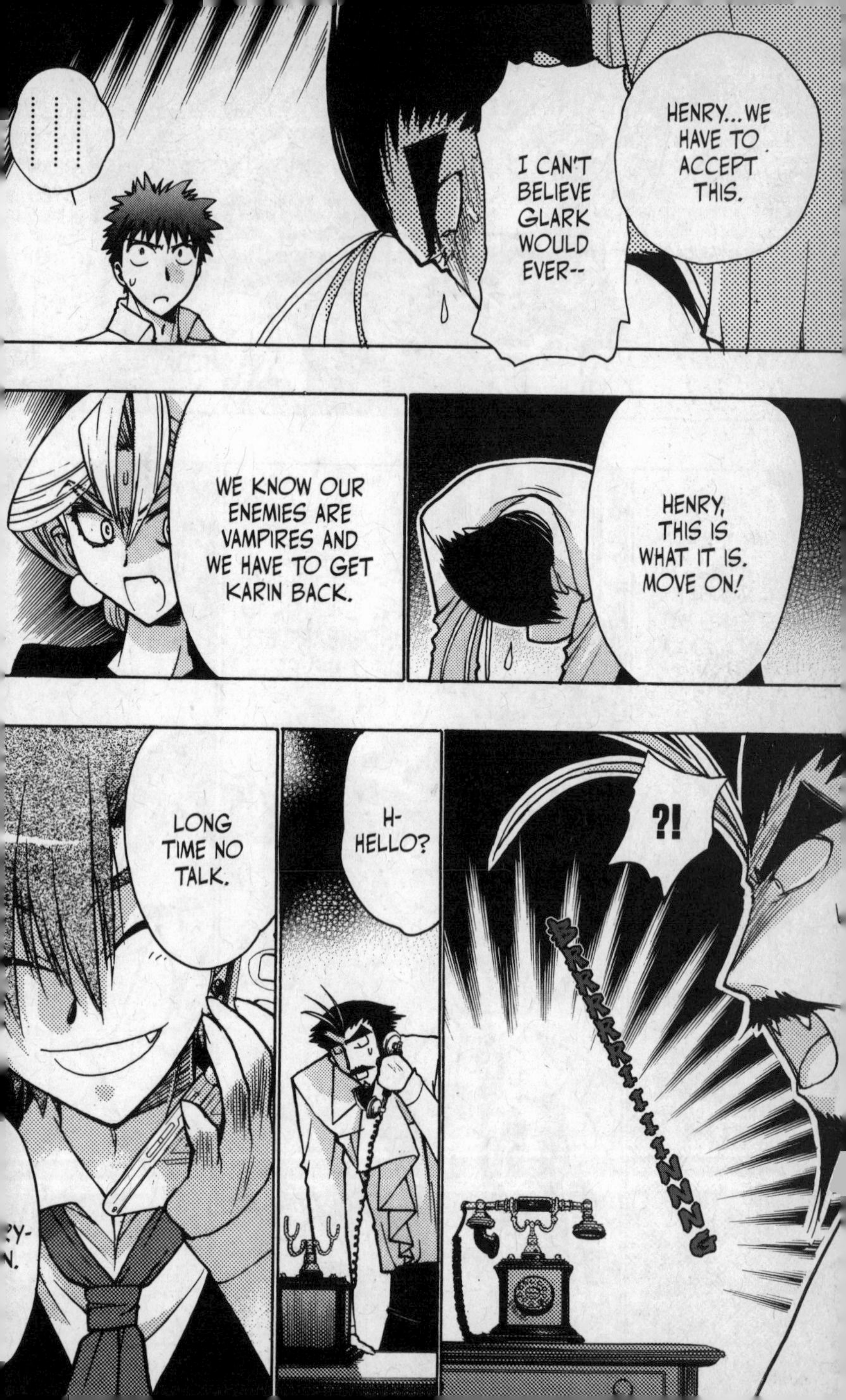
HENRY...WE HAVE TO ACCEPT THIS.
I CAN'T BELIEVE GLARK WOULD EVER--
......
HENRY, THIS IS WHAT IT IS. MOVE ON!
WE KNOW OUR ENEMIES ARE VAMPIRES AND WE HAVE TO GET KARIN BACK.
?!
BRRRRRIIIINNG
H- HELLO?
LONG TIME NO TALK.

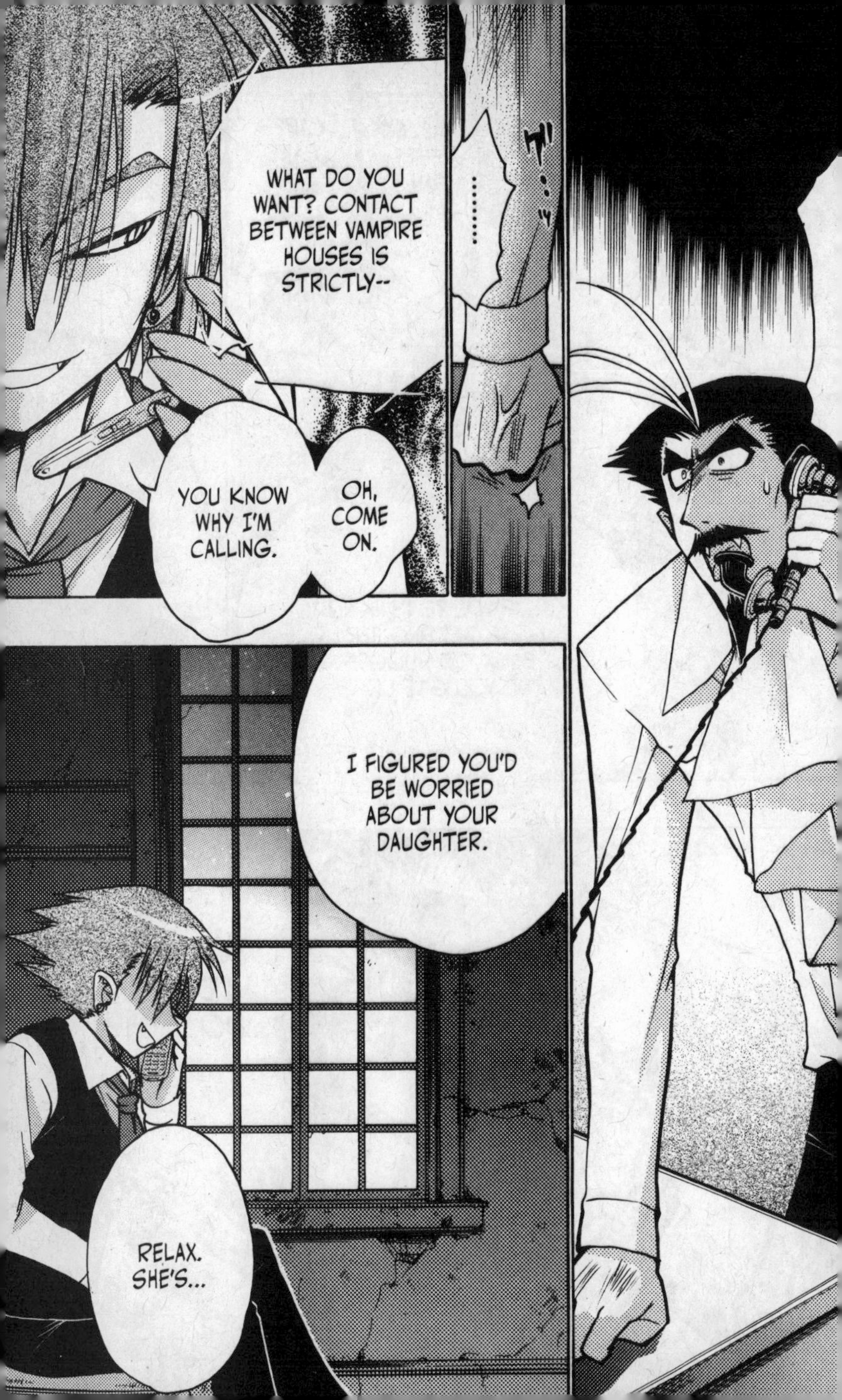
......
WHAT DO YOU WANT? CONTACT BETWEEN VAMPIRE HOUSES IS STRICTLY--
OH, COME ON.
YOU KNOW WHY I'M CALLING.
I FIGURED YOU'D BE WORRIED ABOUT YOUR DAUGHTER.
RELAX. SHE'S...

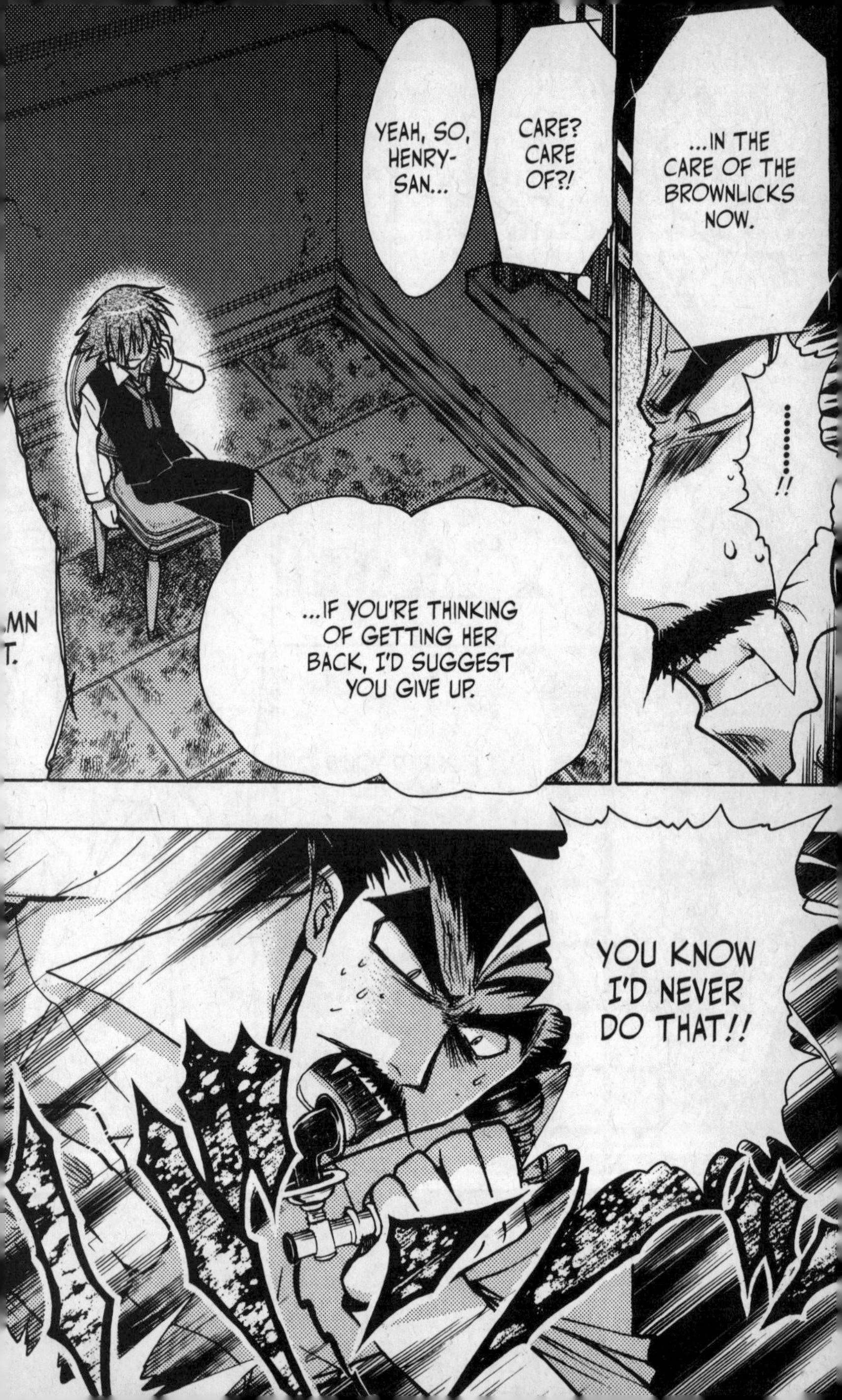
...IN THE CARE OF THE BROWNLICKS NOW.
......!!
CARE? CARE OF?!
YEAH, SO, HENRY-SAN...
...IF YOU'RE THINKING OF GETTING HER BACK, I'D SUGGEST YOU GIVE UP.
YOU KNOW I'D NEVER DO THAT!!

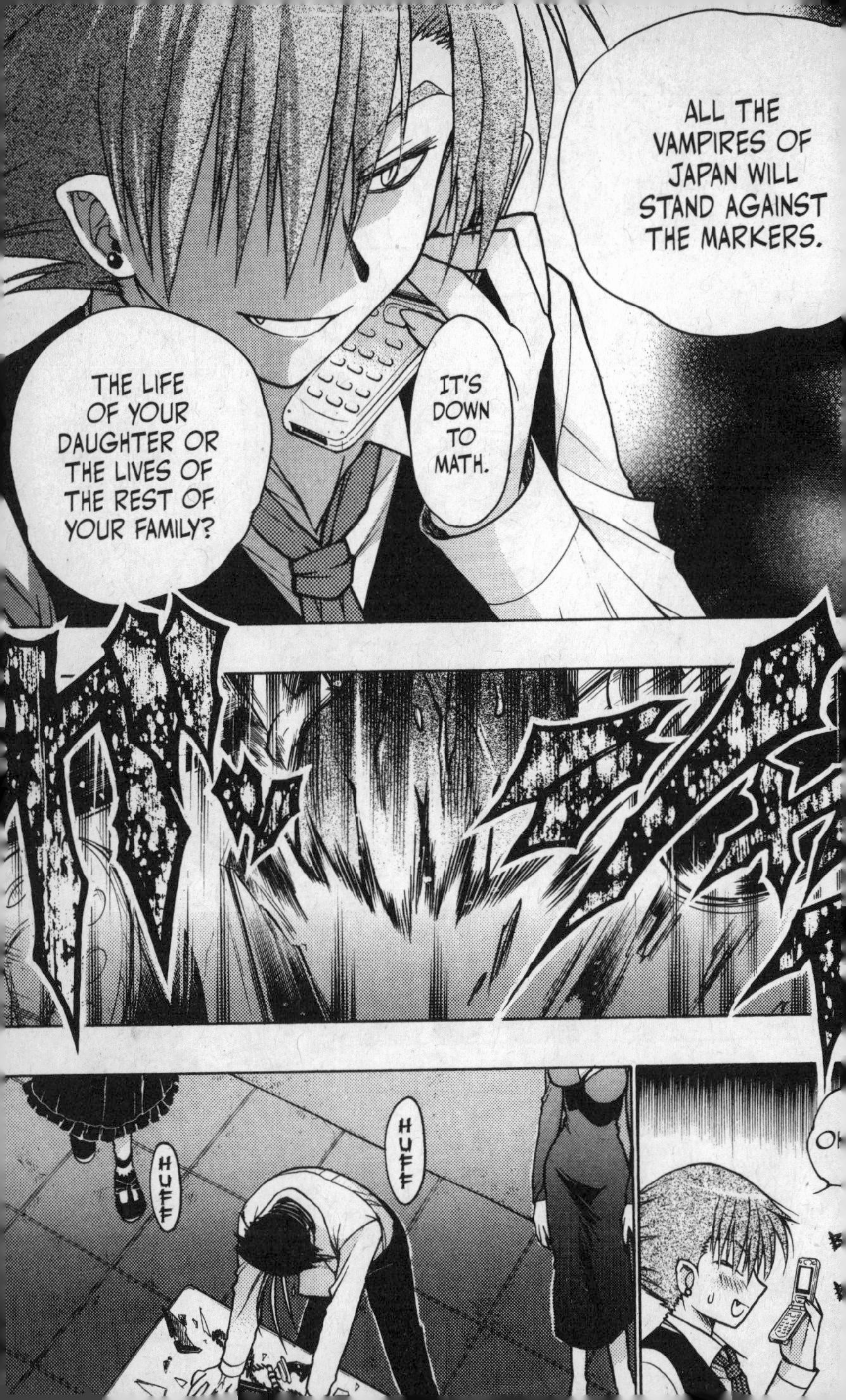
ALL THE VAMPIRES OF JAPAN WILL STAND AGAINST THE MARKERS.
IT'S DOWN TO MATH.
THE LIFE OF YOUR DAUGHTER OR THE LIVES OF THE REST OF YOUR FAMILY?
OH
HUFF
HUFF

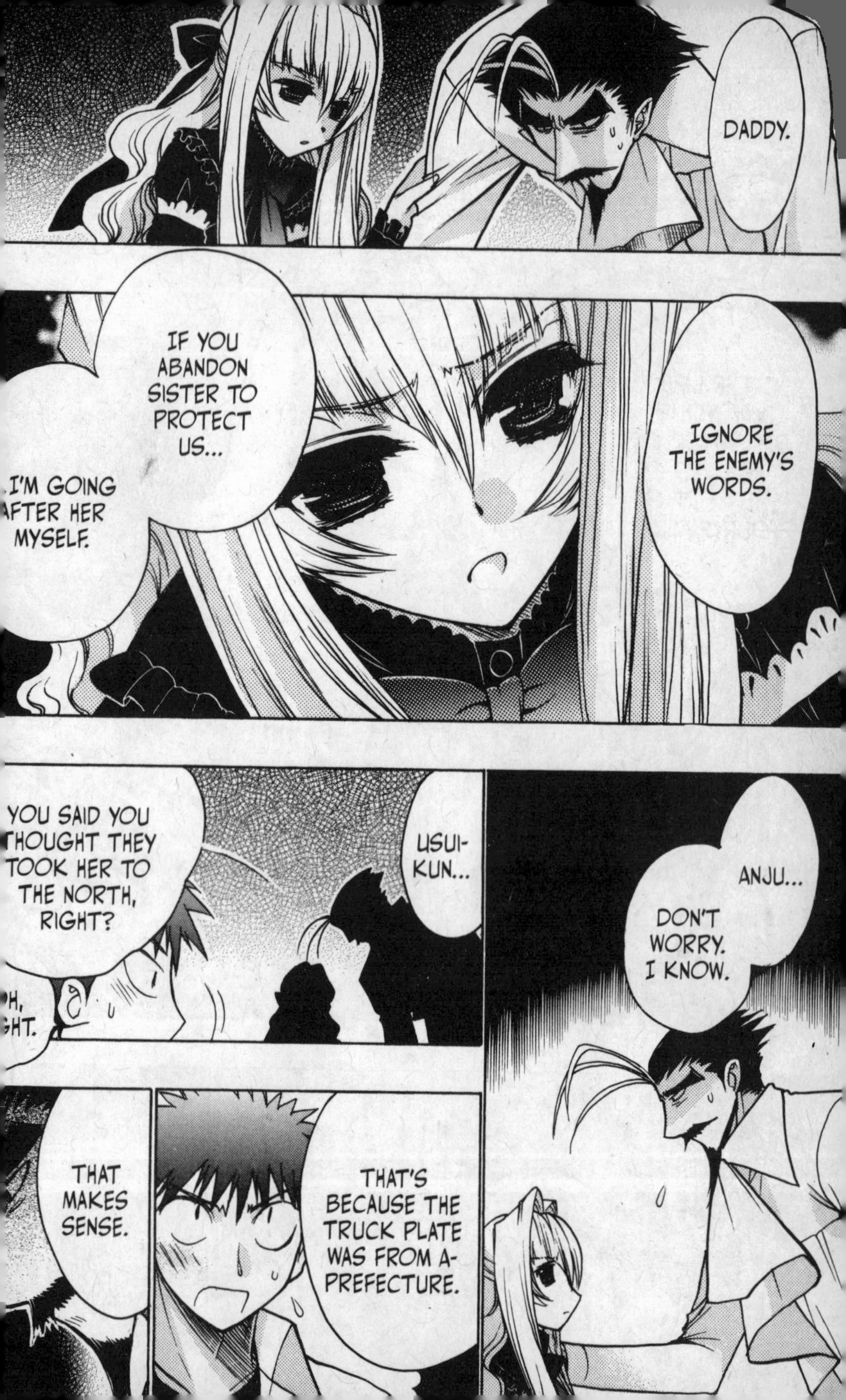
DADDY.
IGNORE THE ENEMY'S WORDS.
IF YOU ABANDON SISTER TO PROTECT US...
I'M GOING AFTER HER MYSELF.
ANJU...
DON'T WORRY. I KNOW.
USUI-KUN...
YOU SAID YOU THOUGHT THEY TOOK HER TO THE NORTH, RIGHT?
THAT'S BECAUSE THE TRUCK PLATE WAS FROM A-PREFECTURE.
THAT MAKES SENSE.

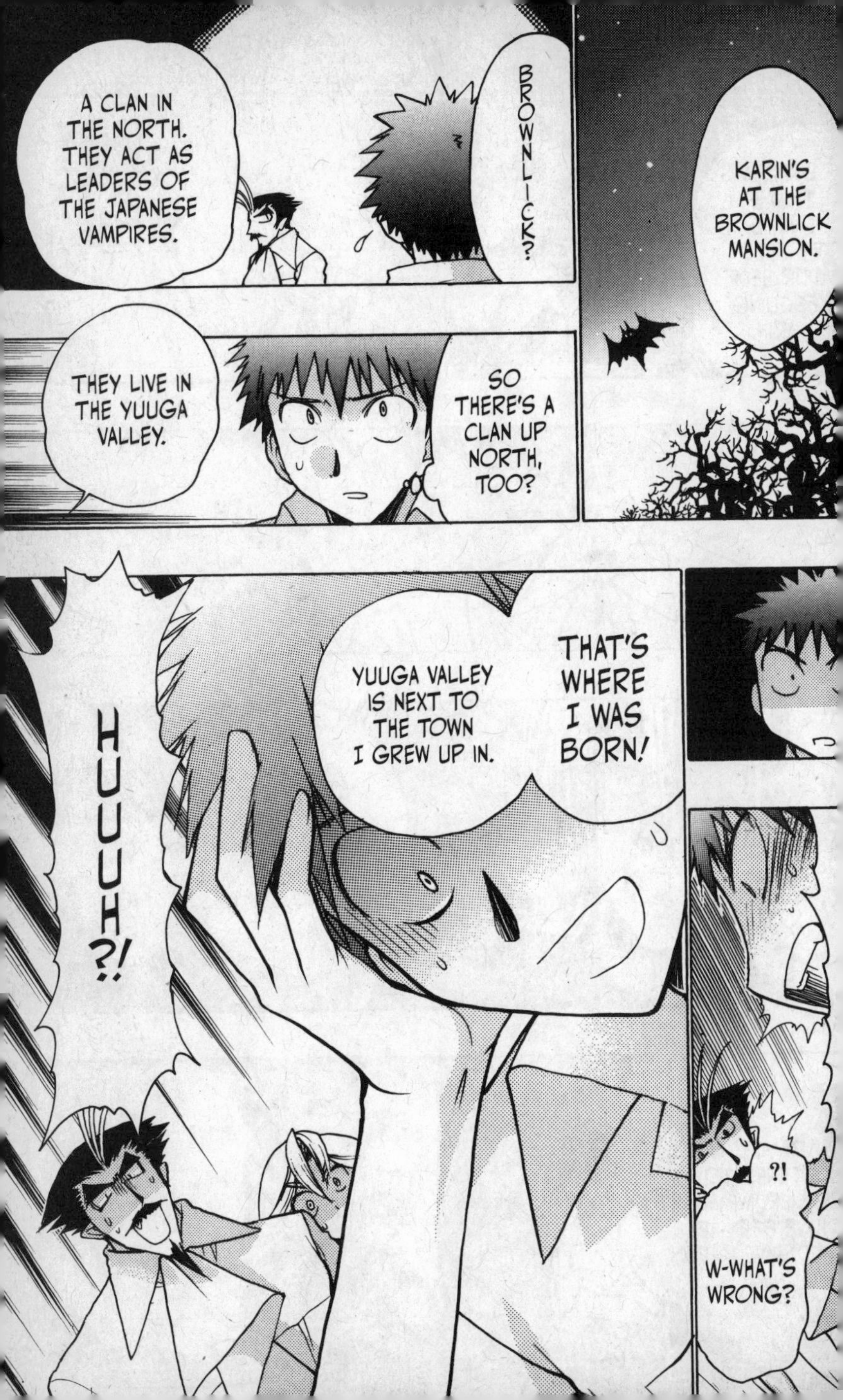
KARIN'S AT THE BROWNLICK MANSION.
BROWNLICK?
A CLAN IN THE NORTH. THEY ACT AS LEADERS OF THE JAPANESE VAMPIRES.
SO THERE'S A CLAN UP NORTH, TOO?
THEY LIVE IN THE YUUGA VALLEY.
?!
W-WHAT'S WRONG?
THAT'S WHERE I WAS BORN!
YUUGA VALLEY IS NEXT TO THE TOWN I GREW UP IN.
HUUUUH?!

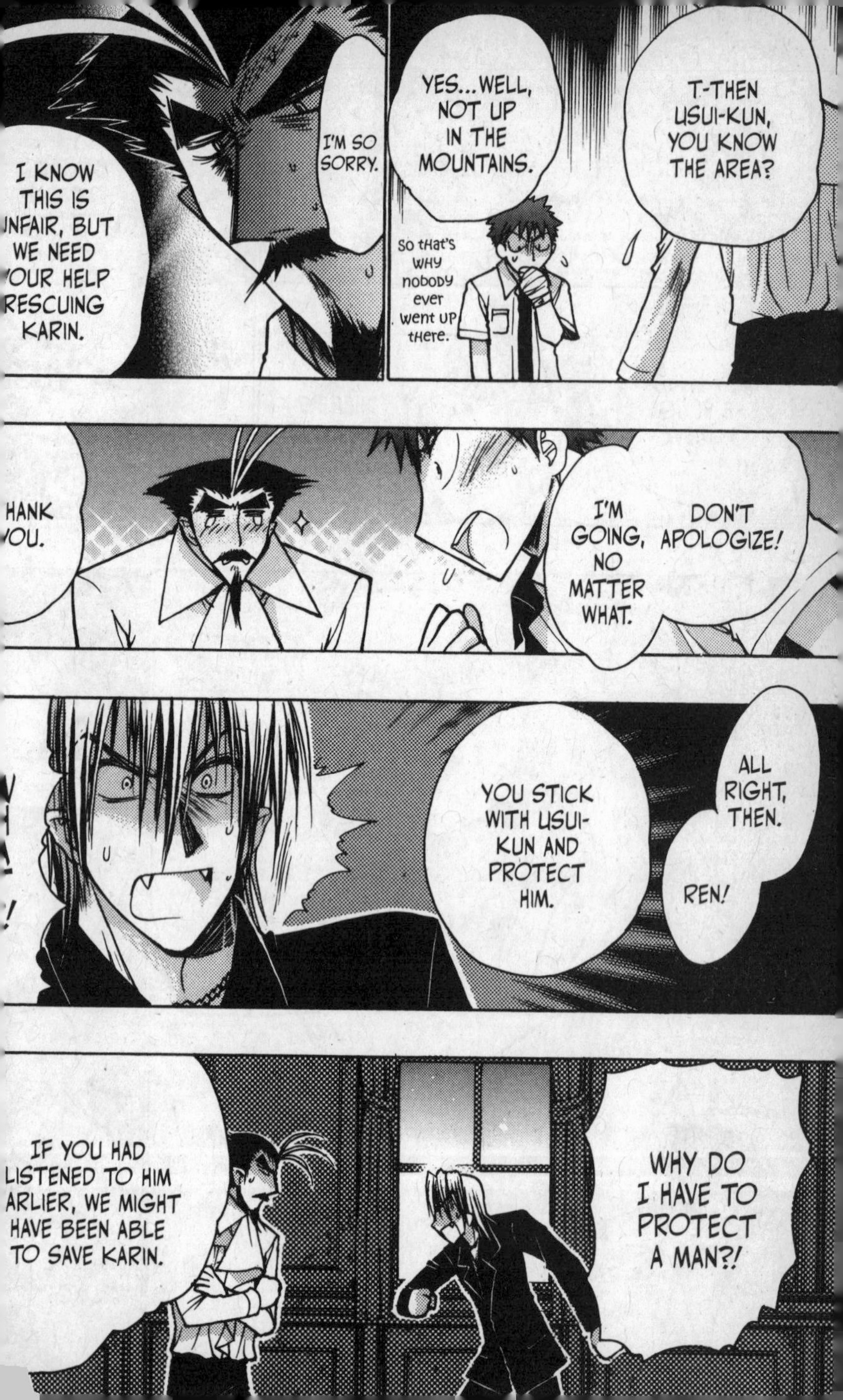

T-THEN USUI-KUN, YOU KNOW THE AREA?
YES...WELL, NOT UP IN THE MOUNTAINS.
So that's WHY nobody ever went up there.
I'M SO SORRY.
I KNOW THIS IS NFAIR, BUT WE NEED OUR HELP RESCUING KARIN.
DON'T APOLOGIZE!
I'M GOING, NO MATTER WHAT.
HANK OU.
ALL RIGHT, THEN.
REN!
YOU STICK WITH USUI-KUN AND PROTECT HIM.
WHY DO I HAVE TO PROTECT A MAN?!
IF YOU HAD LISTENED TO HIM ARLIER, WE MIGHT HAVE BEEN ABLE TO SAVE KARIN.

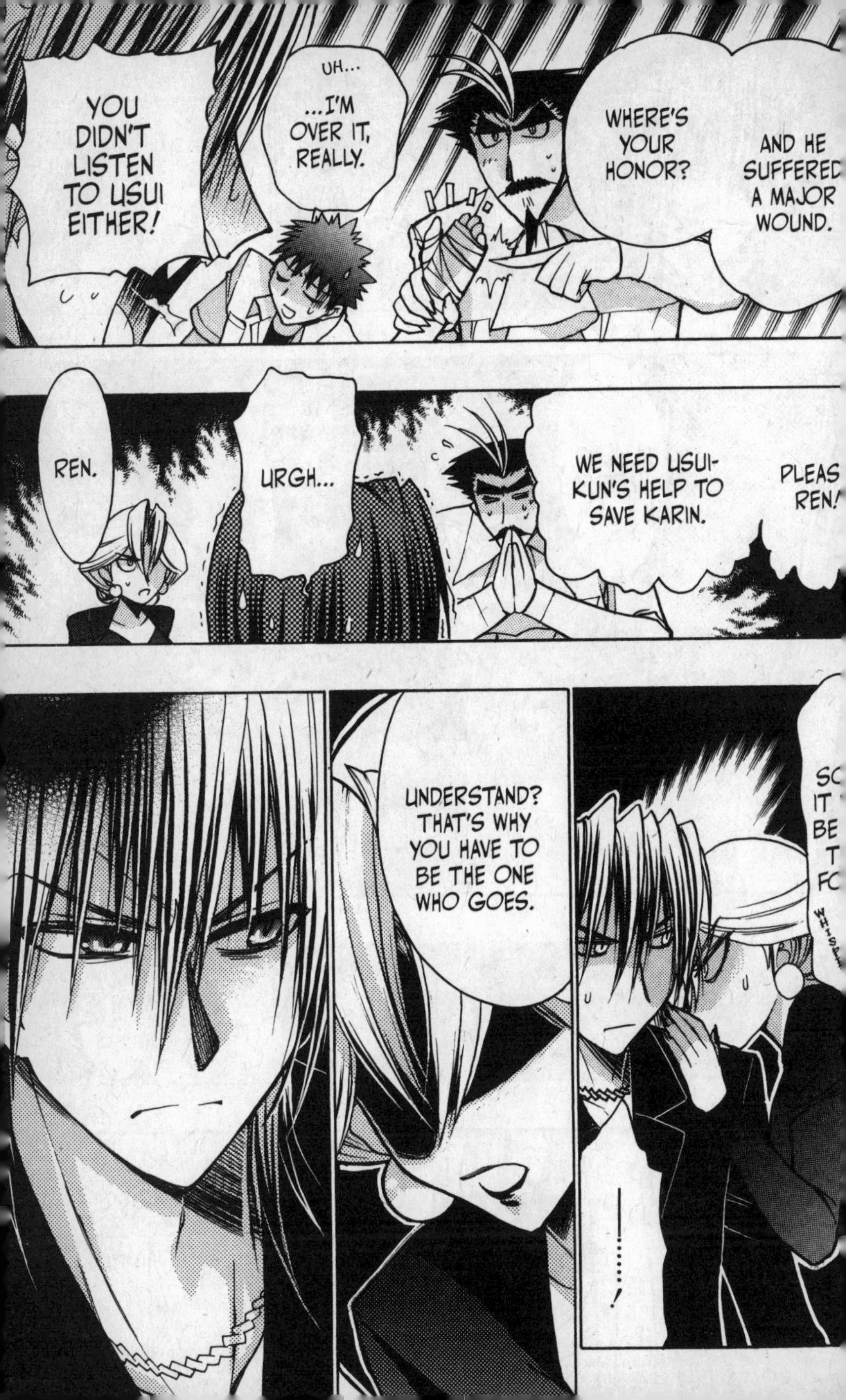
AND HE SUFFERED A MAJOR WOUND.
WHERE'S YOUR HONOR?
UH...
...I'M OVER IT, REALLY.
YOU DIDN'T LISTEN TO USUI EITHER!
PLEAS REN!
WE NEED USUI-KUN'S HELP TO SAVE KARIN.
URGH...
REN.
......!
UNDERSTAND? THAT'S WHY YOU HAVE TO BE THE ONE WHO GOES.

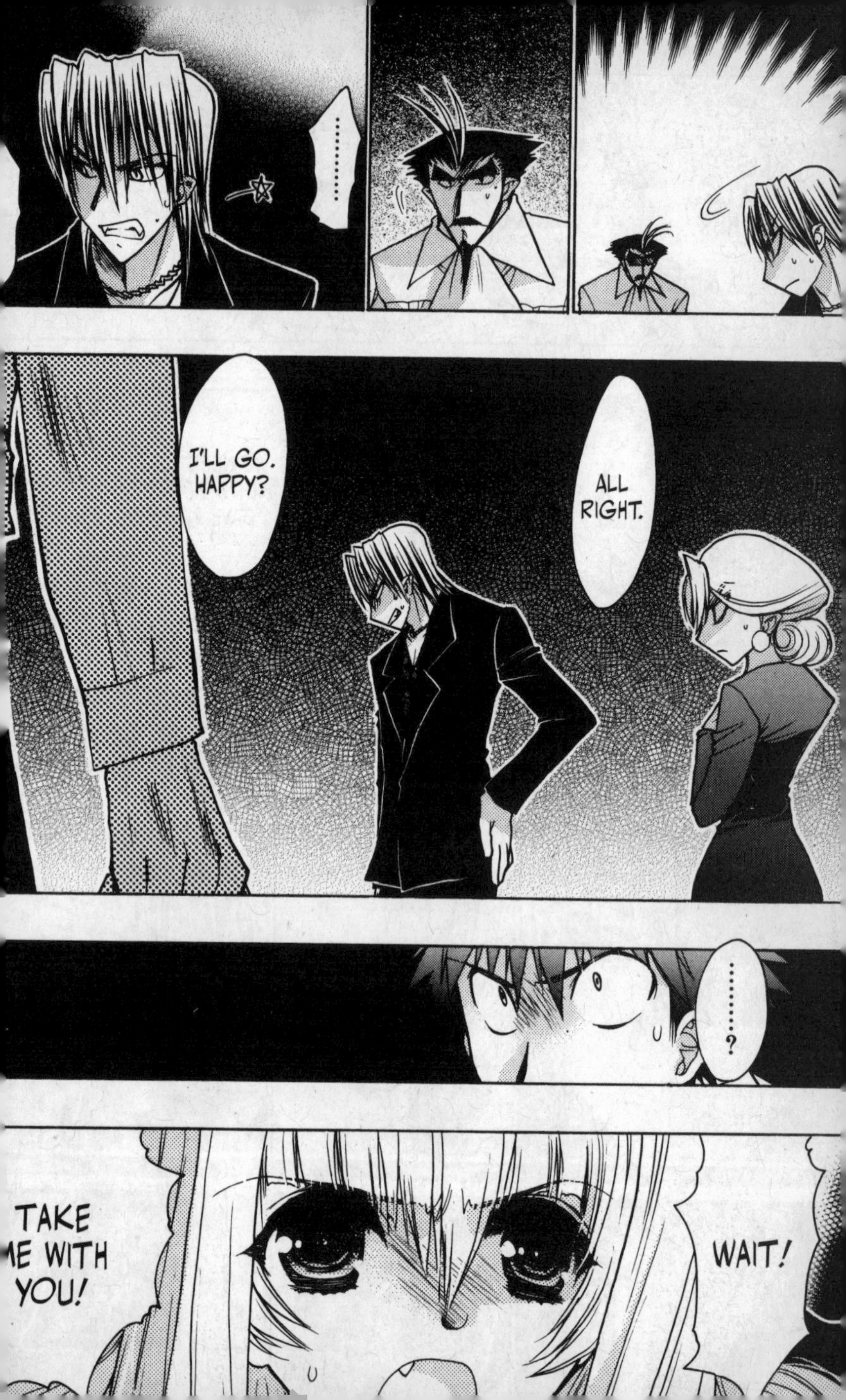
......!
ALL RIGHT.
I'LL GO. HAPPY?
......?
WAIT!
TAKE ME WITH YOU!

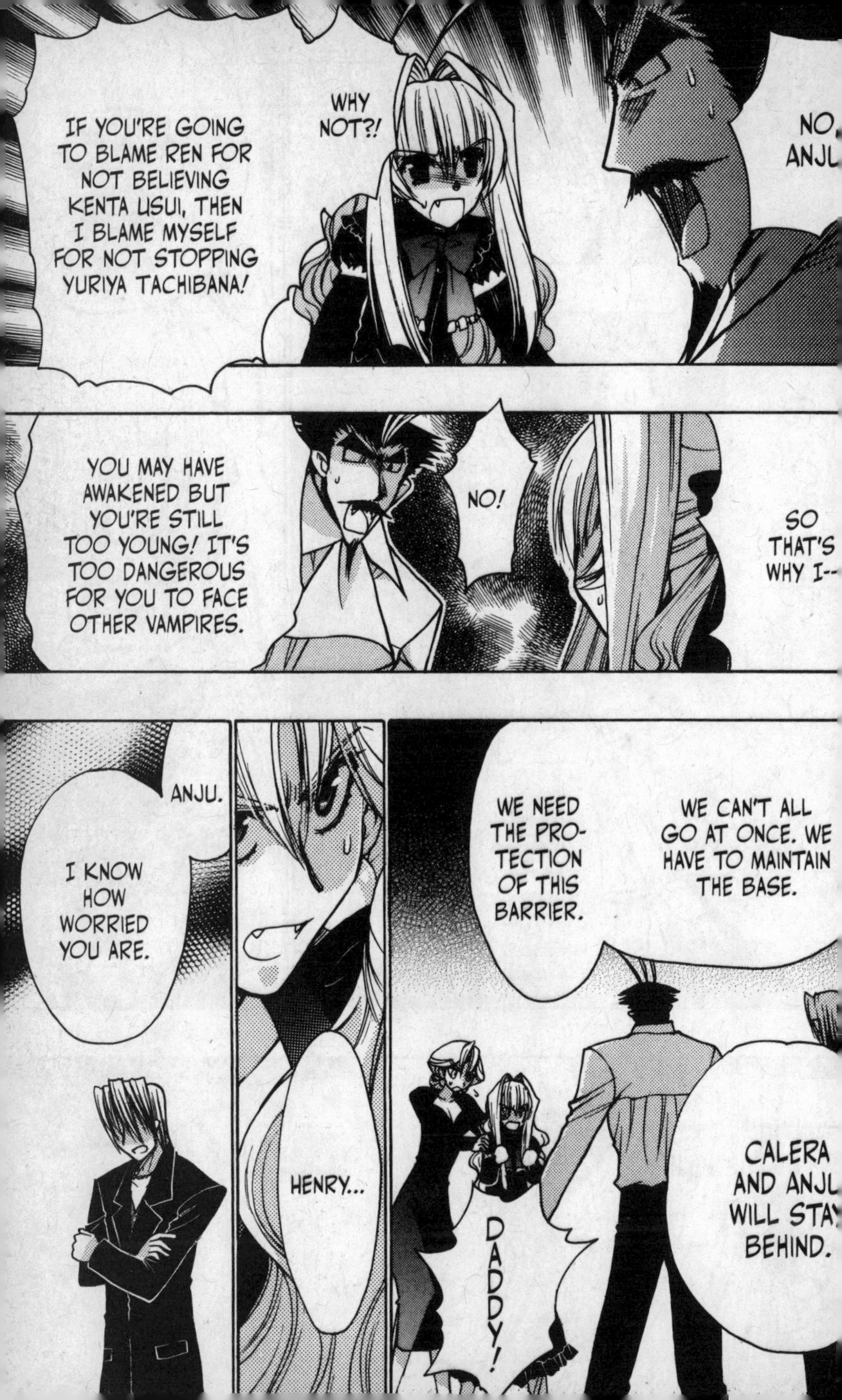
NO, ANJU
WHY NOT?!
IF YOU'RE GOING TO BLAME REN FOR NOT BELIEVING KENTA USUI, THEN I BLAME MYSELF FOR NOT STOPPING YURIYA TACHIBANA!
SO THAT'S WHY I--
NO!
YOU MAY HAVE AWAKENED BUT YOU'RE STILL TOO YOUNG! IT'S TOO DANGEROUS FOR YOU TO FACE OTHER VAMPIRES.
WE CAN'T ALL GO AT ONCE. WE HAVE TO MAINTAIN THE BASE.
WE NEED THE PROTECTION OF THIS BARRIER.
CALERA AND ANJU WILL STAY BEHIND.
DADDY!
HENRY...
ANJU.
I KNOW HOW WORRIED YOU ARE.

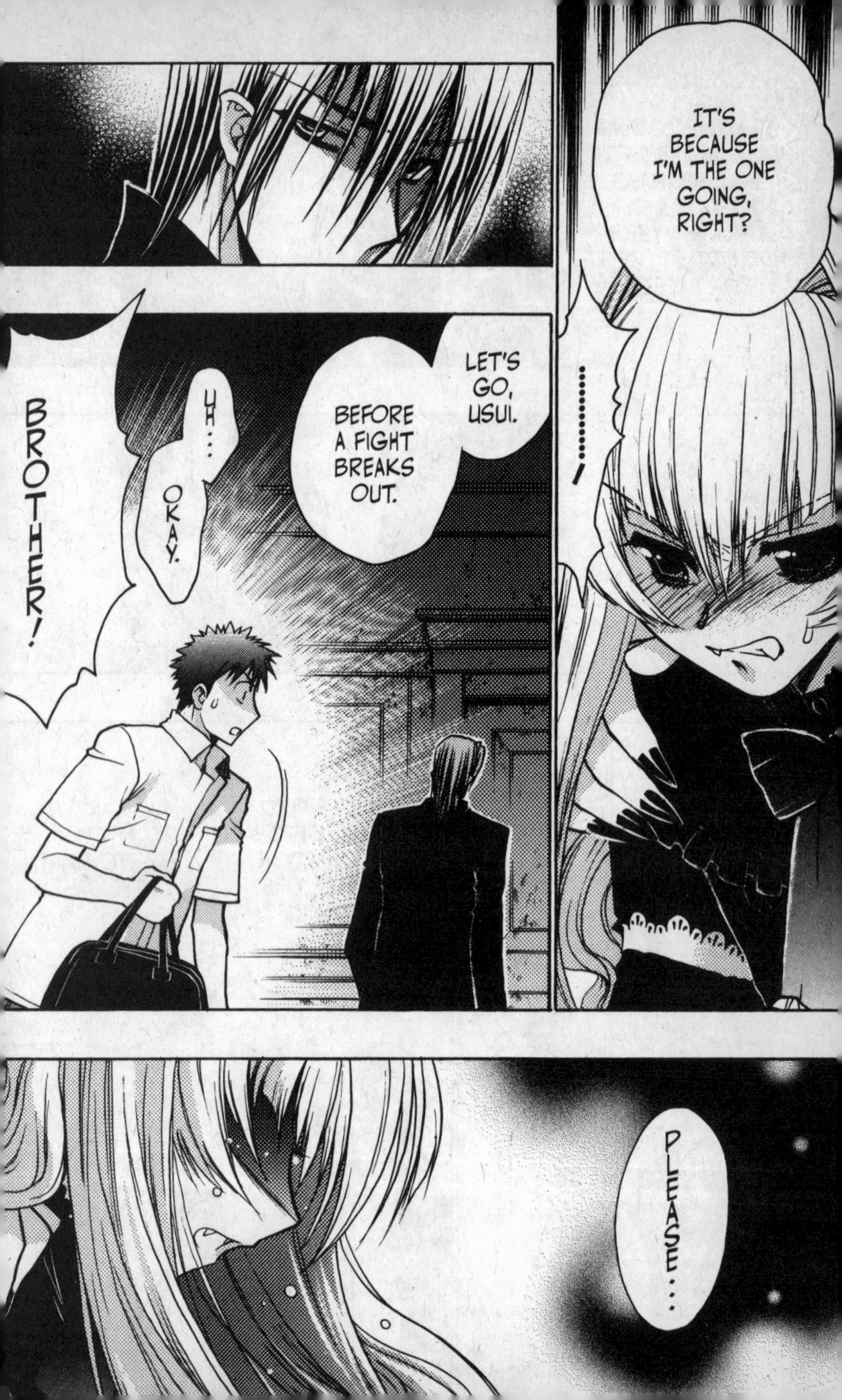
IT'S BECAUSE I'M THE ONE GOING, RIGHT?
......!
LET'S GO, USUI.
BEFORE A FIGHT BREAKS OUT.
UH... OKAY.
BROTHER!
PLEASE...

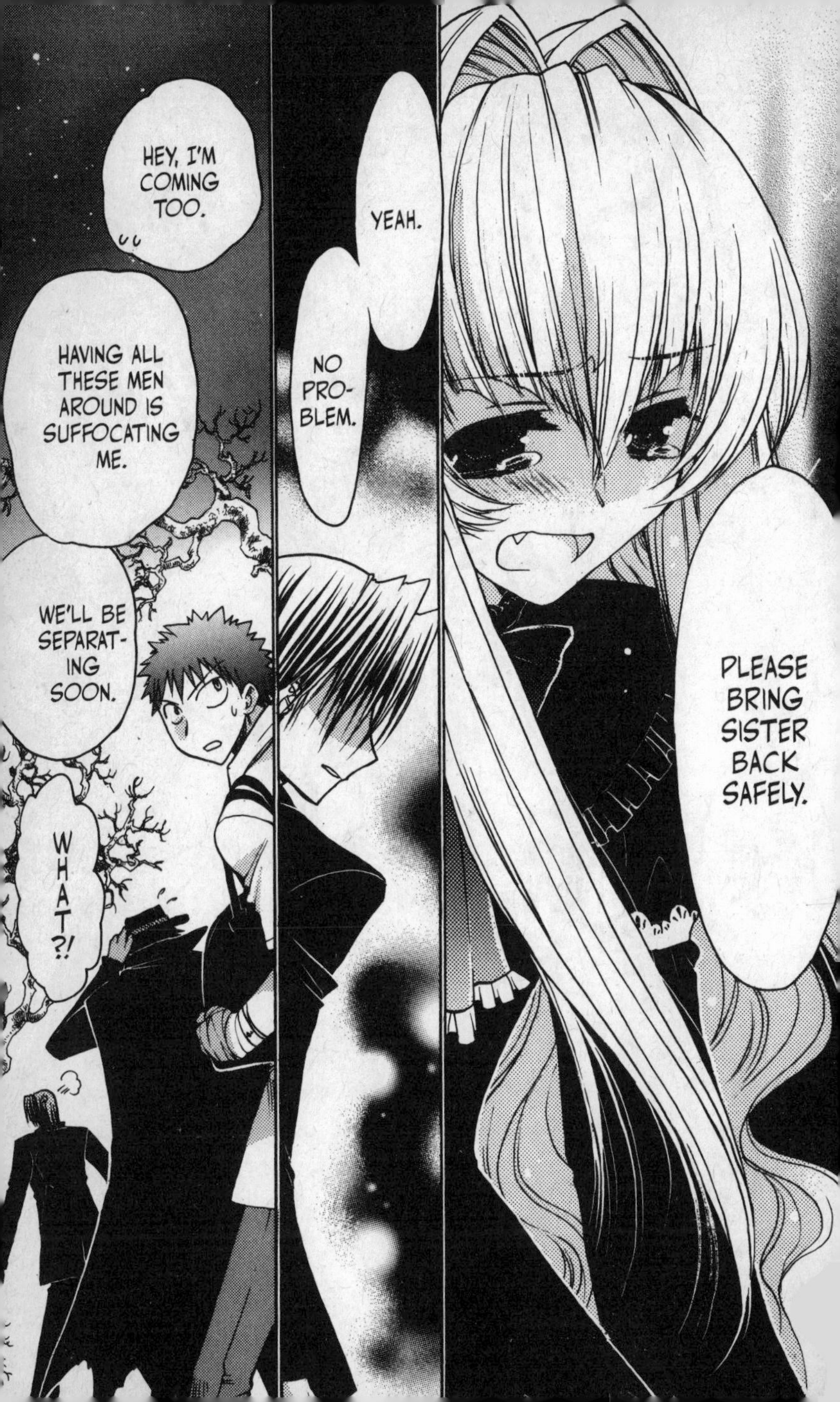
PLEASE BRING SISTER BACK SAFELY.
YEAH.
NO PRO- BLEM.
HEY, I'M COMING TOO.
HAVING ALL THESE MEN AROUND IS SUFFOCATING ME.
WE'LL BE SEPARAT- ING SOON.
WHAT?!

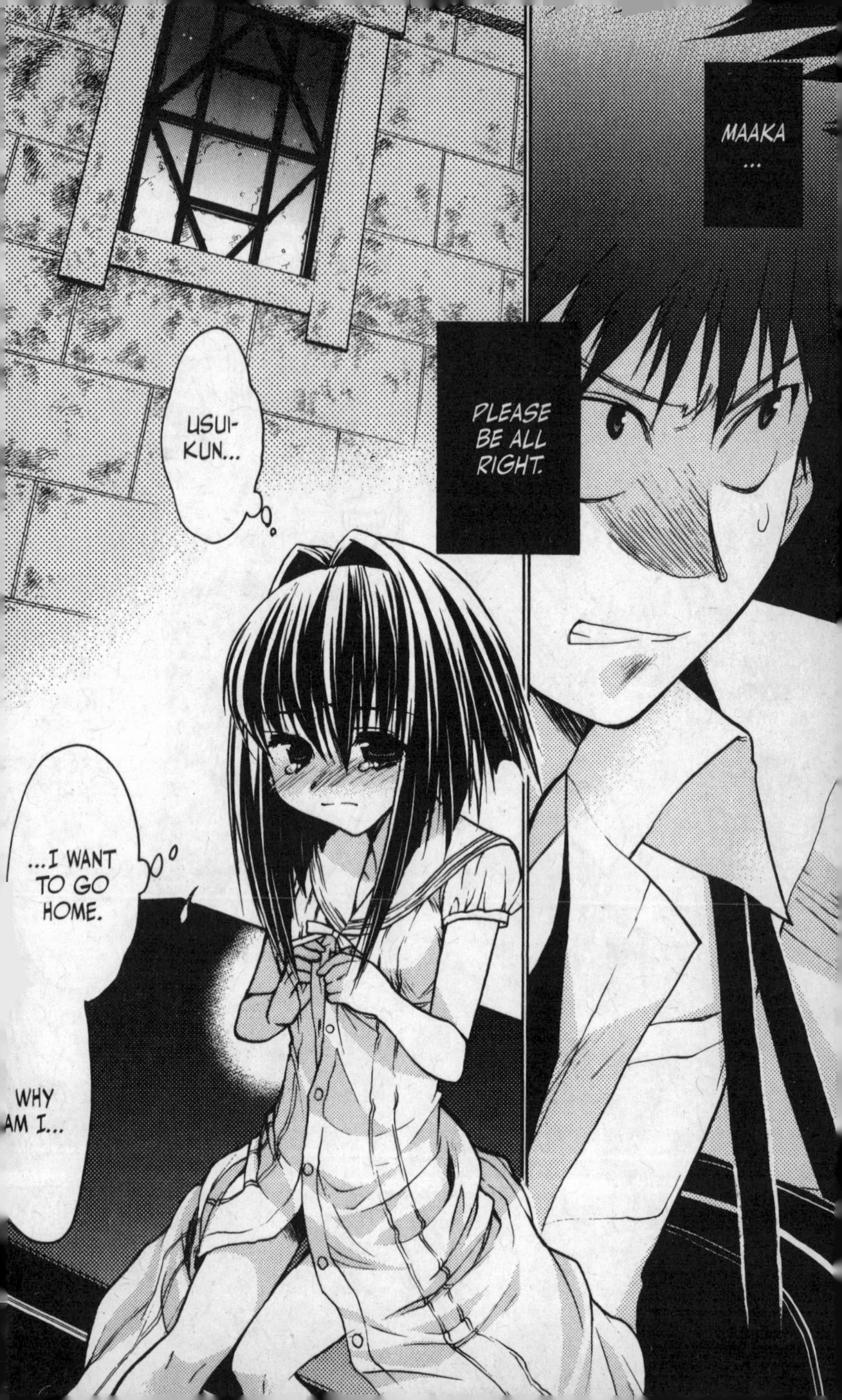
MAAKA ...
PLEASE BE ALL RIGHT.
USUI-KUN...
...I WANT TO GO HOME.
WHY AM I...

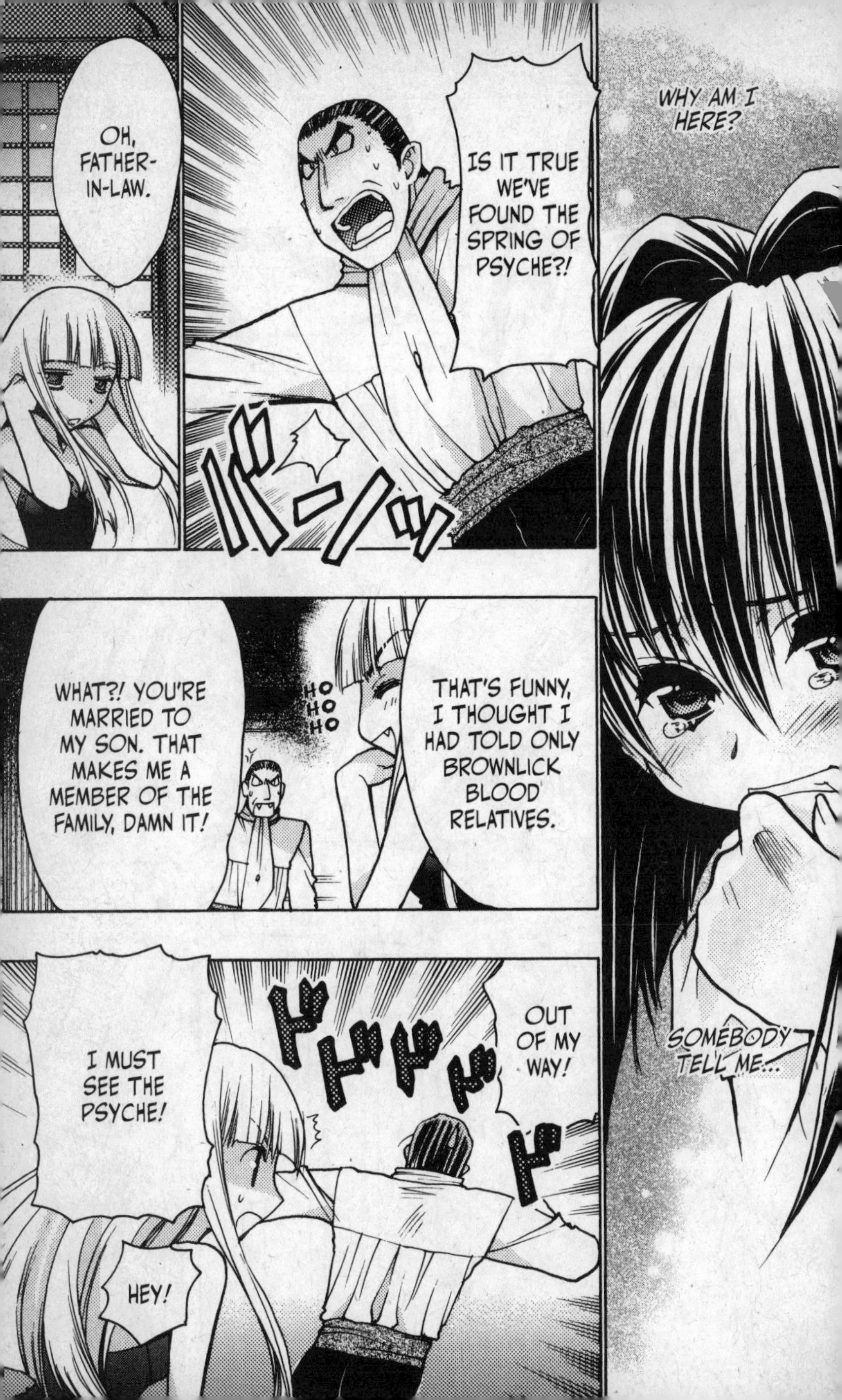
WHY AM I HERE?
SOMEBODY TELL ME...
IS IT TRUE WE'VE FOUND THE SPRING OF PSYCHE?!
OH, FATHER-IN-LAW.
THAT'S FUNNY, I THOUGHT I HAD TOLD ONLY BROWNLICK BLOOD RELATIVES.
HO HO HO
WHAT?! YOU'RE MARRIED TO MY SON. THAT MAKES ME A MEMBER OF THE FAMILY, DAMN IT!
OUT OF MY WAY!
I MUST SEE THE PSYCHE!
HEY!

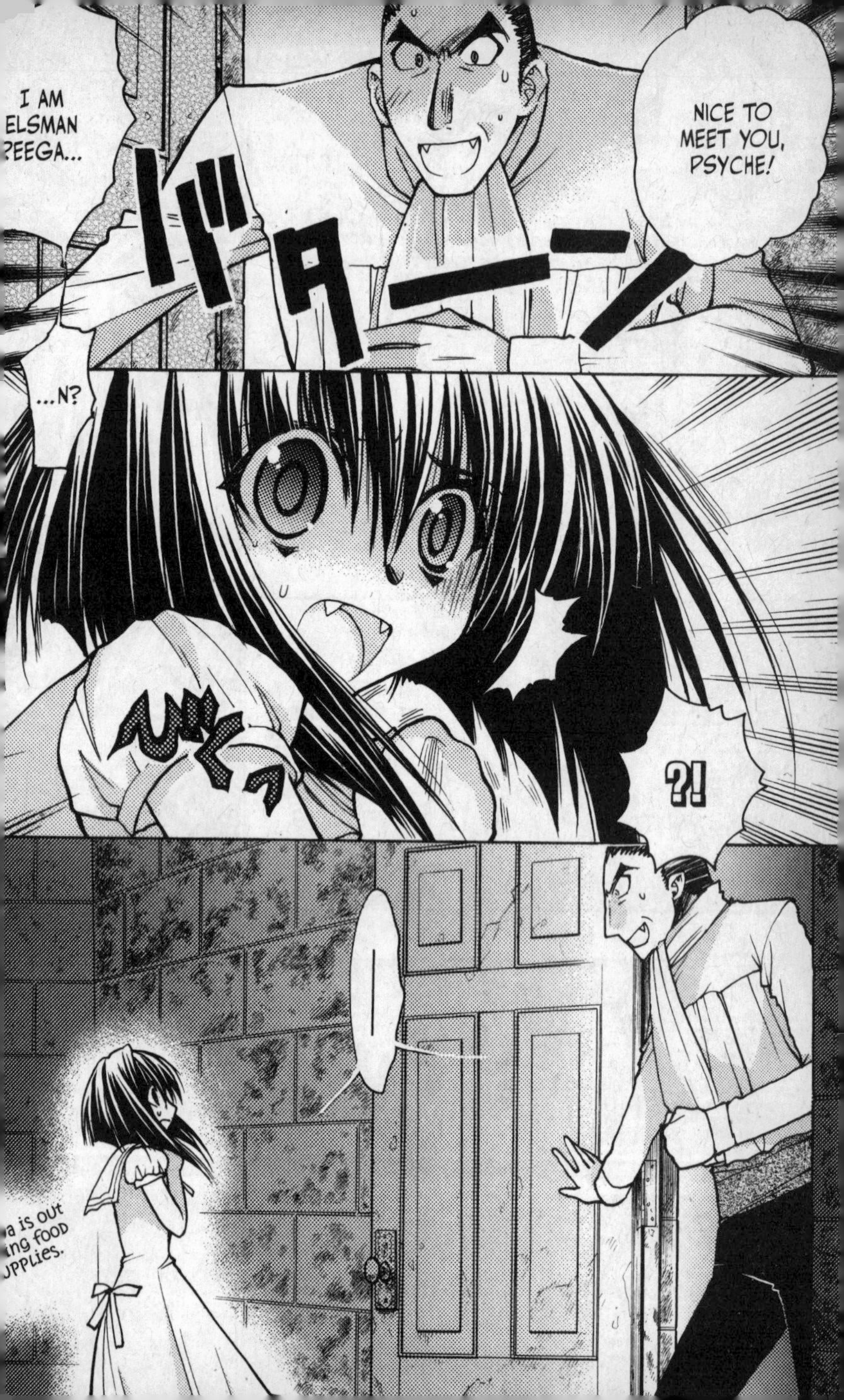
NICE TO MEET YOU, PSYCHE!
I AM ELSMAN PEEGA...
バタ——ン
?!
...N?
びくっ
a is out
ng food
UPPLIES.

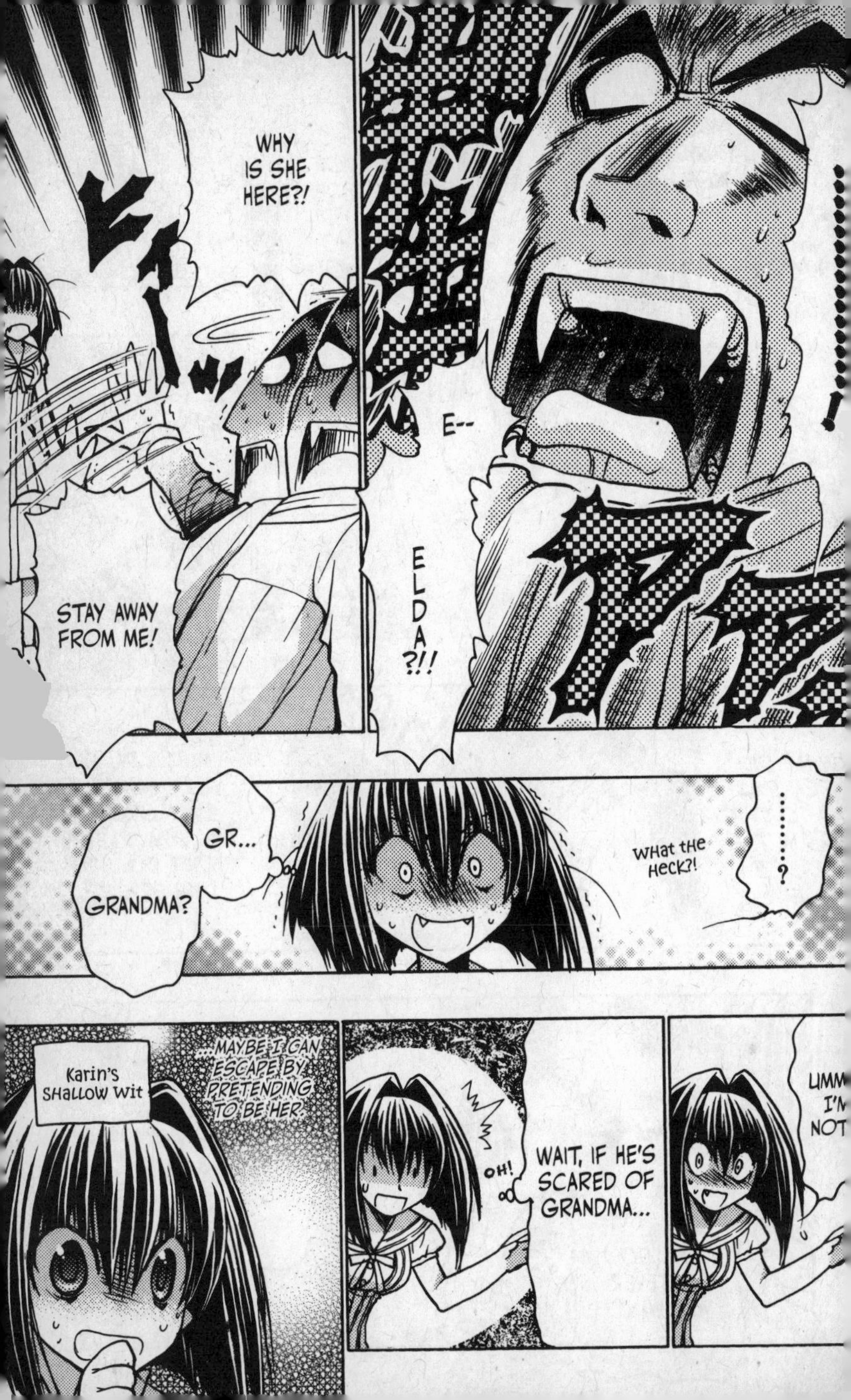
……!
E-- ELDA?!!
WHY IS SHE HERE?!
STAY AWAY FROM ME!
……?
WHAT THE HECK?!
GR... GRANDMA?
UMM I'M NOT
OH!
WAIT, IF HE'S SCARED OF GRANDMA...
...MAYBE I CAN ESCAPE BY PRETENDING TO BE HER.
Karin's SHALLOW Wit

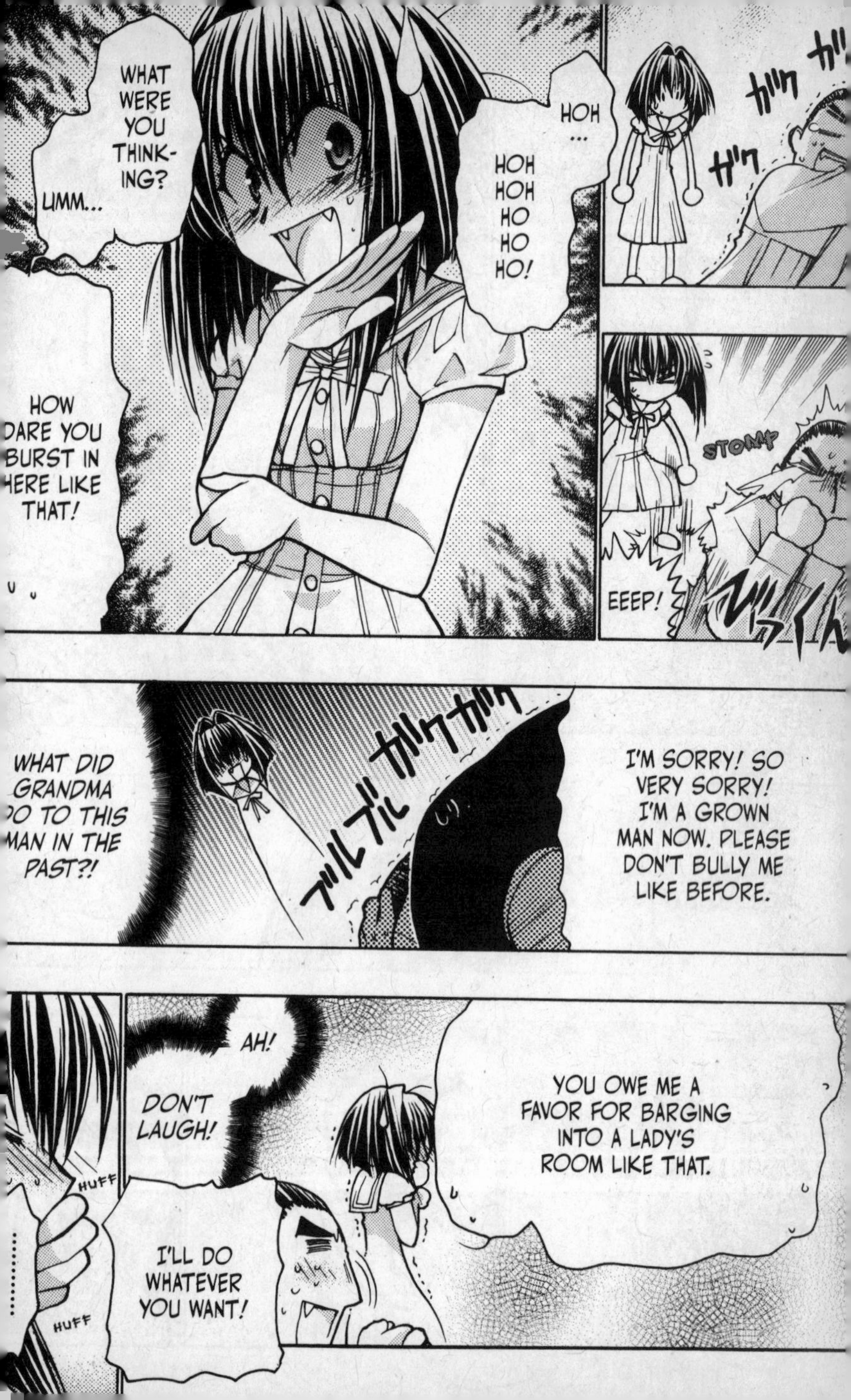

ガク ガク
ガク
STOMP
EEEP!
HOH ...
HOH HOH HO HO HO!
WHAT WERE YOU THINKING?
UMM...
HOW DARE YOU BURST IN HERE LIKE THAT!
I'M SORRY! SO VERY SORRY! I'M A GROWN MAN NOW. PLEASE DON'T BULLY ME LIKE BEFORE.
ガクガク
ブルブル
WHAT DID GRANDMA DO TO THIS MAN IN THE PAST?!
YOU OWE ME A FAVOR FOR BARGING INTO A LADY'S ROOM LIKE THAT.
AH!
DON'T LAUGH!
I'LL DO WHATEVER YOU WANT!
HUFF
HUFF

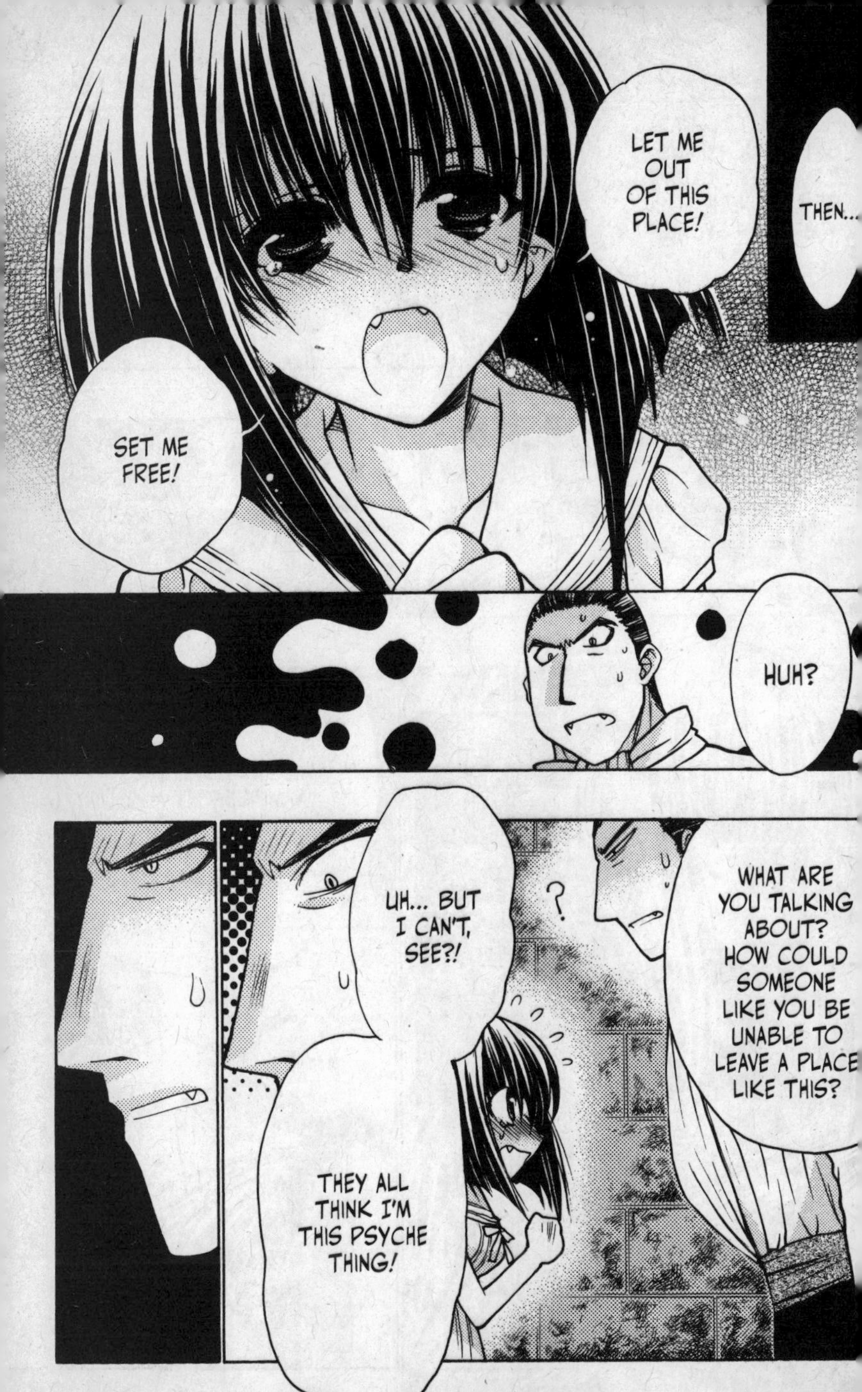
THEN...
LET ME OUT OF THIS PLACE!
SET ME FREE!
HUH?
WHAT ARE YOU TALKING ABOUT? HOW COULD SOMEONE LIKE YOU BE UNABLE TO LEAVE A PLACE LIKE THIS?
?
UH... BUT I CAN'T, SEE?!
THEY ALL THINK I'M THIS PSYCHE THING!

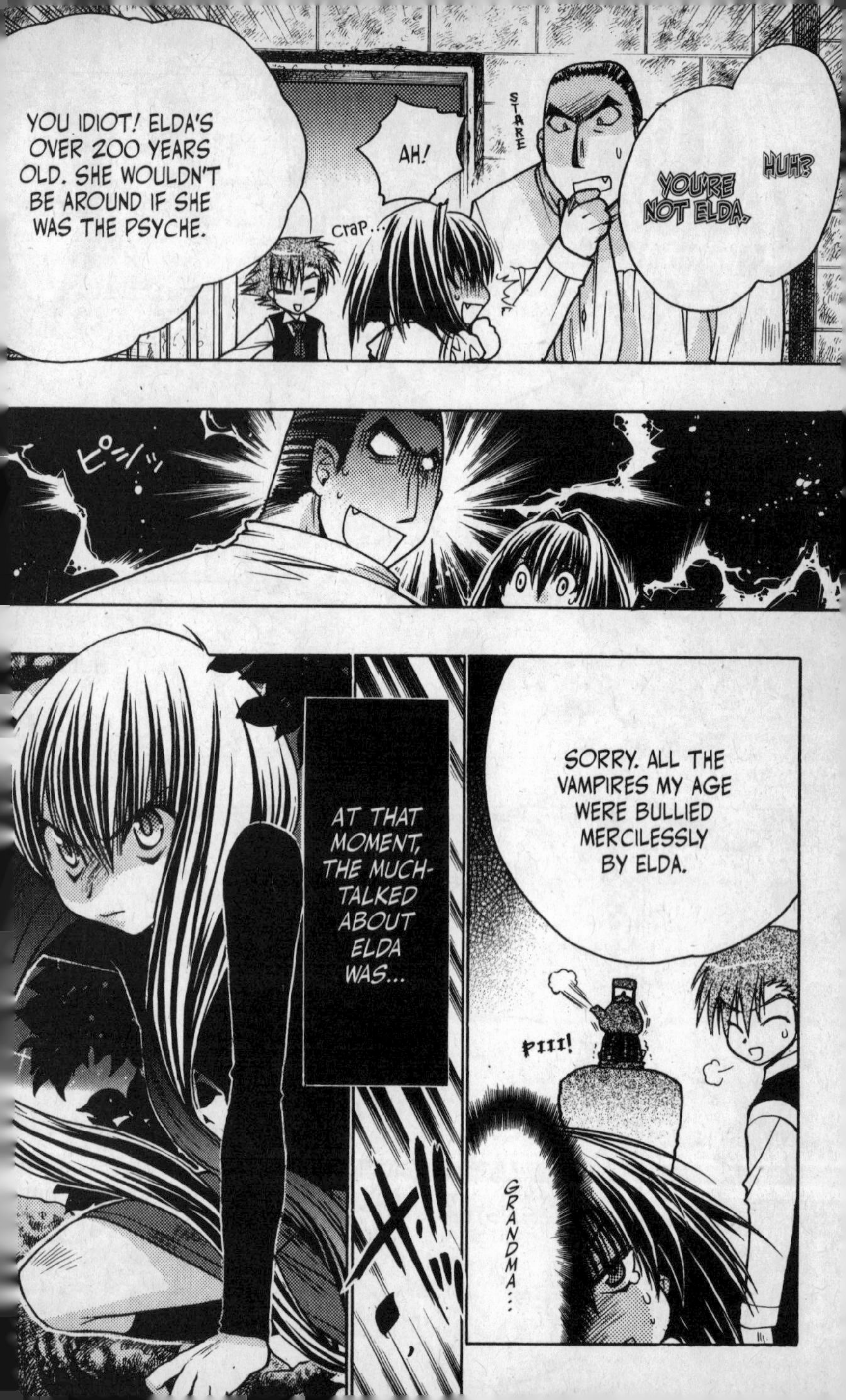
HUH?
YOU'RE NOT ELDA.
STARE
AH!
Crap...
YOU IDIOT! ELDA'S OVER 200 YEARS OLD. SHE WOULDN'T BE AROUND IF SHE WAS THE PSYCHE.
SORRY. ALL THE VAMPIRES MY AGE WERE BULLIED MERCILESSLY BY ELDA.
PIII!
GRANDMA...
AT THAT MOMENT, THE MUCH-TALKED ABOUT ELDA WAS...

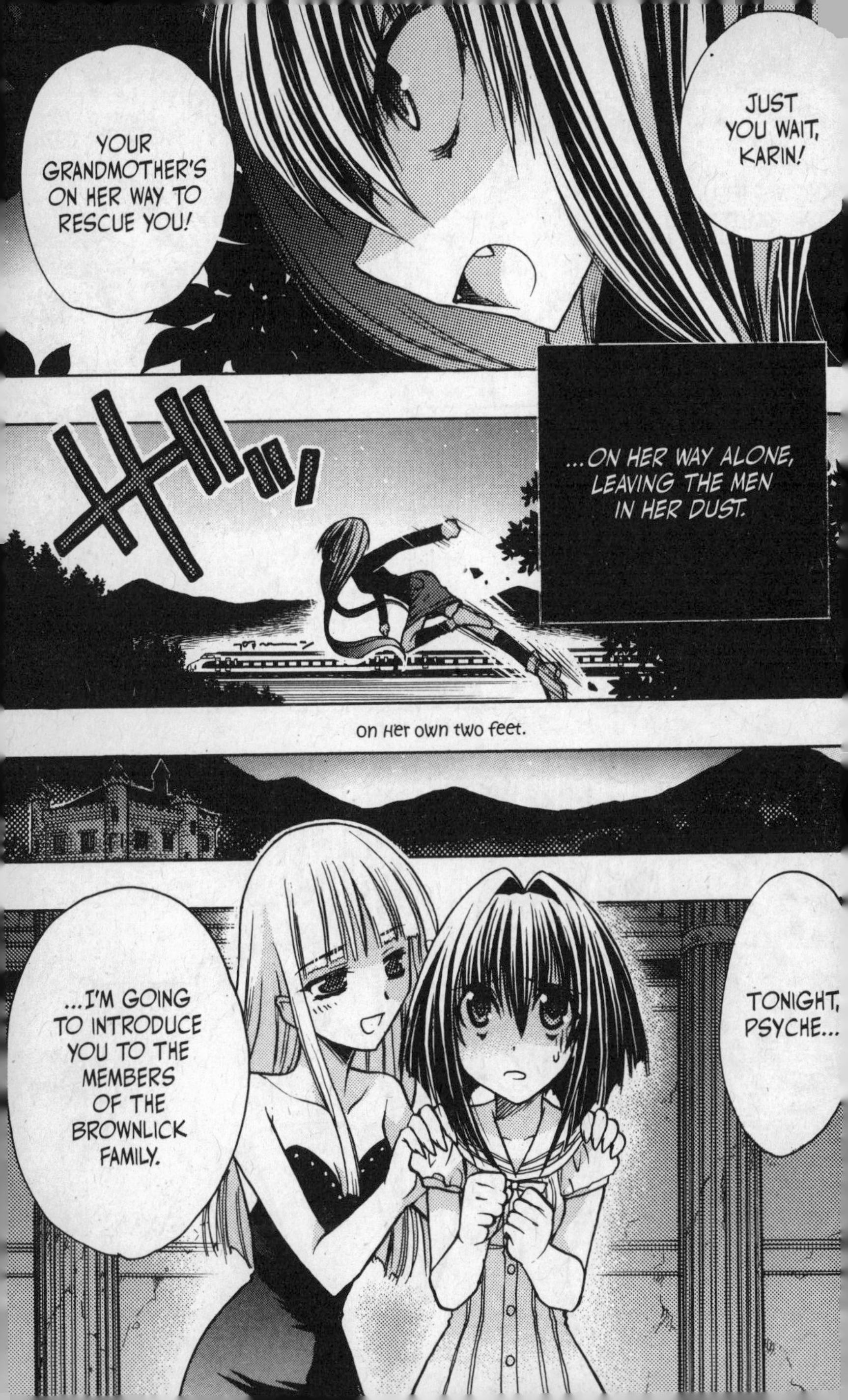
JUST YOU WAIT, KARIN!
YOUR GRANDMOTHER'S ON HER WAY TO RESCUE YOU!
...ON HER WAY ALONE, LEAVING THE MEN IN HER DUST.
on Her own two feet.
TONIGHT, PSYCHE...
...I'M GOING TO INTRODUCE YOU TO THE MEMBERS OF THE BROWNLICK FAMILY.

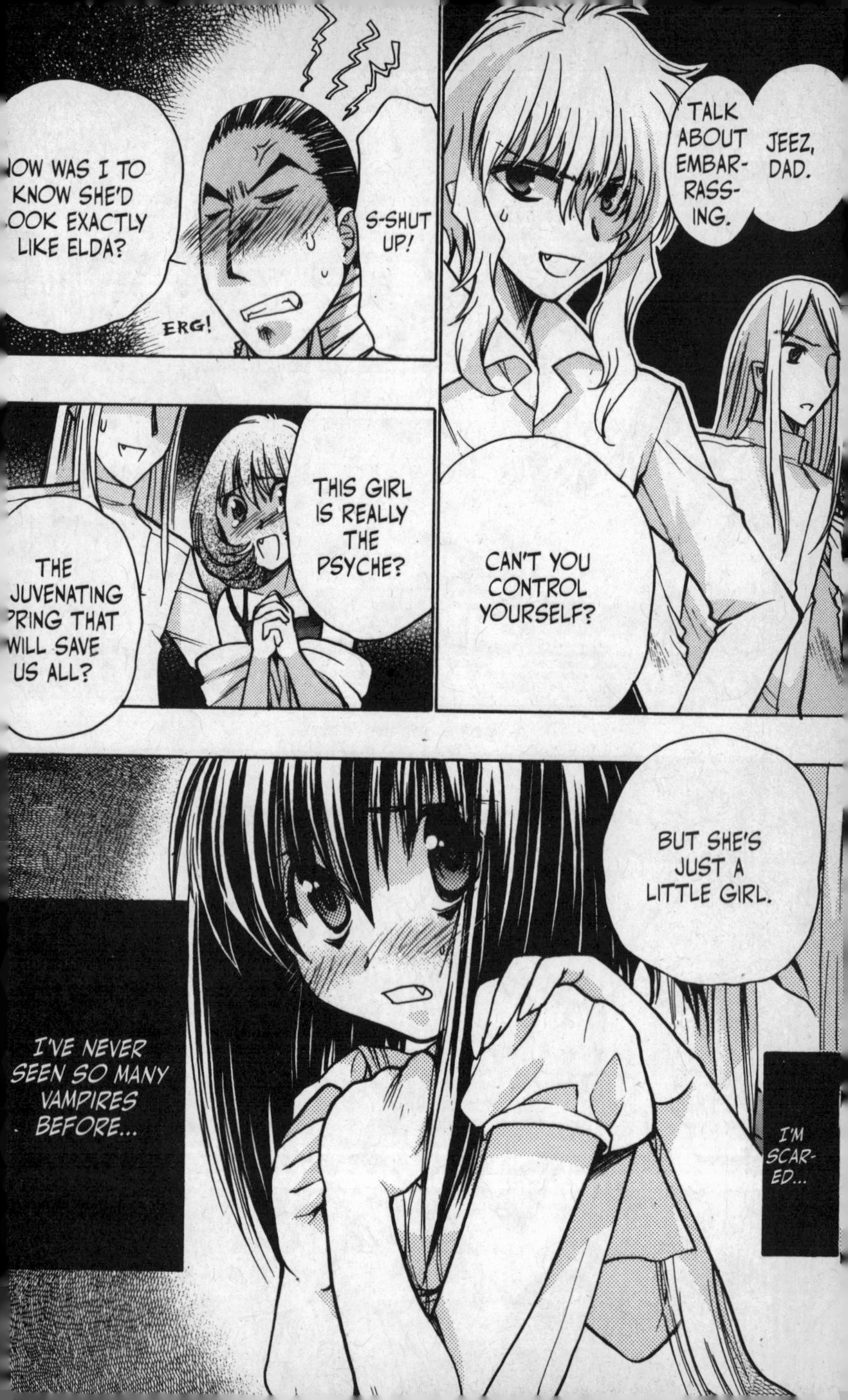
JEEZ, DAD.
TALK ABOUT EMBAR-RASS-ING.
CAN'T YOU CONTROL YOURSELF?
S-SHUT UP!
OW WAS I TO KNOW SHE'D OOK EXACTLY LIKE ELDA?
ERG!
THIS GIRL IS REALLY THE PSYCHE?
THE JUVENATING PRING THAT WILL SAVE US ALL?
BUT SHE'S JUST A LITTLE GIRL.
I'M SCAR-ED...
I'VE NEVER SEEN SO MANY VAMPIRES BEFORE...

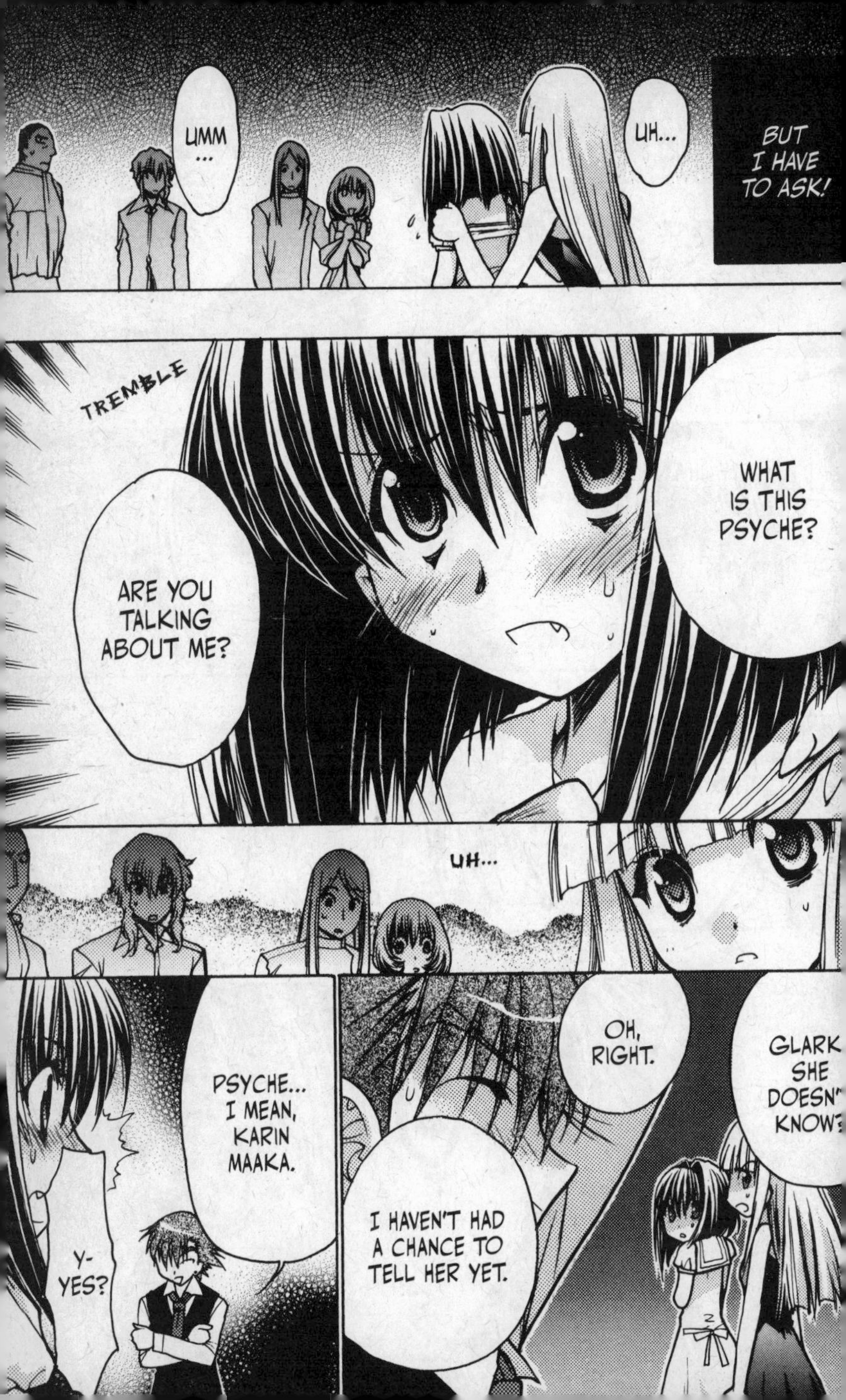
BUT I HAVE TO ASK!
UH...
UMM ...
WHAT IS THIS PSYCHE?
TREMBLE
ARE YOU TALKING ABOUT ME?
UH...
GLARK SHE DOESN' KNOW?
OH, RIGHT.
I HAVEN'T HAD A CHANCE TO TELL HER YET.
PSYCHE... I MEAN, KARIN MAAKA.
Y-YES?

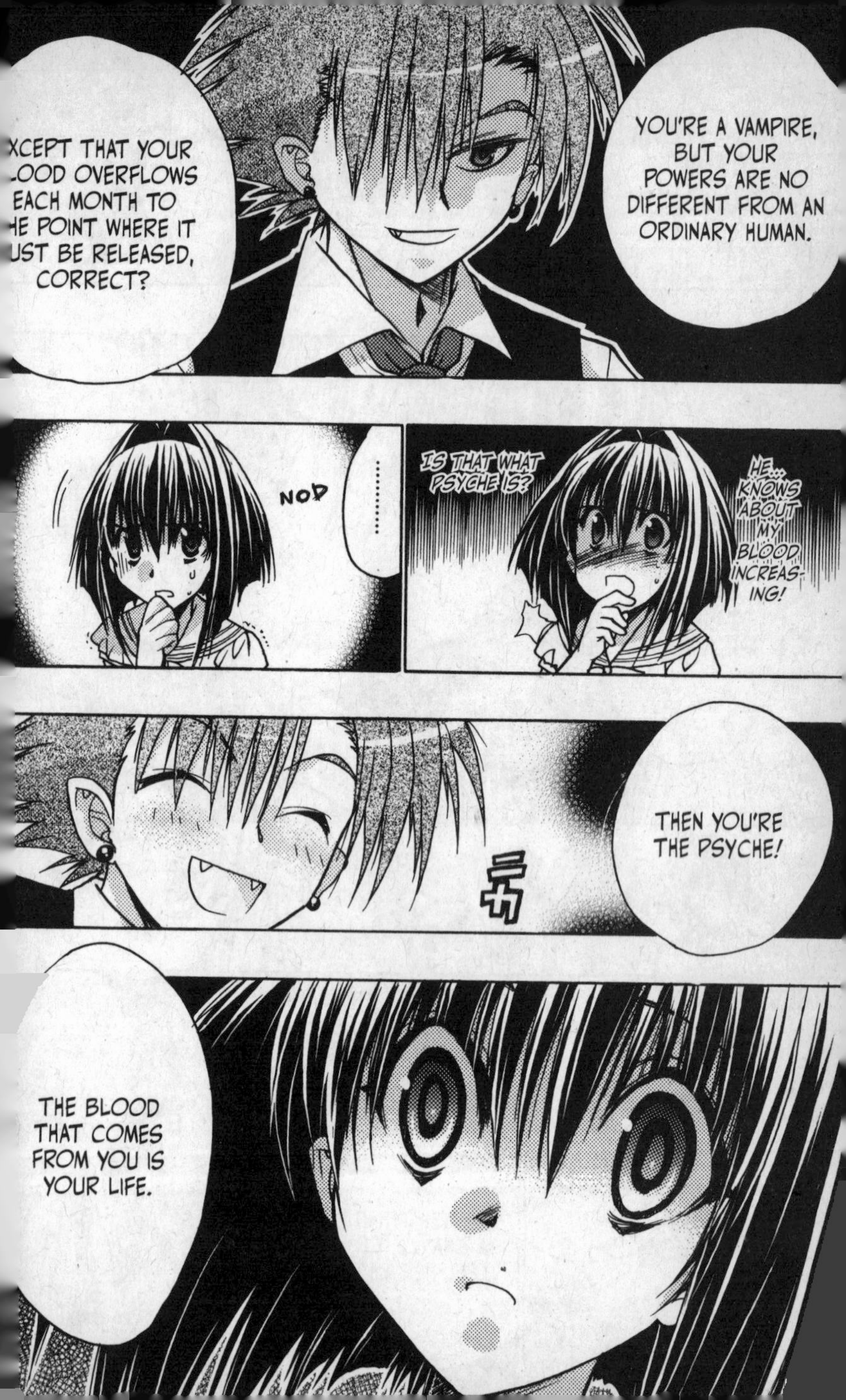
YOU'RE A VAMPIRE, BUT YOUR POWERS ARE NO DIFFERENT FROM AN ORDINARY HUMAN.
XCEPT THAT YOUR LOOD OVERFLOWS EACH MONTH TO HE POINT WHERE IT UST BE RELEASED, CORRECT?
IS THAT WHAT PSYCHE IS?
HE... KNOWS ABOUT MY BLOOD INCREASING!
......
NOD
THEN YOU'RE THE PSYCHE!
ニカ
THE BLOOD THAT COMES FROM YOU IS YOUR LIFE.

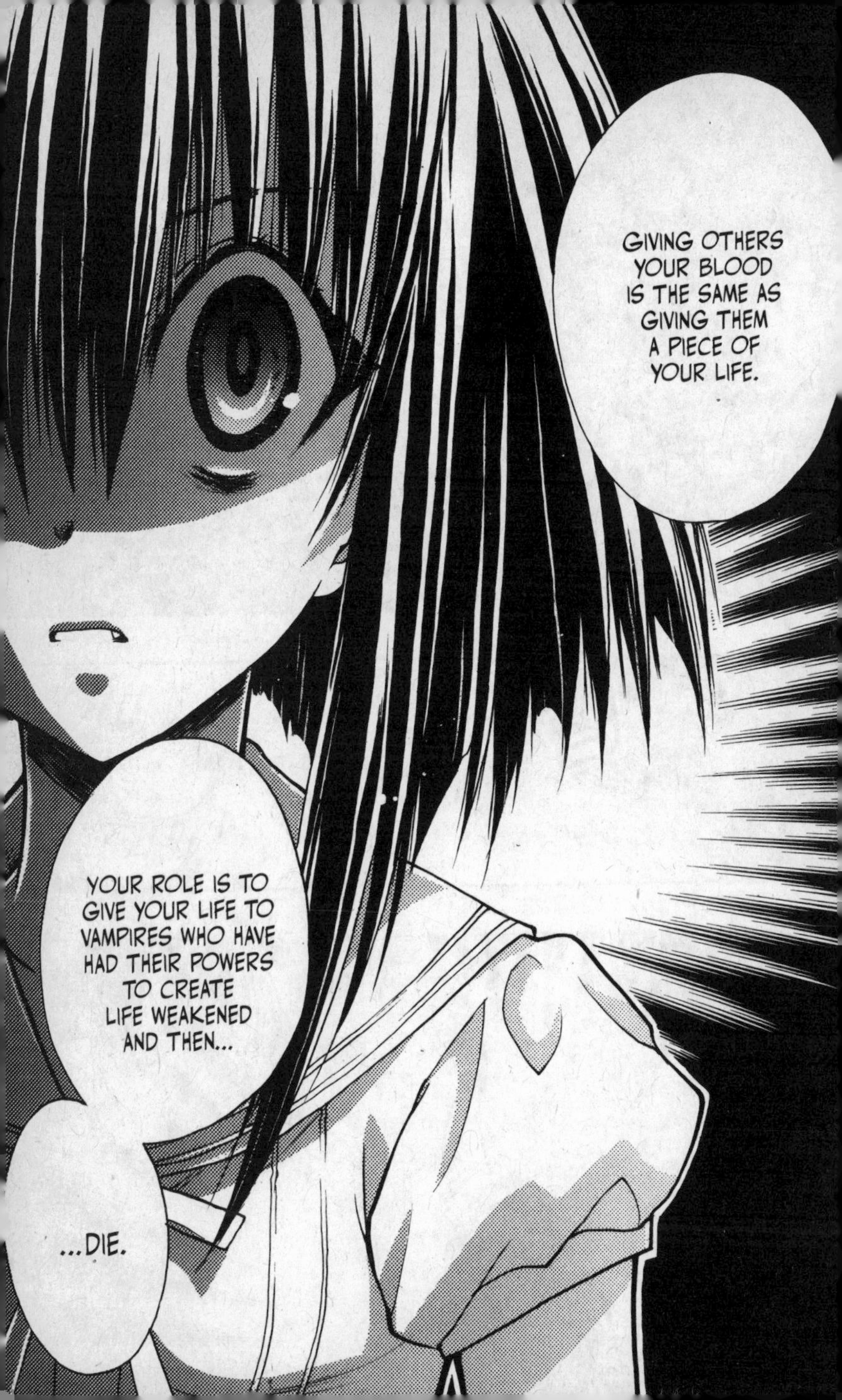
GIVING OTHERS YOUR BLOOD IS THE SAME AS GIVING THEM A PIECE OF YOUR LIFE.
YOUR ROLE IS TO GIVE YOUR LIFE TO VAMPIRES WHO HAVE HAD THEIR POWERS TO CREATE LIFE WEAKENED AND THEN...
...DIE.

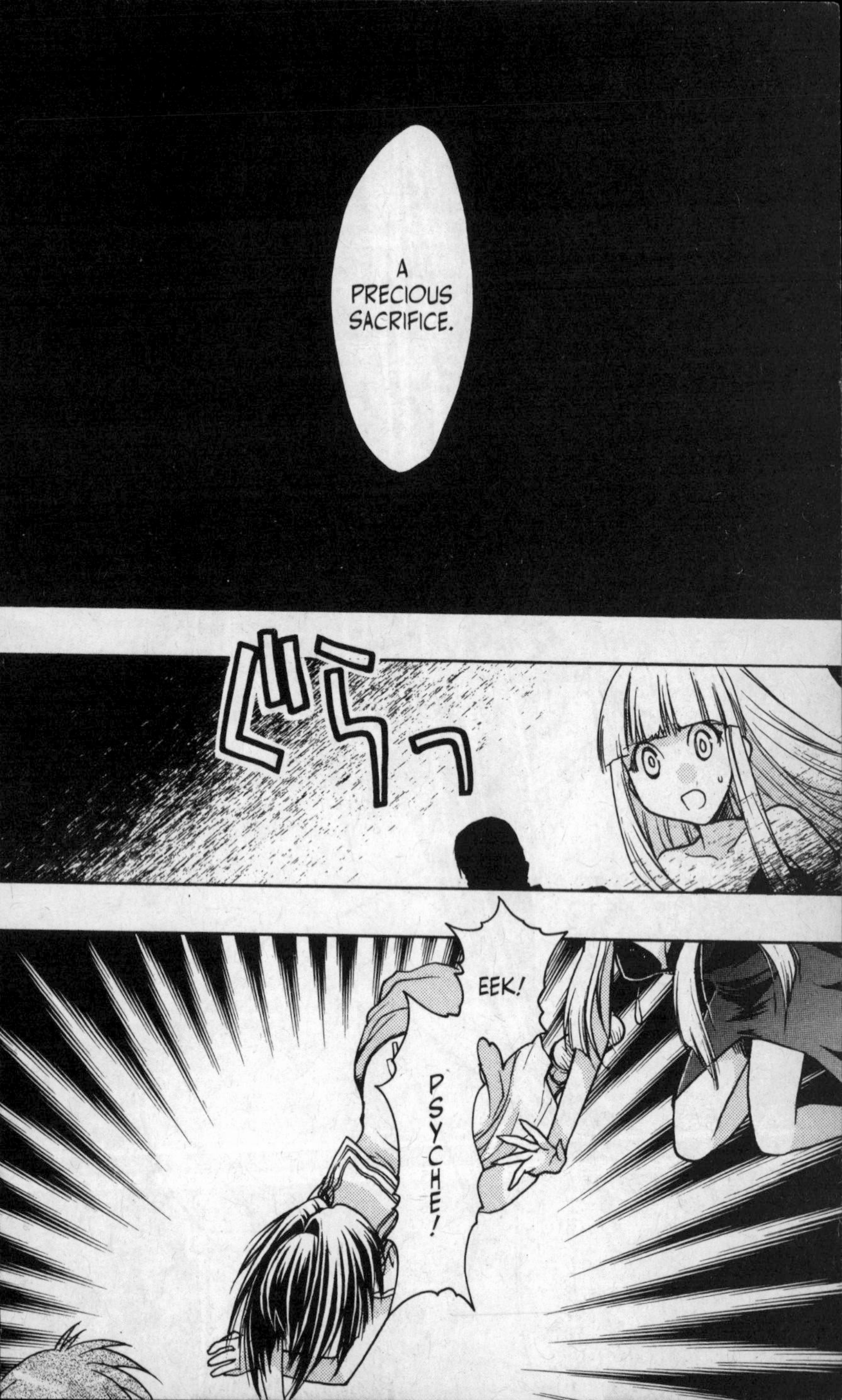
A PRECIOUS SACRIFICE.
ぐらっ
EEK!
PSYCHE!

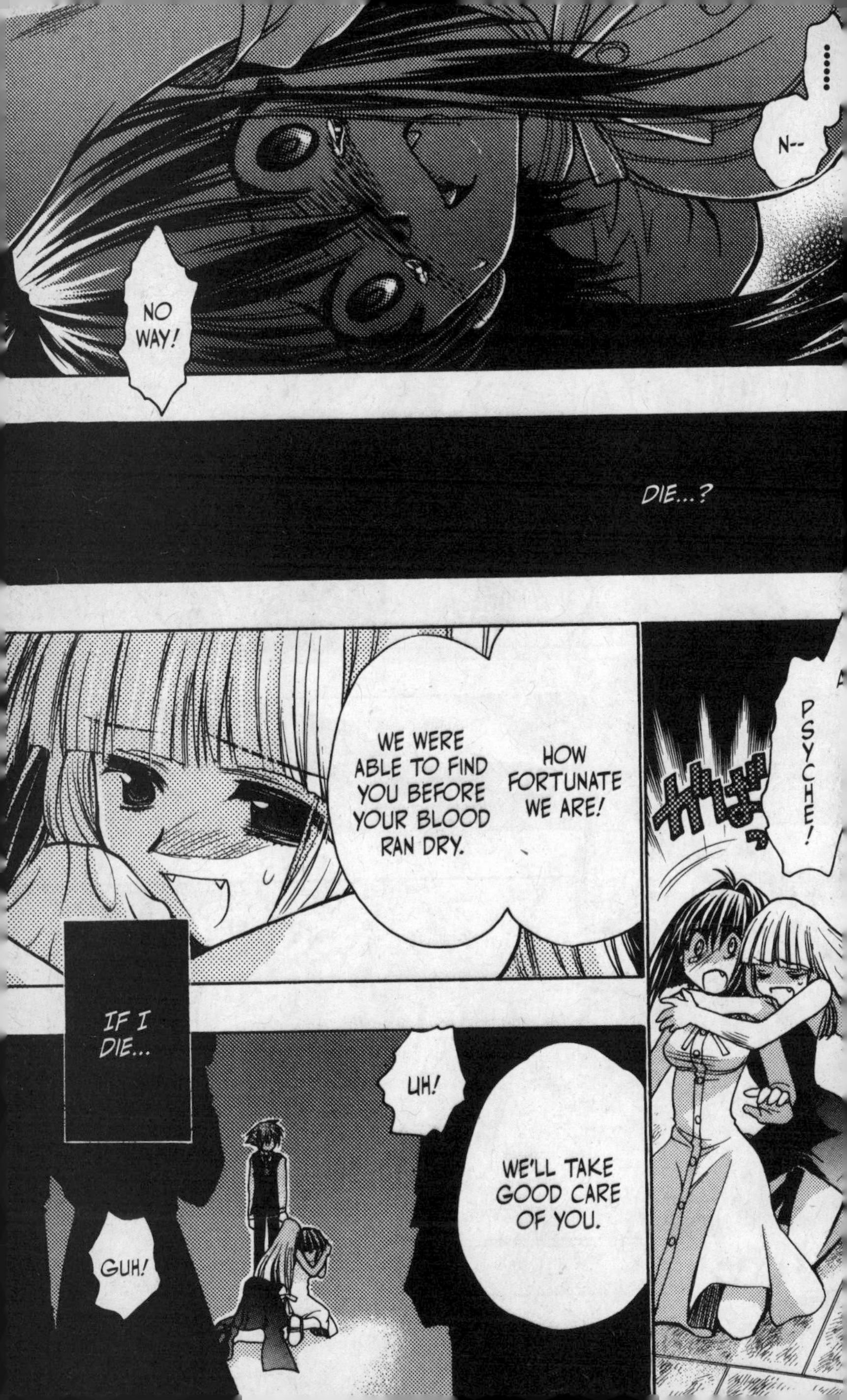
......
N--
NO WAY!
DIE...?
PSYCHE!
HOW FORTUNATE WE ARE!
WE WERE ABLE TO FIND YOU BEFORE YOUR BLOOD RAN DRY.
UH!
WE'LL TAKE GOOD CARE OF YOU.
IF I DIE...
GUH!

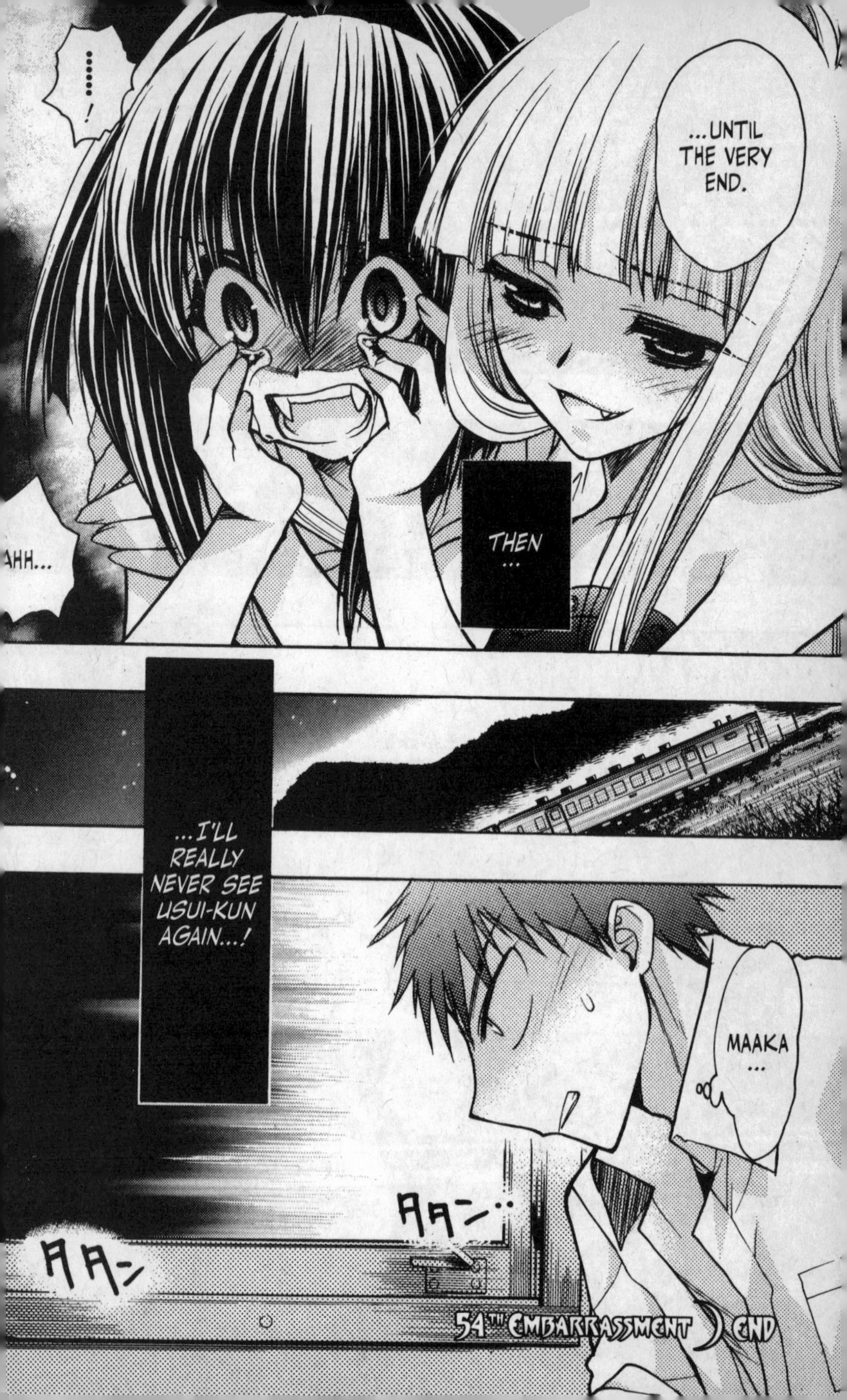
...UNTIL THE VERY END.
......!
THEN...
AHH...
...I'LL REALLY NEVER SEE USUI-KUN AGAIN...!
MAAKA...
タタン‥
タタン
54TH EMBARRASSMENT) END

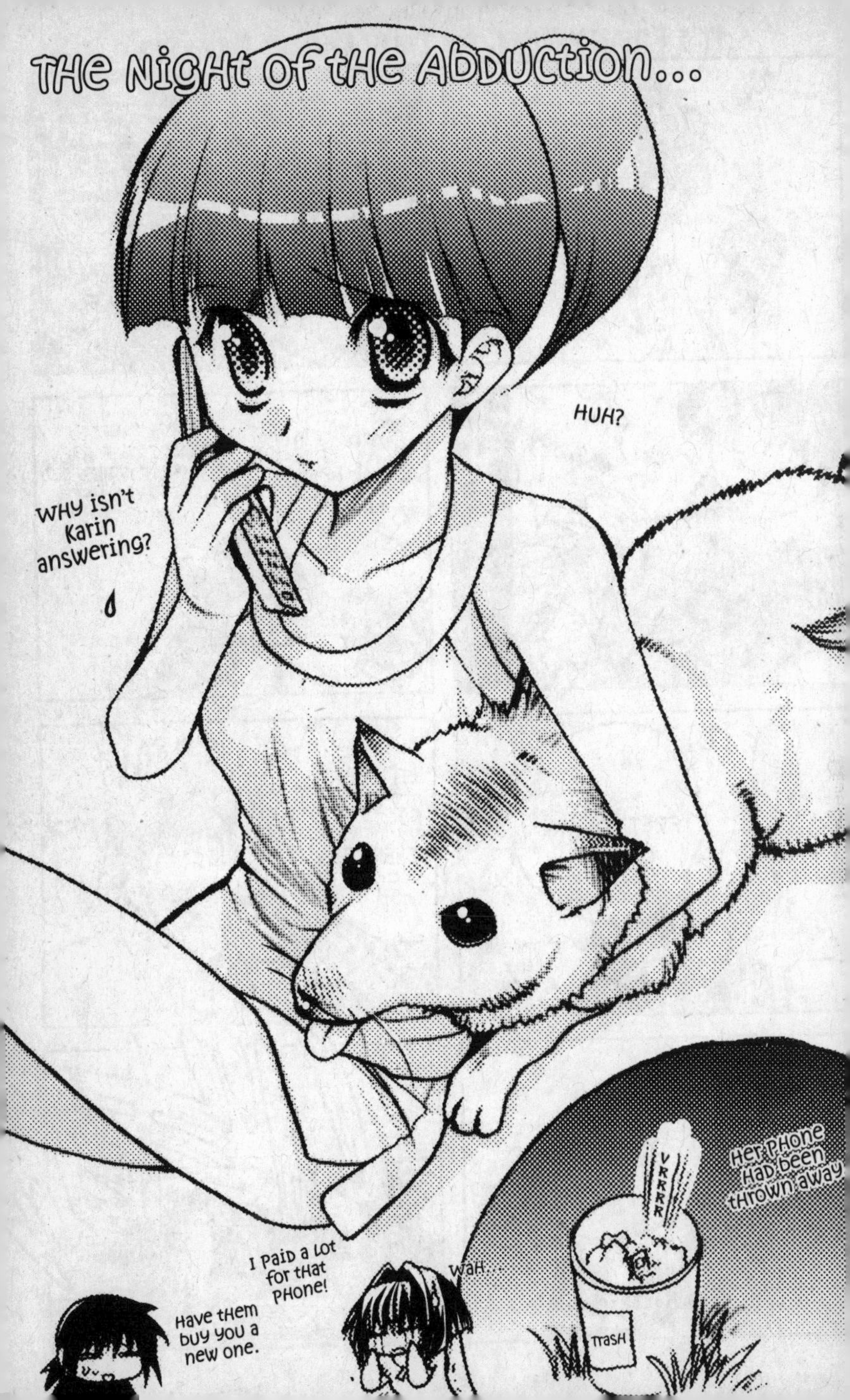
THE NIGHT OF THE ABDUCTION...
HUH?
WHY isn't Karin answering?
Her PHONE HAD been tHrown away
VRRRR
TRASH
WAH...
I PAID a Lot for tHat PHone!
Have tHem buy you a new one.

It's Finally Time to Talk About Breasts

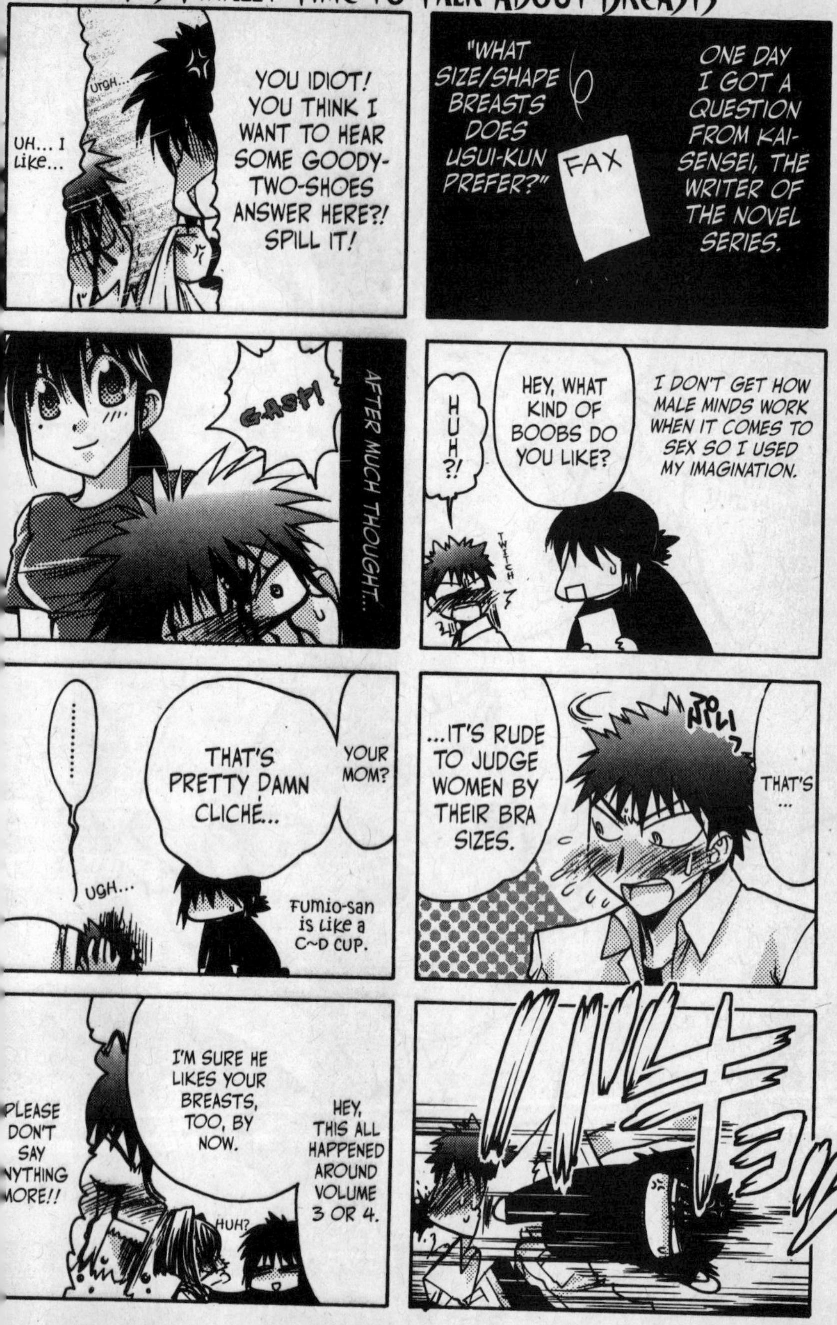

ONE DAY I GOT A QUESTION FROM KAI-SENSEI, THE WRITER OF THE NOVEL SERIES.
"WHAT SIZE/SHAPE BREASTS DOES USUI-KUN PREFER?"
FAX
YOU IDIOT! YOU THINK I WANT TO HEAR SOME GOODY-TWO-SHOES ANSWER HERE?! SPILL IT!
UTGH...
UH... I LIKE...
I DON'T GET HOW MALE MINDS WORK WHEN IT COMES TO SEX SO I USED MY IMAGINATION.
HEY, WHAT KIND OF BOOBS DO YOU LIKE?
HUH?!
TWITCH
AFTER MUCH THOUGHT...
GASP!
THAT'S ...
...IT'S RUDE TO JUDGE WOMEN BY THEIR BRA SIZES.
YOUR MOM?
THAT'S PRETTY DAMN CLICHÉ...
Fumio-san is like a C~D cup.
......
UGH...
HEY, THIS ALL HAPPENED AROUND VOLUME 3 OR 4.
I'M SURE HE LIKES YOUR BREASTS, TOO, BY NOW.
HUH?
PLEASE DON'T SAY NYTHING ORE!!

FREEDOM

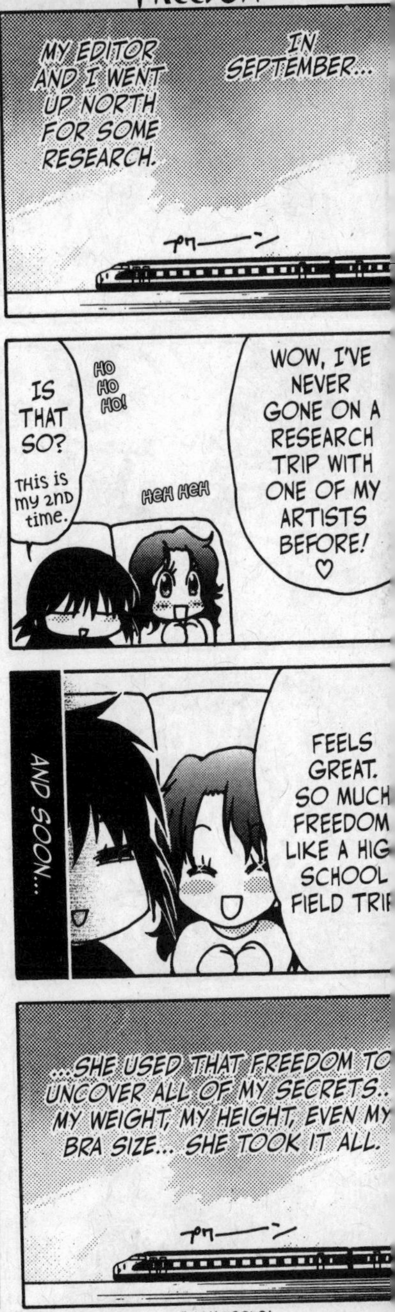
IN SEPTEMBER...
MY EDITOR AND I WENT UP NORTH FOR SOME RESEARCH.
WOW, I'VE NEVER GONE ON A RESEARCH TRIP WITH ONE OF MY ARTISTS BEFORE! ♡
HEH HEH
HO HO HO!
IS THAT SO?
THIS is my 2nd time.
FEELS GREAT. SO MUCH FREEDOM LIKE A HIG SCHOOL FIELD TRIP
AND SOON...
...SHE USED THAT FREEDOM TO UNCOVER ALL OF MY SECRETS.. MY WEIGHT, MY HEIGHT, EVEN MY BRA SIZE... SHE TOOK IT ALL.

SUCH regret...

PEEKING

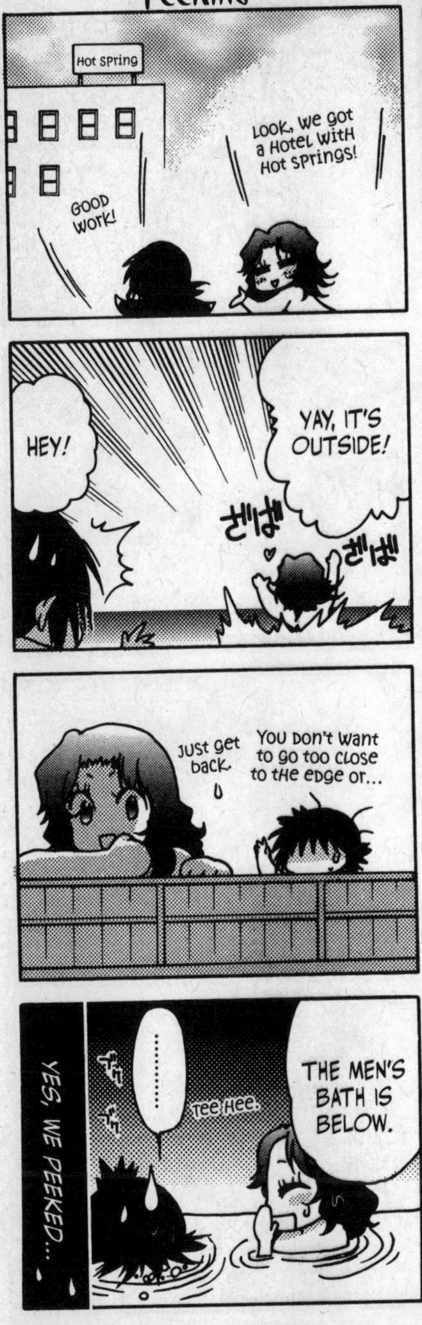
LOOK, We got a Hotel With Hot Springs!
Hot Spring
GOOD WORK!
YAY, IT'S OUTSIDE!
ざば
ざば
HEY!
YOU Don't Want to go too close to the edge or...
Just get back.
THE MEN'S BATH IS BELOW.
Tee Hee.
......
YES, WE PEEKED...

A ROTTEN NIGHT

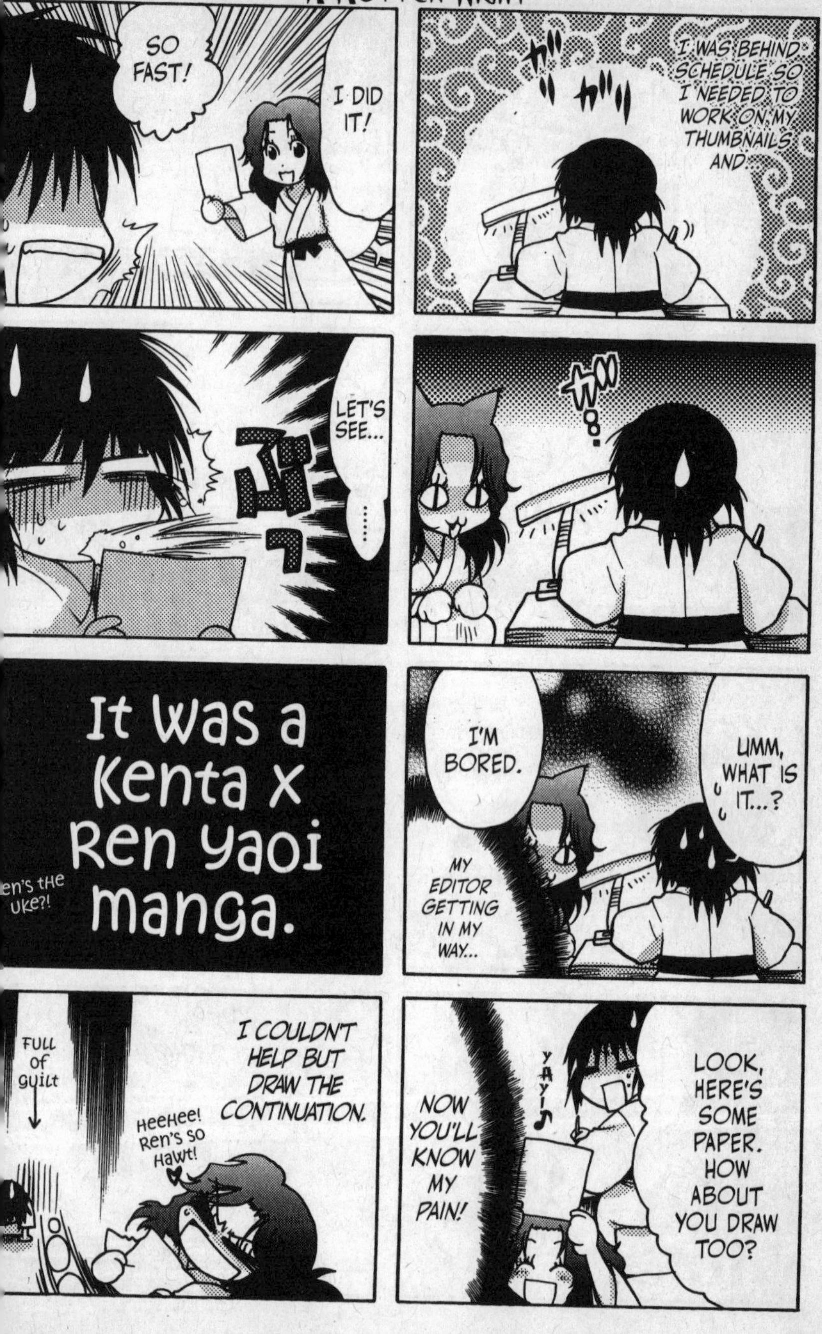
I WAS BEHIND SCHEDULE SO I NEEDED TO WORK ON MY THUMBNAILS AND...
I DID IT!
SO FAST!
LET'S SEE...
......
UMM, WHAT IS IT...?
I'M BORED.
MY EDITOR GETTING IN MY WAY...
It Was a Kenta x Ren yaoi manga.
en's tHE uKE?!
LOOK, HERE'S SOME PAPER. HOW ABOUT YOU DRAW TOO?
YAY!♪
NOW YOU'LL KNOW MY PAIN!
I COULDN'T HELP BUT DRAW THE CONTINUATION.
HeeHee! Ren's so Hawt!
FULL of guilt

RECORD RAINS IN THE NORTH

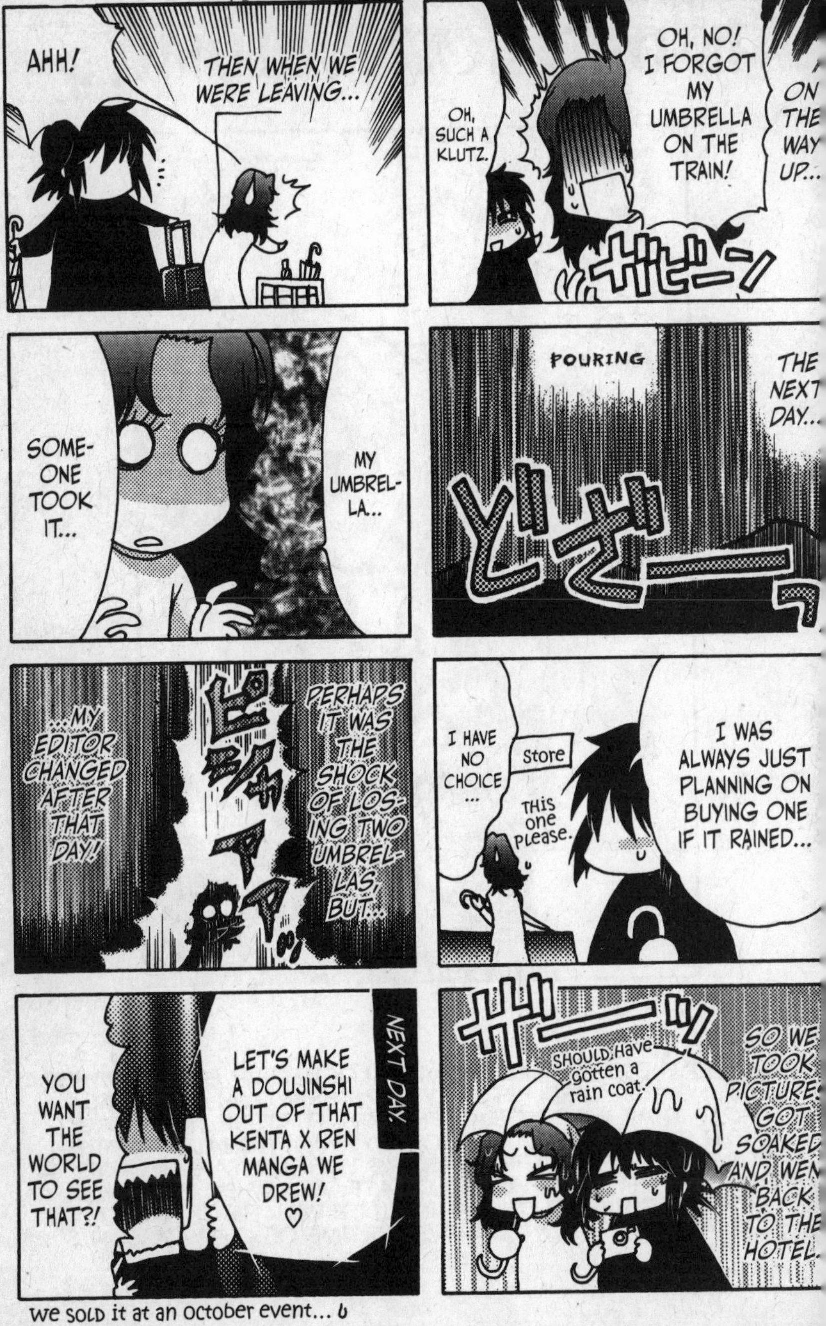

ON THE WAY UP...
OH, NO! I FORGOT MY UMBRELLA ON THE TRAIN!
OH, SUCH A KLUTZ.
THE NEXT DAY...
POURING
どざーーっ
I WAS ALWAYS JUST PLANNING ON BUYING ONE IF IT RAINED...
Store
I HAVE NO CHOICE ...
THIS one PLease.
SO WE TOOK PICTURE GOT SOAKED AND WEN BACK TO THE HOTEL.
ザーーッ
SHOULD Have gotten a rain coat.
THEN WHEN WE WERE LEAVING...
AHH!
MY UMBREL-LA...
SOME-ONE TOOK IT...
PERHAPS IT WAS THE SHOCK OF LOS-ING TWO UMBREL-LAS, BUT...
...MY EDITOR CHANGED AFTER THAT DAY!
NEXT DAY.
LET'S MAKE A DOUJINSHI OUT OF THAT KENTA X REN MANGA WE DREW! ♡
YOU WANT THE WORLD TO SEE THAT?!

we sold it at an october event... ↄ

IN OUR NEXT VOLUME...

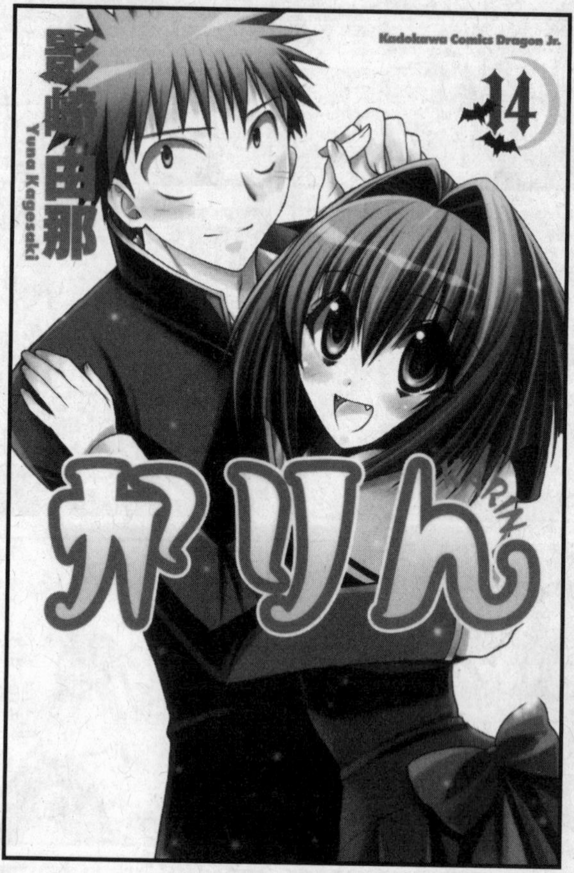

影崎由那
Yuna Kageasaki
Kadokawa Comics Dragon Jr.
14
かりん
KARIN

KARIN HAS BEEN ABDUCTED AND LOCKED UP BY VAMPIRES WILLING TO BLEED HER DRY FOR THEIR OWN SURVIVAL. AND IF THAT WASN'T BAD ENOUGH, FURTHER HORRORS ARE IN STORE FOR OUR POOR DYSFUNCTIONAL VAMPIRE. IT WILL BE UP TO THE MARKERS WITH KENTA'S HELP TO RESCUE HER FROM HER SAD FATE. AND WHEN THE FINAL TWIST IS REVEALED, KARIN'S LIFE WILL BE CHANGED FOREVER IN THE CONCLUDING VOLUME OF *CHIBI VAMPIRE!*

BARE SKIN

WHY DID YOU BITE HER BREAST?!
Sexual Harassment!
OH, SHUSH.
I WANTED THE BITE MARKS HIDDEN.
SO THEN...
YOU'D RATHER I BITE HER THIGHS OR ARMPIT?
ERR... NOT REALLY...
That's worse...
HOW ABOUT HER STO-MACH?
OH...
THAT WOULD BE NICE...
WELL, WHAT'S CLEAR IS THAT YOU'RE AN OLD PERVERT...
SHOW SOME CLASS, OLD MAN!

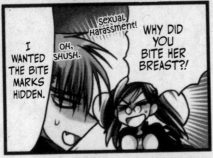

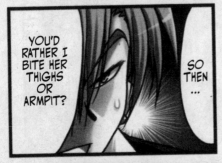

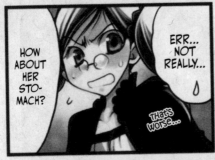

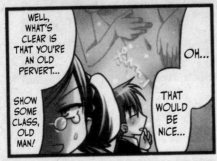

TOKYOPOP MANGA PREVIEW

FUTURE DIARY

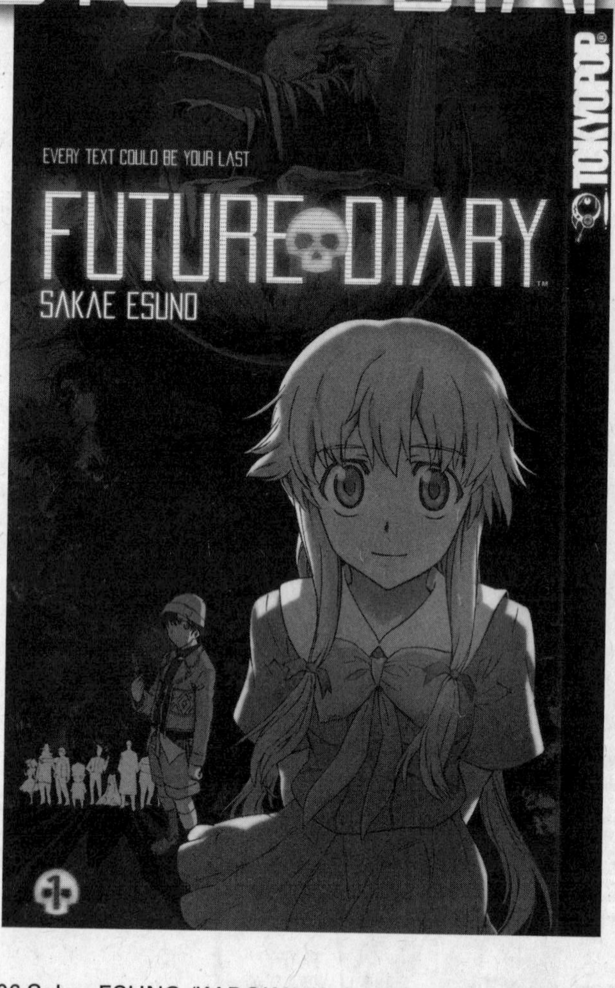
EVERY TEXT COULD BE YOUR LAST
FUTURE DIARY™
SAKAE ESUNO
TOKYOPOP
1

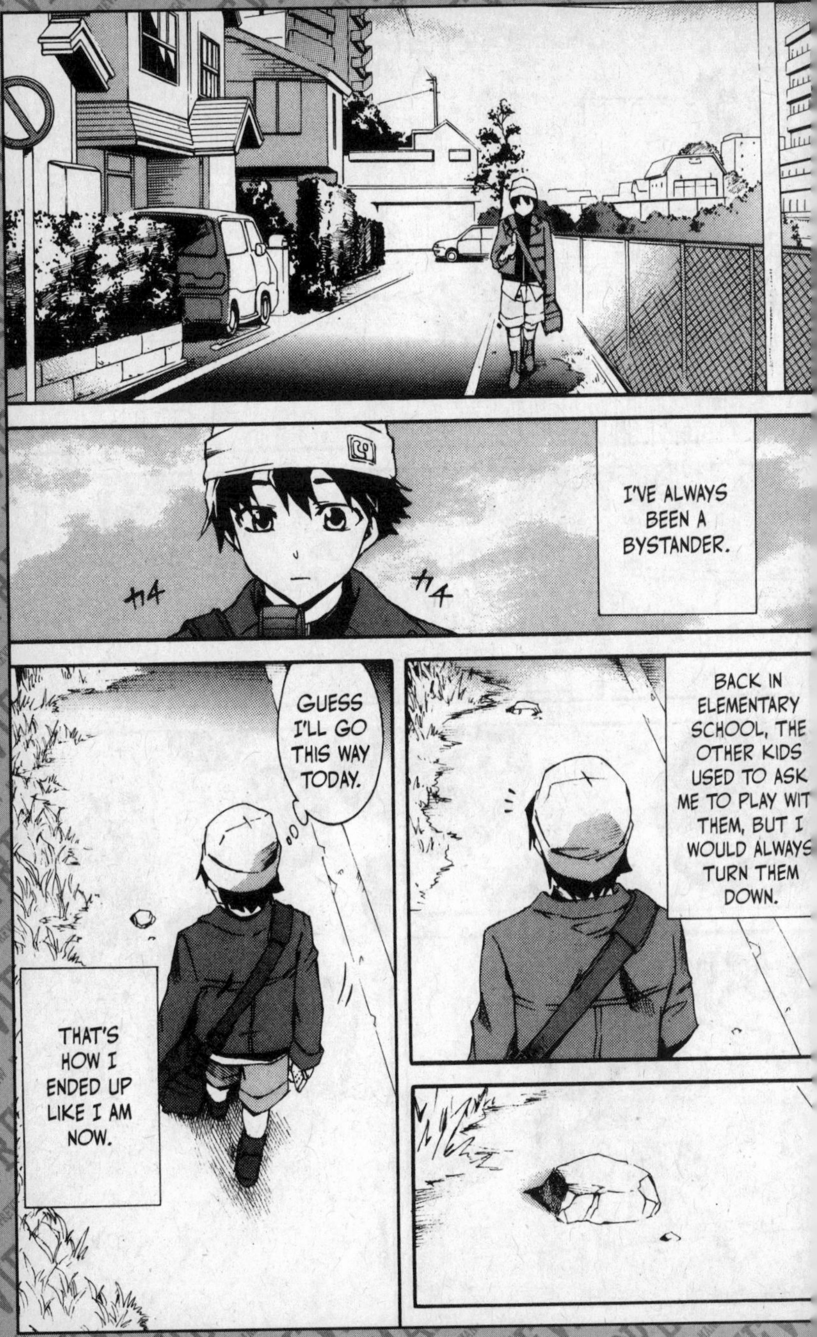
I'VE ALWAYS BEEN A BYSTANDER.
BACK IN ELEMENTARY SCHOOL, THE OTHER KIDS USED TO ASK ME TO PLAY WIT THEM, BUT I WOULD ALWAYS TURN THEM DOWN.
GUESS I'LL GO THIS WAY TODAY.
THAT'S HOW I ENDED UP LIKE I AM NOW.

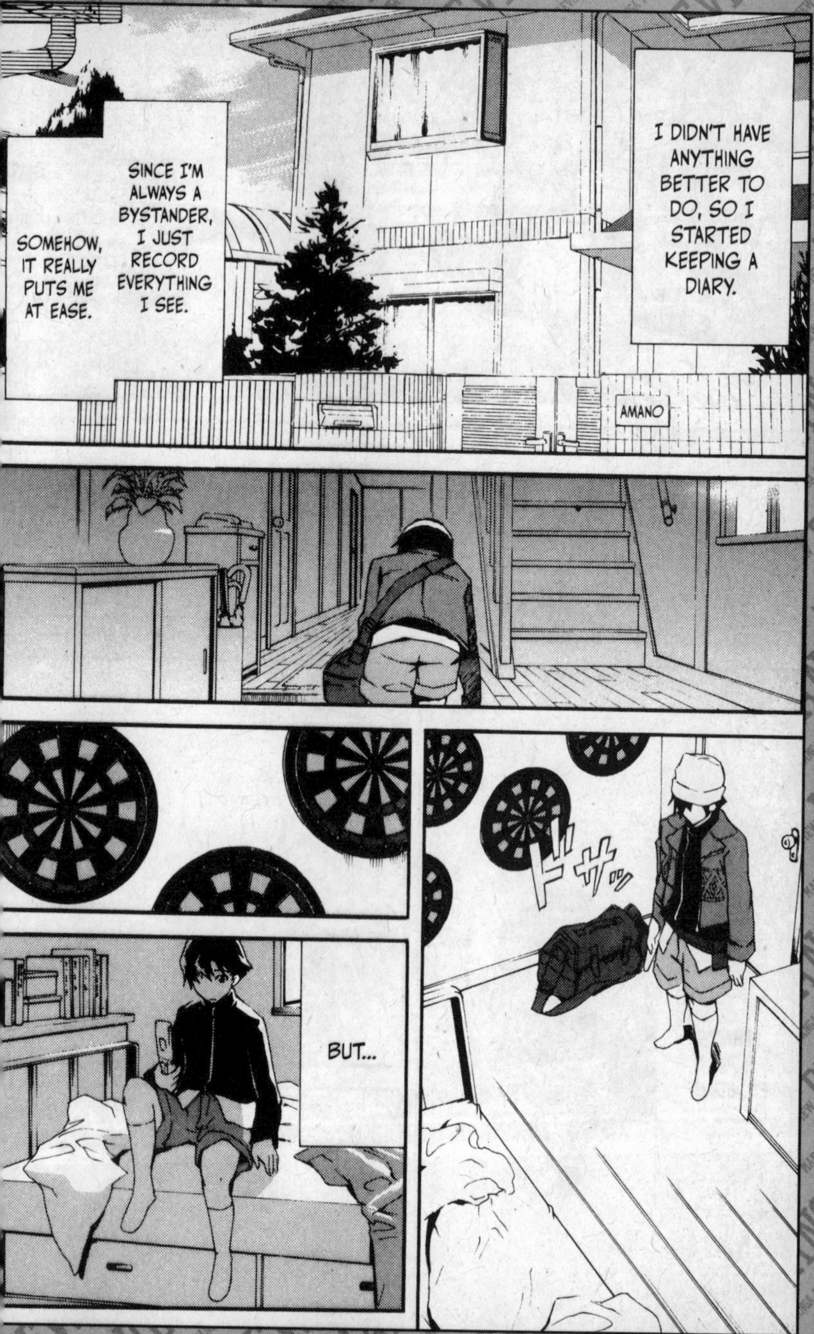
I DIDN'T HAVE ANYTHING BETTER TO DO, SO I STARTED KEEPING A DIARY.
SINCE I'M ALWAYS A BYSTANDER, I JUST RECORD EVERYTHING I SEE.
SOMEHOW, IT REALLY PUTS ME AT EASE.
AMANO
ドサッ
BUT...

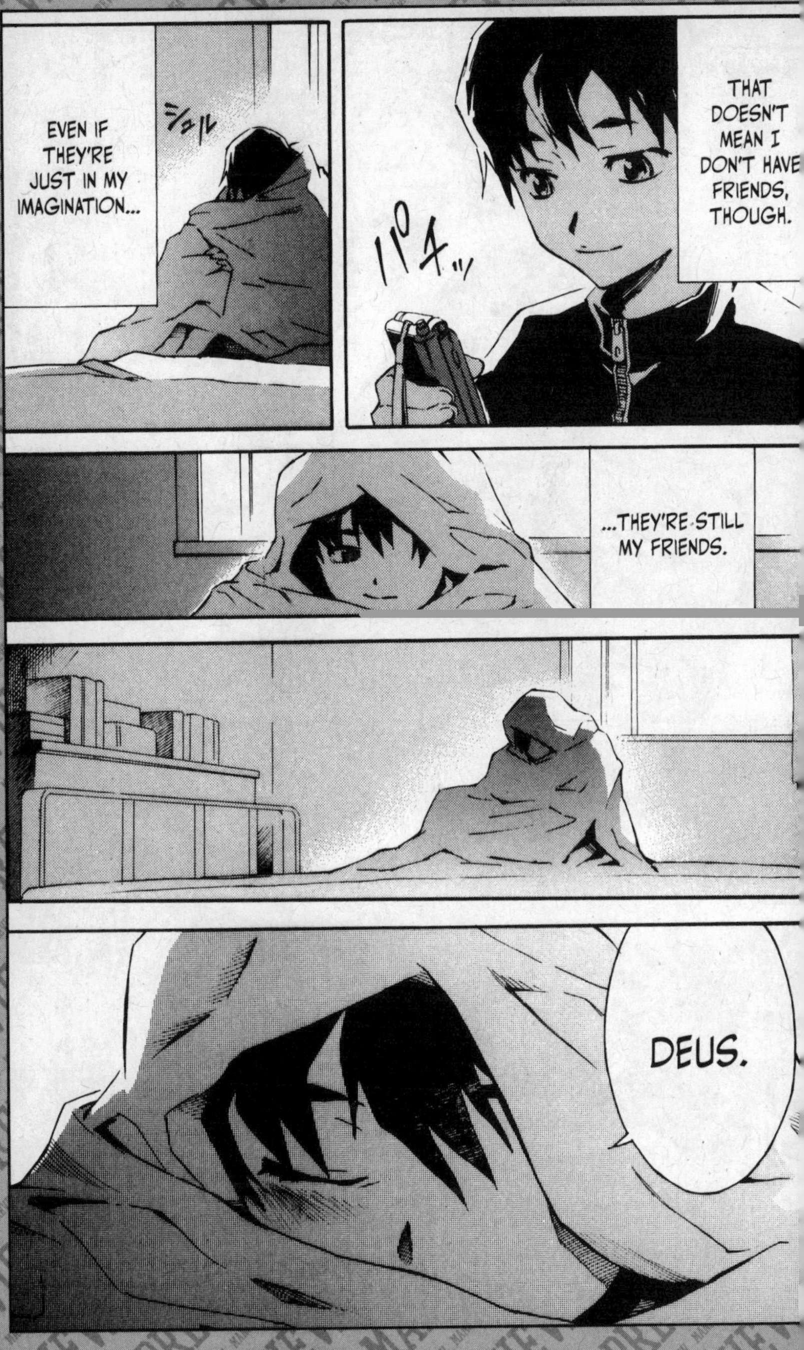
THAT DOESN'T MEAN I DON'T HAVE FRIENDS, THOUGH.
パチッ
EVEN IF THEY'RE JUST IN MY IMAGINATION...
シュル
...THEY'RE STILL MY FRIENDS.
DEUS.

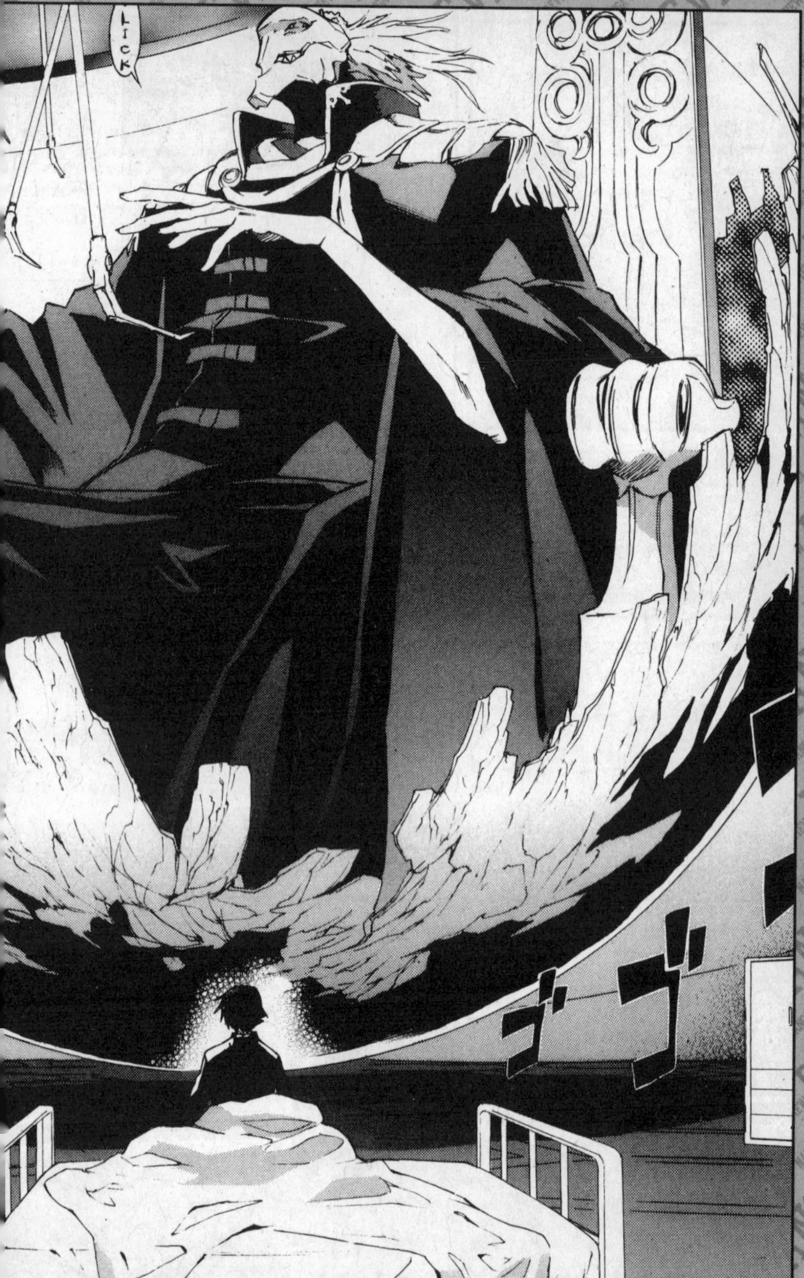
LICK
ゴゴ

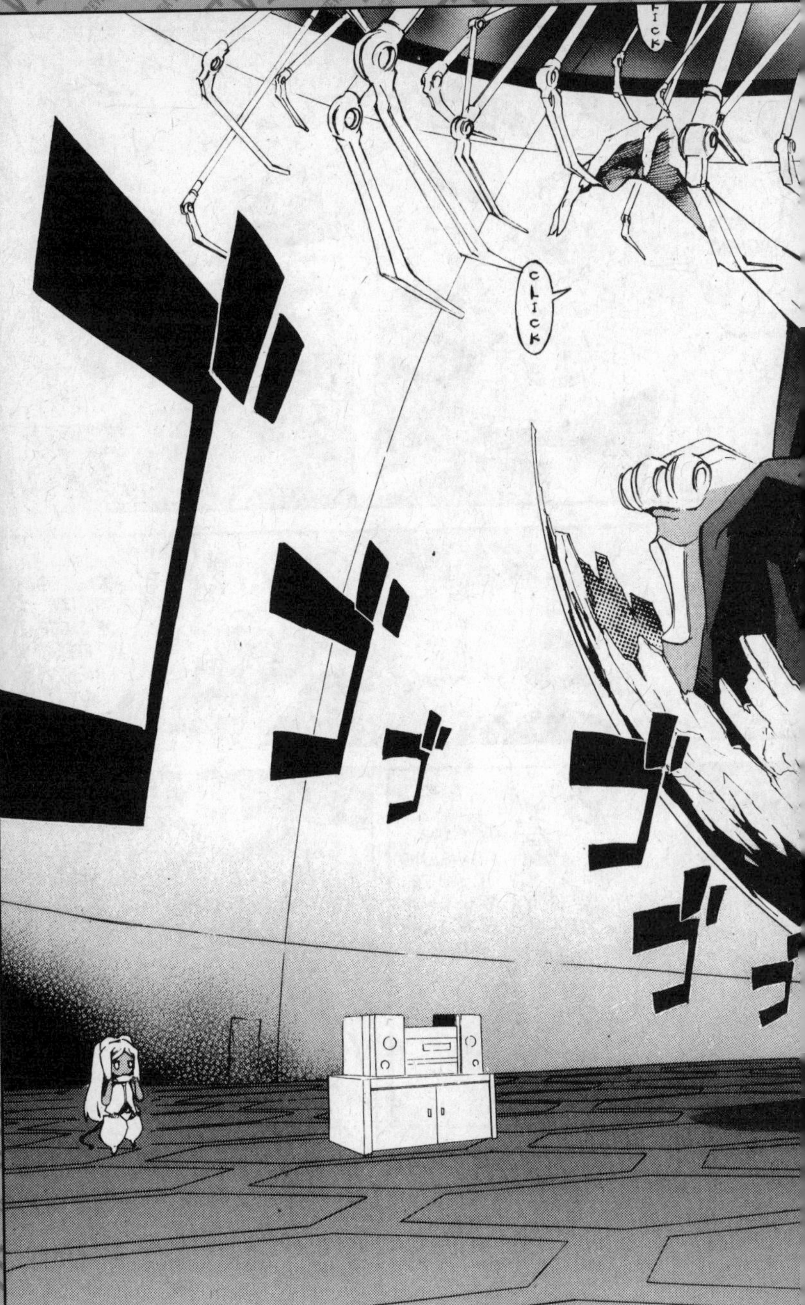
CLICK
ゴゴゴゴゴ

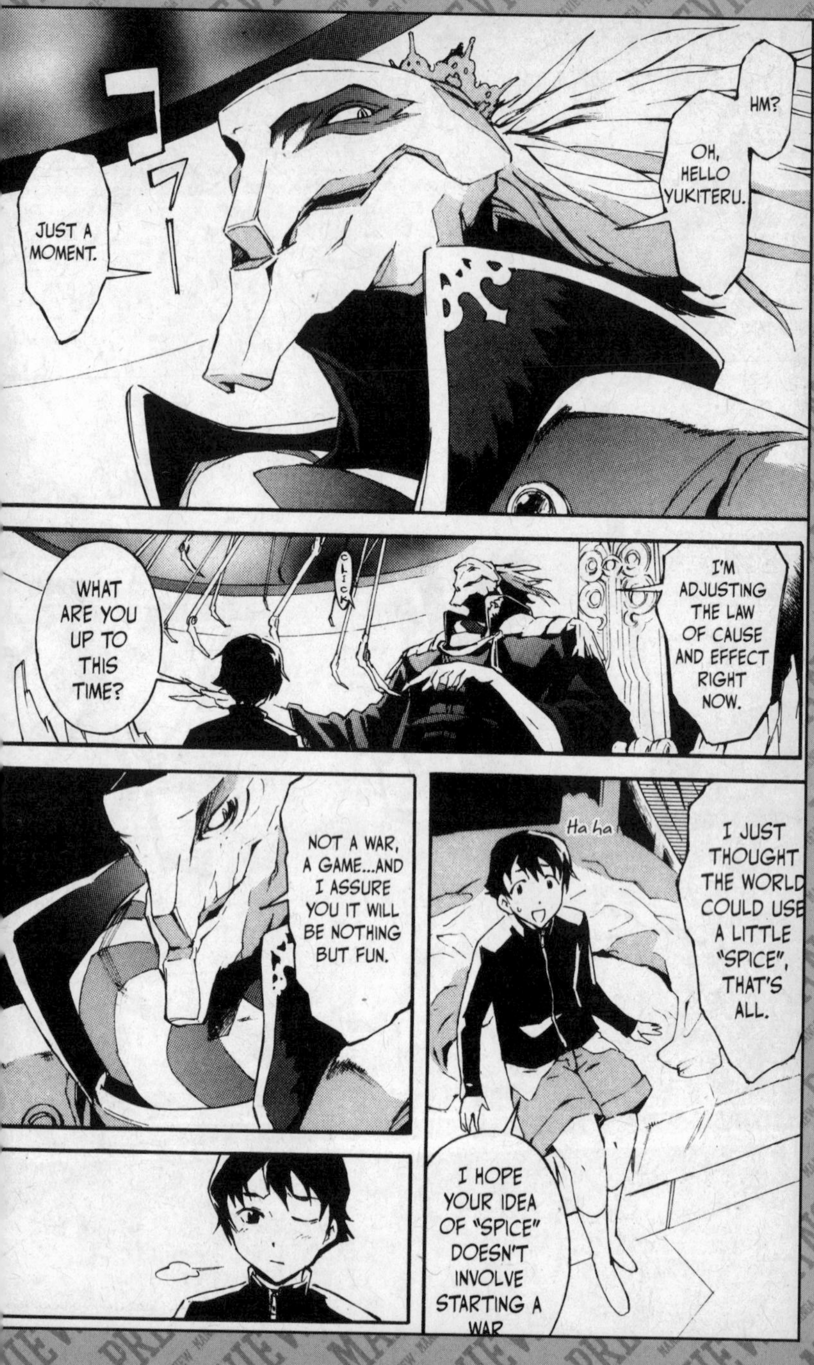
HM?
OH, HELLO YUKITERU.
JUST A MOMENT.
I'M ADJUSTING THE LAW OF CAUSE AND EFFECT RIGHT NOW.
CLICK
WHAT ARE YOU UP TO THIS TIME?
Ha ha
I JUST THOUGHT THE WORLD COULD USE A LITTLE "SPICE", THAT'S ALL.
I HOPE YOUR IDEA OF "SPICE" DOESN'T INVOLVE STARTING A WAR
NOT A WAR, A GAME...AND I ASSURE YOU IT WILL BE NOTHING BUT FUN.

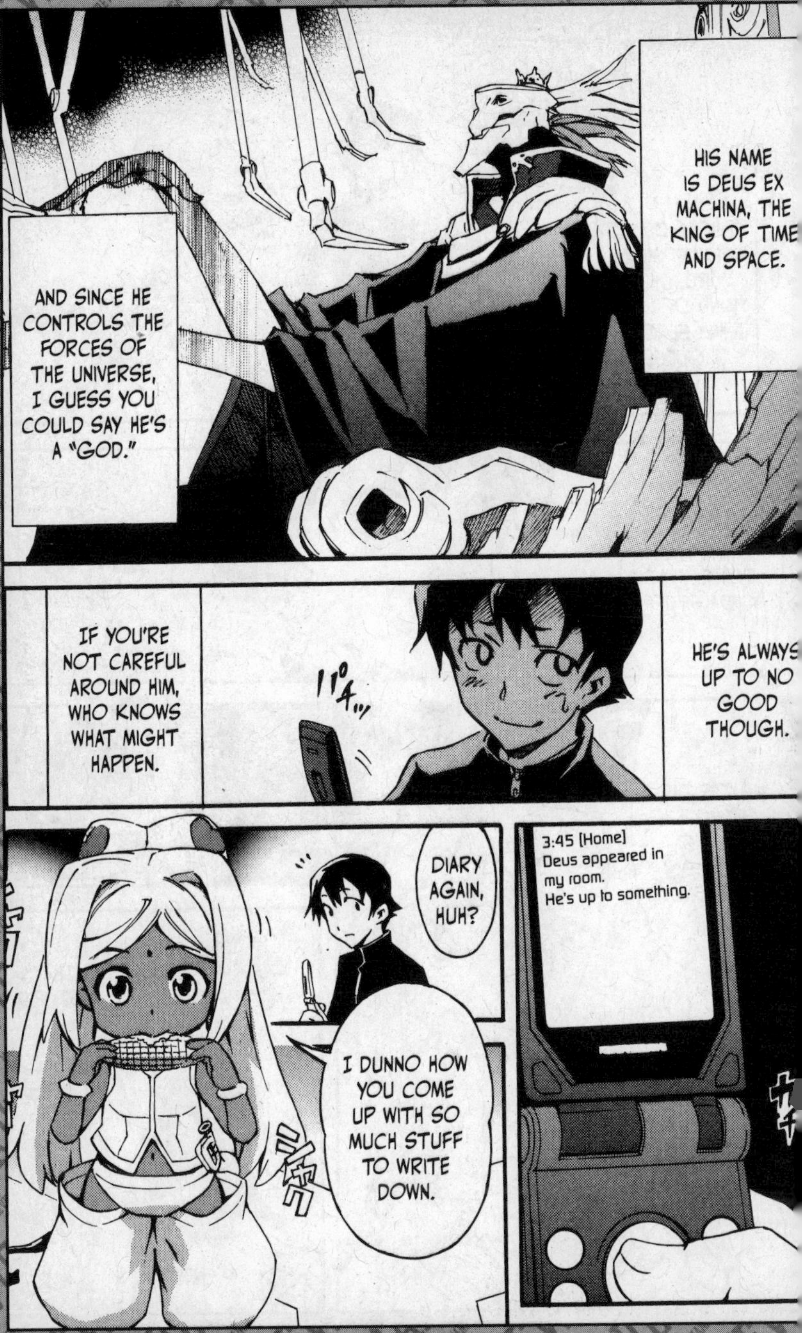
HIS NAME IS DEUS EX MACHINA, THE KING OF TIME AND SPACE.
AND SINCE HE CONTROLS THE FORCES OF THE UNIVERSE, I GUESS YOU COULD SAY HE'S A "GOD."
HE'S ALWAYS UP TO NO GOOD THOUGH.
IF YOU'RE NOT CAREFUL AROUND HIM, WHO KNOWS WHAT MIGHT HAPPEN.
3:45 [Home]
Deus appeared in my room.
He's up to something.
DIARY AGAIN, HUH?
I DUNNO HOW YOU COME UP WITH SO MUCH STUFF TO WRITE DOWN.

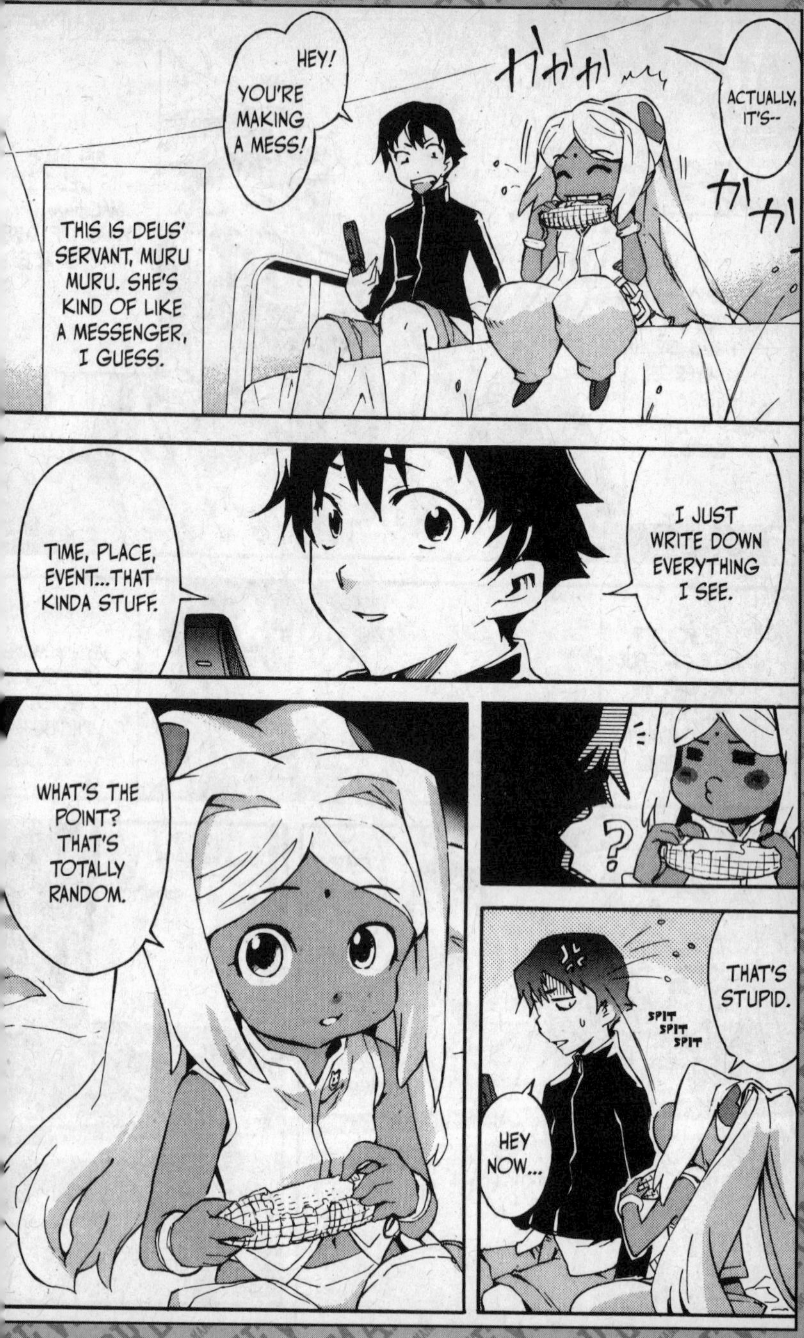
ACTUALLY, IT'S--
HEY! YOU'RE MAKING A MESS!
THIS IS DEUS' SERVANT, MURU MURU. SHE'S KIND OF LIKE A MESSENGER, I GUESS.
I JUST WRITE DOWN EVERYTHING I SEE.
TIME, PLACE, EVENT...THAT KINDA STUFF.
?
THAT'S STUPID.
SPIT SPIT SPIT
HEY NOW...
WHAT'S THE POINT? THAT'S TOTALLY RANDOM.

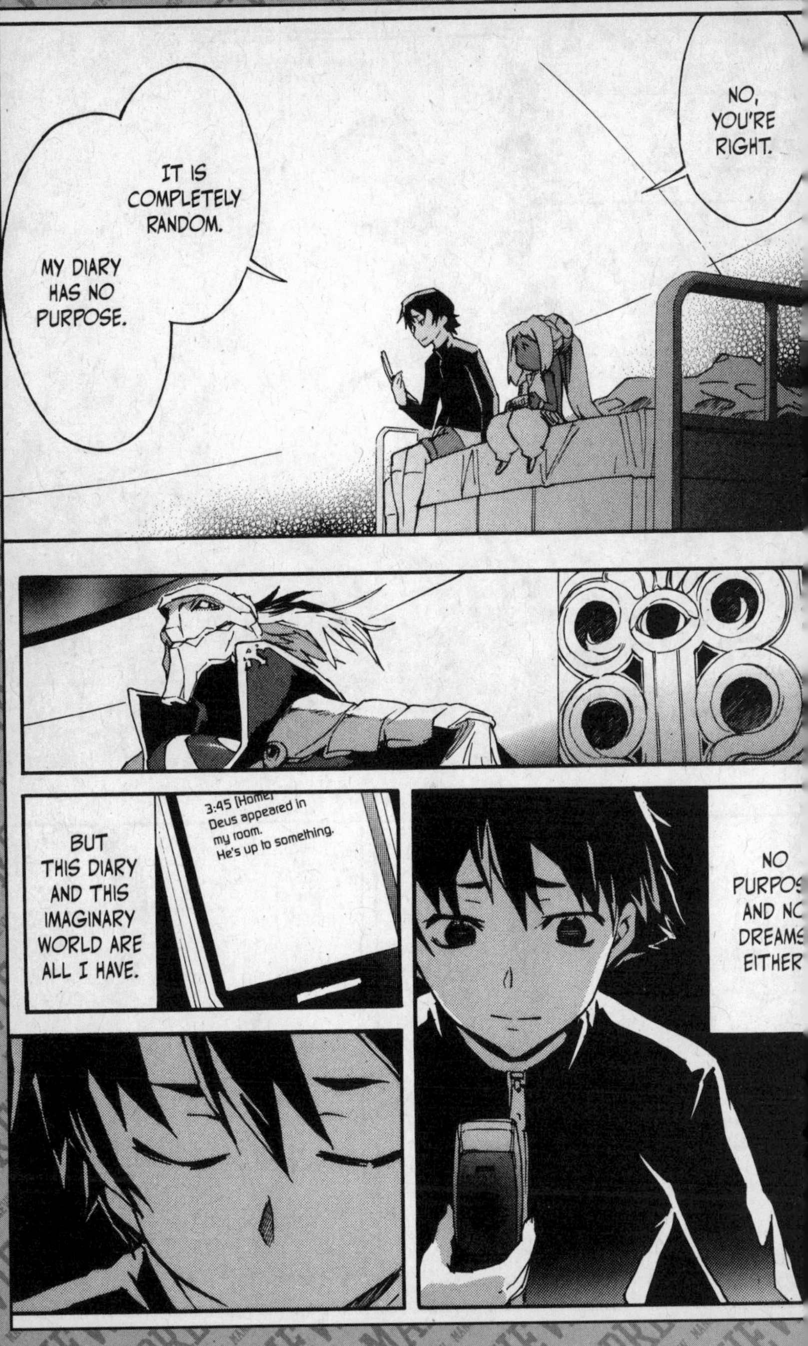
NO, YOU'RE RIGHT.
IT IS COMPLETELY RANDOM.
MY DIARY HAS NO PURPOSE.
NO PURPOS AND N DREAMS EITHER
3:45 [Home] Deus appeared in my room. He's up to something.
BUT THIS DIARY AND THIS IMAGINARY WORLD ARE ALL I HAVE.

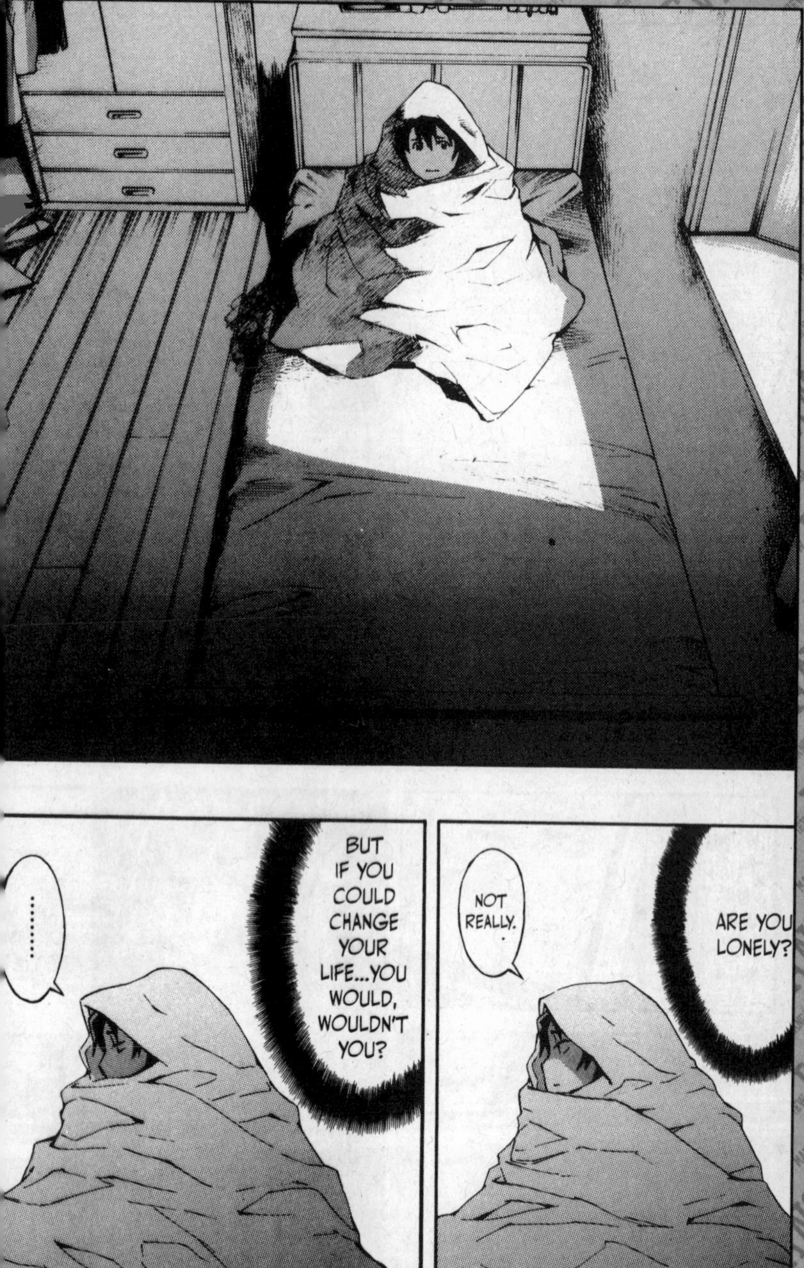
ARE YOU LONELY?
NOT REALLY.
BUT IF YOU COULD CHANGE YOUR LIFE...YOU WOULD, WOULDN'T YOU?
....

VERY WELL.

I SHALL ENTRUST YOU WITH *THE FUTURE.*

WHAT DO YOU MEAN?

?

ISN'T THAT JUST MY CELL PHONE?

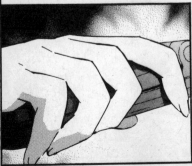

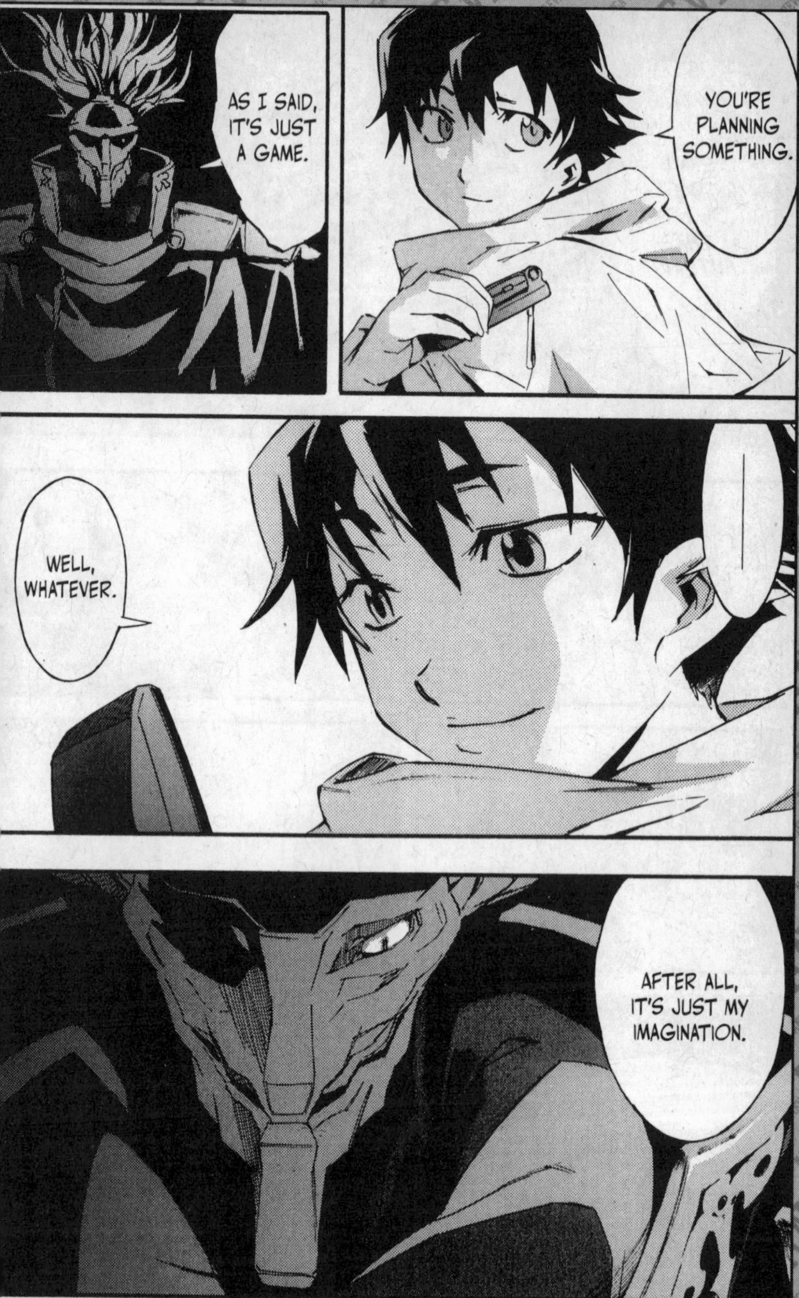
YOU'RE PLANNING SOMETHING.
AS I SAID, IT'S JUST A GAME.
WELL, WHATEVER.
AFTER ALL, IT'S JUST MY IMAGINATION.

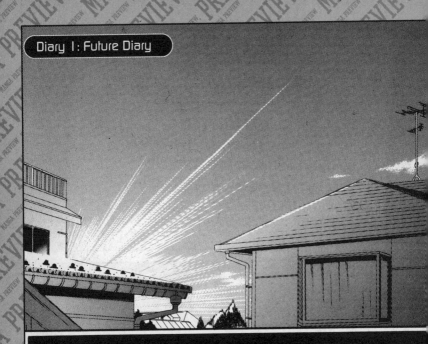

Diary 1: Future Diary

20XX/4/22 6:57 [My room]

HUH? THAT'S WEIRD.

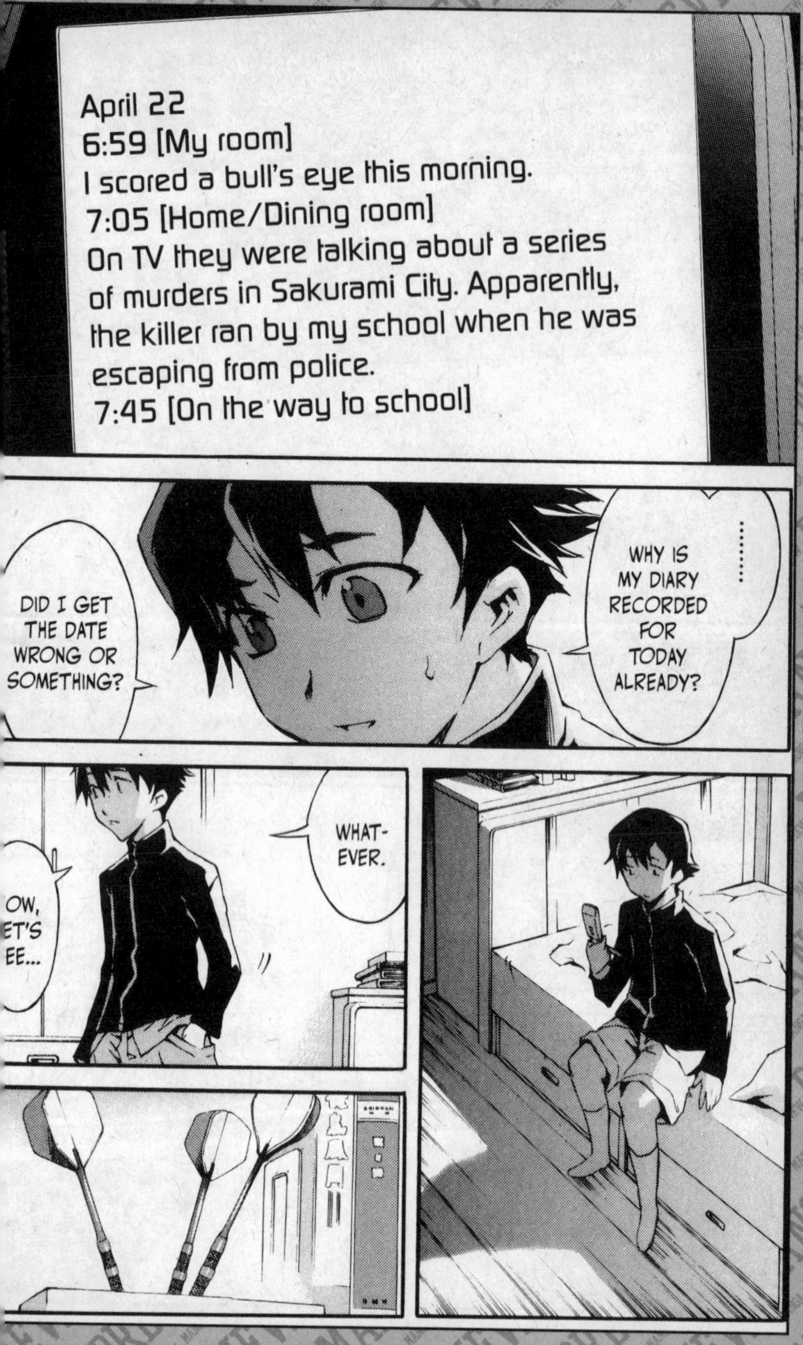
April 22
6:59 [My room]
I scored a bull's eye this morning.
7:05 [Home/Dining room]
On TV they were talking about a series of murders in Sakurami City. Apparently, the killer ran by my school when he was escaping from police.
7:45 [On the way to school]
....
WHY IS MY DIARY RECORDED FOR TODAY ALREADY?
DID I GET THE DATE WRONG OR SOMETHING?
WHAT-EVER.

EVERY MORNING, I TELL MY FORTUNE WITH DARTS.

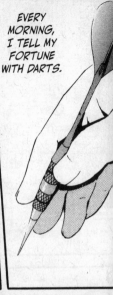

WOW... NOT BAD.

.....

ril 22
59 [My room]
scored a bull's eye this
orning.

:05 [Home/Dining room]
n TV they were talking about
series of murders in Sakuran
City. Apparently, the assailant
an by my school when he wa
escaping from police.

7:45 [On the way to school]

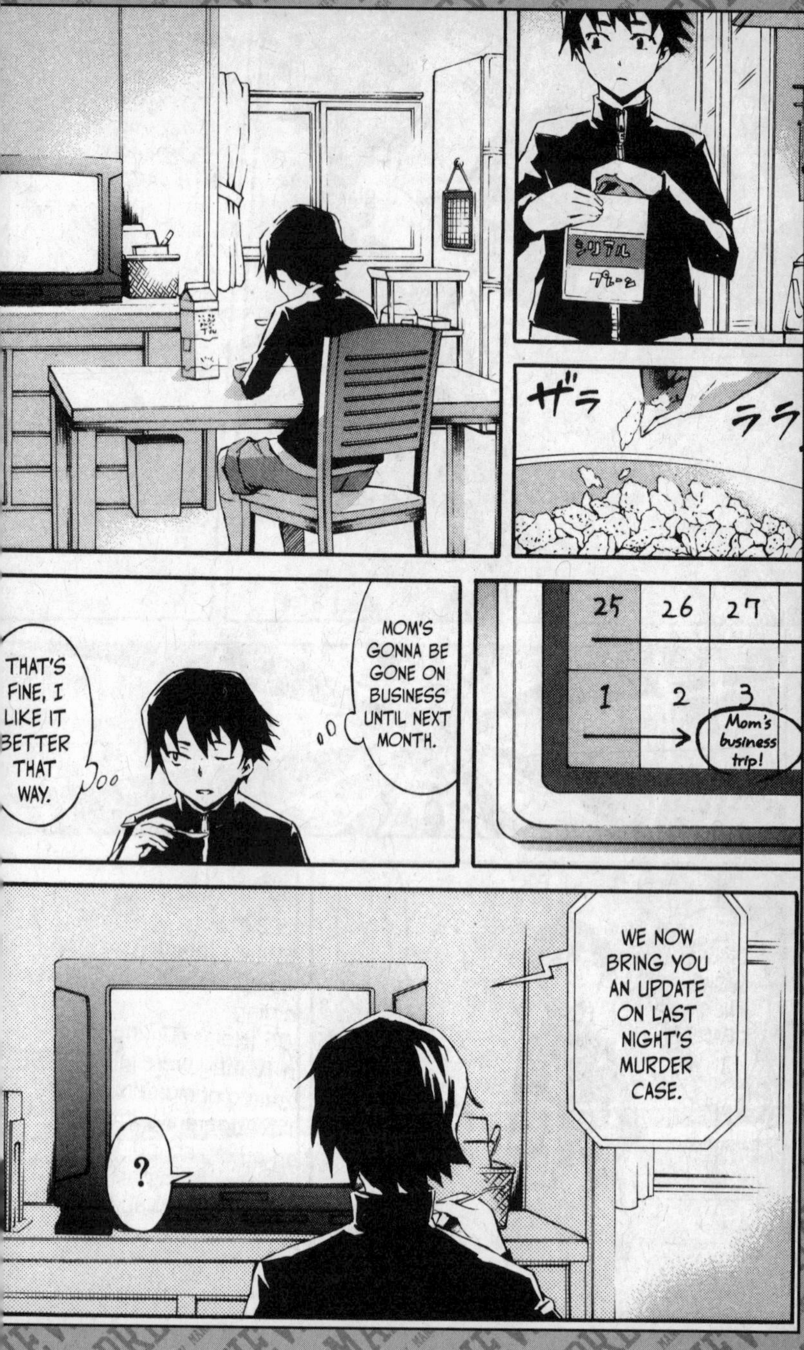
ザラ
ララ
25 26 27
1 2 3
Mom's business trip!
MOM'S GONNA BE GONE ON BUSINESS UNTIL NEXT MONTH.
THAT'S FINE, I LIKE IT BETTER THAT WAY.
WE NOW BRING YOU AN UPDATE ON LAST NIGHT'S MURDER CASE.
?

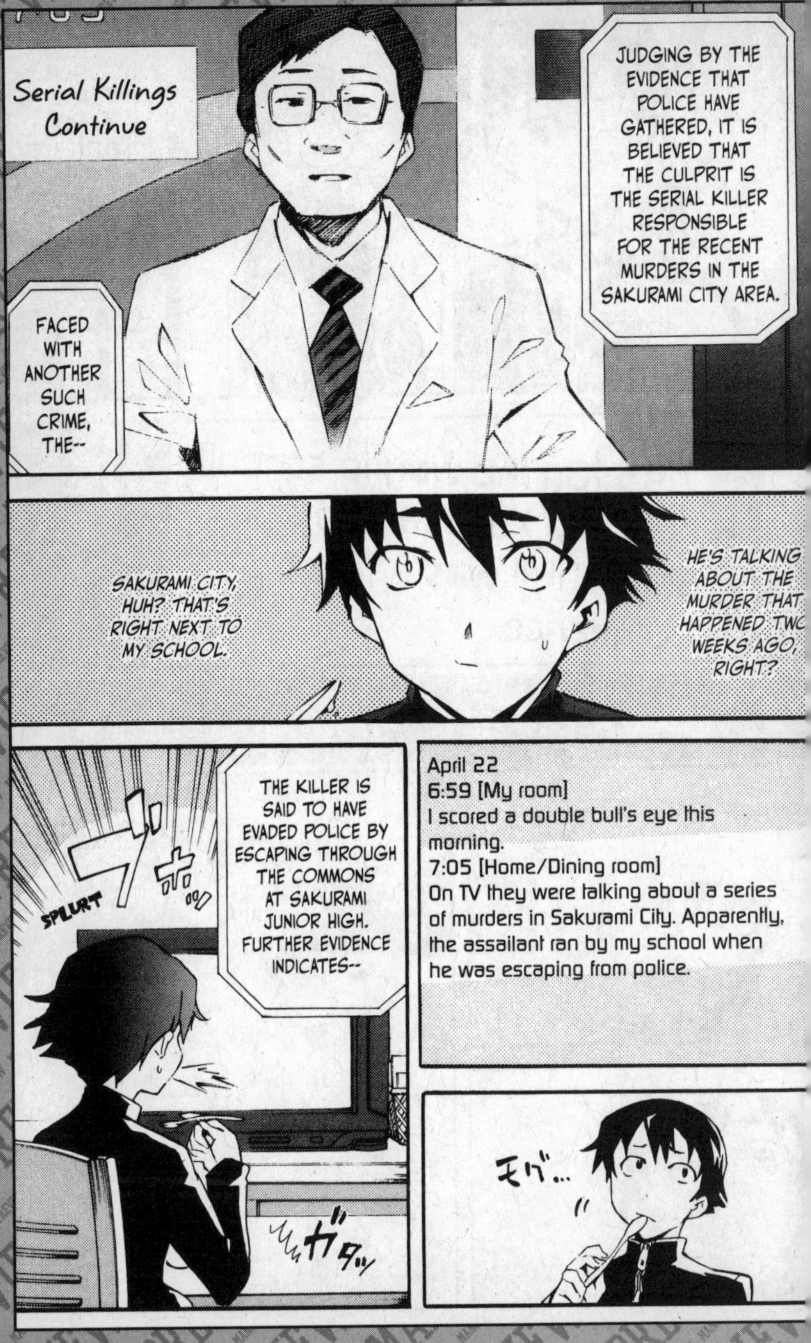
JUDGING BY THE EVIDENCE THAT POLICE HAVE GATHERED, IT IS BELIEVED THAT THE CULPRIT IS THE SERIAL KILLER RESPONSIBLE FOR THE RECENT MURDERS IN THE SAKURAMI CITY AREA.
Serial Killings Continue
FACED WITH ANOTHER SUCH CRIME, THE--
HE'S TALKING ABOUT THE MURDER THAT HAPPENED TWO WEEKS AGO, RIGHT?
SAKURAMI CITY, HUH? THAT'S RIGHT NEXT TO MY SCHOOL.
April 22
6:59 [My room]
I scored a double bull's eye this morning.
7:05 [Home/Dining room]
On TV they were talking about a series of murders in Sakurami City. Apparently, the assailant ran by my school when he was escaping from police.
モグ...
THE KILLER IS SAID TO HAVE EVADED POLICE BY ESCAPING THROUGH THE COMMONS AT SAKURAMI JUNIOR HIGH. FURTHER EVIDENCE INDICATES--
SPLURT
ガタッ

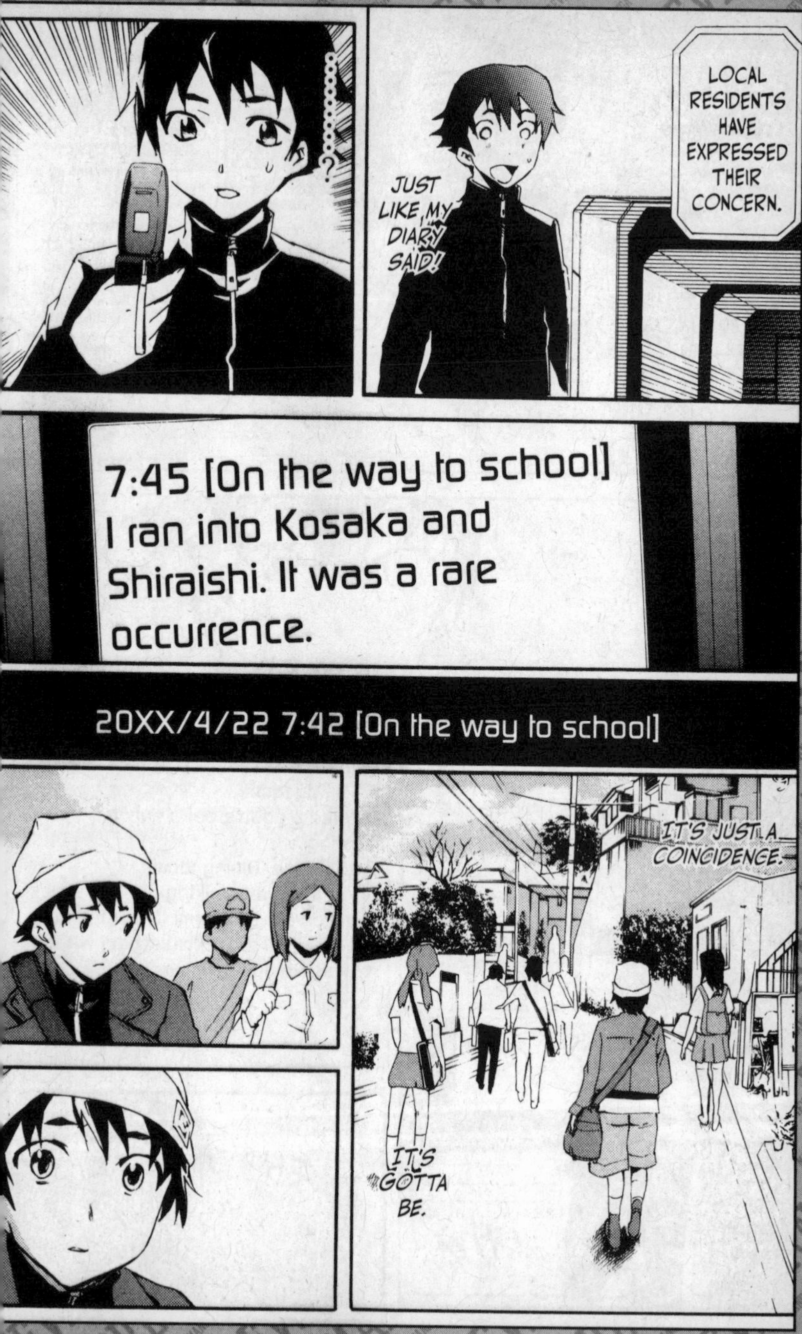
LOCAL RESIDENTS HAVE EXPRESSED THEIR CONCERN.
JUST LIKE MY DIARY SAID!
7:45 [On the way to school]
I ran into Kosaka and Shiraishi. It was a rare occurrence.
20XX/4/22 7:42 [On the way to school]
IT'S JUST A COINCIDENCE.
IT'S GOTTA BE.

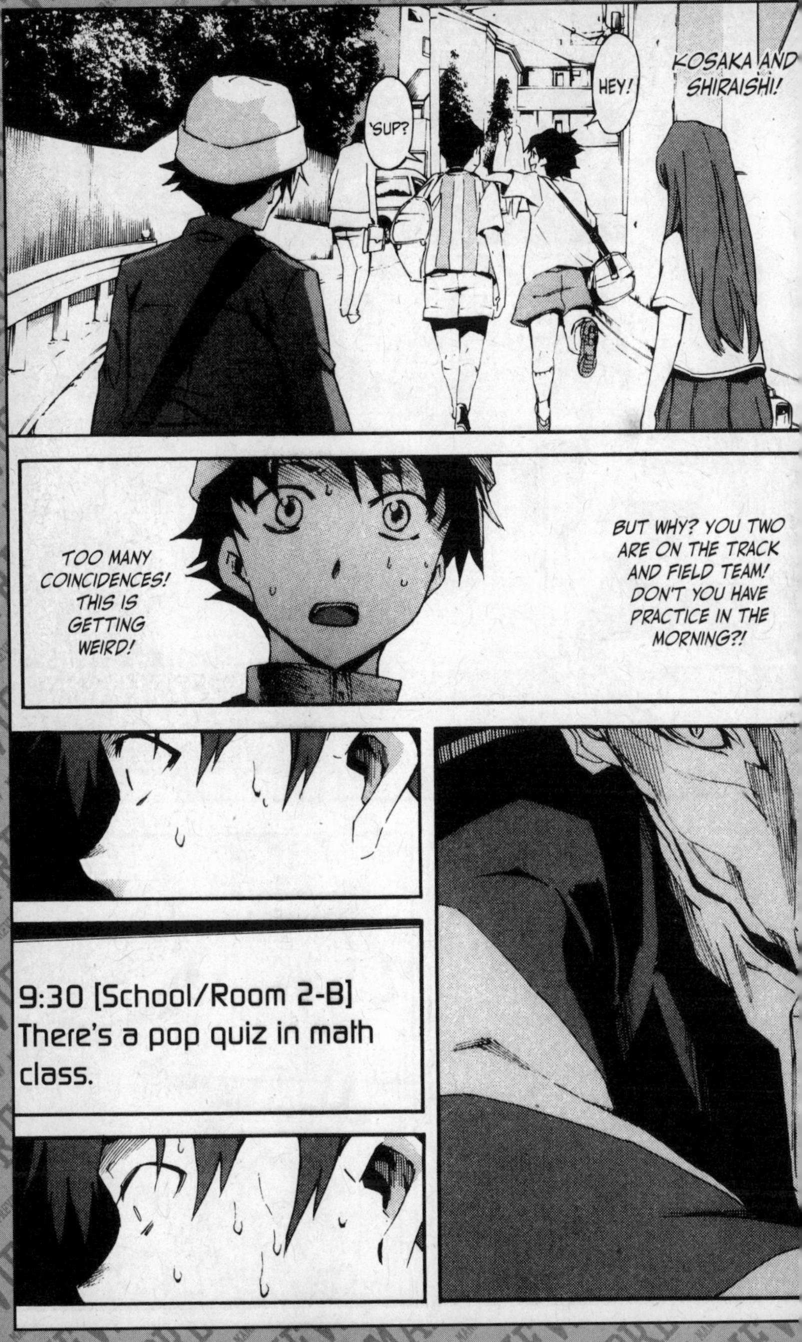
KOSAKA AND SHIRAISHI!
HEY!
'SUP?
BUT WHY? YOU TWO ARE ON THE TRACK AND FIELD TEAM! DON'T YOU HAVE PRACTICE IN THE MORNING?!
TOO MANY COINCIDENCES! THIS IS GETTING WEIRD!
9:30 [School/Room 2-B] There's a pop quiz in math class.

Test

NO...

...THIS CAN'T BE A COINCIDENCE!

20XX/4/22 9:30
[School/Room 2-B]

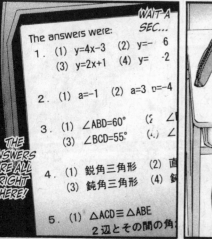

WAIT A SEC...

The answers were:

1. (1) y=4x−3 (2) y=− 6
   (3) y=2x+1 (4) y= -2

2. (1) a=−1 (2) a=3 b=-4

3. (1) ∠ABD=60° (2) ∠
   (3) ∠BCD=55° (4)

4. (1) 鋭角三角形 (2) 直
   (3) 鈍角三角形 (4) 鋭

5. (1) △ACD≡△ABE
   2辺とその間の角と

THE ANSWERS ARE ALL RIGHT HERE!

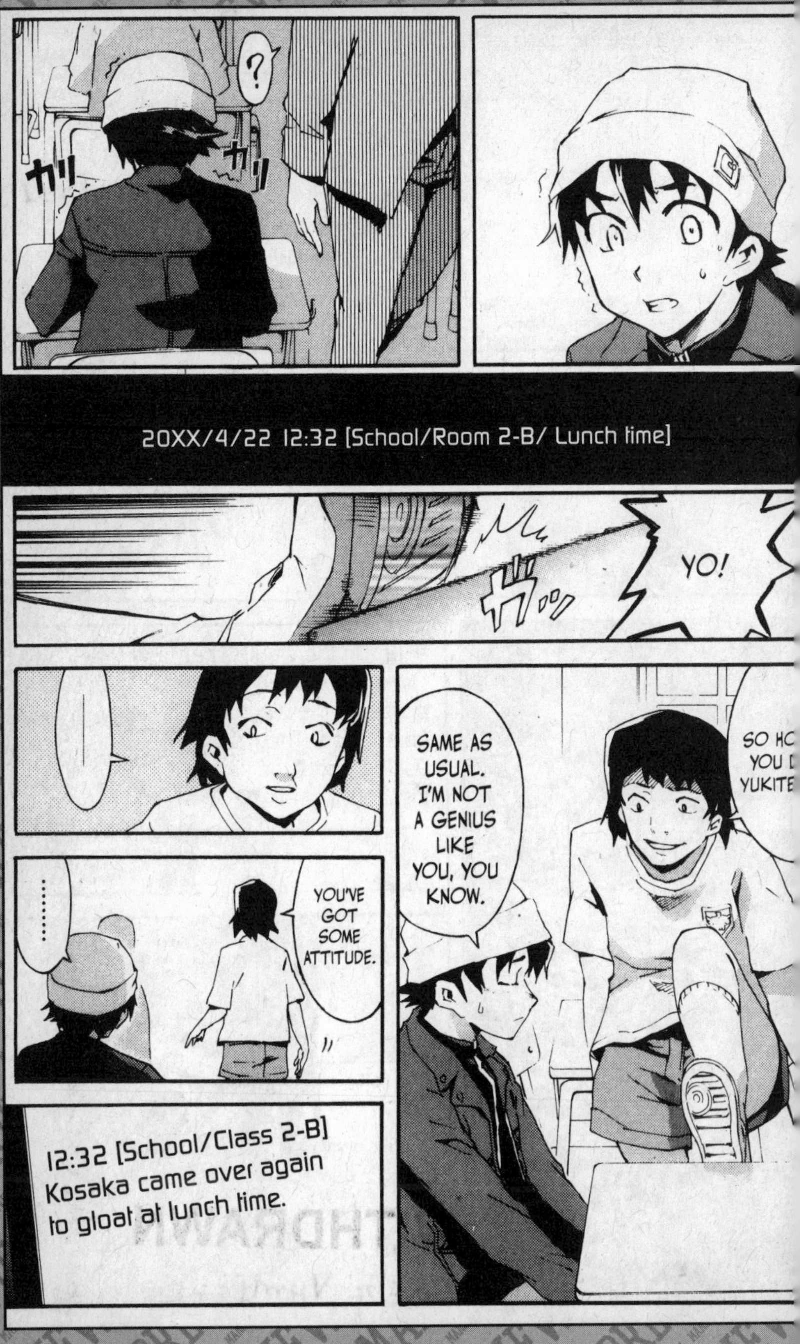
?
カリ
カリ
20XX/4/22 12:32 [School/Room 2-B/ Lunch time]
YO!
ガッ
SAME AS USUAL. I'M NOT A GENIUS LIKE YOU, YOU KNOW.
......
YOU'VE GOT SOME ATTITUDE.
12:32 [School/Class 2-B]
Kosaka came over again to gloat at lunch time.

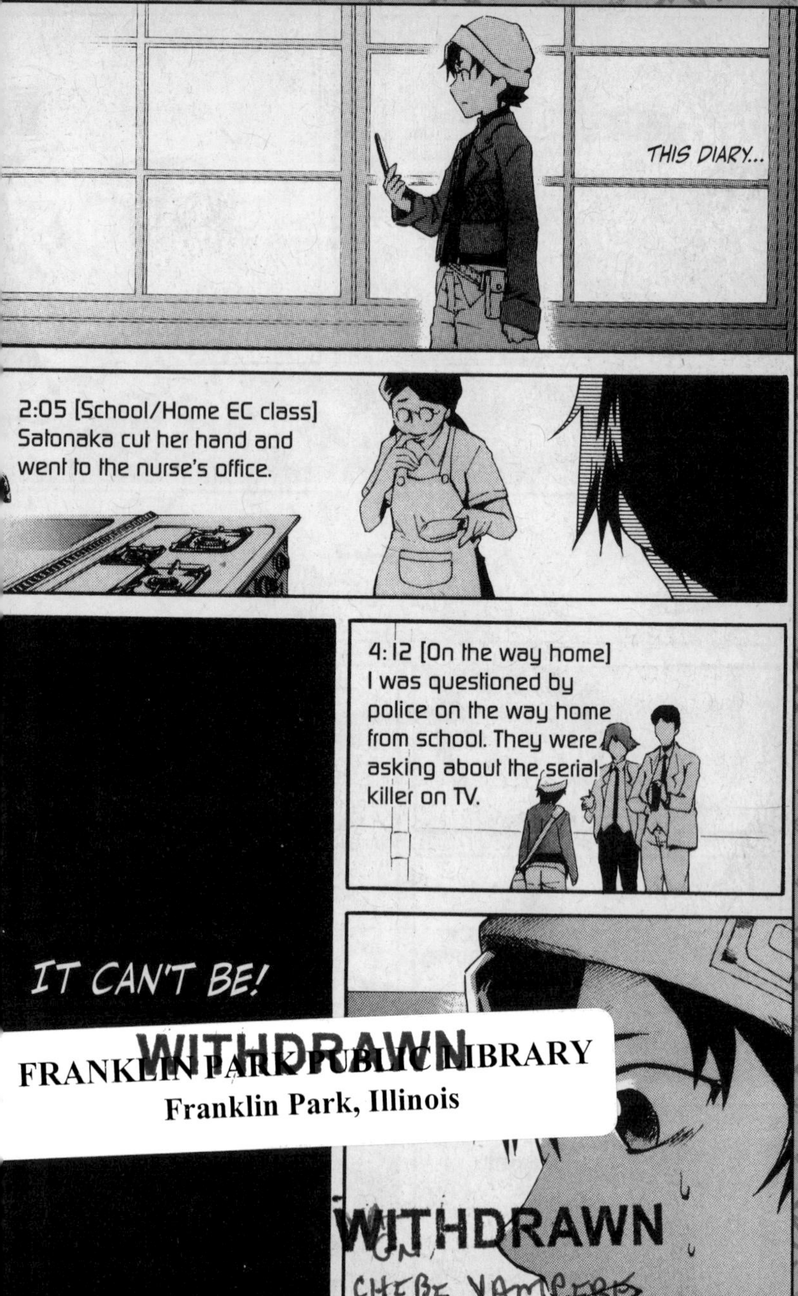
THIS DIARY...
2:05 [School/Home EC class] Satonaka cut her hand and went to the nurse's office.
4:12 [On the way home] I was questioned by police on the way home from school. They were asking about the serial killer on TV.
IT CAN'T BE!

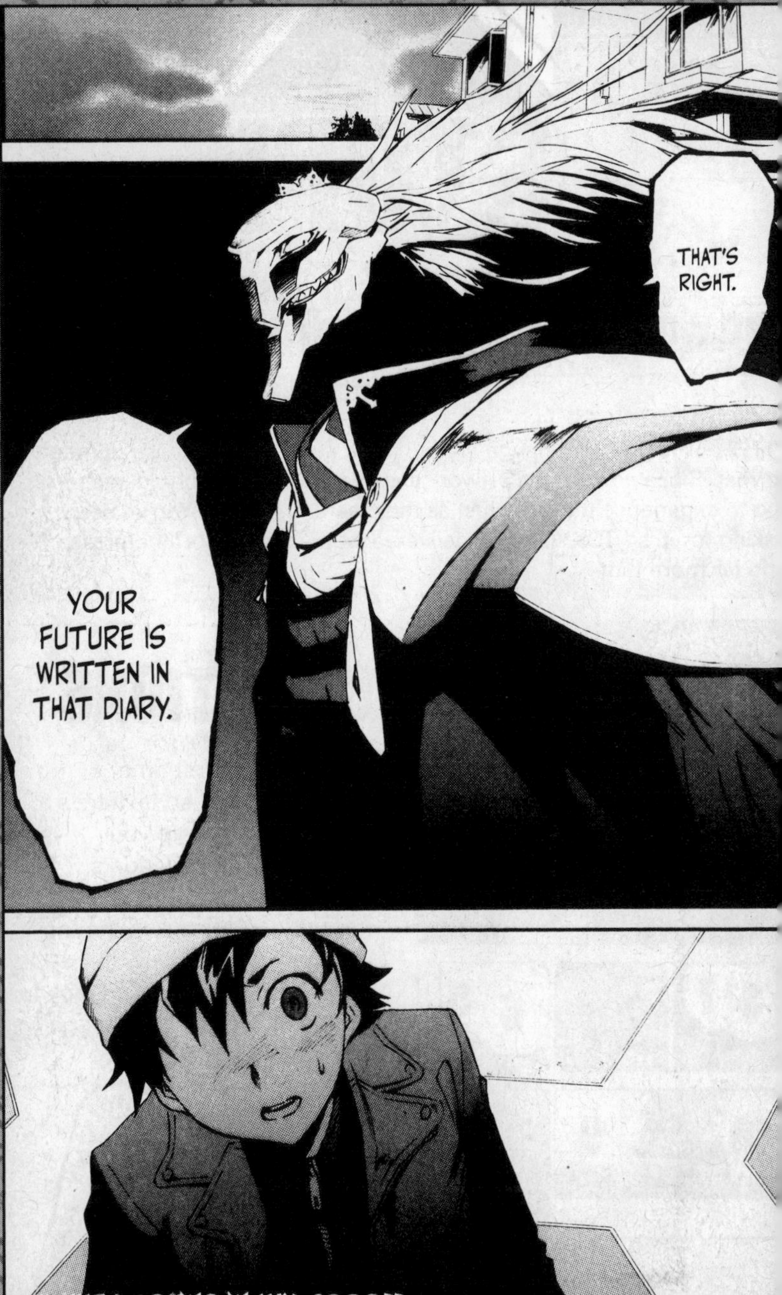
THAT'S RIGHT.
YOUR FUTURE IS WRITTEN IN THAT DIARY.
—VOLUME 1 COMING IN MAY 2009!!

STOP!

This is the back of the book.
You wouldn't want to spoil a great ending!

6/11

This book is printed "manga-style," in the authentic Japanese right-to-left format. Since none of the artwork has been flipped or altered, readers get to experience the story just as the creator intended. You've been asking for it, so TOKYOPOP® delivered: authentic, hot-off-the-press, and far more fun!

DIRECTIONS

If this is your first time reading manga-style, here's a quick guide to help you understand how it works.

It's easy... just start in the top right panel and follow the numbers. Have fun, and look for more 100% authentic manga from TOKYOPOP®!

LEADING • THE MANGA REVOLUTION • LEADING • THE MANGA REVOLUTION • 漫画革命